DEADLY INTENT

JAMES P. SUMNER

BOTH
barrels
PUBLISHING

DEADLY INTENT

Third Edition published in 2021 by Both Barrels Publishing
Copyright © James P. Sumner 2015

Editing and Cover Design by: bothbarrelsauthorservices.com

ISBNs:
978-1-914191-13-8 (Paperback)

Visit the author's website: jamespsumner.com

A new chapter begins...

DEADLY INTENT

ADRIAN HELL: BOOK 4

1

I'm lying in bed, staring at the ceiling. Outside, the morning light is gradually getting brighter. It's shining through the thin curtains covering my bedroom window. I glance over at the clock on my bedside table. It's almost six a.m.

I rub my eyes, clearing them of any grit, and look to my right. The woman next to me is lying on her back. The thin bedsheet is at her waist; her exposed breasts slowly rise and fall with each breath as she sleeps. I look farther down the bed, following the sheet as it rests gently over her naked body.

I smile to myself and look back at the ceiling, thinking about how lucky I am. My mind flicks to the checklist of things I need to do this morning. I'm not going to get any more sleep, so I may as well start. I throw the cover back and swing my legs over the side of the bed. I sit there a moment, then stand and pad across the carpet, over to the bathroom.

A few minutes later, I come back out, feeling more

refreshed and wide-awake. I walk over to the nightstand and put my jeans on. As I move to the dresser to get a new T-shirt out of the drawer, a voice disturbs me.

"Hey, sexy," says Tori. "Where d'you think you're going?"

I smile at her. "Sorry. I didn't mean to wake you."

She smiles back. "You didn't. What time is it?"

"Just after six."

"You're up early?"

"Couldn't sleep." I shrug.

"You have the nightmare again?"

I take a deep breath and nod silently.

For the past couple of years, I've rarely slept more than a few hours a night. I keep having the same recurring nightmare. The details change, but what happens is always the same. Someone is in trouble, and they're screaming for me to help them. I reach out to rescue them, but then a gun appears in my hand, and I shoot them instead of saving them. As they die, their skin falls off their body, and the skeleton falls to the floor. I look down and see that I'm walking through a graveyard. As far as I can see in every direction is a field of bones, with a river of blood flowing through it. I want to escape it, but I sink into the ground as I try to run. As my body disappears completely, that's when I wake up, covered in sweat.

The same dream every night.

"Come here," Tori says.

I walk back over to the bed and sit down on the edge. She moves over to me and puts her arms around my waist, pressing herself against my back and squeezing gently. I put my hand on her arm and smile.

Tori Watson is beautiful. She's thirty-five years old but could easily pass for ten years younger. She has an incredible body, and I know every man in town has a crush on her.

She has captivating brown eyes and a smile that can light up the room. Her long, curly hair is flame-red and rests on her shoulders. She's absolutely flawless. I have no idea how I managed to get a woman like her, but I'm sure as hell not complaining.

She kisses my back. "It's okay. They're just dreams, Adrian."

I turn to gaze into her eyes, then smile and lean in to kiss her soft lips. It feels like kissing Heaven itself.

After a moment, she pulls away, a mischievous look on her pretty face. "You don't gotta rush away just yet, do you?"

"I can spare a few minutes for you," I reply, smiling.

She pulls me on top of her, and we kiss and laugh like people in love ought to do.

06:31 CDT

A few minutes turn into twenty, but I eventually get dressed and head downstairs while Tori takes a shower.

I live in the apartment above the bar that I own, which I've named The Ferryman. I love running the place, and it's the most popular drinking establishment in town. The locals are great, and the out-of-towners who pass through are nearly always friendly. I've made the place look exactly the way I think the perfect bar should look. After all, it's not like I'm short of capital to invest in it. It's the kind of place I'd drink in. Pool tables, good beer, a jukebox full of classic rock music, and saloon doors, like in the Old West.

I guess you could say I've changed.

It's been two and a half years since I killed Wilson Trent and Jimmy Manhattan. I spent a week or so afterward trying to go about my business as I used to—working with Josh and killing people for money—but it didn't last. When I finally put my family to rest, I buried my demons too. I had no reason—and more importantly, no desire—to keep killing after that. I had a quarter of a billion dollars in my bank account and absolutely nothing to do. I talked with Josh, and he was genuinely happy that I'd reached this place in my life.

But he explained that while he felt the same way about our old job as I did, he needed a new challenge. He wasn't ready to give up and retire just yet. We shook hands and parted company. While we still speak occasionally over the phone, I haven't seen him since that day. I think of him often, but now we simply live in different worlds. I don't know what he's doing, and I suspect he doesn't know what I've been up to. He wouldn't believe me if I told him, either.

I came to Devil's Spring, Texas, bought a derelict building, and turned it into The Ferryman. It took me six months, but the unlimited budget helped, and it didn't take long to start doing really well.

I met Tori here. She applied for a waitressing job a couple of weeks after I opened. She made me laugh. I loved the fact that I was starting over. She didn't know Adrian Hell. She only knew the guy who was new in town and had recently opened the bar. We got on really well and soon became friends.

One night, after she'd been working for me a few weeks, a couple of guys came into the bar. They were loud and drunk, and one of them used to date Tori. It had ended months before, but the guy had trouble letting go. I could understand *why* a guy would find it hard to move on from Tori, but I couldn't tolerate them causing trouble in my bar. I gave them a warning to calm down when they got a bit rowdy with some of my locals. Then Tori went to collect their glasses and one of them grabbed her. He started shouting at her, calling her names.

For a brief moment, the old me came back. I walked over and dropped the guy with a couple of well-placed punches. Then I threw him and his friend out on the street, with the clear warning never to set foot in my bar again, unless they had an overwhelming urge to vacate this mortal coil.

I took Tori into the back to see if she was all right. She slapped me across the face, angry that I'd stood up for her and insistent that she could handle herself. I told her I had no doubt that she could, but the gentleman and proprietor in me felt compelled to step in, and if she had a problem with that, it was tough. She smiled, then we kissed, and two years later, we're living together above the bar.

As I walk into the bar, I hear the scratching of claws on wood as Styx walks over to me.

Styx is my dog. He's a big, white and gray husky. He was a stray who randomly wandered into my bar one night as I was closing up. He stood his ground and bared his teeth, snarling at me. I just stared back at him. I let him see the animal that once lived beneath the surface, and he soon backed down. He lay motionless and let me approach him and stroke his head. I then gave him a bowl of water, and he licked my hand to thank me. He never left.

I spent some time trying to train him, but it wasn't necessary. I don't know how old he is or where he came from, but he's a great dog and intensely loyal to me. It's like we're kindred spirits. He sleeps in the bar at night and sits in the corner by the door when we're open for business. The locals were scared of him at first but soon learned to love him. They know he's placid and friendly as long as they're respectful. Any trouble in the bar, and he'll chase you out in a heartbeat.

He rubs his head against my leg and looks up at me with his tongue hanging out of his mouth. I lean down and pat his head. "Hey, boy. Quiet night?"

He barks once and walks off into the back, where his water bowl is. I need to remember to buy him some more food later...

I stand near the bar, looking out at the room. The doors are over to the left. The open expanse of the bar area is quiet, with chairs stacked upside down on tables. The lights above the pool tables are off, as is the jukebox against the right wall, just before the restrooms.

I reach behind me and feel for the light switch just inside the door to the back room. I flick it on and the bar lights up. I smile to myself like a proud father as I walk over to the doors. I unlock the shutter and raise it, ready for the day ahead.

2
———

In a small town like Devil's Spring, businesses open up early. I figure I'll get an early start on my shopping.

I walk out to the street. The early morning sun is still pale and harmless. Directly across from me is The Fire Pit, a small, family-owned restaurant. It's easily the best place I've ever eaten at. I take Tori there on the odd occasion neither of us has to work. Two brothers from Argentina run it. I can't pronounce their names, but they're real friendly, and they always save a table for us by the window. They have a large, open fire pit in the center of the restaurant, where they cook the food. Their steak is the best around, and the way they marinade their chicken is exceptional. Tori's a big fan of their wine as well.

I see one of the brothers in the window, mopping the floor, and he turns and waves. I wave back as I walk left toward the end of the street.

The crossroads at the main junction isn't busy at this

time, but a few cars and trucks pass by. My first stop is the grocery store. I need to stock up on snacks for behind the bar. I've got a delivery coming in a few days, but the last couple of nights have been extra busy, and I'm running low.

I cross the street and head into the store. It's the closest thing to a franchise we have in Devil's Spring. It's no Walmart, but they have everything I could ask for at a decent price. I pick up a basket and head for the snack aisle. I'm thinking of getting some nuts and maybe some small bags of chips.

"Hey, Adrian," says a voice behind me, interrupting my train of thought.

I turn and see Bob standing before me. He's a friendly local who runs an auto shop a few streets over. He's a big guy with a massive beard, and he always wears dungarees over a checked shirt. He couldn't be more Texan if he tried. He's a regular in The Ferryman and was in last night with a few of his friends.

"Hey, Bob," I say. "How are you feelin' today?"

He sighs heavily. "Man, lemme tell ya, I'm feelin' a little delicate today, Adrian."

He chuckles, and I smile along with him. "Glad I could help."

He laughs some more. "Yeah, you kept servin', so I kept drinkin'. God love ya. Listen, I'm glad I bumped into you. Me and some of the boys were wonderin' if you'd reconsider your stance on legal substances in your bar?"

I take a breath and let it out, trying to come across as sympathetic. But I shake my head. "Sorry, Bob. No can do. You know how I feel about it, and I don't want that going on in my bar."

"Oh, c'mon, man. Get with the times. It's not like it's illegal to take a little coke anymore."

"Honestly, Bob, I don't care if the president himself walks into my bar and gives me his blessing. I don't agree with it, and it's not against the law for a business owner to reserve his right to prohibit the consumption of narcotics on his premises."

He's silent for a moment, then shrugs. "Hey, no problem, Ady. Your house, your rules. Ain't gonna stop me from drinkin' in there!"

He pats me on my shoulder and walks off, laughing to himself. I watch him go, then resume my shopping.

A couple of years back, not long after I moved down here to Texas, a new president was elected and sworn in— Charles Tobias Cunningham the sixth. He's a real media darling, this one. An Ivy League educated, handsome guy bred for politics and destined for the Oval Office. He got elected by the largest majority since FDR.

His campaign was weird, though. At a Republican conference, he asked why no one thought to legalize drugs and prostitution. An unquestionably bold move. But then he produced the figures. Cocaine was a trillion-dollar industry. He said that if we made it legal, imposed tax on it, and then used the revenue to provide better healthcare and education, not only would we climb out of the recession, we'd nearly double the GDP within five years. Suddenly, people weren't so skeptical. It's amazing the difference the almighty dollar can make.

He had the same argument for prostitution—another multi-billion-dollar industry. He suggested removing the taboo factor, legalizing it, and unionizing it. He said if we offered a safe working environment, provided good healthcare, and taxed companionship—as they now call it—the money the country could make was mind-boggling.

His winning personality and, frankly, brilliant marketing

campaign meant that he soon won over his peers and his public. Surprisingly, he was right. Within his first three months in office, the crime rate dropped by sixty percent. Unemployment dropped by eighty percent. International relations with South America strengthened. All the cartels that monopolized the illegal drug trade were given a choice —either agree to work alongside the U.S., legitimately, or face a prison sentence longer than Route 66.

I've never seen such an era of peace and prosperity in this country. In *any* country. Ever. President Cunningham made the world sit up and take notice. But he was smart. At the same time, he said he's not forcing anyone to participate in any of these now-legal activities. He just wants the people who do to feel like they're still contributing to a better America.

That's why I exercise my right to stop any drug use in my bar. While I appreciate everything the guy's done for the country, I'm still pretty old school. Drugs are never going to be good for you, and I want no part of them. If you don't like it, you don't drink in my bar—simple as that.

And I'm not the only one to think that way. But while people exercised the First Amendment, there was never any trouble. No rioting or protesting. People just discussed it and decided as communities what they wanted to do, and Cunningham's White House encouraged it.

The guy is a genius.

And that's the world we live in now. It's certainly made it easier for me to start over. Everybody is, to some extent, so it doesn't feel strange for me to leave my old life in the past and begin a new one.

08:06 CDT

. . .

I'm walking back down the street toward my bar, a bag of groceries weighing me down. A few doors before The Ferryman is a companion club. The place looks amazing, to be fair. The facilities are clean, there's healthcare advice at the front desk, and a few of the people who work there often come in for a drink after their shifts are over. They're nice. One of the girls, Laura, is a good friend of Tori's. She always fusses over Styx when she comes in.

Some people struggled to change their perception of companions, but they soon came around. Now working there is no different from working at a gas station or the local supermarket.

Crazy days we're living in.

I walk back into the bar and see Tori behind the counter, cleaning some glasses from the night before.

"Hey, babe," she says with that earth-shattering smile of hers. "You get everything?"

I look at her admiringly. She's wearing denim shorts and a Metallica T-shirt. Could a woman be any hotter?

I hold up the two bags in my right hand. "Sure did. This should cover us until the delivery at the end of the week."

"Just put it on the bar. I'll fill the shelves when I'm done with the glasses."

I smile and do as she says. "You want some breakfast? Bacon and eggs?"

"Sounds great," she replies.

I catch a glimpse out the window at a car parked across the street. It's white and clean and anonymous. Most likely a rental. It's facing to the right with the window down, so I can see who's sitting in the passenger seat. He's wearing mirrored sunglasses and has thick, dark hair and a couple of days' worth of stubble. He's staring straight at me, through the window. Our eyes meet, and he holds my gaze for a few moments. Then he turns to the driver, whom I can't see. They drive off casually.

"You okay?" asks Tori. She must have seen me looking distracted.

"Huh? Oh, yeah. I'm fine, darlin'. Bacon and eggs comin' right up."

I smile and then walk into the back. I have a small kitchen area set up there. I get some bacon out of the refrigerator and put four slices in the frying pan.

I try to focus on what I'm doing, but my mind's fixated on that car. It's been a while since my spider sense tingled, but something definitely wasn't right. I've scoped a place out enough times to be able to spot someone else doing it. I've never seen the car or the passenger before, and he was definitely checking my bar out. I know everyone in town. I don't know him, and that worries me.

Ah, I must be going crazy in my old age.

I smile to myself and think how far I've come in the last couple of years. So what if I get a little paranoid once in a while? After the life I've had, can you blame me?

3

The day passed the way most others do—quickly and stress-free. The sun's beginning its descent outside, and the bar's filling up nicely as the working day comes to an end and the need for a good beer takes hold.

Besides Tori and me, I employ a couple of other bar staff. Phil's a great guy. He's hardworking and usually serves behind the bar. He's also a doorman over at the companion club down the street. He's a big guy. About an inch taller than me. Well put together, too. He always has his black hair styled with different products. I poke fun at him regularly, but he's a tough guy and can back me up when I need him to.

Nicki's a nice girl. A student by day, she takes every spare shift she can while studying at college. Something to do with psychology, I think. She tried to tell me about it once, but I didn't understand a word of it. I remember laughing because it reminded me of working with Josh. She's cute and ridiculously friendly; all the locals love her. Even Styx says hello when she walks in.

It's a quiet night so far, compared to the last couple. Most of the tables are full, but no one is standing. The jukebox is silent. Tori and Nicki are working the floor, collecting empties and delivering new drinks. Standing behind the bar, I listen to the low, idle chatter from people's tables.

I turn to reach for a clean glass off the shelf as the door swings open behind me. As I look back and put the glass under the pump, ready to pull a beer, I see three guys standing in front of me. I recognize the one in the middle immediately. He's the guy with the shades from the car this morning.

I should never question my spider sense.

On either side of him are the hired muscle to his diplomat. I look at each one of them in turn, briefly, then go back to pulling the beer. I do my best to keep calm and resist any temptation to act before I think, like the old me would've done.

"What can I get you gentlemen?" I ask.

The one in the middle replies, "A few minutes of your time, Adrian Hell."

Huh. I've not been called that in a long time. Looks like the old me is in demand all of a sudden. How do they know who I used to be?

My eyes narrow. I focus on his accent, trying to work out where he's from. He sounds Russian... no, Ukrainian. Definitely Ukrainian. His two friends say nothing, but I study them anyway. Oddly, neither looks like they're the same nationality as the guy in the middle. The one on the left looks like he could be Middle Eastern, while the one on the right is Caucasian.

There goes my spider sense again.

I finish off the beer and set it down on the bar. "I think you're in the wrong place, friend. Nobody by that name here."

The middle guy's jacket is open, and he brushes it to the side, revealing a holstered gun. It looks like a Glock.

"I think I'm in the *right* place," he says, firmer this time. "Don't make things hard for yourself."

I smile as I glance over his shoulder, watching Tori talk to a table of locals. "Only thing 'round here that makes things hard for me is serving a customer behind you. I'll say again, there ain't no Adrian Hell here. You're in the wrong place, and you should leave... now."

"I was told you might be a little reluctant to talk to us. Do I have to convince you?"

I quickly survey the room—twenty-two customers and three staff, plus me and Styx. Three unknown hostiles, and one of them definitely armed. There's a bar between us, and I'm not as young as I used to be, so vaulting over it is out of the question.

Not the best situation I've ever been in but far from the worst.

I glance back over at Tori, who's looking over at me with a concerned expression. She can read me like a book. She knows when something's bothering me, and right now something's *really* bothering me. Namely, the safety of everyone in my bar. And not just that. Tori doesn't know anything about my past. She doesn't know I used to be married, nor that I had a daughter. She doesn't know I've been in the military for over half my life, and she doesn't know I used to be the world's most elite assassin. All of that is information I'd rather *stay* unknown to her.

I look at the guy again. I tense my jaw muscles, controlling my emotions. I take a deep breath and let it out heavily. I don't really have much choice.

"Okay, let's talk. Just leave these people alone, yeah?"

"No problem," he replies with a smile. He lets his jacket fall back into place, covering his gun.

"Wanna come into the back?"

He smiles. "Sure."

I look over at Tori again, who silently asks me if I'm okay. I nod back and point to the bar, signaling I need her to watch it for a few minutes. She nods and walks over. By the door, Styx is standing on edge, silently staring at the three men. I see him and click my fingers, so he turns his attention to me. "Easy, boy. It's all right."

He tilts his head questioningly to one side, then turns away and sits back down by the door. He keeps one eye on the three men as if to tell me that his spider sense is tingling too.

He's a good dog.

The men walk around the bar and step into the back. I follow them and stand just inside the doorway, making sure I keep my body between them and my customers. They stand in front of me in a loose semi-circle, their backs to the door leading up to my apartment. The men on either side stand like they're trying to intimidate me— one hand holding the other in front of them, legs shoulder-width apart. The guy in the middle's more relaxed, with one hand in his pocket and the other loose by his side.

I say, "So... talk."

"My employers have asked me to come and speak with you," the man in the middle begins. "They are interested in offering you a position within our organization. They feel you could be a tremendous asset to us and our cause."

I shake my head. "No, thanks. I already have a job, which I enjoy. Sorry you boys wasted your trip."

I step to one side, gesturing to the door to signal that the conversation's over, and it's time for them to leave.

He smiles almost apologetically. "Adrian, my employers are not people you say *no* to. It is a great honor to be chosen to work for them."

I feel the tension slowly building. I sigh and briefly massage my forehead with both hands. "Let me be honest, guys. You blew it the moment you said the words *our* and *cause*. I'm not that guy anymore. And even if I were, I'm not and never have been a terrorist, an extremist, or whatever it is that *you* are. You should be grateful I'm not that guy because if I were, you'd all be dead by now. We're done here. Leave my bar and don't come back. If your employer has a problem with that, he can come here himself and take it up with me. I'll happily tell him the same thing."

The men on either side of him step forward.

The man in the middle says, "At best, you are a relic of an old world, Adrian. You should get with the times. Big talk means nothing anymore. We feel your experience would be beneficial to us, but make no mistake—you're not a threat in any way. You will come with us right now, or we'll shoot you."

He moves his jacket to reveal his gun again.

Well, this went south pretty quick, didn't it? I never was much good at talking my way out of a situation. That was always Josh's forte. I tend to be slightly more aggressive in my approach to delicate situations.

The guy on my right takes another step forward, and I feel my brain revert to survival mode. Without a second thought, I step forward to meet him, swinging my left leg low and kicking the outside of his right knee, hard. He loses his balance. I throw a hard, straight right punch, hitting him across the face and dropping him to the floor. He's not out, but he's hurting.

The guy on my left then comes at me, his arms already raised. I react a second too slow, and he grips me with both hands around the throat.

I'm definitely out of practice.

I lean my head back and bring my arms up. I slam them down on his elbows, forcefully bending his arms, which loosens his grip. As he does, I push him away and immediately step toward him, launching a hard kick to his stomach. He doubles over as the wind is knocked out of him. I bring my right elbow down hard on the back of his exposed head, and he joins his friend on the floor. Again, he's not quite unconscious, but he won't be getting up for a few minutes.

The middle guy has his gun drawn, aimed at me, when I turn to him. I knock his right arm up as he fires, causing the bullet to fire into the ceiling. I hear gasps of shock and concern from the bar, followed by the scrambling of people trying to get outside. I hope Tori's one of them.

I grab his wrist with my left hand, twisting it away from him. He has no choice but to lean with it, so it doesn't break. He drops his gun. I kick it away, then jab him twice in the face. I switch hands and twist his arm back across him with my right, then straighten it out and turn it, so his elbow is facing me. Without warning, I smash my left forearm down and dislocate it. He screams in agony as he crumples to the floor, his elbow hanging loose at an unnatural angle.

I quickly move to the two guys who are already down. I drag them both up by the back of their necks and march them out to the bar area. Styx sees me and is up straight away, snarling viciously.

I throw them both to the floor, just in front of the saloon

doors. Styx circles them, barking wildly. "Keep 'em there, boy. Don't hurt 'em."

Around me, the people still here are looking on, wide-eyed and slack-jawed. I ignore them. They knew I don't stand for any trouble in my bar but not that I could take out three guys at once.

Well, now they know.

I walk quickly around the bar, avoiding the surprised look on Tori's face as I head into the back room again. I retrieve the gun and aim it at the middle guy. "Get up."

He struggles to his feet and stumbles out into the bar area, holding his broken arm close to his body. I follow, keeping the gun on him the whole time. The other two haven't moved. Styx is doing a great job of keeping them in check. I push the middle guy over to them, and he falls.

I release the magazine from the gun, letting it fall to the floor. I eject the round from the chamber, which I catch and drop next to the magazine. Finally, I throw the empty gun over to them as a message.

"Leave now, while you've still got the use of your legs. Tell whoever sent you to forget about me. Forget about Devil's Spring. The next person that comes here looking for trouble leaves in a body bag."

I cross my arms and glare at them until they stand. The two bodyguards hold the diplomat up.

"You're making a big mistake," says the man with the broken arm.

"Like I haven't heard *that* before?" I look at Styx. "Show 'em the door, boy."

The fur on his back rises. He bares his teeth, snarling and barking, rounding them up like he's herding sheep. He chases them out of the bar, then returns moments later, much calmer. He pads over to Tori and rubs his head on her leg, then walks over to me and sits down.

I glance around. Everyone's staring at me, waiting for an explanation. Tori walks over and throws her arms around me.

"You okay?" she whispers.

"Never better." I smile at her, then at the room. "Come on, folks. Show's over. Next round's on me."

Laughter and cheering quickly erupts as people take their seats. I walk over to the bar, get a clean glass down from the shelf, and start to pull the first beer.

4

I'm in bed, sitting propped up against the pillows with my hands behind my head. In the bathroom, Tori's brushing her teeth. She was concerned after the showdown in the bar earlier in the evening, but I think I've managed to appease her for now.

I'm trying to think who those guys could've worked for. It's hard to imagine they could represent any significant criminal organization. Everything that made criminal empires any money is legal now, so they've all but disappeared.

It's a good thing I'm not still working as a hitman. I'd be facing a recession of my own.

I had to expect things like this to happen occasionally, though. It's a drawback of being who I used to be, I guess. The man might be long gone, but the legend clearly lives on.

I dismiss it from my mind as Tori appears at the bathroom door, wearing a cropped T-shirt and panties. She leans seductively on the frame.

"Hey," she says with a killer smile.

"Hey yourself."

She walks over. As she nears the bed, I reach up and put my hands on her waist, whisking her off her feet and onto the bed next to me. I roll over on top of her and lean down to kiss her. She meets me halfway, pressing her lips tenderly against mine. After a few moments, we part, our heart rates slightly higher than they were before. We smile at each other and I lean in again, but she puts her hand on my chest and pushes me back. She props herself up on her elbow, looking at me. "What happened tonight, Ady?"

I sigh. "They were just three assholes lookin' to cause trouble."

"I know. You said that. But why would you invite them into the back room first?"

"One of them had a gun. He said they wanted to talk to me, so I did what I thought was right to protect the people in my bar."

"And that's real thoughtful of you, baby. But you sometimes forget that A... I know you, and B... you can't lie for shit."

She smiles, and I can't help but smile back. She's not mad at me. She's just looking out for me and wants me to be honest with her. And I hate lying to her. I briefly think whether I actually need to. I mean, she's crazy about me, and she's a genuinely great woman. Would she understand if I told her about my former life?

Probably not.

"I honestly have no idea who they were, Tori. I just didn't want anyone getting hurt."

She traces her finger over my chest. "What did they wanna talk to you about?"

"One of them said something about his boss offering me a job. I don't know what that entailed. I didn't give them the chance to tell me."

"Yeah, I saw that part. Did you really beat the crap outta *three* guys?"

I shrug. "It's no big deal. I—"

"Adrian, look..." she says, interrupting me. She sits up and stares straight into my eyes. "I know you don't like talking about your past, and I respect that, and I don't ask. It honestly doesn't bother me. I didn't know you back then. I know you *now*. And I love you now. That's all that matters to me. But please give me something... some idea of who you used to be. Most ordinary people can't beat up three guys without even breaking a sweat. I worry about you."

I think for a minute. I look at her beautiful face, full of care and concern. I decide to tell her something. Just enough to put her mind to rest. I owe her that much. God knows why, but this woman loves me. And damn it, I love her right back.

I nod. "Okay. I used to be in the military. I did some... special operations, back in the day. I'm well trained and can handle myself. After I quit, I worked as a consultant in the private sector for a few years..."

I trail off as I think back, momentarily realizing that this is the same lie I told my wife and daughter to keep them from knowing I was an assassin. I feel a pang of guilt, but I continue.

"I retired with a good pension and came here to Texas to start over. Maybe those guys were with a government contractor? It's not uncommon to hire ex-soldiers for private security firms."

She's silent for a moment, processing the information.

"So, you were some kind of special forces, action hero-type guy, huh?"

"I... I guess, yeah."

She pushes me down beside her, climbs on top of me, straddling my waist, and takes off her T-shirt.

"That is *so* hot..." she says, smiling as she leans down and kisses me.

April 8, 2017 — 06:31 CDT

I wake up early the next morning. The dawn light shines through my curtains like always. Tori is fast asleep, lying on her front with her arm and leg draped over me. I gently slide out from under her and pull my jeans on. I make my way downstairs and put on a pot of coffee before walking out into the bar. Styx greets me with his standard head rub on the legs, then wanders off to the back in search of food. I crack my neck and set about taking the chairs off the tables, ready for the day ahead.

After a few minutes, I hear a banging on the shutters from outside. I get the keys from behind the bar and walk over to open it up. Having just the saloon doors on the place, I need some proper security at night.

I raise the shutter and see a man standing there. He has shoulder-length, dark gray hair and a handlebar mustache. His face is rough and tired, hardened and grizzled after countless years of doing what he does. The morning sun reflects off his badge. He tips his hat up slightly, revealing his eyes. "Mornin', Adrian."

Sheriff John Raynor has been in charge of Devil's Spring since God Himself was in kindergarten. He's old but in that timeless kind of way—doesn't matter how aged he might look, he always moves, speaks, and thinks the same way. Everybody in town knows him well, and they respect him without question. He has an old-school state of mind, much like myself.

"Mornin', John." I step aside to invite him in. "Early start for you, isn't it?"

"No rest for the wicked." He smiles a friendly but humorless smile as he takes off his hat. "Sorry to disturb you. I know you're an early riser, so I took a chance you'd be up and about."

I smile politely. "I'll sleep when I'm dead. Coffee?"

"Sure. Thanks."

"Black, no sugar, right?"

'Is there another way to drink it?'

"So people tell me."

"Sick bastards."

We laugh like old friends, and he follows me into the back. I gesture to a chair.

"What can I do for you, Sheriff?" I ask as I pour the coffee.

Raynor sits down and rests his hat on the table, then takes the mug from me. "I hear there was some trouble here last night?"

I shrug. "It was nothin', really. Just a couple of guys trying to cause problems, and they didn't like it when I asked them to leave."

"So, what happened?"

"I made 'em leave."

He nods and takes a sip of his coffee. "Fair enough."

"Why are you really here, John?"

He regards me for a moment. "A few hours ago, a white rental car was found parked on the side of the road leading out of town. One of the truckers coming in from San Antonio called it in. Inside the car were three men, all executed. Single gunshot wound to the head on each of 'em. No evidence of a struggle. Keys in the ignition, engine running."

That's not good. Don't get me wrong—I lose sleep over many things, and the fact those three assholes are dead isn't ever going to be one of them. But a lot of people saw me tussle with those guys last night, and now they're corpses. The good sheriff is here in an official capacity, no matter how friendly he's being.

I raise an eyebrow. "Any idea what happened?"

He shrugs slightly, as if unsure about sharing his theories with me. "What do *you* think happened?"

I take a sip of my coffee and think about it. "Well, calling it an execution is right. I don't know the ballistic details, but I'd guess the angle of the entry wounds supports what I imagine your current working theory is—that they knew the shooter. He probably leaned in through the passenger window when they pulled over to speak to him. You won't find any shell casing in the vehicle or forensic evidence of any kind—the shooter will have worn gloves. Fast, accurate shooting at close quarters isn't easy, so the guy's a professional."

Raynor strokes his mustache and smiles to himself. He takes another sip of his coffee but remains silent.

I shrug and smile wryly. "I'm just guessing, though. So, am I a suspect?"

Raynor stands, picks up his hat, and laughs. "Christ, if your bar ever closes, I hope to God you consider becoming a

26

deputy. No, you're not a suspect. If you were, I wouldn't have had coffee with you. And if you were guilty, you wouldn't have given me a professional—and frighteningly accurate—theory about what happened. Military?"

I nod.

"You can take the man outta the Army..." he muses. "I appreciate your time, Adrian. Sorry to trouble you so early in the morning."

"No trouble, John. Any time. You need anything else, just holla."

"I appreciate that. Thanks for the coffee. I'll see myself out."

"Take care."

Raynor walks out and across the bar. I hear him fuss over Styx, then the doors swing open and shut.

I turn to head upstairs and see Tori in the doorway, smiling at me. "Was that Sheriff Raynor?"

"Yeah, he just called in for coffee."

"Uh-huh... what's happened?"

I smile at her. "Those three assholes from last night were found dead in their car on the outskirts of town early this morning. Sheriff just had a few questions. He'd heard what happened in here last night."

"Jesus. What did you say to him?" she asks. She moves over to the side and pours herself a coffee, adding cream and sugar.

Shaking my head in playful disgust, I reply, "I just told him exactly what happened. He said he was just following procedure and it was nothin' to worry about."

She walks over to me, stands on her tiptoes, and kisses my cheek. "Well, if he needs you to provide an alibi for your whereabouts last night, I'll gladly give him a full statement!"

She winks and walks back upstairs with her mug of

coffee. I watch her go, smiling to myself, then turn and walk back into the bar. I sit down on a stool in front of the counter and whistle to call Styx over to me. He obliges and sits at my feet, looking up at me. I stroke his head and pat his nose.

"I got a bad feelin' about this, boy. A real bad feelin'..."

5

It's another busy night tonight. Phil, Nicki, and Tori are rushed off their feet. The atmosphere is loud and happy, the jukebox is blasting out some classic songs, and the beer's flowing out as the money flows in. I'm not here for the money, but it's nice to know what I'm doing is working.

I haven't been able to shake the sense of impending doom after the events of last night and this morning, and it's now driving me to distraction. Tori's been great, as always. She keeps telling me not to worry and that it was just a bit of bad luck and coincidence. And she's probably right. It's been well over two years since I dropped off the grid and started afresh down here. Maybe it's just a case of old habits dying hard.

I do my best to put it behind me as I open a couple of beers for a young couple who've just walked in. I've seen them a few times. I think they're new in town, so I make a point of making them feel welcome when they come in. So far, they keep coming back, so I must be doing something right.

As always, the night's gone by quickly with no trouble. But then I look over at the door, and the sheriff enters. With him are two men in dark suits, who look around the bar conspicuously.

Feds. They might as well wear an A-board and ring a bell.

Shit.

He takes his hat off and surveys the bar before walking over to me. "Evenin', Adrian."

"Sheriff," I reply with a nod. "Get you a drink?"

He shakes his head. "Not tonight, thank you. Listen... is there somewhere we can talk?"

I look at him, then at the two men with him, and let out a heavy sigh. "Yeah, we can go in the back." I turn to Phil, who's standing next to me, serving customers. "You okay to watch the bar on your own for a few?"

He shrugs casually. "Sure thing."

I turn back to Raynor. "Follow me."

We walk to the back room, and I offer the good sheriff a seat. I don't acknowledge the two suits that are with him, and they seem happy enough standing.

"What can I do for you, Sheriff?"

He lets out a heavy sigh and strokes his mustache. "Adrian, these boys are from the FBI."

"I never would've guessed."

He ignores the quip.

"They just got here and came straight to me, asking after you. They need to—"

"Mr... Adrian, we have a few questions for you regarding the murder of three men in this town last night," says one of the agents. They're both standing side by side in front of the door. The one on the left is doing the talking. "Do you mind first confirming where you were last night?"

I smile to myself, thinking about what Tori said this morning. "I was in bed from about ten-thirty."

"What time did you fall asleep?" asks the other agent.

I shrug. "I dunno. About eleven, maybe?"

"Can anyone verify that?"

"My girlfriend can. She was with me the whole night."

"I see," says the first agent. They seem to be taking it in turns. "Tell us about what happened in the bar earlier in the evening."

I sigh, already tiring of going over it. "Not much to tell. Three guys walked in and asked to speak to me. They started making trouble, so I threw them out."

"Three guys? You threw them out single-handedly?"

"Yeah..."

I still don't see why that's so hard to believe, but never mind.

The guy on the right produces a cell phone from his pocket. It has a bigger screen than normal. Looks more like a small tablet. He taps the screen and turns it to show me. Displayed on it are black and white pictures of three men, presumably from existing files they have on them.

"Are these the gentleman you evicted last night?"

I look and nod. "That's them, yeah."

"Our crime scene report of the shooting suggests the man in the back seat had a dislocated elbow..."

I smile. "*That* was me. But if you're looking for the shooter, you're in the wrong place. I didn't kill them."

"But you threatened them?"

"Yes."

"What did you say?"

"I said the next the time they come into my bar and

cause trouble, they'll leave in a body bag. But I wouldn't read too much into that. Confrontations like that are usually won by words and a strong physical presence, not by actual violence. I was just saying what I needed to in order to make my point."

"But you *did* use violence..." says the agent on the right.

I nod again. "That's right, but only because one of them pulled a gun on me. I grew concerned for the safety of the people in my bar, so I imposed what force I deemed necessary at the time."

I look quickly at Raynor, who looks genuinely sorry that he's putting me through this.

"Okay," says the first agent again. "You're not a suspect for the shooting."

"So, why *are* you here? There's no need to tell me I didn't do it. I already knew that."

"Adrian, the men who were found murdered were on our watch list. They had known links to a suspected terrorist named Yalafi Hussein. Does that name ring any bells with you?"

I shake my head.

"Not surprising," says the second agent. "He's notoriously camera-shy and keeps a low profile. However, he's thought to have orchestrated multiple attacks around the world over the last few years."

"That's all tragic, but why are you telling me?"

They get nervous and look at the sheriff before responding.

"Adrian, we... have your file," says the first agent. "We know what happened in San Francisco a few years ago."

Oh.

"We understand you've started over down here..." says the second, looking at the sheriff again.

Raynor gets to his feet, presumably sensing the awkward reluctance of the agents. "Adrian, this ain't none of my business now that these boys are here. I know you're a private person. If you'd prefer me to wait outside, I won't take offense."

I think for a minute. If they have my FBI file and they know about San Francisco, then they know exactly who I am. Or who I used to be, anyway. I don't want any mention of Adrian Hell in Texas. I've worked hard to bury him and done a damn good job. I'm not about to jeopardize that now.

"Sorry, John. Would you mind?"

He retrieves his hat from the table and gives a courteous nod as he leaves. I watch him go back out to the bar. He's one of the good guys. I feel bad asking him to step out, but it's necessary.

I look back at the agents. "I appreciate your discretion. Now get to your point, so I can get on with my life."

The first agent stepped forward. "Adrian, we believe those men were here to recruit you."

I frown. "They said they wanted to offer me a position in their organization, but I didn't ask for more details. What were they trying to recruit me for?"

"Well, we don't honestly know. There's chatter about a terrorist network hiring a lot of heavyweights. If that's true, we can only surmise there's a large attack being planned, but we have next-to-nothing to work with. We don't know if the CIA has more to go on because they're not sharing anything with us."

I raise an eyebrow. "Well, their files are out of date. I'm retired."

The agent at the back steps forward this time.

"Maybe it's not as easy as you think to get out of that line of work?" he offers, sounding surprisingly sympathetic.

I take a deep breath and think about how good a point that is. "What's the bottom line here, guys? Why come and see me?"

"Just... be careful," says the first agent. "We don't know who we're dealing with here yet, but it's likely they won't take too kindly to being refused and then attacked. We don't know who shot those men last night, but the smart money would be on this terrorist network assuming it was you. Which means you might not have seen the last of them."

"Okay, well, I'm glad you fellas came to see me. And seriously, if there's anything I can do to help you out, let me know. But don't worry about me. I can handle myself. And rest assured, I won't be signing up to any extreme causes any time soon."

They both nod and we all file out back into the bar. The agents head for the door. Raynor, who must've been sitting at the bar waiting, stands to follow them. He turns to me and says, "I hope everything's all right, Adrian."

"You got nothin' to worry about, Sheriff. You have my word."

He nods and puts on his hat. "See you around."

No one in the bar seems to have paid any attention—except Tori. She heads straight for me. I sit on a stool and rest an arm on the counter.

"Phil, get me a beer, would you?"

He obliges without a word, and I take a long pull on the bottle he passes me.

"What was all that about?" asks Tori. "You all right, baby?"

"It was nothin'," I reply, trying to sound as relaxed and dismissive as I can. "The FBI is investigating the shooting, and the sheriff thought it'd help them if they spoke with me."

She looks at me for a minute, then smiles. "My super-hero action man working with the FBI! I'm so hot for you right now."

She winks and kisses my cheek, then walks off with an empty tray in her hand. She puts an exaggerated wiggle in her hips, knowing damn well I'm watching her. I smile and think briefly about the good times that inevitably lie ahead for me once we close up for the night. But I can't stop my mind from drifting back to what those agents said.

Maybe it's not as easy as you think to get out of that line of work...

What the hell would a network of terrorists want with me?

I have an uneasy feeling I'll find out soon enough.

6

I take another sip of my coffee as I sit at the bar. Styx is at my feet, looking sleepy. It's after five. I didn't sleep well. We had a good night last night—it was busy right up until closing time. Tori dragged me to bed the moment we locked up. But I can't stop my mind from worrying about what the FBI said to me. The last thing I want to do is put anyone in this town in any danger.

Especially Tori.

God, I love her. She lights a fire inside me that hasn't burned in a long time. I'm not going to let anything happen to her.

I need to clear my mind and stop worrying.

I walk back upstairs and into the bedroom. Tori's still sleeping. When I get out of bed, she stretches and rolls over to the middle, spreading herself out, seemingly aware that I'm no longer there. I look at her for a moment, then put my jogging pants and running shoes on. I pull a T-shirt on and quietly make my way back downstairs and through into the bar.

"Coming for a run, Styx?"

He tilts his head to the side again, as if asking if I'm joking.

"Don't look at me like that. Come for a run, you lazy mutt."

He growls at me, then stands. He stretches before walking over to the door. He looks back at me, as if to say, *Come on, then. Let's get this over with...*

He's a pretty cool dog.

I step outside. The first rays of the morning sun streak across the sky as it readies itself to rise for another day. Styx appears next to me, looking around and sniffing the air. I stretch my legs for a few moments, then set off jogging down the street. I can tell Styx is running slower than he'd like to, purely so he can keep pace beside me.

I'm heading in the opposite direction to the grocery store and the companion club. I cross the street and take a left at the end. There's a slight rise that leads to the station house. I'll swing by and see if the sheriff's around while I'm out. Plus, the uphill run will be a great workout.

I haven't turned into a fitness fanatic, but I do have a punching bag at the back of The Ferryman, and I enjoy a run a few mornings a week. I'm not getting any younger, and Tori can be a handful sometimes—in the best kind of way.

I reach the top of the rise and follow it to the right. The station house is across the street from me. Two squad cars are in the parking lot out front, but there's no sign of life. Must be too early for the sheriff today.

I continue with my run. A couple of cars pass me going the other way. It's getting lighter, and the town is starting to wake up. I run past the drug store, which is now more than just a place to pick up aspirin. I bet they make a fortune. Marijuana and cocaine are the new alcohol and tobacco. Not too expensive that the lower and middle-class can't afford them but priced high enough that it's a profitable business. The taxes from their sale continue to fund both the new America and Cunningham's re-election campaign.

A few doors farther along, I see the local barbershop. It's a small business but one that's been around longer than most people around here. An old-timer named Ray Hooper owns the place. He comes in for a drink every Thursday evening without fail. He's pushing eighty, with tight gray curls on his head and a permanent coarse beard on his face. He always wears a shirt with the sleeves rolled up and suit pants. He's sweeping the street out front.

"Mornin', Adrian," he says as he bends down. "Hey, Styx."

I stop for a moment to catch my breath. Styx isn't even breathing heavy. He sits in front of Hooper, waiting for the inevitable patting his head's about to get.

"Mornin', Hoops," I say between deep breaths. "You're up early. How're things?"

"Oh, y'know... same ol', same ol'. You and Tori keeping well?"

I smile. "We're all right, Hoops. I'll tell her you were asking."

"Hear you got a visit from some suited gentlemen last night..."

"You gotta love a small town," I say with a wry smile.

Hooper laughs. "You know how it goes, man. So, everythin' all right?"

"Yeah, everything's fine. Just procedure after I threw those assholes outta my bar."

"Well... you jus' watch yaself, y'hear? Whole town likes you, son. Wouldn't want nothin' to happen to you."

"Thanks. I'll be fine, I'm sure."

He turns and heads back inside his barbershop. "I mean, if you left, where would we drink?"

I shake my head and laugh, then set off running again. I turn left at the end of the street. I'll head back down to the main strip and take a left, back to The Ferryman. I've done a good circuit, and I'm suitably tired now.

A car passes me, heading in the same direction. After a minute, I see another one. Styx growls at the second one as we come up to the end of the street. We turn left again, and I see The Ferryman up ahead on the right. Both cars that just passed us are parked outside. Styx growls again and speeds up. Something about those cars seems to have spooked him.

I keep pace as best I can, heading for the bar. As I get closer, my spider sense starts tingling. I don't like those cars either. I don't know why, but with everything that's happened in the last couple of days, my paranoia is working overtime.

I reach the front door and find it open. I know I shut it...

Styx starts growling louder.

"Easy, boy. Keep quiet now."

I look at the cars. Both sedans, both white. Definitely rentals. Potentially up to eight guys, four in each. As I push the door open and step inside, I hear a woman scream.

Tori!

Without thinking, I rush across the bar and into the back. I can't think of anything else except getting to her. I don't know who these guys are or what they want, but I swear to God, if they hurt her, I'll kill them.

I round the bar at full speed, heading for the back, but I run straight into a fist. The shock of the impact sends me staggering backward, but I manage to keep my balance and lean on the bar for support.

I really should've thought about this before running in.

I look up as four men walk out. Big guys wearing jackets and jeans. A quick assessment tells me they're all different nationalities, so I can only assume they're associates of the three recently deceased men who came to see me the other night.

Styx is barking wildly. I hold my hand up to him, signaling for him to stand down.

"It's all right, boy."

I look at the men in front of me. I take a few paces back, moving into the open space of the bar. They fan out around me. I hear another scream from upstairs and clench my jaw muscles, fighting to contain the anger building inside me.

"Whatever you're after, just take it and go," I say to no one in particular. "Just leave the woman out of it."

None of them make a move; they just smile and stand their ground.

I reckon I can take them. They don't have any weapons that I can see. I just need to get to Tori.

Three more men appear in the doorway from the back and stride purposefully toward me. The last one in has Tori with him. He's standing behind her with his hand over her mouth. She's wearing a thin T-shirt and her panties. The bastards must have dragged her out of bed as she slept.

My heart rate's increasing, and I'm finding it hard to focus on anything other than my anger. It feels like a volcano bubbling away inside of me, waiting to erupt and spew violence across the land. Her eyes are wide with shock, and I see the fear as she struggles to stop herself from crying.

"Tori, are you okay? Have they hurt you?"

She doesn't react—it looks like the guy's got a strong grip on her, holding her still. The new arrivals join the semi-circle of men in front of me. The guy with Tori stands in the center. He's average-looking, just under six feet tall. He probably weighs around two-ten, maybe two-fifteen. He has a Mediterranean look about him. Possibly Turkish. I'm not sure.

He's the one who speaks.

"I'm sorry it's come to this, Adrian, but you should have taken the first offer we gave you."

I look along the line, left to right. A real mixed bag of bad guys. Whoever this supposed terrorist network is, they aren't picky about who works for them. In fact, the only criterion for employment seems to be that you have to be a known badass. Or at least *think* you are, judging by these guys.

Styx is by my side, his fur raised and teeth bared. He's not going to attack until I tell him to, but he's ready.

"Like I told your friends the other night, I'm not inter-ested in any job offers. I run this bar and have no intention of doing otherwise. I didn't kill your friends, but I *am* gonna kill *you* if you don't let her go and leave here right now."

The line of assholes start laughing, not taking me seriously.

I'm out of practice. Problem is, I don't want to get back in the swing of things in front of Tori. She doesn't need to know what I'm capable of. But I can't see any other way out of this.

Shit.

Shit, shit, shit...

Think, Adrian—*think*!

I take a few deeps breaths and look at the line again.

This time, I'm looking professionally. I try to forget about Tori for a moment and focus on what I'm good at.

They all look capable, which is a concern but not a big one. At the end of the day, if they push me, I'll push back. I might not have an Inner Satan anymore, but that doesn't mean I've forgotten what it's like to be Adrian Hell, even if I no longer live his life.

I sigh heavily. "Okay, last chance. Let her go and walk away. Tell whoever sent you that this town and I are off-limits. Then maybe, *maybe*, I'll forget all about this."

Another ripple of laughter.

The man holding Tori speaks again. "I can see why he wants you. But what makes you so confident? You're outnumbered seven to one."

"True, but from where I'm standing, you boys don't have weapons, whereas I have three."

He frowns, and the rest of them look at each other. "Three?"

I hold my hands up one at a time and ball each one into a fist. "There's two... and the third is standing next to me, looking at your throats."

It's funny, but they hadn't paid any attention to Styx. He's a wild-eyed wolf that's almost six feet tall when he stands up on his back legs. Styx is an impressive beast. Definitely cause for concern if he's snarling.

They stop laughing. I think they're finally taking me seriously. About time!

The trick with a large group of attackers is to hit the one who's talking. Whoever talks first is the leader, and if you crush the strongest member emphatically, the rest tend to back down quickly.

The problem I have is the one talking is holding Tori,

and I imagine he's smart enough to keep her next to him too. That leaves me with the other six.

I need to hit hard, hit fast, and hit first.

I look at Tori. I hold her gaze until I'm sure she's thinking about nothing else beside me. Then I wink at her. She visibly relaxes, and I feel better knowing she knows I'm about to save her.

Then I take a step forward. Just one. It's always enough to prompt an attack in these situations. Someone will always step to meet you, like an instinct, to maintain the appearance of strength and control.

This time, the two guys on the left step to meet me.

Now I *know* I'm going to win. These idiots just showed me their hand. If they had any training or common sense whatsoever, the guys at each end would've come forward, immediately surrounding me and creating two separate targets and making it harder for me to fight. But they didn't. Two guys standing side by side came at me, giving me one easy target.

Merry Christmas, me!

"Styx... lunch time!"

I step toward the two men on the left. He barks and sets off charging behind me. The first guy, on the far left, goes straight for my throat, but I grab his wrist and twist it away from me to my left. As he moves his body with it, I jab him twice on the nose, breaking it and causing his eyes to water, impairing his vision.

I whip my right leg forward, kicking the guy next to us hard in the groin, then smash my right elbow into the first guy's throat. Both are down for the count in a matter of seconds. I quickly glance behind me to see Styx clamping his jaws on the left thigh of the man on the far right.

That'll keep *him* busy...

The two on the right of the guy with Tori step forward next. Their lack of organization and tactics baffles me, but I'm not complaining.

As the first one gets within reach, I thrust my left hand into his throat, then step in close to him, bringing my right elbow into his face. He drops to the floor, and I start to spin counterclockwise, crouching as I do. I turn around and punch the second guy in the gut. Then I stand, using my elbow to smash him in his face. He crumples to the floor next to his friend.

I look over again to see how Styx is doing. He's staring at me with shreds of flesh hanging from his fangs. The guy he went for is on the floor, unconscious, with blood pouring out of his leg.

The remaining guy, to the left of Tori, hesitates and looks at his leader, who shouts at him in a foreign language, gesturing at me with his head. The other guy sighs and reluctantly walks toward me.

I let him throw the first punch because I almost feel sorry for him. I block it easily, knocking his arm away with one hand, then punch him hard in the sternum with the other. I move close to him and use my right elbow to hit him again, knocking the wind out of him and sending him to the floor in a heap.

I look back at the one remaining guy, who's moved Tori directly in front of him. He's peering over her shoulder, looking shocked and concerned.

"Let her go."

He moves his hands, positioning one on her jaw and the other at the base of her skull. I look him in the eye, searching for a sign that he's bluffing and that he doesn't really intend to break her neck.

"Fuck you!" he shouts.

He's not bluffing. Shit!

I can't rush him because he's standing a good ten feet away from me. He'll snap her neck before I can get close enough.

Styx starts growling again, but he holds steady.

I'm running every outcome through my mind. I keep eye contact with Tori to reassure her she'll be fine.

A few tense moments silently pass before noises from outside distract me. I look out of the window and see two more cars screech to a halt outside the bar. Eight men get out, forming a line. They're all holding assault rifles.

The guy holding Tori smiles, like he knows he's just beat me.

I look at her. "Tori, I'm so sorry."

Then the shooting starts.

7

As the bullets start flying, I race over to Tori, keeping as low as I can. The guy holding her moves, dropping for cover, but I get to him first. I grab his hand from around her jaw and break two of his fingers. As his grip loosens, I push her to the floor.

"Stay down!" I shout over the noise.

I watch as she moves into a fetal position, covering her ears with her hands and screaming in fear. I feel terrible that she's been dragged into all this, but I stay focused on the guy. I punch him hard in the stomach and across the face, then grab his collar and spin him around, launching him into the center of the bar. I dive for cover behind the counter and look over. He stands, disoriented for a brief second, before being riddled by the bullets peppering the building from outside. He flails backward and lands a few feet away, looking like Swiss cheese. Blood escapes from his lifeless body, quickly forming a large pool around him.

I sit on the floor with my back to the side of the bar, looking at Tori and thinking about how we're going to get out of this in one piece. I guess I should accept the fact that I'm not going to be able to hide my past from her anymore. She's just seen me take out seven guys, and she's about to see me take out eight more...

I crawl behind the bar and reach under the counter, retrieving the custom Beretta 92FS with the engraved butt that I have taped under there. Now isn't the time to think about how much I'd *actually* moved on. I'm just glad I still keep some of my old habits, like preparing for every eventuality. As I check the mag's full and flick the safety catch off, I briefly contemplate what it says about me that I must have subconsciously known that something like this would happen at some point, regardless of how much I tried to move on.

I sigh and lean forward, resting my elbows on my knees and my forehead on the barrel of my pistol, thinking about what comes next. Tori seems to momentarily overcome her fear as she opens her eyes and crawls toward me.

"You can't stay here," I shout to her. "It's not safe."

"What about you?" she yells back. "And where did you get that gun?"

"Don't worry about me. I'll be fine. Just get into the back and go upstairs. Get in the bathroom, barricade the door shut, and lie down in the tub with the cover from the bed over you. Stay there until I come and get you. I'll shout to you, and I want you to shout back and ask for the code word. Do you understand? The code word is *hellbound*, and if I don't say it, don't let me in."

"Adrian, I don't—"

"Just trust me, please. Let me handle this. Now *go*!"

She looks at me, confused and afraid, then nods slowly.

She turns and scrambles across the floor, into the back. As soon as she's out of sight, I stand and fire off a few rounds out the window, catching two of the gunmen to the left of the line and dropping them. I duck back behind the bar and take a few deep breaths, controlling the adrenaline rush I've not felt in a long time.

Six left, but the gunfire seems relentless.

I can't stay here. I'm a sitting duck, but I don't know where else I can go. I just have to bide my time, wait for them to change mags, and be accurate when I return fire.

The bar's starting to disintegrate around me from the perpetual onslaught of bullets. Another minute passes before I get an opportunity to return fire. I quickly poke out the side of the bar, keeping low, and pick off a guy on the right.

That's another one down...

But I know my little resistance is just prolonging the inevitable. I know a shitty situation when I see one, and this couldn't get much shittier.

I move to stand, intending to get another couple of shots off, but the sound of a shotgun blast makes me hesitate.

Crunch-crunch... BANG!

I chance a look over the bar. I see the guy now standing on the far left explode and go flying off to the right, knocking into the guy next to him.

What the...

I wait a second longer, then stand and fire off five more rounds. I take out three of the four remaining guys before clicking down on an empty chamber. The last guy stares at me through the smoke for a moment, then he quickly disappears off to the right in a red mist—the result of another shotgun blast.

Silence falls. I step out from behind the bar and walk

cautiously over to the door, holding my gun ready, despite being out of ammo. The smell of gunpowder in the air stings my nose. The smoke catches my throat, but I fight to suppress a cough. From the left, Sheriff Raynor appears, shotgun in hand and his hat on a slight angle.

"Looked like you could use a hand," he says.

"Yeah, thanks." I tuck the gun into my waistband behind me and step outside. I stand next to him and turn to look at the front of my bar, which now resembles a war zone. "Jesus..."

"So, you mind tellin' me what all this is about?" he asks.

"Would if I could, Sheriff. I have no idea."

Raynor rests the shotgun on his shoulder, the barrel still smoking. "Adrian, you're a good guy, and I consider us friends. But cut the crap and level with me. I just helped you take down eight fellas emptying their machine guns at your bar. Somethin's goin' on here, and you know more than you're tellin' me."

I sigh. I've reached the point I always knew would come, where I can no longer outrun my past. I walk over to the nearest dead guy and pick up his gun. I feel its weight as I turn back to show it to Raynor.

"This is a Steyr AUG A3 SF assault rifle. Manufactured in Austria. It fires nineteen mil' cartridges at a rate of about seven hundred rounds per minute. It's been used by the Austrian Special Forces for the last decade."

Raynor takes off his hat, rubs his hand across his head, then replaces it and strokes his mustache. "Now how the hell d'you know that kinda shit about those kinda guns? What exactly did you do in the military?"

"Sheriff, I'm being straight with you here, and I'd appreciate you keeping what I'm about to tell you between us."

He nods.

"My full name is Adrian Hughes. I'm ex-military and used to head up a black ops unit for the CIA. I did a lot of things that no one kept any record of, and when I retired, I became a professional assassin. I was the best there was, and I made a lot of money doing it. I had a global reputation for being the greatest. But I also made a lot of enemies. I lost a wife and daughter because of that job, and when I finally avenged their deaths, I found my passion for the business had gone. I *was* Adrian Hell, but I buried him alongside my family and hung up my guns."

I pause so that he can process what I'm saying. He just kind of nods along, like none of it is really *that* hard to believe... like it explains a lot. But I continue.

"Those three guys the other night came here looking for me, trying to recruit me for something. I don't know who sent them or what they wanted me for. I just explained I'd retired and that they shouldn't come back. Then when you said they'd been found dead, I started to worry that maybe there was more to it than just my old reputation coming back to haunt me. Next thing I know, I have seven guys in my bar holding Tori hostage, saying I shouldn't have refused their offer, and now I was a liability of some kind. But they came with no weapons..."

"So, you took out seven guys? On your own?"

I shrug like it wasn't a big deal, though I guess it probably was to the sheriff of a small town in Texas. "Just as I was about to get Tori to safety, these boys turned up outside and started raisin' hell. I appreciate the save there, Sheriff."

He raises an eyebrow. "Surprised you needed it, given your past. So, why are you here, Adrian?"

"Starting over, somewhere small and anonymous. I've got plenty of money and no ties anywhere else. I've been real happy here. But you have my word, Sheriff. When all this is over, I'll move on. I don't wanna put the people of this town in any danger. I guess there's never any escaping a past like mine…"

He scoffs. "Cut the shit, you self-righteous son'bitch. I couldn't give a rat's ass about your past, and if you think this is your fault, you're dumber than you look."

"Thanks, John."

"Where's that girl of yours?"

"Shit, Tori! I'll be right back." I turn and run through the bar, into the back, and up the stairs. "Tori! It's me. Are you all right?"

There's silence for a moment, then a muffled voice says, "Wh-what's the password?"

I smile to myself. She's a smart girl. "It's *hellbound*. Now get your ass out here, baby. It's all over."

The bathroom door flies open and she jumps into my arms, wrapping her legs around my waist and burying her head into my shoulder. Tears flow down her cheeks, wetting my T-shirt.

"It's okay," I say, to reassure her. "It's over now."

"And you're all right?" she sobs.

"Baby, I'm fine, just like I promised I would be."

We spend a few minutes hugging, then head back downstairs to the bar. The sheriff's sitting on a bar stool, looking at the damage to the interior, which is extensive, to say the least. He stands when we enter. His hat is resting on the bar next to his shotgun.

"Tori, how you holdin' up?" he asks, genuinely concerned.

She nods and smiles weakly.

We stand for a minute, looking at the devastation around us. In the silence, I hear a low, muffled cry. Actually, it's not a cry. It's more of a… yelp.

My eyes go wide.

"Styx!"

I rush over to the far side of the bar, where tables and chairs have splintered and broken, covering the floor in debris. I follow the noise and come to a small heap of wood in the corner by the window. I throw piece after piece to the side and uncover Styx, lying on his side.

I see the bullet hole straight away. It's underneath him, in the fleshy part between his two front legs. It's a bad wound. I feel my heart sink as he whines, looking up at me with his tongue lolling out of his mouth. I place my hand on the side of his face, and he just about manages to raise his paw enough to place it on top of my wrist.

"Jesus... Styx, hang in there, boy. You're gonna be fine." I shout back without looking around, "John, ring an ambulance... or a vet... or someone—just get somebody! Hurry!"

I hear him leave, and a moment later, Tori appears at my side. She places a hand on my shoulder. "Adrian..."

"He's gonna be fine. Aren't you, boy? Yeah, you're gonna be just fine."

I stroke his head. His breathing is fast and shallow, and he lets out a low whine with every exhalation. He moves his front paw, as if holding my hand against him.

"Come on, Styx. Hang in there. The sheriff's getting you help, okay?"

His breathing starts to slow. Tori crouches down next to me, stroking his back as she rests her head on my shoulder. He looks up at me. I swear to God he's trying to say sorry...

"Styx, come on! Stay strong, boy."

His breathing slows even more. The low whines are less frequent and quieter now. I know there's no hope. Not anymore. But I refuse to accept it.

"Styx..."

Raynor comes back in. "All kinds of folk are on their way, so I've got them to rush a vet here as well, Adrian."

Styx lets out another long, low whine. I stroke his head.

Then... silence.

I frown, holding back the emotion fighting to spread across my face. I feel Tori kiss my arm before standing and walking off. I hear her start to cry again.

"Styx?"

But he's gone.

8

***

I'm sitting in my pick-up truck, staring at my phone. There's a number typed in on the screen, but I've not pressed the call button yet. I probably won't, either. But I'm thinking about it.

I had to leave before all the sirens arrived. I wasn't in the mood for answering questions. Tori said she would start tidying up the bar. I said I needed a bit of time, so I got in my truck and drove for a good half-hour. I've pulled over on the side of the road, heading toward San Antonio. I probably won't go there, but I like the drive and need to clear my head.

I have absolutely no idea how my life got turned upside-down so quickly. It started with three men walking into my bar and culminated in my dog being shot and killed. It sounds like a sick joke.

What the hell am I going to do? I've no idea who these people are, nor why they wanted me to work for them before deciding they wanted me dead. So far, they've sent eighteen men after me. I've killed fifteen with Raynor's help, and someone else took out the other three. The FBI told me they think the first three men had ties to some guy called Yalafi Hussein, so a good bet would be that the other fifteen did as well. I should find out who this guy is and why he wants me to work for him.

But I was never great at fact-finding. That's why I'm staring at Josh's number on the screen of my phone.

We lead different lives now. There are no ill feelings between us. I still regard him as family. I just don't want to call him up unexpectedly and interrupt his new life, purely to drag him back into mine.

No, I'll leave it. I'm sure I can figure this out on my own.

My phone rings, breaking my concentration. I don't recognize the number on the screen.

"Hello?"

"Adrian?" asks the voice, which sounds familiar.

"Who's askin'?"

"Son, it's Ryan Schultz."

His name hangs in the silence for a moment while I compose myself. I've not heard from him since... Jesus— since San Francisco! I remember reading in the news that the new president had appointed his own secretary of defense when he got sworn into office, but there was nothing about what Schultz intended to do instead.

"Something else from my past coming back to haunt me. How've you been, Ryan?"

"Better than you, I believe."

"News travels fast."

"Not as fast as we'd like, sometimes."

I frown. "What can I do for you, Ryan? I'm a little busy."

"Can we talk?"

"We are..."

"In person?"

I sigh. "Where are you?"

"I'm standing in what's left of your bar, son."

I take another minute to process. Something definitely isn't right.

"I'll be there in thirty minutes."

I hang up, spin the truck around, and head back to Devil's Spring.

09:21 CDT

I park across the street and walk over to my bar. A whole host of people are rushing around out front. I see Tori standing off to the side, a blanket draped over her shoulders, with an EMT fussing over her.

"How are you holdin' up, babe?" I ask her as I approach.

She looks up, smiles faintly, and then bursts into tears without a word.

I feel awful for having exposed her to all this.

I walk behind and put my arms around her. She buries herself in my shoulder, and I kiss the top of her head. "It's okay, Tori. I'll keep you safe, I promise."

Someone behind me clears their throat. It's Sheriff Raynor.

"Adrian, you got a minute?" he asks apologetically.

"Yeah, sure." I hold Tori away from me and look into her eyes. "I'll be right back, okay? Head around back and get yourself upstairs to bed while all this is going on down here. Get some rest."

She nods and walks off vacantly, aided by the EMT.

Shock is definitely setting in, but she's a tough woman. She'll be fine.

I turn to the sheriff. "How's it going, John?"

He strokes his mustache and takes a long, deep breath. "Getting there. It's all a bit of a circus, I'm afraid, but it's necessary. I've got my deputies workin' crowd control, tryin' to stop the locals from seein' too much. Look, I know this ain't the best time, but there's a guy here askin' after you. After what you told me earlier, I didn't know if he knew you from, y'know... way back or whatever."

I smile, appreciating his tact. "I know. It's okay. He called me to say he was here. That's why I'm back so soon. Where is he?"

"He's inside. Follow me."

Raynor leads me into the bar, signaling to a deputy that it's okay for me to be there. There's an FBI crime scene investigation team over where Styx is still lying. I try not to look over as I gaze around the room. The place looks like a goddamn warzone. I feel genuine sadness that my bar—the symbol of my new life—is in tatters.

Raynor points over to what remains of the jukebox. I follow his finger and see Ryan Schultz standing around, looking like he's in charge.

"Thanks, John."

I walk over to meet him. Schultz looks well. He's dressed casually, wearing a business shirt tucked into dark blue jeans and some brown shoes. He's got slightly less gray hair than I remember him having, and he's definitely put on a few pounds since he left the White House, but it suits him. Being a Texan himself, he probably feels right at home here.

"Adrian," he says. "Been a long time."

I nod. "Indeed. Been keeping yourself busy since getting sacked by our commander-in-chief?"

Okay, so I still think the guy's a dick, despite him reluctantly being on my side the last couple of times I dealt with him. I don't like him or trust him.

He smiles humorlessly. "Like you wouldn't believe..."

"So, what brings you to my recently demolished part of the world?"

"Is there someplace we can talk?" he asks, looking around at all the FBI agents walking back and forth.

"What's wrong with right here?"

"Too many people. What we need to discuss is of a... delicate nature."

I sigh. I'm tired of things happening that I don't understand and have no control over. "Fine. Come on."

I walk outside and get in my truck. He follows and climbs in the passenger side. I drive away without saying a word, turn left at the end of the street, and head up the hill I jogged up with Styx earlier this morning.

Styx...

I'm sad that he's gone. I do my best not to think about it, so I can focus on figuring out what the hell's going on around here. He was a big part of my new life, and nothing will be the same without him.

I turn into the police station parking lot and pull up, then turn in my seat to face Schultz. "Talk."

He's silent for a moment, presumably trying to figure out the best place to start. "Are you still—"

"No, I'm retired," I say, interrupting him. "Talk."

"Okay... okay, son. So, you had a few visitors in the last couple of days?"

"I've had one or two, yeah. No idea why, though."

"The first three guys that came here were the recruitment team. They send them in to coerce you into joining their cause."

"Whose *cause*? Who sends them? Yalafi Hussein?"

"Nah, Hussein's just a middleman, though as best we can tell, he's connected to the people we're interested in."

I regard him silently, listening with a professional ear.

"Next would've been the retrieval team, sent in to take you by force. Not surprising they failed, truth be told. Hell, even *they* must've doubted their success because they sent in the death squads to take you out at pretty much the same time! That's when we knew we had to step in."

"Could've stepped in a bit earlier, asshole. I might still have a bar and my dog."

"You had a *dog*?" he asks with a smirk.

"Yeah, I did. I loved that little guy, and he got shot. I can't say I care for your tone, Ryan. I'd advise you to remember that although I'm retired, I'm no less capable of ripping your throat out. We clear?"

He smiles nervously. "Hell, I meant no offense, son. I'm here to help—our past be damned."

I take a few deep breaths to pacify my anger. "And who's *we*?"

"I'm sorry?"

"You said, 'As best *we* can tell,' and, '*We* knew we had to step in.' Who's *we*?"

He clears his throat but remains sheepishly quiet.

"Ryan, how did you know what was happening here? Who are you working for?"

He hesitates, clearly thrown off whatever game plan he had when he came to meet me. "Adrian, what's important is what's happening, not who I represent. Let me just—"

He stops talking as another car appears behind us in the rearview. It's a black sedan with tinted windows. It pulls up behind us in the parking lot and sits there, its engine still idling.

"Friend of yours?" I ask him.

He sighs. "Yeah."

"Let's go and say hi, then. Maybe they'll give me some straight fucking answers!"

I climb out of the truck and walk toward the car. Schultz is just behind me. As I near the vehicle, the driver's door opens, and a man steps out. He's dressed like Schultz—nice jeans, boots, a fitted shirt tucked in with the sleeves rolled up, mirrored sunglasses. He has short blond hair, styled and spiked. He shuts the door and stands in front of me, smiling.

"Hey, Boss," he says in a ridiculously happy British accent.

I feel my eyes go wide.

"Holy shit! Josh?"

9

"How you doin', Adrian?" Josh asks, smiling.

I'm guessing he loves the look of confusion and surprise on my face right now. I can't think of anything meaningful to say. After everything that's happened, seeing Josh in front of me is just too much of a curveball to deal with at the moment.

"Where's your hair?" I ask him finally.

He laughs. "Figured it was time for a change. Needed to smarten up a bit, y'know. You like?"

"You look less like someone who listens to rock music and still lives with his parents, if that's what you mean."

We look at each other for a moment in silence, then both burst out laughing. We embrace like long-lost brothers and pat each other's backs. "Man, it's good to see you, Josh. What are you up to nowadays?"

"What else?" he replies. "Watching your back!"

I frown. "Something really weird's going on here, and

I'm guessing you know what that is?"

He smiles that knowing smile of his, the way he always did when he knew things and didn't want to tell me *how* he found them out.

"Josh..."

"Okay. You're about to get a lot of information, and you're gonna have questions. Can you please just wait 'til I've finished? I know you want to know everything all the time, but this is big, and it'll take a while to explain."

I shrug and nod. "Whatever."

"Okay. When we went our separate ways, I went and got a job at GlobaTech, working with our old friend, Robert Clark. What I did was really complicated, and I won't bore you with the details, but it had to do with research and development. Anyway, when Ryan here got the boot from the new president, Robert offered him a job as a consulting director." He leans forward slightly. "You ask me, it's one of those jobs they give a fancy title to that requires you to do absolutely nothing. Y'know, the kind of job that they award old people with too much time on their hands..."

He smiles, winks, and stands up straight again. He casts a quick glance to an unimpressed Schultz, who's leaning against the hood of Josh's car. I smile. The more things change, the more they stay the same...

"But seriously, Schultz has done well for us since he came on board, so respect where it's due. Anyway, we were approached about a year ago by a couple of people with... questionable intentions, shall we say. Think Dark Rain but more evil."

"Lovely," I say, remembering clearly how *that* ended.

"Obviously, since the era of Bob Clark began, we don't get into bed with such unsavory characters. But alarm bells rang nonetheless."

He moves over to his car and leans against the door as he talks. I'm standing with my arms folded across my chest, waiting patiently for the part that explains why the last few days have gone to shit.

"We kept a close eye on the movements of these people, using the vast array of technology at our disposal. There's been little to go on until a couple of days ago, when—you guessed it—*you* got involved!"

I shrug innocently. "Hey, I didn't ask for this."

"I know, I know. This shit just kinda finds you," he replies with another knowing smile. "So, anyway, we tracked these people all over the world. They're on some mad recruitment drive, hiring the best and the baddest killers, mercenaries, scientists—you name it."

"What for?"

He holds his hand up. "Ah-ah-ah, save the questions for later. I figured it was only a matter of time before they tried to recruit you. I mean, you're the best assassin there is."

"Was..."

"Whatever. Point is, retired or not, these people knew where to find you and, in keeping with tradition, asked you to join them. Then they tried to kill you when you said no."

"Okay, Josh, the FBI already told me something along these lines. A terrorist network nobody seems to know anything about has been going around recruiting people to work for them, for reasons unknown. The first three guys who came to me were apparently linked to someone called Yalafi Hussein. They were found dead in their rental car, parked at the side of the interstate. Nothing to do with me, by the way. But they then sent two hit squads to kill me, and *those* guys I killed without prejudice. A real mixed bag of assholes too, from all over the world. What's going on, man?"

He sighs and looks at Schultz, who shrugs. "Just tell him."

Josh nods and looks back at me. "We know *who* they are. They call themselves the Armageddon Initiative. They have active cells all across the globe and run their main base of operations from somewhere in Ukraine. Every time we try to track them via satellite, they disappear completely. We've got it narrowed to a thirty mile radius, but—"

"That doesn't sound all that narrow. Are they underground?"

"That's what I think, yeah."

"So, what do these guys want? What's their plan?"

"We don't know. That's why I'm here: to ask you for a favor."

I take a deep breath. I see what's coming. "You want me to sign up with these assholes, don't you? Be the man inside?"

Josh smiles. "That was my original plan, yeah. But that went to shit when you started killing them."

"So, what can I do? I just wanna be left alone, Josh."

"I know, and I hate asking you, but... we have a bead on Hussein. We have reason to believe he's going to be in New York in the next twenty-four hours. We know he's not in charge, but we think he has access to the people who are."

"You seem to have the same information as the FBI. I wonder if they know where he'll be tomorrow. Why don't you just work with them?"

"Because GlobaTech has its own army, its own weapons, and its own planes. We don't answer to the government because we're in the private sector and are, consequently, not funded by them. As long as we work under the radar, we're good at doing whatever we want. The government tends to make things like this public, so they look good killing terrorists. But we both know that killing them doesn't always stop them. We've got no one to impress, so we've taken it upon ourselves to lend a hand."

"So, you want me to go to New York and help capture Yalafi Hussein?"

He nods. "And bring him back in one piece to one of our sites for questioning."

I sigh heavily. I'm retired. I don't want any part of this. But I appreciate that a large, well-funded terrorist organization that hasn't yet made it known what their plans are isn't the best thing to leave unchecked. And I know Josh wouldn't ask if it wasn't necessary.

I think about my bar. I've got no business to run for a while, so I'll only be sitting around with my thumb up my ass anyway...

What about Tori? She needs me, and I don't want to leave her.

I wonder if Josh knows about her.

"I own a bar here, called The Ferryman," I say to Josh, changing the subject. "It's recently been closed, pending some much-needed renovation. A bunch of terrorists shot the place to bits, trying to kill me. You can still see it, though. Plus, there's someone I want you to meet. Come on."

I walk back to my truck, get in, and drive out of the police parking lot. Josh and Ryan Schultz follow behind me.

10:22 CDT

I arrive back at my bar as the chaos is winding down. The FBI crime scene team is still on site, but Sheriff Raynor and his deputies have left, save for one. He's standing outside, deterring anyone who tries to find out what's happened by giving them the official *There's nothing to see here* line.

I walk around back, with Josh and Schultz in tow, and head up the stairs that lead to my apartment above. We walk inside and see Tori sitting on the sofa, hugging her knees to her chest. She turns as I enter and smiles. Her usually sparkling eyes are red, tired from crying.

"Hey. How are you holdin' up?"

"I'm fine," she lies. "You all right?"

"I'm okay." I smile to offer reassurance, walk over to her, and lean down to kiss the top of her head. "I wanna introduce you to someone." I take her hand, stand her up, and move her round to face the others. "Tori Watson, this... is Josh Winters."

She smiles and extends her hand. "So, *you're* the famous Josh, are you?" she says, showing signs of her old self again. "Adrian's told me a lot about you."

He smiles back, taking her hand and gently shaking it. "Whatever he told you is either a lie, or I was drunk at the time..." He looks at me, grinning, like a proud father would look at a son. "I'm happy for you, man. You have a good life here. All you need is a dog and a white picket fence, eh?"

Tori starts to cry and walks off, slightly embarrassed. I sigh and smile apologetically.

"Shit... something I said?"

I shake my head. "I actually *had* a dog. A stray wolf dog I called Styx. He's under a blanket downstairs. He was with me nearly two years, and he caught a bullet in the attack earlier and died in my arms. I loved that dog, Josh."

"Jeez... I'm sorry, Adrian."

I glance over at Tori, who's sitting on the edge of the bed across the room, staring at the floor. I turn back to Josh. "It's all right. You didn't know. Listen, I don't know if I can help you with this. I've got a life away from all that now. I can't leave her, Josh. I love her."

He nods, immediately understanding and respecting my decision. "We'll do what we can to keep you out of it from now on. You have my word."

"Thanks."

Schultz steps forward, holding his phone to Josh. "This is bullshit. He should just do as he's goddamn told! Show him the photo already."

We both look at him.

"Ryan, shut the fuck up, will you?" says Josh.

I love it when he loses his temper and curses. His accent is perfect for it!

"Ignore him," he says to me.

I frown. "What photo?"

"Adrian, forget it."

"What photo, Josh?"

Schultz sighs and thrusts his phone in my face. There's a picture displayed on the screen. I move back slightly and grab hold of it, examining the image.

Josh mutters under his breath. "It's nothing, Adrian, honestly. You've got your life here now. I don't want you involved. It's not fair."

I don't acknowledge him. I'm too busy looking at the image. It's a file photo, black and white, showing a man and woman talking. Judging by the background, it looks like somewhere in the Middle East. I don't recognize the man, but the woman is familiar.

I look up from the phone and stare him straight in the eye. "Josh, is this..."

He lets out a heavy sigh and nods. "Yup... *that* is Clara Fox."

10

I'm not aware of anything around me. It's like the world has shrunk, reducing my existence to nothing except this image on Schultz's phone.

Clara Fox.

I fucking *knew* she was still alive!

I look at Josh, angry. "And when were you planning on mentioning this?"

He looks me in the eye. "Honestly? I wasn't going to. Not after you said you wanted no part of this. I respected the fact that you've moved on, and I was gonna leave you in blissful ignorance."

We both know my anger isn't justified, and I calm down as quickly as I got fired up.

Tori appears next to me. "What's going on? Is everything okay?"

Josh and I exchange a glance, which instantly tells him

I've told Tori nothing about my old life. He discreetly nods his acknowledgement.

"Is this to do with what's been happening here?" she persists.

I turn to her and half-smile. "Yeah. Josh works for a defense contractor who's investigating the organization that's been sending people after me. There's, ah… evidence to suggest a link to an old mission we worked together, back when I was in the military. He's asking for my help to sort it out."

I feel awful lying to her, but it's for her own good. After everything that's happened here, the last thing she needs is to find out her boyfriend's the world's greatest hitman, trying to retire.

To her credit, she doesn't even hesitate.

"You've gotta help them, Ady. It's the only way to make sure we're left alone, isn't it?"

"I'm not leaving you." I gesture to Josh and Schultz. "These guys are professionals. I'm sure they can handle things without me."

She shakes her head. "Ady, I know you. If you let them go without you, you'll walk around here, restless, wishing you'd gone with them. There's nothing to do here that I can't do myself. You won't trust anyone else to stop this, either, so quit worrying about me and go be my action hero."

She smiles and hugs my arm. I look at Josh and raise an eyebrow.

He laughs. "Wow, she really *does* know you!" He turns to her and puts a hand on her shoulder. "Tori, this man is like a brother to me, and I can confidently say, hand on heart, that I've not seen him this happy in a long time. That makes *me* happy, and I thank you for that. And you're right. You know him almost as well as I do, by the sounds of it." He turns back to me, takes the phone off me, and hands it to Schultz without looking. "And you... you should listen to your better half here. We need you on this. Neither of us trusts anyone other than you to fix it, and we both know it."

I turn and walk over to the refrigerator. I take out four beers and place them on the counter. I open the drawer underneath and use a bottle opener on them, then carry them over, two in each hand, and share them among the group.

"Everyone... drink."

They all oblige—even Schultz, which surprises me. I look at the bottle for a moment, appreciating the taste.

"Tori, if I go, I don't want you to stay here, okay? Go and stay with Nicki for a few days. I'm sure she won't mind. If you need anything, call the sheriff."

She smiles and kisses me. "Don't worry about me," she says, seeming happier than she was five minutes ago. "I'll be fine. You just need to go and fix this, so we can move on."

She stands up straight and salutes, then laughs. I laugh along with her. Josh looks on with that proud smile on his face again.

I look at him. "New York, huh?"

He nods. "That's where our intel puts him at some point tomorrow. We need to track him, find out what he's doing, *and* who he's meeting. Then we need to apprehend him and get out of there without alerting anyone."

"Sounds simple enough."

Schultz scoffs. "You're still an arrogant son'bitch, ain't ya, son?"

I shake my head and smile. "Not arrogant... just good."

"We've got a plane fueled and ready to go on an airstrip at Fort Worth," Josh announces. "It's a five-hour drive, so the sooner we hit the road, the sooner we can get you fully briefed and in the air. The flight will take around three-and-a-half hours."

I nod and look at Tori. Her flame-red hair is all tangled yet still looks gorgeous. Her brown eyes stare at me, not quite full of life but getting there. She smiles at me like she's so proud of her man, she can't contain it. It makes me think I'm doing the right thing by agreeing to help Josh.

I look at him. He'll be close to fifty nowadays, but he still looks younger than I do. He was always well built, so I figure it's his fitted shirt that makes him look like he's been working out more. His change of image is staggering, considering he's looked the same to me for the last twenty-seven years. But it suits him. It seems he's moved on too, and it's good to see.

"Gimme half an hour guys. I'll meet you out front."

11:20 CDT

I'm packing a shoulder bag with a change of clothes and some essentials. I'm wearing my jeans but no shirt. Tori's lying in bed, wearing nothing. We spent ten minutes saying goodbye the way people in love ought to, then another ten minutes reassuring each other we would both be okay. Whoever this Armageddon Initiative is, they'll go where I go to try to kill me, so there's no reason to come back to Devil's Spring once I've left.

I make sure I pack my Berettas. Until earlier today, I hadn't touched them in over two years. I'm not traveling on a civilian plane, so having them with me won't be a problem.

"Are you *sure* you're okay with me doing this?" I ask Tori as I pull my T-shirt on over my head.

"Will you stop asking me that?" she replies. "If I didn't want you to go, I'd tell you. Josh is your friend, and he's asking for your help. Besides, you're going off to fight terrorists and stuff! That's so exciting!"

I smile at her. It's nice to see that some people still remain innocent to the harsh realities of conflict. Even after everything she's been through in the last twenty-four hours, she's still the same ol' Tori that I fell in love with.

"What would I do without you?"

She shrugs. "Well, you probably wouldn't have as much great sex as you do now..."

We laugh. I lean down, kissing her hard on her lips. When we part, we look into each other's eyes for a moment. "See you soon, beautiful."

"I'll be here waiting..."

I smile, pick up my bag, and leave the room. I walk out my front door and down the stairs to the back of the bar. I walk around to the street. Josh and Schultz are standing side by side, leaning against their car.

I stand in front of them, bag over my shoulder. "You guys ready?"

Without a word, they get in the car. I climb in the back, behind Josh, who's driving. As we set off, I lean forward.

"Swing by the police station, would you? I wanna see the sheriff before I go."

"No worries," says Josh. He turns right at the end of the street and heads up the hill toward the station house.

"Hey, you've got a companion club here, haven't you?" he asks.

I nod. "Yeah. One of the girls there is friends with Tori."

"Really? Might have to come back and visit you when you're back up and running..."

I smile.

"It still ain't right," says Schultz. "Drugs and whores shouldn't be legal."

"I'm inclined to agree with you, Ryan," I say. "But there's no denying the effect it's had on the country since the president got elected."

"Ah, horseshit," he spits, waving his hand dismissively. "I don't trust that prissy, silver-spoon son'bitch any farther than I can throw him!"

"Nice to see you're not bitter about losing your position on the National Security Council."

Josh chuckles. "Been keeping up with your sarcasm lessons, then, boss?"

I shrug. "I learned from the best."

We round the corner and pull over outside the police station, where we all stood just a few hours ago.

"I'll just be a minute, guys."

I get out of the car, walk across the parking lot, and head through the front doors, into the reception area. There's a deputy stationed on the front desk, which runs almost the entire width of the room. His name's Thompson. He's been in the bar a few times—not much of a drinker.

I approach the counter. "Hey, is the sheriff around?"

Thompson looks up from the paperwork he's engrossed in. He's got neat, short dark hair with a side part, and he's clean-shaven and fresh-faced. He's only a rookie and has lived in Devil's Spring his whole life. He's got no clue about the world beyond our modest borders.

"Yes, sir," he replies respectfully. "Let me call him."

He reaches for the phone, but I stop him. "Actually, d'you mind if I go back and see him? I just want a word in private."

He hesitates. "Well... I'm not supposed to let civilians back here unescorted."

"Then escort me. I don't care."

"But I can't leave my post, sir…"

I sigh. I don't have the patience for this. "Listen, I've had a pretty shit couple of days. You've seen the state of my bar, right? Y'know, after it got shot up by eight armed terrorists. I just gotta see the sheriff about something."

He goes to speak, but a voice at the back of the squad room beats him to it.

"It's all right, Thompson," shouts Raynor, who's come out of his office. "Adrian, come on back."

I walk through the hatch to the left of the front desk, past the other two deputies sitting at their desks, and over to Raynor. We step into his office, which is in the back right corner of the building. He offers me a seat, but I remain standing.

"I don't have long, Sheriff. I'm on my way to Fort Worth. I'm flying out to New York straight away."

"You fell off the wagon, then?" he asks with a half-smile.

"Something like that, yeah. You heard of GlobaTech?"

"Those big military contractors? Sure, I heard of 'em."

"Well, an old friend works for them, and they've been tracking the organization that keeps sending assholes to kill me. I'm gonna go help them out, maybe put a stop to all this before it escalates."

He nods. "I'll keep an eye on Tori for you."

"I appreciate that. Thanks." I extend my hand, which he shakes.

He moves over to his desk and picks up a folder. "Adrian… I wanted you to hear this from me in case you speak to anyone else about it. I asked those FBI fellas to give me a copy of your file. I hope you don't mind, but I thought it could be useful for the investigation, in case your character's called into question or somethin'."

I nod. I honestly don't care. I've been upfront with him about my past so far, and there's nothing in that file I have a problem with him finding out about. Not now.

"Thanks for telling me, but I have no issue with it."

"There's, ah... there's some pretty crazy things in here after you left the Army."

I smile. "I've been around, yeah."

"San Francisco... Nevada... Pittsburgh..."

"To name a few."

"And you say you're going to New York to help go after these terrorist bastards who've been trying to kill you?"

I nod.

"Jesus... I'm glad I'm not a goddamn terrorist."

I smile again, and he chuckles for a moment. "I'll take care of things here. You go and save the world, or whatever it is you intend to do."

"Thanks, John. You're a good man."

We shake hands again and I leave. I walk through the station without a word and back out front, where the afternoon sun is assaulting the town. I climb in the back of Josh's sedan.

"You good?" asks Josh.

"Yeah, everything's fine. Let's get this show on the road."

He drives away, and within half an hour, we're halfway to San Antonio. I start to think about the flight and what I'll do when I get to New York. I can't remember the last time I was there. If I find Hussein, I'm going to do everything I can to bring him in alive, so Josh can work his magic on him. But before I do anything, I'm going to make that bastard tell me where Clara Fox is.

She and I have a lot of catching up to do.

11

GlobaTech's private jet is a Lear 85. I've never traveled like this before, and it's a bit weird being the only passenger. There are a handful of seats inside, all large, reclining armchairs in white leather. The red carpet underfoot is thick and looks expensive. In addition to the pilot and co-pilot, there's a stewardess serving me drinks and food upon request.

I arrived at Fort Worth and was ushered across the runway to where the jet was waiting, fueled and ready to go. Josh gave me a laptop and advised me to research the information contained on it during the flight, as well as a comms unit for when I land. He said GlobaTech had taken care of all the private landing fees and secured a priority arrival slot at JFK to minimize any delays. Someone would meet me when we landed and take me directly to a safe house I could work out of, bypassing any of the usual processes involved in flying cross-country.

We've been in the air maybe twenty minutes. The stewardess walks over to me, carrying a large, black duffel bag.

"Sir, this was left for you," she announces, gesturing to the bag as she rests it next to my chair. "I was instructed to give it to you once we'd taken off."

"Thanks," I say curiously.

She flashes me a smile and walks off, leaving me alone again. I reach down and bring the bag up, placing it on the table in front of me. I unzip it and look inside.

"Now you're talking..."

Inside the bag is a whole host of gadgets, courtesy of GlobaTech, which I'm sure Josh had something to do with. There are microphones, tracking devices, cameras, recording equipment, and various other toys. Then I see the explosives—trip mines with laser sensors and remote detonation.

I feel like a kid at Christmas.

There's also plenty of ammunition for my Berettas, plus an FN SCAR-H assault rifle, which is a beast of a weapon. It's a rival for the M4 Carbine and fires over six hundred rounds per minute at almost seven hundred and twenty meters per second. To be honest, it's probably overkill for any confrontations I'm likely to have, but I do enjoy making a statement.

I set the bag aside and boot up the laptop Josh gave me. I look briefly at the information on the Armageddon Initiative. There's not really much to go on, apart from a brief dossier on confirmed and suspected members and hypotheses about what they want. I quickly tire of reading it and load up the internet to look at the recent news. I tend to avoid looking at what's happening in the real world, content with my own little existence in Devil's Spring. With Tori.

God, I miss her. I've only been gone a few hours

—Christ!

I find an article online about the president's most recent cabinet reshuffle, and it makes me think of Schultz. When I first met the guy, he was secretary of defense. He'd served the country well in that role and was a distinguished soldier in his day. Within his first two months in office, Cunningham asked for Schultz's resignation. It was a minor story at the time; it's not uncommon for new presidents to appoint their own people to such positions. But I'm reading a blog here that's detailing all of Cunningham's changes, and people are noticing that he's almost wiped the entire slate clean, starting over with handpicked people of his choosing. Some of them seem to have questionable suitability and experience.

But as I've said, because of everything he's done for the country, he can pretty much do whatever he wants, and no one will question him. Besides, all is right with the world nowadays, so who cares who sits in the room when the president thinks up some more changes to impress Congress with?

22:51 EDT

The flight passed quickly, and we're preparing to touch down at JFK. I get my things ready. We land without incident and taxi to a stop a few minutes later. I look out the window at the illuminated skyline of New York City and let out a sigh. It's been a while since I did this kind of work. I'm worried I'm out of practice.

The stewardess kindly opens the door for me, and I thank her for her hospitality as I exit the plane. I step out onto the staircase, carrying the black duffel bag and my own shoulder bag, and take a quick look around.

We're close to the small hangars at the back of one of the runways, set farther away from the main hub and the commercial flights. There's light airport security around, which is standard. But it's reasonably quiet—presumably because of who owns the plane and the fact everything had been cleared prior to takeoff.

I make my way down the staircase, toward the black Ford MPV that's waiting for me. The windows are tinted, but as I approach, the side door slides open and Robert Clark steps out. He smiles and extends his hand, which I happily shake.

"Adrian, glad to have you with us on this," he says. "How've you been?"

"Good to see you again, Bob. I'm here to help in any way I can. I just want these bastards to leave me alone."

He gestures me into the vehicle, and I oblige. I sit down on the leather seat, facing forward. He climbs in after me, sitting opposite me, with his back to the driver. There's a partition separating the front seats from the back, and Clark taps on it twice as he slides the door closed. We set off.

He looks well, if a little tired. His dark hair still has its side part, but there are flecks of gray showing around his temples and above his ears now.

"Good trip?" he asks.

I shrug. "It was what it was. The plane was nice."

He smiles. "A handy little acquisition from some former associates south of the border. It serves its purpose." He gestures to the black bag and smiles. "I see you got our little care package?"

I nod. "Yeah, thanks. Lots of nice toys to play with. You expect me to run into trouble, then?"

Clark shakes his head. "Hopefully not, Adrian, but I know how you like to be prepared. I hope you won't need any of the weapons in there, and the camera and microphone are for our surveillance of the target and location."

I smile to myself. I try to think of an occasion in the past when a situation has gone exactly to plan, and I've not needed a weapon to resolve things...

None spring to mind.

I take a quick look out the window as we leave the airport and head out into the city along the Van Wyck expressway.

"So, what do you know?" asks Clark.

"Only what Josh and Schultz told me."

"Did they show you the photo?"

I fix him with a hard stare. "Yes."

He nods. "Well, do me a favor. Get me Hussein *before* you go all Charles Bronson on me, okay?"

I can't help but smile. "I'll do my best."

He nods and falls silent for a moment. We carry on past Willow Lake and come off at Flushing Meadows, heading west alongside the Long Island expressway, all the way to Queens.

"Adrian, I... I heard what these people did to your bar back in Texas. I'm sorry you got dragged into all this. Truly, I am."

"Not your fault, Bob, but I appreciate the sentiment. I'll get this guy for you, and hopefully you'll be able to stop these assholes before anyone else gets hurt."

"We'll do what we can."

23:09 EDT

. . .

We navigate the traffic for another ten minutes or so, eventually turning onto 55th Avenue in Queens. We stop outside an anonymous single-story house halfway along the right side of the street.

"Here we are," announces Clark.

I raise an eyebrow at him. "Really?"

He smiles. "It's a safe house. The whole point is to put you where no one will think to look for you."

"Oh, I understand the concept. Don't get me wrong. It's just... I figured that with your budget, you'd have sprung for something a little less run-down."

Clark laughs. "Well, this place has served us well over the years and will do just fine for now. Come on."

We get out and walk to the front door. I instinctively glance around the neighborhood. The street is quiet, and there are no people around. He produces a key, unlocks the door, and steps inside. He holds it open for me to pass him.

I walk down the hall, which runs centrally through the house, toward the kitchen, which covers the width of the building at the back. There are four rooms in between, two on either side. I check each room in turn, like someone on vacation arriving at their hotel for the first time. The first door on the left is a modest bedroom, with a single, ready-made bed against the far wall and a closet on the right opposite the door. Minimal but functional.

I close the door and turn, opening the one across the hall on the right. Inside is a living room, with two sofas arranged in an L-shape facing away from me, aimed at the TV on its stand in the far corner. Again, aside from a small table in the middle of the room, there is little else in there.

I back out again and walk farther down the hall. I open the second door on the right, revealing a bathroom. The toilet is facing the door, with a sink next to it. Against the right wall is a decent-sized shower cubicle. It's basic but serves its purpose.

Finally, I turn to the left and open the second door, opposite the bathroom. It's a dining room, with a table and four chairs in the center. I close the door and turn to see Clark smiling at me.

"Everything to your satisfaction, sir?" he asks sarcastically.

I smile. His sarcasm is obviously a result of his time spent working with Josh, which I can completely relate to. "Just getting a feel for the place."

"Good. I'll leave you to acclimate. I'm staying in another safe house a mile or so away. My number's pre-programmed into the burner phone I put in your goody bag, so call me if you need anything."

I nod. "I will. Thanks. When's Hussein meant to be making an appearance?"

"Sometime tomorrow morning, if the intel is to be believed."

"Is the source reliable?"

"We like to think so."

"Contact me as soon as you have a location. I'll arrange my own transportation and try to stay off anyone's radar as long as I can."

He nods and leaves without saying another word.

I walk into the kitchen and lean against the side, next to the sink, and look out the window at the yard. I let out a heavy sigh. So, this is it. Here I am, in a run-down house in Queens, thinking of the best way to go about taking down a well-guarded terrorist who has, so far, sent eighteen people to kill me...

Doesn't matter how fast I run—the past is always quicker.

12

My phone rings. It's Clark.

"We've got the location," he says when I answer.

I'm already up and dressed. I found a jar of instant coffee in the cupboard, and I'm halfway through my second cup.

"Where am I heading?"

"I've got eyes on Hussein's convoy now, using a remote satellite uplink to GlobaTech's servers. It looks like he's in the middle of three limousines, and he's just stopped outside an apartment in the Upper West Side district of Manhattan."

"Nice. Any sign of who he's meeting?"

"No, but looking at a thermal scan of the building, there are at least half a dozen people inside, so my guess is his contact is already on site."

"How many men does he have with him?"

"Eight men have exited the vehicles with him, but the three drivers have stayed."

"So, best case, I'm looking at Hussein and one other high value target to capture alive, plus thirteen red shirts? Wonderful."

"Red shirts?"

"Yeah, you know, off the old Star Trek show? If the away team beamed down to some planet consisted of three main cast members and a stranger wearing an Ensign's red sweater, you *knew* he wasn't coming back from the trip."

Clark laughs. "You really can tell how many years you and Josh worked together! Try and keep casualties to a minimum. We don't want to attract attention from anyone unnecessarily."

"Hey, who are you talking to? It'll be like I was never there."

"Adrian, surely, even *you* can't believe that?"

I pause. "Fair point. Call you when I have eyes on."

I hang up and move to the front door. I pick up my shoulder bag before leaving. I'd packed the tech into my bag the night before, and I have both my Berettas at my back, just like the good old days. I feel the familiar, reassuring weight of the guns in the holster under my jacket as I lock the door and slide the key under a brick beside the door.

The weather hasn't improved much since yesterday. It's not raining, but it's still dull and windy.

I need to get to Central Park, which is probably a good half-hour from here in traffic, so I should get moving. I quickly glance up and down the street and spy the perfect car for me to borrow. It's a rusted, dirty red Plymouth Road Runner. I'm not much of a car enthusiast, but I'm not going to pass up the chance to drive a true classic, even if it's in such a state of decay.

I stroll casually over, glancing around before I get to it.

Nothing looks more suspicious than checking your surroundings when you're standing next to the car you intend to boost.

I'm in the clear, so I approach the vehicle as if it's my own and use a skeleton key device that GlobaTech included in my black bag of treats. I quickly and naturally open the door, climb inside, and use the device again to start the engine. It's an old car, so I don't expect an alarm.

I rev the engine, check my blind spot, and set off down the street, heading toward Queen's Boulevard. I take a right and follow the long road for five miles or so, until I reach the Queensboro Bridge. I play with the stereo, but I can't find any decent music to listen to, so I have to settle for some talk show discussing the Knicks.

I think about what I need to do when I get there. Assuming the guy's security detail is of a similar standard to his hit squads, I don't expect any major issues getting past them. I'll probably commandeer one of his limos once I have Hussein and his contact with me. I'll sit them both with their backs to the driver. Then I can cover all three of them as I direct us all to the GlobaTech safe house where Clark's staying. He's already texted me the address and has a team on stand-by, should I need support.

It all sounds straightforward enough. The sooner this is over, the sooner I can go back to my anonymous life down in Texas. I've got a bar to re-build and a gorgeous woman waiting for me.

I cross Roosevelt Island and enter Manhattan, turning right, then left off the highway. I follow East 63rd Street until I hit Park Avenue, then take the East 65th Transverse through the park. I come out on the other side a few minutes later, on Central Park West. I continue along the street for almost fifteen minutes but get stuck in some traffic and hit every goddamn red light in the city. I eventually pull into the parking lot at the Museum of Natural History and call Clark.

"I'm in Manhattan," I say when he answers. "Tell me the quickest way to get to Hussein on foot."

"Gimme a minute," replies Clark.

I hear him tapping away on a keyboard.

"Josh would've had the answer by now... just saying."

"Well, Josh isn't here, so you can wait!" I can't tell if he's joking or genuinely offended. "Right, they're on West 81st Street, in a townhouse overlooking the Hudson. It's about ten minutes away if you walk fast."

"I'm on my way." I get out of the car, sling my bag over my shoulder, and set off along the street. I cross Columbus Avenue as I put my earpiece in and connect my phone to it. "Leave the line open. I might need you."

"I'm watching your back. Don't worry. I have eyes on you and a thermal scan running of the building."

"Great. Give me the layout."

"The cars are in a line outside. Two men are standing by the front door. Inside, there's a guy at every downstairs window and a group in a room upstairs. Looks like one guarding the door, and the rest are inside for the meeting."

"I'll need a visual, but it doesn't sound easy to get inside. That's a lot of security."

"Maybe they're expecting you?"

I don't answer, but I hope they're not. Yalafi Hussein will undoubtedly be aware of the failed attempts to recruit me, but I don't think he'd entertain the possibility of me coming looking for him. Why would he? I didn't even know about my link to GlobaTech through Josh until yesterday, so it's doubtful he did.

I'm crossing Amsterdam Avenue and see Broadway ahead of me. "Who do you think Hussein is meeting here?"

"No idea but staying in the U.S. to do it is brave."

"Or stupid..."

"Sadly, Adrian, I think the Armageddon Initiative is many things, but stupid isn't one of them. I think they have a purpose, and that's what worries me—the fact we don't know what that purpose is."

"Well, hopefully, we will soon."

I cross over West End Avenue and see the line of limousines up ahead. I figure I'll go past them, get a quick look at the building from the outside, and then find a spot to do some recon, so I can send any information back to Clark.

I stroll on casually, approaching the first of the limos. They're all the same—shiny and black, with private plates and tinted windows. The driver of each one is inside, sitting still behind the wheel like a mannequin. I throw a sideways glance at the one in the middle—Hussein's driver—as I pass. He's got a Middle Eastern look about him, styled facial hair, and a dark suit.

I draw level with the front doors, which are up a short flight of steps. Walking past, I look casually at the two men standing guard outside.

Something's not right.

They're almost certainly American, wearing black suits and sunglasses. I quickly look them up and down. I can tell they're well built, disciplined, definitely packing inside their jackets, and have earpieces in. I walk on, crossing over to the other side of the street at the end, and then over Riverside Drive. I finally stop by the park.

"We have a problem," I whisper urgently as I sit down on a bench, resting my bag at my feet.

"What is it?" asks Clark.

"Hang on..."

I fumble about inside my bag and retrieve a digital camera and Wi-Fi transmitter. I try to look more tourist than spy as I set the camera up, connecting it to the transmitter so that the feed streams back to Clark's system. Then I aim it at the house.

"I'm no expert, but I'm pretty sure those guys on the door aren't terrorists."

Clark's silent for a few moments, studying the feed I'm sending him. I adjust the camera a little, zooming in to give him a better look at the guys standing guard on the entrance.

"Adrian, I'm running facial recognition software on those two now, but working remotely, it might take some time."

It's my turn to fall silent. I don't know who those guys are, but they look like G-men. Who in the U.S. government could possibly be meeting with Yalafi Hussein? Why would someone from the U.S. government be meeting with someone in charge of recruiting for a large terrorist organization?

"I take it I'm to proceed as planned?"

"We have to," confirms Clark.

"I figured. Okay, I'm going to head around back and see if there's a way in. Any movement inside that you can see?"

"Negative. Everyone's still in position, judging by their heat signatures."

"Okay, give me five minutes."

I put the camera away and stand. I sling my bag over my shoulder and walk down Riverside Drive, toward West 80th Street. I cross over, so I'm on the same side as the apartment. I walk along the side of the property, glancing in the windows as I pass. There's not much to see, but I get a glimpse of another guy in a suit who looks suspiciously non-terrorist-like.

The buildings have terraces, so there's no way for me to access a rear entrance. I walk on, drawing level with the front door of the adjoining property, which appears to be a block of apartments. I look up and see two windows overlooking the street, with the roof of the bay window just below them. To their left is a small ledge underneath a window on the second floor of Hussein's building.

I've just had a really crazy idea...

"Bob? Which room did you say the meeting is taking place in?"

"The front room on the second floor, facing the street and overlooking the limos," he replies.

I look up again. I wonder...

"What about the windows on the opposite side? Facing Riverside... same floor."

"Let me check," he says. Again, I hear the tapping of keys. "It looks like that room is down the hall from the meeting. There's a guy outside the door, but the room is empty. Do I want to know why you're asking?"

I smile to myself. "Probably not. Thanks. Just keep your eyes open. I think I've found my way in."

I walk up to the door of the apartment building and press the buzzer for each number until someone answers. I get lucky with number six.

"Hello?" says a distorted, female voice.

"Oh, hey. I live in number three, and I've forgotten my key. Can you buzz me in, please?"

She chuckles. "Sure thing. It happens to me all the time."

I hear the buzz and the click as the door unlocks. I step inside to a small vestibule, with wooden mailboxes mounted on the right-hand wall, a single elevator opposite on the left, and stairs directly ahead.

"Bob, can you pull up the layout of the apartment building next-door?"

He sighs. "There's only one logical—and frankly insane —reason you would want me to do that..."

"Yes. Yes, there is."

He sighs again. "One second... and... okay. What do you need?"

"The room facing the street—which apartment is it? And please don't say six."

"Let me check." More key-tapping. "It's apartment five."

Phew. Okay, so that's fortunate. I know they're not home, but whoever lives at number six *is*, and they might hear me breaking in, which would be awkward.

"Thanks, Bob. Give me a few minutes."

"I'll be watching..."

I take the stairs, two at a time, to the top floor and come out in a small hallway. I look around. Four is on the left in front of me, with five opposite. I'd need to double-back down the short hallway to get to six. There's a single window at the end facing me, on the wall separating the first two apartments.

I walk over to the door to five and knock once. I place my ear against it, listening for any sign of movement. After a few moments, I'm happy it's empty. I rest my shoulder bag at my feet and reach inside for a lock-picking kit—another handy little gadget, courtesy of my sponsors at GlobaTech. I'm not a master at this, but after a couple of minutes fiddling with the lock, I manage to open the door.

I quickly pack up my things and step inside, then close the door quietly. It's a nice, spacious apartment—must cost a small fortune to live here. The main room is an open plan lounge with a kitchenette on the right-hand side. There are two doors at the opposite end, next to each other. I'm guessing the one on the left is the bedroom, where the windows will be.

I head over and open the door. I step into the bedroom, as predicted. A double bed is on the right, in a small alcove created by the large, fitted wardrobe unit that's dominating the wall. To my left are the two windows. I step toward them and peer out. The roof of the bay window is only a couple of feet down. It puts me pretty much level with the window in the room next-door, down the hall from Hussein's mystery meeting.

I take off my holster and put it in the bag but keep one of my Berettas out. I attach the suppressor to it and tuck it into the waistband of my pants at the back. I then zip up my jacket and put the bag over both shoulders. I lift the bottom of the window and stick my head out. I look up and down the street, seeing if anyone's paying me any attention. The road is busy, but there aren't many people on the sidewalk, so if I'm quick, I should go unnoticed.

I climb out slowly and drop as quietly as I can onto the roof below, landing in a crouch. I look across at the other window, which is about a foot above my eye level. There's a small gap, maybe five feet across, in between. I edge forward, looking down to the ground below.

The fall wouldn't kill me, but the landing sure wouldn't tickle.

I take a deep breath and look back up at the ledge. The window is the same style as the one I just climbed out of, so I'm hoping I'll be able to just slide it up and climb in.

I stand, readying myself for the jump. I take one last look over my left shoulder, down at the street, but anyone walking by hasn't looked up at me yet.

It occurs to me how scary it is that terrorists could meet to plan God-knows-what in the middle of Manhattan, and no one would ever know. They're just walking around in blissful ignorance as, potentially, world-threatening plans are being made right under their noses.

Just as I'm about to jump, Clark's voice sounds in my ear.

"Adrian, wait a minute."

I relax my body again and crouch. "What is it?"

"There's movement inside. The eight guys are still in the meeting, but two of the men from downstairs have gone up. They're walking toward the guy standing outside the room you're about to break into."

"Shit. Any idea why?"

"No. There's been no interior or exterior movement that would've alerted them to anything."

"Where's everyone else?"

"The two outside are still manning the door. There are now four downstairs dotted around, and two have moved upstairs. One seems to have stopped at the top of the stairs. The other is standing with the guy outside the room."

I think for a moment. "Might just be a status update. Like you say, they have no reason to suspect anything's wrong."

"Perhaps. Sit tight and see what happens."

I stay crouched and focus on keeping my breathing slow. I'm still not sure what I'm going to do once I'm inside, but the way I see it, getting inside is the hard part. Once I'm in there, I only need to get a hold of Hussein. I can probably negotiate my way out by holding my gun to his head, without needing to shoot anyone...

I almost kept a straight face as I thought that!

I reach behind me, draw my gun, and check the clip is full. There are sixteen in the mag and one in the chamber.

Including the drivers, I have sixteen potential targets and seventeen bullets. Take Hussein and whomever he's meeting out of the equation, since I can't shoot them, and I'm down to fourteen. That's one bullet each, with three for grace.

I've done more with less.

Clark speaks, breaking my train of thought. "Okay, those two guys are heading back downstairs. Looks like you were right."

"Okay. Let me know when they're gone, and I'll make the jump."

I stand again, readying myself once more. I crack my knuckles and rub my hands together, giving them some extra warmth and checking the blood's flowing, ready for the grip.

"You're clear," says Clark.

I take two steps back and dash forward, jumping as my front foot hits the edge. I step through, clearing the gap with ease, and get a good, solid grip of the window ledge. I brace as the momentum slams my lower body against the building and close my eyes to suppress an involuntary grunt from the impact.

I compose myself and glance down, making sure my legs aren't dangling in front of the window below me. Happy they're not, I relax my arms.

"Any sign of movement?" I ask, my voice straining from the effort.

"No. You're still looking good."

I heave myself up, using my feet to push myself as best I can, and rest my elbows and forearms on the ledge. Happy with my grip, I lift my head up and look through the window into the room. My view is limited; the sun is shining through the low, gray cloud and reflecting off the glass, meaning I can only see myself. But the room appears empty.

I steady myself and press my right palm flat against the glass. I push against it, then try to slide it up, hoping the window will move. It's a struggle, and I put plenty of pressure on it, but it doesn't budge. The window's locked.

Well, shit...

13

"Ah... Bob?"

"What's wrong?"

"The window's locked."

"Oh, shit..."

"Yeah, my thoughts exactly. I'm dangling thirty feet above Manhattan. A little help wouldn't go amiss."

"You should really plan things a little better. Did you not consider the possibility of the window being locked *before* you jumped?"

"Well, obviously, I *considered* it. I just believe positive thinking creates opportunity."

"Adrian, you're an idiot."

"Bob, if I wasn't hanging from a window ledge, I would absolutely kick your ass right now. Enough with the lecture. Fix this."

"What do you want me to do, exactly?"

"I don't know! Josh would've thought of something by now..."

"Well, I'm not Josh, am I?"

He falls silent. My arms are starting to ache.

"Bob, I've clearly hurt your feelings here, and I feel I should apologize. But I won't. Stop being such a fucking old woman and find me a way into the building!"

I can hear him go to say something, then stop himself, audibly catching his breath and his words. There's more silence on the line. My arms are really starting to hurt, to the point where my grip is slowly weakening.

"Any time you want, Bob..." I say, trying to hurry him along without antagonizing him any more than I already have.

"Well, I hate myself for saying this, but given the circumstances... why don't you just break the window, climb in, and shoot anyone who comes looking? You know you want to."

I smile to myself. About damn time.

"Bob, you're a good man."

"Whatever... just don't shoot the targets, okay?"

"Cross my heart."

Using my feet, I scramble up the wall as much as I can, renewing my hold on the ledge. Then I slowly reach behind me to get my gun. Holding it in my right hand, I look left as much as I can to shield my face. Then I slam the butt of the gun, hard, into the center of the window. The glass breaks, and I quickly heave myself up and through, while avoiding the few pieces of glass still sticking out from the frame.

I drop to the floor in a crouch and remain still. I aim my gun at the door, waiting for the guy outside the room to barge in to investigate the noise. My heart rate is increasing as the adrenaline kicks in. I take some deep breaths to try to regulate it, so I can use it to my advantage.

Three seconds pass before the door swings open. The guard stands there, a look of shock and confusion on his face. He must be one of Hussein's men. He looks Eastern European and is dressed in jeans and a sleeveless, insulated jacket. In his right hand is a submachine gun—looks like a MAC-10—with a suppressor attached. Using the split-second of hesitation to my advantage, I fire once, putting a bullet in the center of his forehead. His head snaps back, and he slumps straight to the floor. A crimson stain appears on the wall opposite, across the hallway.

I creep to the door and quickly search the dead guy for anything useful. I retrieve a driver's license, which states his name is—sorry, *was* Joseph Jameson, from Ohio.

Yeah, right...

I really dislike the MAC-10 as a weapon, so I leave that where it is. It's bulky and inaccurate, and its hair-trigger means one squeeze practically empties the clip, which is of no use when you're trying to be subtle and effective.

I look right, down the hallway to the stairs. I wait a moment, then turn left and glance at the door across the hall. It's big and made of thick wood, which looks out of place in the otherwise modern apartment. I suspect the last time the place was re-decorated, the owners decided to leave the original wooden door to give it a rustic feel. Again, after a minute of waiting, there's no sign of life.

I step out into the hallway, heading for the meeting room.

"Hey! Who the fuck are you?"

A voice behind me. American. Possibly from Boston.

Shit.

I turn around. Two men are at the top of the stairs. The

one on the left is wearing a suit and an earpiece. My guess is he's the one who just spoke. The guy next to him is dressed in jeans and a black, loose-fitting sweater. He doesn't have an earpiece. He has thick, dark hair and a matching beard, with dark, caramel skin. He's more likely one of Hussein's men.

Clark's voice sounds in my ear. "Adrian, head's up—I think they might have spotted you."

I roll my eyes. "Thanks for the update, *Bob*."

Quickly, I drop to a crouch and fire twice. The first bullet hits the American in his left shoulder, close to the neck, and sends him crashing to the floor. The second bullet hits the other guy square in the chest. He falls backward, and his lifeless body tumbles down the stairs.

I know how it might look, but I'd rather injure someone I can't identify. My spider sense is tingling about all these suited-and-booted Americans who are here. My gut tells me they're not with the Armageddon Initiative, so I don't want to risk killing someone and having a whole other bunch of people pissed at me. I've been there and done that, and it's hard work.

The second guy, however, was *definitely* a terrorist, so fuck him.

I hear commotion behind the wooden door. I'm assuming everyone has been alerted to my presence.

"Adrian, you've got more guys heading up the stairs," says Clark.

Great. So, I can't easily go that way. Plus, I need to get to Hussein and his friend, who are both in a room with six other people whom I can guarantee will be packing.

"Any ideas?"

"I'm thinking... sorry, Adrian. We need Hussein, but you

should maybe consider abandoning the mission, unless you want to risk not getting out of there at all."

"Rule number one, Bob—you never call off the mission. There's always a way out. Just gotta learn to think outside the box a little."

I look around, searching for inspiration. It will be too time-consuming to go back the way I came and too counter-productive to fight my way down the stairs and out of the building. My gaze keeps resting on the wooden door.

Going in that room would be crazy, wouldn't it? I mean, I don't know who's behind that door, where they are in the room, what weapons they have, anything...

It would just be sheer insanity to burst into the room.

I smile to myself.

I've always loved a little crazy!

I run at the door and barge into it shoulder-first. I nearly take it off its hinges, and it swings open, revealing the room. I stand in the doorway, my right arm throbbing from the impact. Everything slows down—split-seconds feel like hours as I take in every detail of the scene before me.

There's a large rectangular table in the middle of the room, lengthways, facing the door. At the far end, standing and facing me with his back to the window, is Yalafi Hussein. I recognize him from the information I read on the flight over here. He's just above average height, wearing an expensive suit and a small, fitted turban. His long, scraggly, black beard obscures much of his face, but when I catch his eyes, I see a glimpse of the hatred that lies beneath the surface. His mouth is open, frozen mid-speech, in shock.

On his left are three men all dressed in suits, with earpieces in and conspicuous bulges underneath their left armpits. All are Caucasian and clean shaven, with a disciplined air about them.

On his right, facing the men in suits, are three more men. They're dressed more casually, with no obvious weaponry, concealed or otherwise. They're all from different ethnic backgrounds, but each has short hair and trimmed beards. Their dark eyes hide the same, underlying anger that I see in Hussein.

Across the table, with his back to me, another man in a suit stands and faces Hussein. He doesn't turn around to look at me, but I can see the glint of military decoration on the left breast of his light brown jacket. He's bald and about my height. His stance is rigid and upright, with his shoulders back to their full width. He exudes confidence.

The suits on the right slowly reach into their jackets, presumably to retrieve their firearms. In front of Hussein is an open laptop.

I assess the situation, looking at the probable outcome of every possible course of action. I decide quickly that I have absolutely no chance of getting Hussein and the guy with his back to me out of here alive.

So, what's the next best thing?

Everyone's guns are almost drawn. Time restarts and I toward Hussein. My gun's already in my hand. I fire off five shots. One goes in the table in front of Hussein to make him duck down, three go at the suited men reaching for their guns, and one goes in the window that looks down over the street.

I reach the end of the table and spin clockwise, closing and swiping up the laptop in one movement. Then I fire off another two rounds in quick succession, aimed at the chests of two of the men there with Hussein, killing them instantly. This also gives me my first real look at the guy Hussein is meeting. It's a quick glance, but I take in his stern, weathered face and his emotionless, dark eyes. He's wearing lots of medals on his suit and stars on his shoulders. We look at each other for a brief moment, then he calmly turns away from me.

Tucking the laptop under my left arm, I jump at the window. I drop my head to the right and roll into it, so my left shoulder and back go first. With the glass already weakened from the bullet, I smash through, rolling naturally and falling the twenty-or-so feet down to the street.

Having developed the useful ability to accurately judge distances with the naked eye from my many years as a soldier and assassin, my calculations are right on the money. I land with a heavy thud, flat on my back on the roof of the middle limousine parked out front. I let out an involuntary grunt of pain from the impact.

My momentum carries me over and I continue to roll, then drop down onto the street. Still holding my gun, I put my right hand on the ground, stopping in a crouch and steadying myself. I quickly check to make sure the laptop wasn't damaged. Luckily, it seems intact. When I look up, a car's speeding toward me. The driver slams on his brakes, and the car screeches to a halt. I can only watch, rooted to the ground and unable to think quickly enough to move. Luckily, the car stops inches from my head.

Jesus!

I'm breathing heavily, and pain is pulsing through my entire body from the exertion and fall, but I manage to get to my feet. The smell of burning rubber from the tires drifts across the street, stinging my nostrils. I move to the driver's door and open it, using my gun to gesture to the driver to get out. It's a middle-aged man wearing chinos and a sweater, and he looks shaken up.

"I'm sorry about this, but I *really* need a ride."

The man says nothing; he just gets out of the car with a

petrified look on his face. I throw a quick glance up at the apartment before I climb in. The men guarding the door outside have disappeared. I'm guessing they've gone inside to see what was going on. I look up at the window and see Hussein standing there. His expression is a mixture of gloating that I didn't capture him and anger that I'd dare try to. I smile at him, then duck into the car, speeding off down West 81st Street, eager to put some distance between the angry terrorists and me.

And who was that guy meeting with Hussein? He looked important and vaguely familiar, but I can't place him.

"Clark, you there?"

"Adrian! What the hell's going on? Did you just get thrown out of a second-floor window?"

"No, I jumped."

"Of course you did! What happened?"

"My only way out of that room was straight down. No way was I getting out of there with Hussein, or his friend. I got a decent look at the guy, but I don't know who he is."

"So, you didn't get either target? I'm glad you're all right, Adrian, but I'm disappointed the mission was such a bust. All that risk for nothing."

I glance at the laptop on the seat beside me. "It wasn't a complete write-off. I managed to swipe Hussein's computer before I jumped. I don't think it's damaged, so we might be able to get something off it."

"That's damn good work, Adrian. Sorry I wasn't more use to you."

"You did fine, Bob, honestly. Where are you?"

"I'm still at the other safe house, over in Brooklyn."

"I'll make sure I'm not followed, then head over to you. See you soon."

I navigate the traffic, head back through Central Park,

and turn right onto FDR Drive. I follow it for over six miles and eventually turn onto the Brooklyn Bridge.

I hope there's something useful on this computer. As it stands, we're still none the wiser as to who this Armageddon Initiative really is, what they want, or who's working with them. We need a victory and fast. After today, they know I'm on their trail.

I can't help but think about Tori, back home in Texas. I need to stop these assholes before they retaliate.

14

I arrived at the secondary safe house about fifteen minutes ago. I ditched the car a couple of blocks away and approached on foot, taking an indirect route to make sure no one followed me.

Once inside, I handed the laptop over to Clark, and he set about hacking into it. I'm standing behind him, watching him work.

"Do you mind?" he asks, glancing over his shoulder.

"Sorry," I say, realizing I'm probably putting him off. "I used to watch Josh do this kind of thing because he'd talk me through it as he went along..."

I trail off when I see the look on his face. I've compared him to Josh a lot in the last few hours. He's probably pissed at me. I hold my hands up in apology and step away, pacing aimlessly around the room.

The safe house is an apartment in a run-down tenement block in Brooklyn. The neighborhood isn't the best advertisement for living in New York. Graffiti riddles a lot of the buildings, and they look abandoned. Plus, most people walking the streets look as if they're affiliated with a local gang. It's a great location for a safe house, but I have to smile at the irony because the place looks anything but safe.

The apartment is on the third floor. It's a simple, three-room place. The living room is spacious—mostly due to the fact it has little furniture in it—with a kitchenette built into one side of it. There's a table against the opposite wall with two chairs tucked under it. Clark's currently sitting in one of them, working away on the laptop. The carpet's worn and discolored. There's no TV and only a battered sofa against the far wall, facing the door. There's also a faint stale odor in every room, a smell of damp and neglect.

On either side of the front door is another door. On the left is a small, barely practical bathroom, complete with stained tiles, a toilet that's not been cleaned in decades, and a shower stall that Norman Bates would've been ashamed of. Opposite, on the right, is the bedroom. There's a single bed, unmade, in the center of the room, but otherwise it's empty.

"Anyway, are you all right?" asks Clark after a few minutes of awkward silence.

I shrug. "I'm fine. I've been in far worse situations than that."

He nods to signify he's listening but doesn't look up from the screen. "You don't need to tell me," he says, sounding distracted. "Anything more come to mind about who was there meeting with Hussein?"

I must admit, that's had my spider sense going haywire. Yalafi Hussein is a typical terrorist, by all accounts. He has a superior and armed men from all over the world—though from what I've seen so far, they seem to predominantly come from Middle Eastern countries. The powers that be are as aware of him as I am, but no one in the intelligence community seems to have any idea what this Armageddon Initiative is actually planning.

That's what I don't understand. With all the funding these people have, how can no one have any solid intel whatsoever on these guys? Plus, for him to be meeting an American, dressed in military garb and surrounded by American-looking, military-trained men in suits and earpieces... *and* on American soil... something isn't right.

"There's something off about all of this. I only got a quick look at the guy, and he wasn't immediately familiar to me. But I'm pretty sure he was a four-star general, and the men he brought to the meeting all looked suspiciously like government agents."

Clark finally looks up from the laptop, concerned and surprised. "Are you sure?"

I nod. "No other explanation I can see as to who the muscle was. And as for him, he was definitely a high-ranking U.S. military official. Either that, or he was really committed to his fancy dress outfit."

He looks back at the laptop, shaking his head slightly. "Christ... this just keeps getting better."

I continue to pace around the room, feeling restless.

"I'm just gonna check in with Josh."

I take out my phone and dial his number. He answers on the second ring.

"How's it going, Boss?"

"It's like you never left..." We share a brief laugh. "I'm just checking in."

"You get Hussein?"

"No, the whole thing was a train wreck. The place was

too heavily defended. All I managed to do was steal his laptop as I jumped out the window."

"You jumped out the... wait, never mind. Of *course* you jumped out the window. So, what's on the laptop?"

"Don't know yet. Clark's working on it as we speak."

"Be patient with him, Adrian. He's not me, but he's a good man."

I glance over at him and smile to myself. "I know."

"So, what about the meeting? Who was there with Hussein?"

"That's what's bothering me the most. I was just saying to Bob, I didn't recognize the guy, but he was a four-star general, Josh. U.S. military. And he was protected by some well-trained guys. I don't know if they were secret service, but they were definitely G-men."

"Holy shit."

"Indeed."

"Adrian, this is getting worse by the minute."

"Tell me about it. Where are you, anyway?"

"Schultz and I flew back to HQ in California after we dropped you off at the jet. Just scanning through our intel and planning the next move."

Clark abruptly stands, pushing the chair backward and knocking it over.

"Fuck me..." he says in a disbelieving whisper.

"Josh, hang on a sec. I think we might have something." I hold the phone against my chest and walk over to look at the screen. "Bob, what is it?"

"I've got in and decrypted the information Hussein had," he explains. "A lot of it is useful but not groundbreaking— financials, locations of safe houses and the like. But then I found this..."

He leans forward, taps a few keys, and brings up something that looks like a blueprint.

I shake my head and shrug. "Looks impressive but means nothing to me."

Clark points at the phone. "You got Josh on the line?"

I nod.

"Put him on speakerphone. He'll want to hear this."

I do and rest the phone next to the laptop. "Josh, you're on loudspeaker. Bob's here and looks distressed."

"Josh, we have a serious problem. Yalafi Hussein has the schematics for Project Cerberus on his computer."

Silence descends. After a few moments, I begin to feel awkward. I should say something, but I don't know what.

"Fuck me..." says Josh.

I frown. "Okay, that's what Bob said. Everyone's doing that thing where they all talk in some sort of code, and everyone seems to understand it except me. And you all know how that pisses me off. Somebody start talking—in Adrian language."

"Adrian, Project Cerberus is a government-funded program for NASA," explains Josh. "It was one of the first things the new president invested in."

"NASA? So, it's a rocket or something?"

"It's a satellite," he continues. "A powerful satellite. Its primary purpose is to act as a roaming firewall, protecting all the important information the U.S. government doesn't want falling into the wrong hands."

"Like..."

"Like information for the Department of Treasury, military strategies and programs, nuclear launch codes..."

I raise an eyebrow. "Fuck me..."

"Exactly! Cerberus is basically a large, floating, unhackable computer in space, looking down and protecting all the important data the U.S. has."

I massage my temples, trying to process the information. I'm far from computer-illiterate, but I'm not technically minded like these two. I'd prefer everything stayed written down and filed away somewhere. I see absolutely no reason to put more and more information on smaller and smaller computers.

"So, the fact a terrorist has the blueprints for this satellite is a bad thing, right?"

"Bob?" Josh says, as if prompting him to add to the conversation.

"That's... not *all* the satellite does," he says, somewhat reluctantly.

I roll my eyes. "Oh, great. There's more..."

"Everything Josh just said is accurate, but that's only what the official statement to the media said about the program."

"And you're about to tell me the unofficial statement, correct?"

Clark sighs. "Cerberus is also capable of monitoring and recording... well, everything. Every phone call, e-mail, text message, photo, video, camera feed... literally *everything*."

"Whose bright idea was *that*?"

"The primary function of the program is to safeguard all critical information in a place no one could break into. That much we all know. But the secondary function is to protect the nation from any potential threats. To do this, it monitors *everything*, all the time. It searches for certain parameters, records everything it finds, stores it on its servers for up to seven years, and transmits directly to the Pentagon. Adrian, there's an obvious moral issue, to say nothing of the legalities of the technology. Even President Cunningham couldn't have sold such a massive invasion of privacy to the American people."

That's a lot of information to take in. I move over to the window and look out to the street below, gazing aimlessly as I wrap my head around it. Cerberus isn't a computer or a shield for the American people—it's a goddamn weapon! And Hussein has the blueprints for it. So, this must be the Armageddon Initiative's goal—to somehow gain control of this satellite. Christ, they'd be able to hold the country ransom!

I walk back over to Clark. "Okay, here's a question: how do you two know all this top-secret shit that no one else does?"

It's Clark's turn to pace the room.

Josh clears his throat on the line. "Adrian, we know because... we built it."

15

I stare disbelievingly at the phone. "What?"

"NASA's budget has always been unjustifiably large," explains Josh. "But most of that is for research, not production. The project was outsourced to GlobaTech for us to physically build the satellite. We had a hand in the design, then once it was completed, NASA launched it and took the credit."

I shake my head. "And you didn't think to question all of these little extras they asked you to put in?"

"Adrian, I know where you're coming from. I do. But it doesn't work like that. GlobaTech is a worldwide company who make weapons and technology and contract out their own private army to countries around the world to solve problems. We're not here to debate the moral implications of what people pay us billions of dollars to do."

I look at Clark, who seems to be doing his best to avoid my gaze. "And what happened to the ethical reign of the mighty Robert Clark?" I clench my fists as I fight to retain control of my short temper, enraged by my own helplessness.

He turns and glares at me, a flash of anger in his eyes. "Hey, don't lecture me on ethics, you self-righteous sono-fabitch! All day, you've been insinuating I'm not good enough to help you, and I'm sick to death of it! Then you have the audacity to question *me* on a morally gray business venture that the U.S. government paid me a small fortune to be part of? Don't you dare start pointing the finger at me and mine over this!"

I don't respond. His confrontational tone takes me by surprise.

Still on speaker, Josh takes in a breath and holds it, stunned into silence. He knows there aren't many people alive today who have spoken to me like that and gotten away with it.

I take a couple of deep breaths, finding it hard to resist lunging for his throat. It takes a moment, but I somehow find a sense of calm. "I'm not pointing the finger at anyone. I'm merely questioning how anyone in their right mind could agree that making something this powerful and this... invasive... could possibly be a good idea. But to call me self-righteous? Bob, I'm only here because you asked for my help. And honestly, the more I find out about this whole thing, the less I feel I can actually do anything. Shouldn't you be calling the Pentagon? Or the White House?"

Silence descends once more, which Josh breaks after a few tense moments, sounding eager. "Okay, Bob, send every-thing you have on that laptop to one of our secure servers. I'll copy it onto my personal computer and set to work trying to figure out how Hussein intended to use this infor-mation. Adrian, get your ass back home to Tori. I'll contact you if I find anything out, or if I need your help any further, okay?"

I notice he said *I*, not *we*, just then. He probably thinks it's best to disassociate himself from GlobaTech when talking to me for now, which is a wise decision.

I nod. "Sounds like a plan. Josh, I'll call you when I get back to Texas anyway, just to see how you're getting on." I turn to Clark. "Bob, if you still want my advice, once you've given all the information off that laptop to Josh, I'd destroy it. Just in case Hussein sends anyone to retrieve it."

Clark nods, which looks like half a *thank you* and, I think, half an apology. I hang up the phone, pick up my shoulder bag, and walk out of the room.

I'll make my own way to the goddamn airport.

22:04 EDT

I decided instead to head back to the safe house in Queens first. Initially I just wanted time with my thoughts, but I ended up catching some sleep. I woke about an hour ago and flagged a cab just down the street from the safe house to drive me to JFK. Thankfully, GlobaTech's hospitality hadn't expired, and the plane was still waiting for me. After minimal fuss getting back on board, our takeoff was given priority clearance, so I was in the air within twenty minutes, heading back home.

There's no stewardess on the flight this time, so I'm sitting alone in the cabin, staring out of the window with my bag at my feet. The co-pilot saw me on board and showed me to my seat before disappearing into the cockpit and locking the door behind him.

I'm staring into space, trying to wrap my head around everything that's happening. I think it's fairly safe to assume that Hussein and his Armageddon Initiative intend to access this Cerberus satellite. God only knows what they're going to do with it, but whatever it is can't possibly be good.

On top of that is their recruitment drive, which I have to assume is still ongoing. I doubt they would stop just because they couldn't get me. Then there's the mystery four-star general, who was meeting with Hussein. I don't know who he is, but if Hussein's managed to negotiate getting a man on the inside, especially one that highly ranked, then they're an even bigger threat than anyone realizes. The FBI is investigating, but they aren't going to know as much as I do right now.

Maybe I should go to them with all this? I think back to my argument with Clark. I know my opinion isn't everybody's, but surely, I'm not the only one who thinks GlobaTech's involvement in this is questionable? And for Josh to be front and center... I know he was just doing a job, but I don't want anything coming back on him. Or Clark, if I'm honest. He's always been straight with me and has had my back when I needed him.

I sigh heavily. I feel a headache coming on.

Oh, and let's not forget Clara fucking Fox! I've got at least one bullet with that bitch's name on it.

I look back out the window. My vision glazed over as I was thinking about everything. As I focus more on the world outside, something strikes me as strange. New York to Texas is a fairly straight line over land. Why am I seeing water below us?

I'm a reasonably well-traveled and well-educated man, but I call on my middle school-level geography from the dark recesses of my mind, just to make damn sure I'm not mistaken. But there's definitely no ocean between New York and Texas.

I take out my phone and use a compass app to see which way we're traveling. I look out the window again, then back at the direction. Using my middle school math as well, I reckon I'm somewhere over the North Atlantic Ocean, approaching Bermuda. Being in a relatively small plane, that could pose its own set of problems.

I get up, walk over to the cockpit, and knock on the door. "Hey, you got a sec?"

I hear movement from inside, but almost a minute passes before the door unlatches and opens. The co-pilot stands in the doorway, holding it ajar just enough for his body to fit. I can't see past him into the cockpit itself.

"Is everything okay?" he asks.

He's a tall guy, almost my height. He looks in good shape physically and is dressed smart, with some designer stubble. Maybe late thirties. But there's something not quite right in his eyes. I make a mental note and carry on.

"Yeah, everything's fine. Just a question, really... and I'm the first to admit I'm no expert here, but I'm pretty sure we don't need to fly over any ocean to get to San Antonio from JFK?"

There's a split-second flash in his eyes, then it's suppressed as quickly as it appeared. I didn't expect it, but I saw it, and I'd recognize it anywhere.

It was fear.

Beads of sweat form on his forehead. He hesitates. "We had to divert via Florida. The airspace isn't clear for a private plane, due to a buildup of commercial flights coming out of Tennessee, so we have to fly around them."

I'm impressed with his answer—technical and extremely plausible. He was calm and professional.

However, I can smell bullshit a mile away, and coupled with everything else I've noticed, I'm now convinced something's not right here. The question is, what do I do? I'm probably seventeen thousand feet up, and with guns not being an option, I'm left depending on my skills in diplomacy and tact to deal with whatever happens next.

I'm so screwed...

"That makes sense. Fair enough." I pause, making like I'm about to walk back to my seat, but I've just thought of something else to say. "Is everything all right, man? You don't look so good."

Before he can answer, I hear movement behind him, and then the co-pilot grunts as he's struck on the back of his head. His eyes roll up in his skull, and he wobbles momentarily before falling heavily and landing at my feet.

I knew something wasn't right, but I didn't expect that. I take a couple of steps back, momentarily distracted.

Another man steps out from inside the cockpit, strides over the body, and stands in front of me. He's pointing a Glock at me, aiming right between my eyes. His arm is steady, his breathing is normal, and his stance is relaxed and comfortable. He's definitely well-trained. He's about my height, with an average but well-built, frame. He's wearing unmarked, black and gray camo overalls and thick work boots. He's got thick stubble, and his dark eyes stare at me, not blinking and not interested.

I take a deep breath, preparing myself for a fight that I hope won't happen. Too many things can go wrong on a plane. I stand my ground but don't make any movement.

When in doubt, antagonize and capitalize...

I raise an eyebrow. "Just for my own peace of mind, before we go any further... there's still someone flying the plane, right?"

His gun doesn't move an inch. He smiles. "Yeah, the pilot's fine. For now."

He's definitely American, although I can't place his accent. My spider sense is telling me he's not with Hussein. I wonder if he's with our mystery four-star general?

"That's a relief. So, are you gonna introduce yourself?"

He shakes his head. "Nope."

"Oh... okay. Well, I'm Adrian Hell."

"I know who you are."

"Of course, you do. Or do you simply *think* you do? I mean, no offense, but let's be honest here—you're still vertical and awake purely as a courtesy because I want to know what's going on. Should I deem it necessary, you'll quickly be laid out on the floor."

He smiles at me again. "I know *exactly* who you are. But you seem to be missing the point. You don't know who I am, or why I'm here. You're also approaching your third year of retirement, right? You're not a threat to me. And *no offense*, but you're only alive because my orders are to ensure you stay that way until we land. But make no mistake—you *will* behave. My orders *don't* specify whether you need to be conscious when we land, just breathing."

"Nice speech."

I stand in front of him a few moments longer, then turn my back and walk over to my seat. I want him to know I'm sitting down because I choose to, not because he ordered me to. I sit casually in the seat and stretch my legs out, crossing my ankles and resting my arms across my chest.

"So, where are we really going?"

He says nothing.

"Okay, how about telling me who you work for?"

Still, he remains silent.

"Well, the rest of this flight isn't going to drag at all..."

I close my eyes and let my head relax. I doubt he'll move from covering me. The pilot can't do anything. He's going to fly where he's told. I suspect any communication with people on the ground is out of the question as well. But we're on a plane in a pressurized cabin, so there's no way he's firing his gun at me, which means I can simply dismiss him as a threat until we land. The total lack of respect and credibility I'm affording him as my apparent captor will likely start to eat away at him before much longer. Then he'll get all emotional and make a mistake. Then I'll pull his arm off and beat his brains out with the wet end.

But until then, I might as well get some sleep.

April 11, 2017 — 00:16 CDT

I wake up, still sitting in the same position as when I dozed off. I glance out the window and gather my senses, gently rubbing my eyes as I come to terms with consciousness once more. My body clock says I've been out nearly three hours.

Across the aisle, slumped in the chair with his wrists and ankles bound, is the co-pilot. He's alive, but I'm guessing he's taken at least one more blow to the head since I last saw him. I doubt he'd still be out after all this time from the initial shot he took.

The cockpit door is closed again. Our mystery guest must be in there, probably pointing his gun at the pilot. I look down and see my bag's missing, which has my phone in it.

Great.

I stand up and stretch, then bend down to look out the window properly. I don't recognize anything that I can see, but we're not over the ocean anymore. The ground is close, so we're making our descent.

I sit back down just as the cockpit door opens. The mystery man walks in. "Get your beauty sleep?"

I shrug. "I'm beautiful enough. I was just bored of talking to you."

He smiles humorlessly, then reaches behind him and produces his handgun again. He holds it loosely at his side. "We'll be landing soon. When we do, you'll exit the plane, kneel on the ground, cross your ankles behind you, and place your hands behind your head, interlocking your fingers. If you don't, I'll shoot you. Is that clear?"

Huh. They were professional instructions. I get the impression he's used to dealing with hostages. He seems comfortable and confident giving out commands. I reckon he's American military of some kind. I suspect he's special ops, as this is a bit too risqué for a standard grunt. He's not the leader, but he's high-ranking and probably respected by his peers. Experienced. Not intimidated.

Maybe I should be worried.

I nod silently, shifting in my seat to get comfortable. There's bound to be a team waiting for me when we land. If we *are* looking at an off-the-books operation to apprehend me, the team will consist of four or five guys, who will take me to an undisclosed location to either meet with someone more important, or simply to torture and kill me.

The guy sits in the chair opposite me, regarding me impassively. His gun rests on his leg. Next to us, the co-pilot stirs, groaning quietly.

I'll test my luck.

"So, you not gonna give me any clues as to who you are and what you want with me?"

"When we land," he replies matter-of-factly. "My job's to get you there, not tell you why."

"Get me where, exactly?"

He smiles but says nothing. The pilot's voice interrupts our little exchange, sounding over the speaker system. "We'll be landing in a few minutes. Please stay seated until we're on the ground."

He sounds terrified. I hope he's not so shaken up that he crashes...

He's not, thankfully. A few minutes later, we land unscathed and taxi to a stop. I look out of the window. We're on an abandoned runway. It's dark, but there are a few floodlights around the perimeter, bathing the area in a faint glow.

Like lightning, my captor is out of his seat. He turns slightly and fires his gun, putting a bullet in the co-pilot's head. His body lurches away from us, hits the side of the cabin, and falls to the floor, leaving a crimson stain in its wake.

He then dashes into the cockpit, and I hear another bullet. The pilot clearly met the same end. Before I can move, he's back in the cabin and aiming his gun at me. "Move to the door, nice and slow."

I do as he says. I don't have any real alternatives. He's keeping his distance from me, anticipating an attempt from me to disarm and disable him.

"Now open it," he instructs.

I spin the handle in the center of the door, unlocking the metal levers from the top and bottom, and push it open. It hisses as the cabin depressurizes. The door swings out and down automatically. Steps unfold from it and rest on the ground.

I feel the barrel of his gun push against my lower back.

"Move," he says.

I sigh heavily. I clench my fist and tense my jaw muscles in frustration as I realize how helpless I am right now. But I descend the stairs nevertheless.

As I step onto the blacktop, I look around, trying to find some clue as to where I am. The moon is high and clear, contributing to the pale glow around us. There's a small building just ahead of me with an array of antennas on the roof. It looks abandoned; the wood and brick is damaged and discolored from years of neglect. To my left, the runway stretches back to the line of trees surrounding the small airfield. To my right, a little way off, is a chain-link fence with a gate on wheels, standing open.

I think about my options, but there aren't any that spring to mind that don't result in my death.

"On your knees," says the man with the gun. "Ankles crossed, hands on your head."

I obey, working on the assumption that I'm going to, at the least, be asked some questions before any violence breaks out. I'll use that to buy myself some time, so I can think of a way out of this.

After a few moments of kneeling there, four people appear from inside the abandoned building ahead of me. They walk purposefully, side by side, across the tarmac toward me. Then they stop a few feet in front of me and fanning out. They're all dressed in the same unmarked camo as my captor. They're not wearing masks, so I can see their faces quite clearly. There are three men and a woman, all holding weapons ready and loose, staring at me impassively.

The guy from the plane steps around from behind me and joins his team, standing on the far right of the line.

The man on the far left of the group steps forward. He's

a monster—easily six-five, maybe six-six. He's built like a tank, with clean good looks and a military buzz cut.

"Adrian Hell?" he asks, somewhat rhetorically.

"Used to be..."

He levels his weapon at me—a FAMAS-G2 if I'm not mistaken. Nice gun. Shame it's French.

"Welcome to Colombia."

16

"On your feet," says the big guy, whom I assume is in charge.

I stand, still trying to figure out why anyone would kidnap me and take me to Colombia, of all places.

"Now where's the laptop?"

I keep my expression neutral. "What laptop?"

"The one you stole approximately fourteen hours ago. It's government property, and you're going to hand it over immediately."

"So, you work for the government?"

He doesn't say anything.

"You guys have me confused with someone else, clearly. The laptop *I* stole belonged to a known terrorist. I'm actually trying to *help* the government that you may or may not work for. But it's okay. You didn't know. I'll just get my things and be on my way. I... ah... I don't suppose one of you can fly this plane, can you?"

The other four in the line gesture with their weapons in

unison, looks of impatience etched on their faces.

"I won't ask you again," says the big guy. "Give me the laptop."

I relax and see the first flicker of doubt in his eyes. He's in charge of the unit and presumably experienced. He'll be able to tell I'm not lying, which will be making him question his orders.

"Like I said, I stole a laptop off a terrorist, not a government employee. I did so on behalf of a private military contractor as part of an ongoing operation. And you people obviously wouldn't be interested in that, would you?"

I smile, daring them to give me more information.

"What operation?" he asks.

Bingo. I'll give them just enough to reel them in.

"I've been targeted by a terrorist group who want to recruit me. As you say, I'm Adrian Hell, retired or not. I refused, and they came after me. Some friends of mine happened to be investigating these assholes anyway, so I agreed to help them out. I managed to get in the same room as one of them and steal his laptop, which I've since handed over to my PMC friends. But that's got nothing to do with the government, so I'm at a loss as to why you'd be sent after me..."

The big guy's eyes narrow, and I see him working everything out in his head. I have no doubt the orders he received were based on the assumption I'm still in possession of the laptop I took from Hussein. This tells me that the guy Hussein was meeting in Manhattan is definitely a big deal because this operation to hijack my plane must've been put together within a matter of hours. Now he has me, and I have information that directly contradicts what his superiors must've told him.

It also confirms my suspicions about the suited Americans and the mystery four-star general at the meeting. Whatever relationship they have with Hussein, they seem eager to keep it a secret. That means the laptop is just a cover to justify killing me in the middle of nowhere.

I need to persuade these people that I'm not the mission here.

"Who sent you after me?"

The big guy remains silent.

"Come on. Get on the comms and ask the question. You know you want to."

His jaw muscles clench. He takes a deep breath and turns to the rest of the group.

"Watch him," he says. He walks a few paces away from us, presses his hand to his chest, and activates his comms unit. I can just about hear what he's saying.

"Sir, we have the target. There's no package—I repeat, no package. Please advise. Over."

He nods, listening to the reply.

"He says he stole a laptop from a known terrorist on behalf of a PMC he was working with. He doesn't have it on his person anymore... I understand, sir, but can you please clarify the threat here? If what he says is true, we should contact the PMC and follow up from there... Say again, sir..."

He sighs heavily, glancing over at me.

"Understood, sir."

He walks back over and stands reluctantly in front of me.

"My orders are to kill you," he says matter-of-factly. "But I want to know who you're working for."

I shrug. "Why?"

"Because there's an ongoing mission that I think could benefit from that information."

Out of the corner of my eye, I see the guy from the plane touch his ear, as if receiving a communication. Nobody else in the group acknowledges their comms. But I dismiss it as quickly as I noticed it.

"What's the mission?"

"Are you serious?"

I shrug. "Worth a try. I know you have your orders, but I'm not the enemy here. You have my word."

"And what is the word of a two-bit hitman worth, exactly?"

"Two-bit?" I scoff, genuinely offended. "Try *world's greatest*, you ignorant prick. And I'm many things, but I'm not a liar. I'm trying to help. I don't trust you enough to give you everything I know, but I *can* tell you I have seen solid intel that suggests a pending terrorist attack that nobody else currently knows is coming."

Everyone in the group exchanges glances, but the big guy keeps his eyes fixed on me.

"I'm trying to help, and I'm offering my help to you now. I'm not the enemy, and given what I know, I suspect your orders are bogus, unjustified, and given by someone who doesn't want the world to know they're implicated in a terrorist attack."

"And you can prove this?" he asks.

"Yes."

He levels his gun at me for a second, then lowers it again, wrestling with his conscience. I watch the internal debate in his eyes. The soldier in him has his orders and knows he shouldn't question them. But the smart, experienced leader in him wants all the information to satisfy the ounce of doubt plaguing his mind.

He kind of reminds me of me.

I feel a glimmer of hope that I might have managed to

buy myself some time and talk my way out of a firing squad death.

The guy from the plane, standing on the far right, quickly spins around and aims his gun at the big guy. Without hesitation, he fires. The bullet hits their leader in the forehead, and he falls to the ground, turning away from us and landing heavily. Blood pools around him from the wound.

The team looks at him with a mixture of shock and excitement.

"I've been given the authority to execute Alpha Protocol," he announces. "The parameters of the mission have changed, based on the opinion that Jericho is no longer fit to lead this team. I've been placed in command, and you now report to me. Any questions?"

He's met with silence, which he seems to take as a sign they're all on the same page. He then turns back to me. "If you don't have the laptop, you'll give me all information relating to Yalafi Hussein and the people you're working with, or I will shoot you."

And there it is—unequivocal proof that I'm screwed. I need an exit strategy right now.

My eyes narrow. "I never said the terrorist was called Yalafi Hussein. Who *are* you guys?"

The guy from the plane looks away, cursing himself. Then he turns back to me. "Kill him!"

My primeval, long-buried survival instincts immediately kick in. I dive to the left, pick up the big guy's FAMAS, and run around the plane for cover.

What did they say his name was? Jericho?

I hold the rifle in my left hand, aiming it behind me as I run, firing blind to buy myself some time. I need to get on the plane and get my bag.

I carry on running away from the group, putting as much distance as I can between us. I aim for the trees, thinking I can lose them in there and then double back to the plane for my things.

I chance a look behind me, but the team isn't in pursuit. I see two of them, one on either side of the plane, planting explosives along the fuselage. The other two are aiming at me but holding fire. Behind them, where I was just standing, I see the body of their former unit leader—the man known as Jericho.

I actually quite liked him. It's a shame he's dead.

But I need to focus. If that plane goes up, I'm as good as dead myself. I skid to a halt, turn around, and drop into a crouch. I bring the rifle up, taking aim. Tucking it into my shoulder, I look down the sight. I must be a good few hundred yards away by now. I set it to fire in three-round bursts and squeeze the trigger twice. The first burst peppers the ground next to the man on the left of the plane, and he scurries away around the other side for cover. The second burst scatters the two arming the explosives, who both do the same.

Knowing they'll be re-grouping behind cover, I run back over to the plane. I crouch down behind the front wheel and glance up at the first explosive charge.

Shit.

They've armed it, and the timer says two minutes and counting. They clearly didn't intend to hang around, so I shouldn't either.

I peer around the wheel to get their positions, but they're gone. I look around and see the four of them disappearing behind the abandoned building at the opposite end of the runway.

Not wishing to waste another second, I stand and run

onto the plane. I quickly find my shoulder bag in the cockpit. I put it over both arms and head back outside. The explosive charge on this side of the fuselage, next to the steps, has got thirty-four seconds left.

I need to get out of here!

I set off, but as I draw level with Jericho's body, I hear something. It's only faint, but it's definitely a murmur. I look down at him.

Jesus Christ, he's alive!

After a split-second of deliberation, I decide I can't leave him lying next to a plane that's about to explode. I crouch and roll him on his back. The bullet hit his forehead but must have gone clean through the front part of his skull. I'm not a doctor, but I imagine the consequences of such an injury are severe, even if the guy *is* still breathing. The wound looks nasty, and blood's pouring down his face.

I grab his left hand and pull, in an effort to drag him clear of the blast.

"Jesus, what do you eat? Bricks?"

I continue to drag him across the runway, building up speed and momentum as I go. There's maybe ten seconds left before the charge on the plane goes off. I'm a good few hundred yards away, but I need to keep going as far as I can.

I'm breathing heavily, and my back and arms are aching from dragging Jericho's motionless body across the ground.

Another few seconds pass, then a deafening explosion sounds out. The ground shakes, and the force of the blast knocks me off my feet. I land maybe twenty feet away, hitting the ground hard. My head ricochets off the concrete, making me momentarily dizzy.

Ah, shit!

Lying on my back, I look over at the plane, which has disappeared in a ball of fire and smoke. I feel the heat from the blast stinging my skin. I struggle to catch my breath; the rapid increase in temperature has sucked all the oxygen out of the air around me.

I lie still for a moment, staring at the blackening sky. My ears are ringing loudly and my back screams from the impact.

I let out an involuntary groan. "Oh, man, that sucked..."

I look over to my right and see Jericho's still motionless nearby. I did what I could for him, so my conscience is clear. But to be honest, given the head wound he has, I doubt he'll last the night. He might get lucky, and someone might call the fire department.

Having said that, I'm on an abandoned airstrip somewhere in Colombia. I doubt anyone who could've heard the blast is likely to care.

I roll over on my stomach and push myself up on all fours, looking ahead of me at the building. I can't see anyone, so I'm guessing the team sent to kill me has left the area. That buys me a little time at least.

I take the bag off my shoulders and open it. I retrieve my cell phone, which is thankfully still in one piece. I check the screen and see I have a weak signal. I dial Josh's number, then take one last look at Jericho's body before walking slowly toward the building ahead. He answers after three rings.

"Adrian! Are you all right? Why aren't you back home yet?"

"It's a long story, man. The short version is the jet was hijacked. I'm in Colombia, and the jet's all blown up. I've just survived a run-in with a pretty deadly special ops unit. Don't know whose books they're on, but the guy who took the plane just shot his unit leader and assumed command."

"Jesus... why?"

"I don't know. The leader was a guy named Jericho. Not sure if it's a codename or not. He wanted the laptop I stole from Hussein... said it was government property."

"How did they even know about that?"

"Not sure, but it must have something to do with the four-star who was at the meeting. My guess... whoever he is, he's important and doesn't want his involvement with terrorists becoming public knowledge. He or someone he works with sent that team to kill me, using the laptop as justification. The leader started asking questions when I told him who I was, and the next thing, his second-in-command shot him in the head. Said something about Alpha Protocol. Does that mean anything to you? Anyway, the guy's still alive but barely. Nothing I can do for him."

"Holy shit, Adrian! This is just getting bigger and bigger. Look, just get your ass back to Texas, all right?"

"Yeah, about that... where the hell am I, Josh?"

The line goes quiet for a moment and then I hear muffled voices in the background.

"Josh, is everything all right there?"

"Adrian, look... I'm sorry, but I kinda got something going on here. I don't want to say any more over an unsecure line. Just... just get back to Texas and wait for me there, okay?"

He hangs up before I can say anything, leaving me standing here, staring at my phone. I put it away and then sling my bag back over my shoulder. I look around for any clue as to where to go from here. I'm not going to get anywhere until morning, so I head over the abandoned building. I just hope the fire doesn't attract any unwanted attention before I can get out of here.

17

I managed to get some sleep underneath a desk in the old control tower, on the second floor of the building overlooking the airstrip. A commotion outside woke me up, so I'm peering out the window at the scene. Fire crews and ambulances blast their sirens, dealing with the immediate situation. There's an EMT checking on Jericho, who's now gesturing frantically at his colleagues for a gurney, so he must still be breathing.

Tough bastard. I'll give him that.

While much has changed in the last few years, especially the relationship between North and South America, I'm still not sure it's worth heading out there. The drug trade around these parts might be a legitimate business nowadays, but that doesn't mean crime and corruption don't exist anymore. No police down there, though, which tells me all I need to know.

I'll wait for everyone to clear out before trying to find my way back stateside as soon as possible.

Five minutes pass. I hear a noise from outside the airstrip, and a moment later, three convertible Jeeps race through the gates. All of them are rusty, battered, and full; four men are in each, with one driving and three armed with AK-47s. They all do a lap around the scene, then screech to a halt next to the firetruck. There are three firemen I can see, plus three EMTs, so they're outnumbered.

So, who the hell are these new guys? All the cartels have either disbanded or gone legit, thanks to President Cunningham's influence. There's no rebel activity in this part of the world that I'm aware of, either. They could be local militia, I guess. But would this situation warrant military intervention? Even in Colombia?

I should go down there. It doesn't look like the EMTs and firemen are going to survive otherwise. Plus, I might be able to convince the guys with guns that I'm an ally, which might lead to me getting out of here. Granted, me going down there might result in everyone getting shot too, but I can't just sit here with my thumb up my ass, waiting. God knows what Hussein and his powerful friends are up to right now, and the longer I'm out of the game, the more chance they have of disappearing and getting their hands on Cerberus.

I massage my temples and take a deep breath, trying to focus my mind on the task at hand and forget everything else for now. With that done, I stand, gather my bag, and head for the door. Instinctively, I touch the barrels of both Berettas, which are holstered at my back.

Just in case.

I walk out of the building, holding my arms in the air. Time to play my part and get the hell out of here.

"Hey, guys! I need your help here!"

Everyone turns to look at me, and all the guns immediately aim in my direction. One of the men shouts back in Spanish, and I don't understand him. I make sure my palms are facing him and my arms are wide, giving the impression I'm on the defensive and not a threat to them.

I stop a few feet away from the nearest EMT. "Does anyone here speak English?"

A man on the right of the group gestures at me violently with his rifle. "American?"

"Yes, American! Do you understand me? Can you help me?"

The man quickly translates to another in the group, whom I assume is in charge. He then says something to me, which the first guy interprets. "Who are you? What are you doing here?"

I point to the flaming ball of metal behind them. "That was my plane. It was hijacked, and I was brought here. I managed to escape, but I need to get back home urgently."

He explains what I just said to his boss, who eyes me wearily. He lowers his rifle and walks toward me, and a few of the group follow him. He shouts something to me again, and I look to the first guy for clarification.

"Who hijacked your plane?" he asks.

I shrug. "I don't know, but they were American, like me. Definitely military. Possibly special forces."

This causes urgent murmuring among the group, which is finally silenced by the man in charge, who says something. His friend translates once more. "You will come with us. We will talk more."

"Thank you." I gesture to the firemen and EMTs. "Do you intend to let these people go?"

"What's it to you?" he asks after a moment of discussion.

"I just don't want anyone getting hurt because of me. I'll come with you and answer your questions if you agree to let these people leave here unharmed.'

The man smiles. "And what if we don't agree?"

I take a deep breath, preparing to go for my guns if I need to. "Then we'll have a big problem. There are people looking for me—important people, with lots of resources. I don't want to have to tell them you were anything other than accommodating. That would be bad for you."

A hushed discussion ripples through the group of armed men. The firemen and EMTs look nervous, glancing at each other and at me. I remain calm. I'm not too worried. Whoever these guys are, I suspect we're simply on their turf, and they want to know why. Any local presence will operate on fear, but I doubt they'll kill anyone they don't have to.

After a few moments, the boss shouts to all the firemen and EMTs in Spanish. They all nod, quickly get into their vehicles, and drive away. I watch until they're gone, leaving twelve armed, unidentified hostiles and me.

I look at them. "So, where are we going, fellas?"

The one who speaks English walks over to me. Before I have a chance to react, he raises the butt of his rifle and hits me on the side of—

??:??

I open my eyes slowly. My head is pounding from the impact earlier. I've got no idea how long I've been out, but it's light outside, so I'm guessing a few hours. I look around and see I'm sitting in a room filled with expensive décor. There are six men around me, covering the exits and windows—all of whom I recognize from the airstrip. I'm in a comfortable cream armchair in the center of the room. There's a nice rug underneath my feet with a glass table on it. There's a matching chair opposite me and a large sofa completing the set to the right.

In front of me, along almost the entire wall, are tall windows overlooking the ocean, with trees just outside. The ceiling is high and made up of wooden beams. Works of art and expensive ornaments adorn the walls of the room on all sides.

I'm confused, but I remain silent and seated. I figure it's best to say nothing and wait for the owner of whatever mansion I'm sitting in to introduce himself.

I don't have to wait long. A man walks in from the left, tall and probably on the rough side of fifty. He's got short black hair and a thick mustache, both flecked with gray. He's wearing an orange silk shirt, white trousers, and sandals. He's smiling at me, which is a little weird, but at least he's not likely to kill me in the next five minutes.

"I'm sorry for the way in which you were brought here," he says to me, sitting down in the chair opposite. His accent is thick, but his English is good.

I smile weakly, rubbing the base of my neck. "Beats getting shot..."

He laughs loudly, looking around the room at his men, who all join in on cue. Then he looks back at me. "My friend, have we met before?"

I look at him, genuinely trying to remember him... but I don't. I shrug. "Not that I know of."

"Hmmm. You look familiar to me. Tell me, what is it that you do for a living?"

My eyes narrow. Does he know me? Is he playing with me? Am I in immediate danger here?

I decide there's no point in being anything other than honest. "I own a bar in Texas."

He laughs. "Excellent. A businessman, like myself. But please, indulge me. What did you do *before* you owned a bar in Texas?"

Now I'm suspicious. I look at him again, doing my best to remember him from somewhere, but the throbbing in my skull is making thinking difficult. "Why the interest in my life story?"

His smile fades slightly. "Because I like to know who's trespassing in my domain."

I relax into the chair a little, casually glancing at the armed men in the room. There's a palpable tension in the room now, and I know I'm not getting out of here by fighting.

Shit.

"Okay, fine. My name is Adrian Hell. I'm—"

The guy claps his hands and laughs, looking around for an audience. He shakes his finger at me, as if he knew all along who I was and was just waiting for me to admit it. "I *knew* you looked familiar! An old friend of mine hired you once, many years ago."

I smile uncomfortably. "Huh... small world."

"I'm Carlos Vega. Welcome to my humble home." He gestures to the room around us, which is anything but humble. "What brings you to Colombia, my friend?"

I shrug. "It's a long story..."

Vega turns to one of his men and says something I don't understand. The guy disappears, only to return a moment later with two bottles of beer, dripping in condensation. He hands me one and his boss the other.

"Drink. Tell me," says Vega.

I'm not one to turn down a free beer, even if it *is* for

breakfast. I take a long, refreshing swig, using the natural silence to quickly figure out how to explain—as vaguely as possible—what I'm doing in Colombia.

"My plane was hijacked by a small military unit and re-directed to the airstrip where your men found me. I was flying back from New York, where I'd been working a contract. I'm retired, but it was a favor for an old friend, so I felt obliged, y'know? Anyway, my target managed to escape, annoyingly. I was heading home to plan my next approach. These soldiers accused me of stealing something from the U.S. government—which I hadn't. We argued and then they killed their own leader and blew up my plane, leaving me for dead."

Vega finishes his beer and puts the bottle carefully down on the glass table. He regards me silently for a moment. "That is... quite a story, my friend. Tell me, why would they think you'd stolen something if you hadn't?"

I shrug. "You got me."

"They don't sound like the kind of people who would make a mistake about such things. They must've been pretty certain you were their man, no?"

I try to play things as innocently as I can.

"Maybe there's more to my contract than I realize?" I try to make it sound as if I'm discussing the situation with a colleague. "The friend that I'm doing the job for has always been somewhat questionable, as far as his business dealings are concerned."

Vega is silent for a few moments, then he stands and smiles. "Well, my friend, you can relax. You are my guest here, and I will help you as much as I can."

Taking my cue, I also stand. I extend my hand, which he shakes. "I appreciate that, Carlos. Thank you. I don't suppose you've got my bag, have you? I need to make a call, and my phone's in there."

"But of course." He nods at another of his men, who leaves the room without a word. "Though, I must warn you, there are eyes everywhere here. I have a jamming system in place, stopping any signal coming into my house. Your phone will not work here, Adrian Hell."

"Bit extreme, isn't it?"

"I value my privacy."

The man returns holding my bag, which he hands to me. I throw it over my shoulder and notice immediately it's a lot lighter than I remember.

Vega must've seen the look of confusion on my face. He holds his hands up and smiles. "My apologies. We *did* search through your belongings, purely as a security measure. Your weapons have been confiscated while you're a guest in my house. I have no issue returning them to you when you leave."

I give him a curt, understanding nod, trying to hide my frustration. "That's fair enough."

There's something not quite right here, but I can't put my finger on it. Typically, in my limited experience, men who live in big Colombian houses surrounded by armed bodyguards aren't usually this friendly toward strangers.

He smiles. "Come, my friend. Let me show you around."

He places his right hand on my shoulder and gently guides me toward the door on the left, facing the chair I woke up in. I'll play along for now. Besides, I don't really have much choice. I'm unarmed, completely surrounded, and cut off from the outside world. I just hope an opportunity presents itself soon for me to get the hell out of Dodge.

We walk out of the room side by side. His men don't follow us, and as we walk along a wide hallway, I can see why. Vega has men *everywhere*. Large windows fill the right-hand wall, offering a stunning view of the ocean, as well as the forestry on the property. On the left wall are various closed doors—each with a man stationed outside, holding an AK-47 loosely at his side.

"You have a lot of security, Carlos. Do you get much trouble in these parts?"

"Not so much nowadays, but one must keep up appearances all the same. I run a profitable business here, Adrian. Sometimes people get jealous of what they don't have. You understand?"

I nod slowly. "All too well."

We walk into another large living room, which looks as equally opulent as the last one. Four bikini-clad women sit huddled together on a large, brown leather sofa in the middle of the room. There's a rectangular block of silver foil on the table in front of them, sliced open with a knife. Cocaine is spilling out of it. The women are all laughing and look up as we enter.

"Ladies, I want you to meet my guest." Vega walks over to them and gestures to me. "This is Adrian Hell."

They all look over at me, smile, and wave coyly. Then they whisper among themselves, giggling and glancing back at me. I want to say they're checking me out, but they're speaking so fast in Spanish that I honestly have no clue what they're saying.

I wave reluctantly at them. "Hi, ladies."

There are no armed men in this room, but there are three large floor-to-ceiling windows on the far side, offering a great view of the gardens behind the house. I'm aware that Vega is saying something to me, but I've zoned out. I'm too busy looking out the window and piecing everything together.

The armed guards, the women, the drugs, the remote location, and the lavish house...

I can't see how this is possible, but I'm almost certain Carlos Vega is a cartel drug lord.

But I thought all the cartels had shut down or turned into legitimate businesses following President Cunningham's economic revolution? Why on Earth would a cartel still be operating in Colombia, like it was the good ol' days? They can't possibly be making any money. The main source of income from any cartel was cocaine, and nowadays you can buy that over the counter from the local 7-Eleven. But Vega's clearly doing well for himself, so how's he making money?

A voice appears, interrupting my thoughts.

"Adrian?"

"Hmm?" I look up and see Vega staring at me patiently. "Sorry, I was miles away. This is a beautiful view."

He smiles. "I often lose myself staring out across the expanse of my empire. I was just saying, how is business for someone in your line of work?"

I shrug. "I'm trying to put the killing business behind me if I'm honest. But even in this day and age, somebody always wants somebody else dead. The work's there, should I ever want it."

"True, Adrian. *Somebody always wants somebody else dead...* I like that!" He walks across the room, kissing one of the women on the head as he passes by the sofa, heading for a door at the far end. "Come. There is something I want to show you."

I follow him out of the room, growing more skeptical with each minute that passes. I've got a bad feeling about this, but I still can't put my finger on it.

We enter another, smaller room with a glass door on the

right that leads outside. Vega gestures for me to pass him and step out into the garden. I feel a light breeze at the door, which is refreshing. The sun is high already, shining bright and hot, and the grounds surrounding this massive house look absolutely—

18

Goddammit! I got hit in the head again, didn't I?

I haven't opened my eyes yet, but my arms and shoulders are killing me. I'm hanging from something—my arms are above my head, my wrists tied together, and my feet can't touch the floor.

I slowly open my eyes and blink quickly to remove the fog of unconsciousness.

It's dark, and there's a strange smell nearby. It's familiar, but I can't place it just now. Chemicals, maybe? I recognize it, but the source of the strong odor eludes me.

It's cold in here too. I look down and see I've been stripped to the waist. There's no sign of my bag—not that it'll be much use anyway.

I look up to see what I'm hanging from. There's an old, tough-looking leather band around my wrists. It's pulled tight and hooked on the end of a chain, which is attached to a wooden beam running along the ceiling. I'm guessing I'm in a shed or garage. I grip the chain in my hands and pull against the restraint, trying to heave myself up. My shoulders are screaming, but the beam supports my weight, so that's good to know.

I relax as much as I can, trying to think how I can get out of here. Then I hear a door slide open behind me. There's laughter and footsteps, and the door is slid shut again. There's a click, and a bright light bathes the room, forcing me to squint and look away as best I can.

As my eyes are adjusting, I can make out more of the room. It's definitely a garage. There's a rusted car on bricks off to my left, and along the three walls I can see are racks and shelves full of tools. In the right corner, I see a body slumped in a sitting position on the floor. The flesh is discolored and in the preliminary stages of decomposition.

That explains the smell...

Three men appear in front of me, standing in a loose arc. They're staring at me and mumbling to each other in Spanish. I recognize two of them from the airstrip and, later, in Vega's house. The guy in the middle I haven't seen before. His face is pockmarked and ugly, and his dark eyes are full of menace.

I suspect the next few minutes are going to suck.

I look at each of them in turn. "Hey, fellas, there appears to be some kind of misunderstanding. How about you let me down, and I'll go straighten things out with your boss?"

The guy on my right unleashes a big right hand, swung from down by his knees, and connects with the side of my stomach. I grunt and wheeze as the punch knocks the wind out of me, sending me spinning on my restraints like a punching bag.

I feel hands on my back, turning me back around to face the line-up. As I cough and struggle for breath, the guy on my left takes his turn, throwing his own right hand and catching me on the other side of my torso. Again, I wheeze, cough, and splutter as I'm sent spinning around. And again, I'm turned back to face the three amigos.

The man in the middle smiles at me.

"Okay, hold up a minute, Curly," I say, keen to delay another blow to my gut. "Larry and Moe have had their fun, and that's fine, but before you go following the trend, can you just tell me what the hell's going on?"

They look at each other in turn, shrugging and laughing. Then the man in the middle smiles again and produces a blade from behind him; it must've been tucked in the back of his waistband. It's a rusty, stained knife, maybe seven inches long. It's narrow and looks sharp. He holds it up to me, waving it menacingly at my chest, then says something I don't understand.

"Oh, come on, guys," I say, still struggling for breath. "Sending non-English-speaking people to torture me is just plain unfair!"

He's still waving the knife at me and talking in Spanish, as if he's toying with his food before he eats it. I need to get out of here. I grip the chain again in my hands, tensing my arms and preparing to lift myself. Thankfully, my ankles are still free, so this next part is going to be a lot easier.

The men on either side take a step back. The guy in the middle changes his grip on the knife, holding it upside-down and to the side, with the blade facing away from him, ready to slash across me. I see him shift his weight to his right side and drop his right shoulder slightly, turning away from me and preparing to strike.

With my upper body stinging from the blows I've just taken, I grit my teeth through the pain as I heave myself up on the chain. I pull my body as high as I can in one movement, then lash both legs out, catching the man with the knife square in the face with both feet.

He stumbles backward, dropping the knife on the floor. The man on the left rushes toward me. I swing both legs up again, grab his head between them, and squeeze, crossing my ankle and holding him in place. I let him struggle for air for a few moments, then jerk my hips to the right, breaking his neck. The sound of his vertebrae snapping echoes loudly around the garage.

As his lifeless body drops to the floor, the guy on the right makes a move for the knife. Moving as quickly as I can, I heave myself up and grab the edge of the roof beam, struggling to unhook the leather restraints from the metal chain. Keeping one eye on my attackers, I finally manage it and drop to the floor, landing in a crouch.

I stand as the man on the right approaches me, having given up his pursuit of the knife in favor of attacking me. As he raises his right arm to punch me, I duck under and jab him with both fists in the stomach. I then move behind him and hook the leather restraints joining my wrists together around his throat, pull him tightly toward me, and yank back as hard as I can. He chokes, spits, and claws at my hands, but it's the restraints doing all the work, so doing that is futile. It doesn't take long for him to stop moving, and I discard his body to my right.

The man in the middle is left staring at me. His face shows signs of swelling from the kick, and his confidence is shaken, having just seen me kill his two friends. The knife is off to my left, just in front of the old car. He's got his back to the shelving unit with an array of tools on it—any one of which could be used effectively in a fight...

Thankfully, the guy's an idiot. He chooses to run at me, screaming, his arms raised above him like something out of a bad horror movie. I meet him with a swift, accurate right foot to his stomach, which stops him in his tracks. He doubles over, then stands and resumes screaming. I step into him, pushing my left foot down and through his right kneecap, breaking his leg. As he crumples to the floor, he rolls on his side, holding the gaping wound caused by the snapped bone protruding through the skin. I look down quickly at his exposed head and neck, then bring my right foot down hard on the side of his throat, crushing his windpipe and killing him instantly.

I crouch down, resting on my haunches and catching my breath. The pain currently pulsing through my torso starts to subside as my heart rate returns to normal. The bitterness in my mouth from the adrenaline makes me cough.

I walk over to the knife, pick it up, and use it to cut through my restraints. With my hands free, I search the garage for anything useful, but other than the blade I'm holding , there's nothing practical.

I head over to the door and push it open just as Carlos Vega pulls it from the other side. We bang into each other and freeze momentarily in surprise. He wasn't expecting me to not be swinging from the roof with my guts hanging out, and I honestly wasn't expecting to see him come and do his own dirty work.

We're standing inches apart—him in his nice silk shirt and white pants and me with no top on, covered in dirt and bruises. Acting on instinct, I drop my shoulders and let my neck take the dead weight of my head, whipping it forward and slamming my forehead squarely onto the point of his nose. He grunts as blood explodes across his face, his nose shattered. He stumbles backward and falls over. I move toward him, bend down, and grab him by his collar, dragging him to his feet and ushering him inside the garage. I quickly look around to make sure no one's seen us, then close the door behind us.

I throw him to the floor and stamp down on the side of his right leg, hard enough to stop him from running away but not hard enough to break anything.

"Okay, Carlos, you and I are gonna have a little talk."

Blood runs from his nose to his mouth, and he spits it to the floor. "Fuck you!" he snarls. "You have no idea who you're fucking with!"

"Yeah, I've been hearing that a lot in the last week or so, and it's starting to piss me off."

I lean over him and jab him in the face with my left hand, connecting with his busted nose. He lets out a cry of pain and holds his face in his hands.

"Now you can start by explaining what your problem is with me," I say to him. "I've given you no reason to consider me a threat, so why knock me out and tie me up?"

"I'm not... telling you nothin'!" he yells, struggling to breathe properly.

"Uh-huh... let me see if I can't persuade you."

Knowing he can't go anywhere, I walk over to the right-hand wall and look through the various tools lying around haphazardly. I rummage through and find a pair of pliers, discolored from years of neglect.

These will do nicely...

I walk back over to Vega, who hasn't moved. I put my left hand on his forehead, holding his head still, and wave the pliers in front of his mouth. His eyes go wide and he clamps his lips together, clearly sensing what's coming.

"Ah-ah, don't go getting all shy on me now," I say, then jab him hard in the ribs with the pliers.

He lets out a sharp yell of pain, and as he does, I quickly grab one of his front teeth between the head of the pliers and squeeze them tight. He's making all sorts of funny noises as he panics, but he can't do anything.

"Carlos... be quiet and try to retain at least an ounce of dignity," I say. "Now are you going to tell me why you tried to torture me, or am I going to have to cause you severe pain?"

His eyes are still wide, and he just manages to shake his head from side to side.

"Fine, have it your way."

I'm more than adept at the fine art of torturing people for information, but to be honest, I've never taken any pleasure in it. I find it more of a hindrance. It's much better if people just tell me what I want to know in the first place. Plus, I've been out of the game quite a while, and like these pliers, I'm a little rusty. So, I try not to drag it out too much.

I yank my right arm up and over his head, snapping his front tooth and ripping it from his mouth. Blood spurts all down his chin and onto his shirt, and he screams with genuine agony.

I throw the pliers down next to me and rest my right hand firmly on his throat.

"Why torture me?" I ask again.

He struggles to talk, but this time, he's more than happy to reply.

"I wa' tol' to," he says.

It takes me a moment to work out what he said.

"You were told to? Who by?"

"P'ease... 'ey'll 'ill 'e..."

His accent isn't helping the situation...

"They'll kill you? Who will?"

He waves his hands at me, silently asking me to give him a minute.

"I'll 'ell 'oo. Jus' gi' 'e a 'econ'..."

I stand and gesture for him to talk when he's ready. He sits up and uses his shirttails to wipe the blood from his mouth. Tears are streaming down his face from the pain in his nose and mouth. He spits blood out on the floor next to him, looking up at me with hatred and defeat in his eyes. He composes himself and starts talking.

"I was 'old 'o expec' you," he says, speaking a little better now that he's calmed down.

"By?"

"By my con'ac' in 'he U.S."

"Give me specifics, Carlos. Who's your contact?"

"I don' know, hones'ly. He uses a codename, and I never me' him in person."

"Okay, so what does he do? What do you even have a contact for?"

Vega hesitates. I kick him hard on his leg again.

"Tell me!" I yell.

"Go 'o hell!" he yells back. "Do wha' you wan' 'o me. No'hin will change."

I walk off, massaging my temples. I don't think he's going to say anything more to me. Why would he have a contact in the States? What does he even do here? There's no way he's funding his cartel from drugs because that's a legal business nowadays. Even if he's still farming it, distribution companies in the U.S. will essentially pay him a salary. There's no way he'll be able to charge the kind of prices he used to because he's far from the only game in town.

No, the only way he's funding this operation is by doing something he shouldn't. But what? And he said he'd been told to expect me... but who knew I'd be in Colombia? *I* didn't even know! The only people who did were the special ops unit...

Holy shit.

Wait a goddamn minute.

What if Vega's contact has access to the special ops team? That would mean they'd have to be senior government or military... perhaps a four-star general? They redirected me here, knowing I'm likely to try to find my way home, thinking the cartel would be an ally...

I look back at Vega, who's sitting on the floor, mopping blood from his mouth and looking really pissed off.

My mind's racing, trying to fit together all the information I have like a jigsaw puzzle, but the pieces aren't shaped right. Not yet, anyway.

I storm back over to him and grab his collar. I yank him up, pushing him against one of the sides.

"What do you do for your contact?" I demand. "What's your role in all this?"

He's breathing heavy and panicking, seeing the look I know I have in my eyes. It's a look so dark, you can see Hell itself in my baby blues. I've perfected it over years of dealing with demons. Good to know I can still turn it on and off when required, despite burying those demons long ago.

"I 'upply guns," he says finally. "I ge' paid 'o 'ranspor' weapons in'o the coun'ry and all over 'he worl'."

Gun-running?

"Who are the guns for?"

"Whoever wan's 'em, I guess. I dunno who he gives 'em 'o, hones'ly."

"What's your contact's name?" He hesitates, so I lean in and press my forearm against his throat. "His name?" I yell.

"He calls hi'self Ares," he says, looking more afraid.

Ares. The god of war.

Whoever Ares is, my money's on him being the same person who green-lighted the mission to hijack my plane and bring me here. So, he's paying Carlos Vega and his cartel to smuggle weapons into the States? But why?

I look at Vega. I've got all I'm going to get from him. I believe what he's told me. I glance quickly at the side we're leaning against and spy a screwdriver.

Without another word, I grab it and jam it hard into the side of Vega's neck, all the way to the handle. His eyes widen in shock, and he clutches at his throat, gargling as blood spurts from the wound. I step back, allowing him to sink to the floor. He falls sideways, dead.

"Goodbye, Carlos," I mutter to myself, then look at the door. "Now how do I get out of here?"

19

I'm outside the garage, leaning flat against the side of the small building, staring over at the main house. I'm in the corner of one of the gardens at the back. I imagine any vehicles are parked out front, so I have to get into the house, find my bag and guns, and make my way through unseen.

Well, I'll settle for just getting through the house. *Unseen* is probably asking a bit much.

I compose myself, then sprint over to the door I remember standing at earlier. I keep as low as I can, looking around for anyone patrolling the grounds. It's probably close to three hundred yards, and I cover the distance quickly, ignoring the dull ache in my torso as my heart rate increases.

As I approach the house, I see a man turning the far corner, coming toward me. I drop to the floor and slide across the grass. I stop by a small wall with white, cast iron railings in it, which makes up the large patio area at the rear.

I crouch down close to the steps and listen for the sentry's footsteps. Ideally, he'll head down the steps toward me, but it's no issue if he doesn't.

I wait for a few moments and hear him passing me as he crosses the width of the patio. I chance a peek over the wall and through the railings. The man is level with my position, walking away from me. He's carrying his AK-47 loose at his side, with one hand resting on it.

Slowly, I stand and creep up the steps. Staying low, I move behind the guy, pausing a moment to make sure he's not heard me. Happy he hasn't, I pounce forward, placing my left hand over his mouth. I pull him into me as I pinch his nose with my right hand. I drag him backward away from the house and down the steps, clamping down on his face tightly. By the time we're standing down by the wall again, he's dead. I release him and he drops to the floor. I take his weapon and quickly frisk him for spare ammo, then head back up the steps. After a few steps, I pause and look back at the corpse.

His upper body looks a similar shape to mine...

I quickly bend down and take off his shirt, then throw it on and fasten all but the top two buttons. It's hideous, but it fits. I pick up the gun and head inside the house.

Standing in the doorway, I think back to what I've seen of the house. I know what's to my left because that's where I woke up the first time. I could go straight or right, but I think I'm best sticking with what I know.

I head left and down the hall to the large living room with the brown leather sofa in it. The women are still sitting there, with their backs to me, laughing and giggling. I take one step into the room just as two men enter from the opposite side. Our eyes meet, and we all freeze.

I raise my rifle and fire a few rounds before they can

react. The one on the left catches the brunt of it and drops to the floor. His trigger finger twitches as he dies, enough to fire off a few rounds himself, but they're not aimed. The second guy has enough time to react, and he dives behind the sofa.

The women's giggles turn to screams, which is the last thing I wanted. Nothing attracts people more than screaming.

Except maybe gunfire, I guess. Shit! This place will be crawling with cannon fodder any second.

I run into the room, firing blind and hitting the second guy as he positions himself on the floor. I hear the squelches as the bullets hit his body. I rush over and retrieve his rifle, taking care not to slip in the pooling blood seeping out from underneath him.

With an AK-47 in each hand, I exit the room the way they had entered and head to where I woke up. Nearby but out of sight, I hear raised voices and commotion, so any element of surprise I had was now gone.

I enter the room and skid to a halt. Seven men all spin around and look at me, their rifles primed and leveled at me.

I chuckle nervously. "Has anyone seen my bag?" I ask, then lift both rifles and fire from the hip in their direction.

They only weigh about eleven pounds apiece, but when you're holding one in each arm and firing while running, it quickly strains your muscles.

The rifle isn't designed for accuracy, and I'm in no position to take aim. I just fan both rifles back and forth across the room, soon hitting everyone in front of me. They all flail to the floor; not one of them, thankfully, had enough time to get a shot off.

I take a second to regain my composure, then run across

the room to the door at the opposite end. It leads into another hallway. The large double front doors are ahead of me, and I see my bag resting at the side, which is a stroke of luck. They must've put it there after taking me to the garage.

I rush over to it, checking quickly before I drop the rifles and open it up. Both my Berettas are inside, along with all the other equipment I had. They must've put all my stuff back in there after I'd left with Vega.

No sign of my cell, though, which is a pain in the ass.

I sling it over my back, tuck one of my guns at the back of my waistband, and keep one in my right hand. Quickly, I look around to make sure no one's nearby. Then I slowly open the front door, trying not to make a noise.

A voice shouts behind me as I turn the handle. I look over my shoulder and see a man at the top of the staircase gesturing at me with his rifle. I quickly raise my Beretta and fire once, hitting him in the throat, then open the door and step outside.

I was right. There are indeed several vehicles parked in front of the house. There are also, however, five men standing in a line with their AK-47s aimed at the front door, blocking my exit.

I don't even think about it; I just run to my left and start firing blind. I somehow make it to the corner of the house and dive around the bend as I click down on an empty chamber. I lean against the wall, breathing heavy. I switch my Berettas around, making a mental note to remember the one at my back is now empty, and peek around the corner at the main courtyard.

It's mostly gravel, bordered by a short wall with a space where the driveway ends. There are four convertible Jeeps over there. The one closest to me has a few fresh bullet holes in it now, so I'll avoid that one.

Four bodies are on the ground, so I must've done all right during my tactical retreat. The last one must be hiding behind the Jeeps. Conscious of how much time I've lost since leaving New York, I forego the majority of my training and walk out toward the vehicles. I've got my Beretta aimed steadily with both hands, ready to snap to my target.

Sure enough, after a few seconds, the guy's head pops up from behind the hood of the Jeep farthest away from me. I quickly aim and fire, putting a bullet between his eyes.

Happy there's no one else nearby, I search the bodies for anything useful. I finally catch a break—one of them has a cell phone on him, so I take that with me. Then I climb inside the second Jeep from the left, for no reason other than it's facing the way out. The keys are inside. I speed down the drive and turn right onto the main road at the end.

I have absolutely no idea where I'm heading, so I'm making my way to the coast. I'll figure it out from there. After a few minutes, I slow down a bit, disappearing into anonymity on the roads as I hit the countryside. I pick up the phone and call Josh.

"It's me," I say when he answers.

"You managed to get home yet?" he replies.

"Not quite. It's a long story, my friend. Listen, first thing's first—can you get me on GPS by tracing this phone?"

"Sure, gimme a sec..." The line goes silent for a moment. "Okay, you're about twenty miles southwest of Barranquilla." He pauses. "So, why *exactly* are you in Colombia?"

"That would be the long story. Can you get me out of here?"

"Yeah, hang on. Right, just follow the road signs to Barranquilla, and you should be fine. Once you're there, you should be able to get across to Panama easily enough. It's a popular trading route. I can get you a flight from there back to the States."

"Thanks, Josh. So, is everything okay with you?"

"Not really, but that can wait. Why are you still in South America, Adrian?"

I navigate the light traffic and see the first sign for Barranquilla, which announces that it's eighteen miles away.

"The special ops unit blew up the plane. After I dragged that Jericho guy away from the blast, EMTs and firemen arrived and took him away. But that's when the cartel showed up."

"Cartel? Are you sure? I didn't think they existed anymore. Maybe it was some local rebels?"

"Nope, definitely a cartel. I was taken to meet the drug lord who ran it, Carlos Vega. Lived in a huge mansion teeming with armed guards. I approached them as a hitman seeking sanctuary, but they got the drop on me, tied me up, and intended to torture me."

"Jesus... I thought cartels operated with drug money, but they can't anymore—not since Cunningham was sworn in and ruined it for them. What were they doing?"

"That's what I thought. Had a little chat with Mr. Vega, who finally admitted he was running guns around the world for a mystery contact in the U.S. who goes by the codename Ares. He was paid a small fortune for doing it too."

"I'll start searching for potential candidates," he says. "So, what do you make of it all?"

"Well, Vega said he was told I'd be coming, which means Ares knew about the mission to re-route my plane. My guess is he's a high-ranking official of some kind."

"Like a four-star general, perhaps?" he asks excitedly, coming to the same conclusions I had.

"That's what I think. Doesn't explain why the guy was meeting with Hussein, but if he *is* Ares, it certainly adds a few more pieces to our puzzle."

"It does. And I might have a few answers for you."

"Finally! What have you got?"

"Since we spoke last, I did some digging on this Jericho character. I wasn't sure if it was a codename either, so it took some time. Turns out, his name is Jericho Stone. He's a real big deal from the military who, a few years ago, took command of a non-existent CIA unit..."

"Jesus, how do you find this stuff?" I ask.

"Ah-ah, don't be silly. Anyway, do you want to know the name of this unit?"

"Hit me."

"D.E.A.D."

I drift off in shock for a moment but quickly snap back to the present as I feel the Jeep swerve off the road. I regain control and re-focus.

"Josh, that's not possible."

"Oh, it is," he replies, laughing.

"You think this is funny?"

"A little bit, yeah!"

D.E.A.D. stands for *Doesn't Exist on Any Database*. It was a CIA black ops unit created back in '93 for operatives around the world to come together and do things for the greater good that people probably didn't want to know about.

I know this because I used to run that unit. It was how I met Josh. After we left, they closed the program down, but it appears someone's re-opened it.

"Well, it's certainly an unexpected trip down memory lane. I'll give you that."

"Isn't it just! So, now we know for sure that the CIA is after us."

"Wonderful."

I'm still trying to wrap my head around the bittersweet irony of someone sending my old unit to kill me.

"There's something else," says Josh. "I've found out a bit more about Cerberus…"

His words trail off. I get the impression he's been spooked by something, which doesn't happen to Josh.

"So, what is it?"

"In addition to it doing everything we already know, both advertised and otherwise, it also does something else. Something *we* didn't build it to do, which means it was a feature added after we handed it back over to NASA."

"I'm guessing this new feature isn't a good thing?"

"Adrian, it not only protects our *own* nuclear arsenal, but it has the ability to remotely hack into and control anyone else's. It potentially has access to every nuclear weapon on Earth."

His words hang in the air for a few moments. I zone out of the conversation, letting his revelation sink in as I re-focus momentarily on the road ahead.

"Josh, that's…"

"Yup."

"But that means…"

"I know."

"Man, we have to…"

"I'm trying, Adrian. We're still at square one—no idea where to find the key members of the Armageddon Initiative, no idea how they intend to do what we assume they're trying to do, and no idea what any of this has to do with a U.S. general."

My mind's racing again, and I have no idea what any of the answers are. I fly past another sign that tells me I'm just a few miles away now, and my thoughts quickly turn to Tori.

I've missed her like crazy, and I'm mad at myself for not thinking about her during all of this. My survival instincts took over, and I've been doing whatever I needed to in order to get home. But now that home is in sight, I can't get her off my mind.

"Okay, keep doing what you're doing, Josh. I'm almost there, so I'll contact you when I reach Panama."

"No worries. Watch your back, yeah?"

"You too."

I hang up and throw the phone out of the Jeep, just to be safe. In another few minutes, I'll be in Barranquilla and one step closer to Tori.

20

I open my eyes slowly, stretching and cracking my back and legs. I feel like I've just slept for a lifetime. I need a minute to get my bearings. I'm sitting on a comfortable chair, slightly reclined, with a pillow behind me. I turn my head and look out the window on my left. I see blue skies around me and white clouds below.

After I arrived in Barranquilla, I made my way to a small airfield and bribed the pilot of a cargo plane bound for Panama to let me sneak on board. I didn't get any rest on the journey. There was nowhere to sleep, and my mind was doing a hundred miles an hour, trying to figure out the shit-storm I've found myself in.

It took about two hours to reach Panama. I contacted Josh when I landed. He directed me to another airfield, where he had arranged for another GlobaTech jet to fly me home. He said it would take some time to get to me, and he sounded stressed, so I didn't push him or stay on the line any longer than I needed to.

It took quite a while for the plane to arrive, and I used the time to get some much-needed rest. There was a small office on the airstrip, and I got some sleep on the sofa in there. And even once I was on board, as soon as my ass touched the seat, I was straight back out like a light.

There's a stewardess on the flight. She smiles at me as I look around, slowly emerging from my deep sleep.

"Are we there yet?" I ask, smiling.

She laughs. "We'll be on the ground in fifteen minutes or so. You've been asleep well over three hours. Is everything okay?"

I take a deep breath. "That's a broad question. I'm alive, and if we can make it home without another plane I'm on being hijacked, I'll consider that a victory for the day."

Her face changed immediately to one of concern.

"*Another* plane?"

"It's, ah… it's been a rough few days," I say with a weak smile. I stand and stretch again. "You haven't seen my bag, have you?"

"It's stowed at the back of the cabin," she replies, now sounding distracted. "Oh, and Mr. Winters requested a change of clothes be made available for you as well."

As she says that, she looks me up and down. I realize I still have on the shirt I stole, which is both insulting and offensive to all other shirts in the world.

"Thanks," I say, a little embarrassed.

I walk to the back and see a new outfit hanging in a small, open closet space opposite the bathroom. My bag and a change of shoes are underneath.

I step inside the bathroom and put on the fresh pair of jeans, tan work boots, and a plain black T-shirt.

I leave my old stuff in the trash and step back out, picking up my bag on the way past. I walk back to my seat. The stewardess isn't there, so I assume she must be in the cockpit, talking with the pilot.

I take my Berettas and back holster out, load the guns, click the safety on, and slide them into place. I put the holster in the bag again and relax back in my seat. I feel better now that I've changed my clothes and I'm on my way home.

I hope Tori's doing okay. As soon as this mess is over, I'm going to take her on a vacation somewhere—put some distance between us and the real world for a while. And then, once the FBI and God knows who else have finished dissecting my bar, I'll get the place back up and running. It shouldn't take long to do. It might sound crazy to say, but I sometimes forget I have a quarter of a billion dollars in my account. I'm a simple man with simple tastes and needs—I took that money more out of principle than necessity. But I'll get the place looking brand-new in no time.

The stewardess reappears, smiling professionally and looking a little more relaxed.

"We'll be landing in San Antonio in ten minutes," she announces. "There'll be a vehicle waiting to take you home."

"Thanks. Do you mind if I drive myself? I could do with the alone time."

She smiles. "I'm sure that won't be a problem."

07:49 CDT

We land just over ten minutes later. There's a black rental car waiting on the runway with the driver standing by it, resting on the hood. I thank the stewardess and the pilots for their service and step off the plane, feeling the early Texas sun on my face. Without a word, the driver hands me the keys, then turns and walks across the runway toward the terminal building at the far end. I climb in, crank up the air conditioning, and set off.

I'm excited to see Tori again but also a little nervous. I've spent the last two and a half years burying Adrian Hell and starting over, and I've just spent the last seventy-two hours resurrecting him. In a strange way, I feel like I've betrayed Tori. I'm going home with so much blood on my hands. Regardless of how necessary it might have been, it still wasn't me—not anymore.

I let out a sigh. I need to stop worrying. I've got enough on my mind as it is. I lean over and turn the radio on, fiddling until I find a station playing something half-decent. After a moment, I stumble across the opening line of *I Wanna Rock* by Twisted Sister. I smile, wind my window down, and drive a little bit faster.

I soon reach Devil's Spring. I feel a warm sense of familiarity and comfort as I drive through the center of town, truly feeling like I'm home. I stop at a red light. If I go right, it'll take me up the hill toward the station house.

I wonder how Sheriff Raynor's doing. He handled the truth about me really well, which I'm grateful for.

The lights change, and I turn left, following the road around to the right. I finally pull up outside The Ferryman. I get out and stretch, looking around for a moment and soaking it all in.

Jeez, it's quiet around here...

I get my bag out of the trunk, sling it over my shoulder, and then head around back and up the stairs to my apartment. The first thing I notice is that the door is open. I place my bag quietly on the ground and take out one of my Berettas, holding it firmly in my hand. I push the door open gently and step inside.

The place is a mess. All the furniture is either upturned or broken, scattered across the floor.

Jesus... when did this happen? I'm just glad Tori wasn't here.

I walk over to the bed. The mattress is on the floor, and the frame is on its side. I check the other door, which leads down to the bar area, but that's still locked.

Strange. Whoever did this was coming to my home specifically, not the bar.

I hear a noise behind me and spin around, bringing my gun up to aim.

Sheriff John Raynor is standing in the doorway at the top of the stairs outside. He looks like shit—a couple of days' worth of growth is on his chin, and his right arm is in a sling.

He holds his left arm up when he sees my gun.

"I'm a friendly," he says with a weak smile.

I relax, lowering my gun. "Jesus Christ, John. What the hell happened to you?"

"It was... a nightmare, Adrian," he replies. "That's the only way I can think to describe it. An absolute nightmare. There were only five of them too—and I never thought I'd use the word *only* when describing a five-man assault. That's your goddamn influence. Anyway, they came the night you left for New York. It wasn't guns blazing, like the others. It was... it was planned. Meticulous. They came knowing exactly what they intended to do and how they wanted to do it. I got here as soon as I could and brought all my deputies with me. In hindsight, we never stood a chance..."

I look around my apartment again. "It must've been the

bad guys I went after in New York," I say, turning back to him. "If they knew I was coming for them, they maybe tried to pre-empt my involvement by taking me out here. They were just a few hours too late."

Raynor shakes his head. "We arrived as they were leaving your place, but I don't think they were here for you."

I frown. Who would they be after, if not me? A split-second passes, then my eyes go wide.

"John... is Tori all right?"

His mouth forms a grim line of regret. "We exchanged gunfire and then chased them in squad cars... all the way to young Nicki's house. Adrian, I'm sorry, but the woman of the group put a bullet in Nicki's head right there in front of us. Then two of the men bundled Tori into the trunk of their car."

I glaze over, numbed by the news that Tori was taken. But my brain kicks in after a few moments, and alarm bells sound as I process what Raynor had told me.

"A woman?" I ask.

"Yeah, real evil-looking bitch. Dark eyes, bit too much make-up, wore a cat suit..."

Clara Fox!

"What did she say?" I ask.

"Nothing," he shrugs. "She just pulled out a gun so big that I was surprised she could lift it. Had it strapped to her back. She just unloaded at us—destroyed both cruisers. Killed one of us and injured the rest." He reaches behind him and pulls out a disc in a plastic sleeve, then hands it to me. "She threw this at us before leaving. Got your name on it."

I feel a rush of anger explode inside me, waking my Inner Satan from his slumber. It's like a river of heat coursing through me, making me shake with fury. The only thing stopping me from properly losing my shit right now is the sadness and despair I feel. I can't get the image of Tori lying dead somewhere out of my mind.

I shake my head.

No. She's alive. If Clara's taken her, it's to draw me out. She won't kill her only bargaining chip just yet. I pick up the DVD and examine it.

"Come on," I say to Raynor, focusing on the problem and trying to distance myself from it emotionally. "Let's see what she has to say for herself."

I walk over to my TV, which is still in one piece. Clara must've had this planned from the beginning. They destroyed my apartment but left the TV in one piece on purpose, knowing I'd need to watch this DVD.

He follows me, and I put the disc in the DVD player and press play. We stand side-by-side, my arms folded across my chest, watching the TV intently. The video looks like it was filmed on a cheap handheld camera. The picture quality is grainy, and the background noise is hollow.

Clara walks into view. The room she's in is pretty basic and could be anywhere in the world—plain, dirty walls, no carpet on the floor, no visible windows...

"Hello, Adrian," she says.

She stands silently smiling at the camera for a moment. I notice the long scar across her face, running from her right temple across to the left corner of her mouth.

Hope that hurt, you heartless bitch.

Her hair is jet-black now, not blonde like I remember. She definitely has too much make-up on, like Raynor said. Her dark eyes betray no emotion.

"It's been a long time," continues Clara. "What is it? Four years? Four years since you left me for dead in the desert...

four years since you killed my father... and for four years, I've been itching for revenge."

Raynor looks at me out of the corner of his eye. I see it, and I know what he's thinking.

"Yeah, I killed her father," I confirm. "He was a terrorist trying to kill a whole lot of American soldiers. I beat him to death and blew his base off the face of the earth."

"Fair enough," replies Raynor, shrugging.

I re-focus on the video. "...geddon Initiative will soon be able to hold every nation on the planet to ransom. I know Yalafi Hussein has already tried to recruit you, but I told him that wouldn't work, you fucking Boy Scout! But in typical *Adrian Hell* fashion, you had to start asking questions about things that didn't concern you, and now... now we're at the stage where we need to remove you from the picture. If you're watching this video, we have your little girlfriend. We'll make sure she's looked after until you get here."

She's pacing around as she's talking, trying to look scary and intimidating. She looks more like a psychopath than the last time I saw her, and from her body language, she's harbored a grudge toward me that's consumed her entirely.

"I'm sure you won't have any trouble working out where we are, so I'll wait patiently for you to arrive. Oh, and to be clear, our plans will not be delayed any further by your interfering. By the time you see this, we'll be seventy-two hours away from controlling the world, and my vendetta against you will be obsolete. At that point, if you're not here, I'm going to cut your girlfriend's fucking head off and mail it to you. Bye for now." She smiles at the end and blows a kiss to the camera, then walks out of shot.

I turn back to Raynor. "I have to find her."

"What do you need from me?" he asks.

"I'll let you know when I have a better idea what I'm up against."

We're interrupted by the sound of a deep, haunting, foreign voice.

"Adrian..."

We both frown and look at the TV. We had left the video playing, and the camera had obviously been left recording after Clara had gone. On screen is a man sitting cross-legged on the floor. He's Middle Eastern, with a long black beard and a turban. He also has an eyepatch over his left eye. He's hugging his knees as he stares at the camera. I must admit, looking at him makes me a little uncomfortable. The look on his face... it's like he can actually see me.

"Adrian... I am Hamaad El-Zurak. I control the Armageddon Initiative."

Jesus. The man himself.

"I have heard much about you. I need you to understand that you cannot stop what we have started. We will change the world, and I promise you will not be alive to witness it."

He stares at the camera for a moment. It's like he's staring through the screen, right at me. I don't know what it is about him. He doesn't scare me. He's just... I don't know... unnerving.

I'll find him and put a bullet between his eyes, just to be on the safe side.

I turn the DVD off and remove it from the player. I slide it back into its cover, then walk over to the door to retrieve my bag. I bring it inside and rest it on the floor in front of the TV. I open it up, throw the DVD inside, and take out my other Beretta and my custom holster. I stand, strap the holster in place at my back, and then slide the guns inside it.

"They're mighty fine-lookin' weapons," says Raynor approvingly.

I nod. "They do the job. Listen, can I borrow your phone for a minute?"

"Sure," he shrugs.

He reaches into his pocket and passes it to me. I take it and call Josh's number from memory.

"I need your help," I say when he answers. "It's Tori. She's been—"

"Adrian, where are you?" he says, cutting me off. Panic is evident in his voice.

"What? I'm back in Texas. Why?"

"Shit. Adrian, you need to run. Now!"

My eyes go wide. I've never heard fear in Josh's voice before.

"Why?"

"They're coming for you. For all of us. Just run—I'll call you."

The line goes dead. I look at Raynor.

"What was that all about?" he asks.

"I don't know... but Josh was spooked, and he said we should run right now."

He shifts uncomfortably on the spot. "So, where are we going?"

I sling my bag over my shoulder, trying to remain calm and casual, despite everything that's happened. I need Raynor to trust me, and he won't do that if I don't look like I'm in complete control of the situation.

"Across the street," I say with a smile.

21

I walk out of my bar and cross the street, with Sheriff Raynor close behind me.

"I think your friend may have meant for us to run a bit farther than this," he says.

"Aren't you the least bit curious as to who we're supposed to run away from?" I ask.

"Not particularly."

"Ah, John, you have much to learn. If you wanna win the game, you first have to establish who's playing."

"That's surprisingly philosophical, Adrian," he says with a chuckle.

"Don't let the fact I used to be a ruthless sociopath who charged people money to commit murder on their behalf fool you. I'm actually quite intelligent."

"Uh-huh..."

I knock on the door of The Fire Pit, quickly attracting the attention of the owner, who opens up for us. He's in his early sixties and wearing casual clothes with an apron over the top.

"Mister Adrian!" he says, smiling. "We've not turned on the grill yet!"

I push past him without a word. I feel bad because he's a nice guy and always treats Tori and I well when we eat here, but I'm in a hurry. Raynor follows and shuts the door behind us.

"I'm sorry," I say. "This is an emergency. Can we go upstairs?"

"Mister Adrian, I... what is going on?"

Raynor steps forward and takes over.

"Pardon the intrusion," he says professionally, "but this is Sheriff's Department business, and we could really use your help."

He pauses, looking at us both. I see the excitement building in his eyes. He probably watches *Cops*...

"Sure thing. Just head through to the back and up the stairs."

"Thanks," I say. "And whatever happens outside in the next few minutes, just act normal. And remember—we're not here, okay?"

He nods enthusiastically, and I catch Raynor's bemused look.

We head upstairs and position ourselves in the room at the front of the building, overlooking the street and directly facing my bar. It's a storage room with lots of big wooden crates scattered everywhere. We stand on either side of one of the windows, peering cautiously down below.

"So, what now?" asks Raynor.

"Well, Josh seemed pretty keen for us to get outta there, so I'm guessing whoever's coming is close. Once they see we're not there, they'll figure we got tipped off and cleared out as quickly and as far as possible. So, we can stay here and get a good look at who we're dealing with."

Raynor strokes his chin with his left hand, then scratches his right shoulder.

"Is this what your old life used to be like?" he asks.

I shake my head. "Nah, back then, people used to run away from *me*."

09:10 CDT

We've been waiting over half an hour. I'm getting impatient. Every second I stand here is a second less I have to find Clara and rescue Tori. And time's running out.

"Maybe they got tipped off and aren't coming?" offers Raynor.

I shake my head. "Not likely, the way Josh was acting."

I hear vehicles coming from both directions. It's been like a ghost town since I got back, so the engines are quite loud.

"Head's up."

Five large black SUVs screech to a halt at all angles in front of my bar. Men in black suits pile out of them, guns drawn—there must be nearly thirty guys in total. A line of them form a loose perimeter around the street, facing away from the bar. Four gather around the door, running through basic entry tactics. Then they tear down the police tape and storm inside, quickly followed by the rest.

"Jesus," mutters Raynor as we look on. "These boys ain't kiddin' around."

"No, they're not..."

I must admit, I'm concerned. This is a large-scale

government operation, no doubt about it. It's overkill to bring in just one guy, even if it *is* me. And this only leaves me with more questions. Who are they? How did they know to look for me here? Are they the same people that our mysterious general works for? Why is everyone so intent on stopping me from taking out a terrorist? Surely, that is a good thing...

They were been inside just a couple of minutes, but they're starting to re-appear on the street already. They look casually up and down, but they're concluding that I must be long gone. I mean, what sane guy wouldn't be?

I look over at Raynor as they begin getting back inside their vehicles. He's sitting on an unopened box, staring at the floor. The look on his face says it all.

"Trying to get a handle on things?" I ask him.

"Adrian, what the hell are you mixed up in?" he asks.

"John, if I knew, I'd tell you. Look, they don't know you're with me. Wait 'til they've gone, then go back to being the local sheriff. If they come back around askin' questions, just be honest."

"What's happening here... whatever all *this* is..." He points outside. "There's no going back to normal, Adrian. If what you've been dragged into is big enough to warrant *that* kind of response from the government, you're gonna need all the help you can get. Plus, your bad guys have Tori, and she's one of our own. It's my duty as sheriff to help get her back."

I sigh and look at him. His jaw muscles are tense, and his lips form a thin line of determination. I've known him long enough to know when he's made his mind up, so I'm not going to insult him by trying to talk him out of it.

I nod. "Okay, but you know what you're signing up for, right? I mean, you've seen the FBI's file on me. I'm not stopping until I have Tori, some answers, and the body of a dead terrorist. I'm just concerned you might question my methods along the way. This isn't the time for disagreeing with me."

Raynor stands and walks over to me, stopping inches from me. He cuts an imposing figure; I'll give him that. He takes off his hat and rests it on a box next to me. Then he unpins his sheriff's badge and places it down beside it.

"From what I know of you, Adrian—even before I read your file—I can imagine, when it comes down to it, you're not one I'd enjoy disagreeing with. Let's go get your girl back."

He turns and walks out, picking up his hat but leaving his badge. I follow him downstairs and thank the owner for his hospitality and discretion. We walk out and cross the now empty street.

I pause in the doorway of my bar. I take one last look inside before I leave. Every memory I have of this place involves Tori. There's a part of me—a small, *normal* part of me—that wants to just sit down and rock back and forth, angry and upset and confused and heartbroken. That normal part of me wants to let somebody else fight the bad guys, so I can just stay at home and wait for them to return with the woman I love, unharmed.

But I'm not normal. And a much larger part of me is standing on the edge of a cliff, looking out into an abyss filled with violent and deadly intent, holding a gun in each hand and preparing to jump.

Clara fucking Fox has risen from the dead, and she brought my Inner Satan with her. I can't remember the last time I was this pissed.

God help whoever's behind this because Death himself is coming for them... and his name is Adrian Hell.

. . .

09:50 CDT

"Josh, it's me," I say. "Can you talk?"

We're riding in the rental car that GlobaTech provided for me. Raynor insisted on driving, despite having his right arm in a sling, and I have Josh on speaker.

"Yeah, I've got a few minutes," he replies, still sounding flustered. "You manage to get away?"

I shake my head instinctively, even though I know he can't see me. "Nope. I hid upstairs in the building across the street to see who was coming for me."

There's a moment's silence on the line. I'm guessing Josh is questioning my sanity, although that's a debate that's raged on for years between us. He knows damn well that I don't think like normal people.

"And?" he asks eventually.

"And a thirty-strong team of armed, suited-up G-men searched my bar and left again in a hurry."

"Shit."

"That's what I said. There's something else too. I couldn't tell you earlier."

"More good news?"

"Clara's kidnapped Tori."

I let my words hang in the air. After more silence on the line, I hear banging and swearing. I picture Josh hitting everything around him in a fit of rage. He's a passionate and emotional guy. He may well be my conscience and guardian angel, but he still has his own battles to deal with, and sometimes things get to him.

"That fucking bitch!" he yells. "That absolute slag! I'm

gonna kill her, Adrian. I swear, I'm gonna kill her myself. I'm gonna pull out her spine and knock her head off with it! I'm gonna—"

"Josh?"

He pauses, breathing heavily. "What?"

"Calm down and get in line. The bitch is mine."

He takes some deep breaths. "Sorry."

"It's fine. I appreciate the sentiment. And you know I love it when you get mad and cuss. You sound so British!"

Out of the corner of my eye, I see Raynor shake his head and let slip a half-smile.

"Adrian, this whole situation is messed up..." says Josh.

"What have you got, Josh?"

"We're in deep, deep shit. Like, *up to our necks* deep. Those guys who came after you were NSA."

"Great—another acronym joining the party. What do *those* assholes want?"

"I have no idea, but they've raided GlobaTech. They stormed our head office earlier today. They seized control of everything. Not just the systems and information relating to this whole Armageddon Initiative, Yalafi Hussein thing. Everything. They closed us down, seized our assets, put an indefinite hold on all operations and research, and ordered every operative we have overseas back to the U.S. straight away."

"What? How? On whose authority? Does anyone even *have* that kind of authority?"

"According to the suited stiff in charge, their orders were signed off by President Cunningham himself."

"I don't understand..."

"You and me both. Luckily, I was able to get off-site before they could take any of my stuff, and Clark is still in

New York, so the only two copies of the data from Hussein's laptop weren't taken by the NSA."

"Well, that's something. Have you spoken to Clark yet? Do you guys have anything new?"

"No, nothing yet. I got the message about the NSA raid to him, and he's gone dark. We're meeting up at a safe house as soon as we can."

"I've got John Raynor, our local sheriff, with me. We'll join you. I'm gonna need your help getting Tori back."

"Good. I'll text you the location. Memorize it, then ditch your phone. I'm doing the same. We'll just meet you there. If anyone's not arrived in twenty-four hours, we'll assume the worst and carry on without them."

"Sounds fair. Where's Schultz?"

"Ryan went along with the NSA to try to straighten everything out and find out what the hell's going on."

"I don't like this, Josh. Any of it."

"Me and you both, Boss."

"Okay, text me the address. I'll see you tomorrow. Watch your back, Josh. I mean it. No risks."

"Understood. You too."

He hangs up. I look at Raynor. "So, how does it feel to be wanted by the NSA with no idea why?"

He keeps looking at the road, focusing on the light traffic as we hit a nice cruise down the Interstate.

"Pretty shitty," he replies.

I smile.

A text message comes through on the phone. I quickly read it and memorize the address. Then I take the SIM card out of the phone, snap it in half, and throw everything out the window.

"Sorry about your phone. It's for the best."

Raynor shrugs. "At this point, I really don't care."

"Yeah. We need to head for Jonesboro, Arkansas."

He whistles. "That's easily a thirteen-hour drive."

"Keep to the speed limit. Stay off the main roads where we can when passing through any major cities. We don't want to draw any attention to ourselves."

"Smart."

"We need to swap cars too. We're driving around in a GlobaTech asset, so we have to assume they know where it is. We have to go completely dark until we're sitting in a room with Josh and Robert Clark."

I sit back in my seat and close my eyes. I last twenty seconds before I need to open them again. Every time I blink, I see everything that's happening come rushing toward me at once. I can't focus on it yet. I just have to hope that by the time we hit Arkansas, I'll have figured it all out and determined who I need to kill to end this.

22

It was a long drive. It's definitely one thing I *don't* miss from my life as a hitman—the constant traveling. The good sheriff and I took turns driving, doing two- or three-hour stints all the way here.

The journey was mostly uneventful. There was an hour or so as we went through Little Rock where we thought we might have picked up a tail, but in hindsight, I think we were just paranoid—which is forgivable, under the circumstances. We found a cheap motel there for the night and did our best to recharge our batteries. We got some breakfast and made the two-hour drive to Jonesboro.

We're now parked outside the safe house, across the street. We switched cars twice on the way here, and we're currently riding in an anonymous, rusty red pick-up truck that we... *acquired* in Jacksonville. The seats are torn and dirty, and there's a funky smell coming from somewhere, but it'll do for now.

I'm looking over at a warehouse, seemingly long-abandoned. It's a large building that takes up most of the block, and the outside of it is a mixture of boarded windows and illegible graffiti.

"Doesn't look safe," observes Raynor, looking out of his window.

I smile to myself, remembering my conversation with Clark the other day in New York.

"The whole point of a safe house is that it's somewhere you can go where no one will think to look for you," I reply. "This is perfect."

I look up and down the street but can't see any other parked vehicles. I assume that if Josh or Clark are here, they've left their cars somewhere else.

"We headin' inside?" asks Raynor.

I glance once more up and down the street and check the rearview, just to be safe. "Okay, yeah. Let's go."

We get out of the truck, stretching as we stand, and look around. There's a light breeze, but it's not cold, despite the gray clouds masking the sun. The district we're in seems mostly abandoned. There aren't any residential buildings nearby, and any neighboring industrial complexes, like the safe house, look like they've been empty for a while.

I put my bag over both shoulders. We stroll across the street and head around the back of the building. There's a small, empty parking lot surrounded by a chain link fence, topped with razor wire. On the back wall of the building, as we turn left, is a fire escape leading up to the roof, and farther along from that is a fire exit. We approach the scratched, red double doors and see the left-hand side is propped open by an extinguisher. We exchange glances of curiosity and caution and then I draw one of my Berettas, holding it ready in both hands.

"Keep quiet," I whisper. I pull on the metal bar across the middle of the door and step inside.

We enter a narrow corridor, which is poorly lit and damp. A musty smell stings my nostrils. There are two doors on either side of us, closed and caked in a thick layer of dust.

"This place is disgusting..." Raynor mutters quietly.

We walk on, ever alert for the first sign of trouble. My gun is steady in my hands, my finger resting gently on the trigger, prepared for action. At the end of the corridor is a massive, open expanse of warehouse. It's mostly empty, save for a few bits of discarded packaging from years past. In the far right corner is an office room built on metal stilts, with a makeshift wooden staircase leading up to it. I see the light in the window, so someone's home.

I look back at Raynor and gesture to the office. He looks up and nods at me. We walk slowly, as quietly as possible, across the floor of the warehouse toward the corner. We reach the office, and I put one foot on the bottom step, causing it to squeak loudly. I wince and pause as I hear movement in the office above us. I aim up, preparing for anything. Raynor is just out of sight, off to my right. My finger tightens on the trigger as the door above slowly creaks open. Then I see Josh stick his head out from inside.

"Hope you've brought pizza," he says, smiling.

I breathe an audible sigh of relief and holster my gun. I walk up the stairs with Raynor behind me.

"I'm getting paranoid in my old age," I say to him as I reach the top. We shake hands, and I step inside the office.

Robert Clark is leaning over a table in the middle of the room, looking at some paperwork scattered across the surface next to a laptop. He looks up as I enter.

"Glad you could make it, Adrian," he says.

"Likewise, Bob," I reply with a nod, then half-turn and

gesture to Raynor. "Guys, this is John Raynor. He's the sheriff in Devil's Spring."

"Temporarily retired sheriff," he says, correcting me. He extends his hand first to Josh and then to Clark.

With the courtesies out of the way, we all surround the table and get straight to business.

"Okay," I begin. "Here's what we know. There's a terrorist organization who tried to recruit me—then kill me—called the Armageddon Initiative. So far, we know the names of three people who work for them. Yalafi Hussein is the guy who sent people to kill me. He was last seen in New York meeting with someone dressed as a four-star U.S. general, surrounded by government-issue bodyguards. Hamaad El-Zurak is the leader of the terror group. We don't know where he is, or what exactly he's planning, but I have a video message from him telling me I'll be dead before he succeeds. Finally, we have Clara Fox—our old friend. I don't know where she is either, but I know she's kidnapped Tori and killed one of John's deputies, so for me, top priority is finding her and burying her.

"Next, Josh found out it was the CIA that sent a team to hijack my plane, take me to Colombia, and kill me. Obviously, that didn't work. After I got away from them, I found a cartel operation that's smuggling guns around the world for a contact in the U.S. military who goes by the codename Ares.

"More recently, the NSA has gotten involved at the order of the president to raid GlobaTech and seize all assets and information relating to the Project Cerberus satellite. Suffice to say, in the wrong hands, the world could be in danger. Now, as luck would have it, we know that Hussein had blueprints for this satellite on his laptop, so we know their plans involve Cerberus, but we don't know to what end. Have I missed anything?"

Everyone looks at each other and shakes their heads in turn. Raynor looks like he's going to say something but stops himself.

"John?" I say.

He shakes his head and holds his hand up. "It's nothing. I'm just trying to get my head around this. What's all this about a satellite?"

I look over at Josh and raise an eyebrow, giving him his cue to fill in the blanks. He nods.

"Cerberus is a floating firewall that protects the country's nuclear launch codes," he explains. "But it also spies on everyone, monitoring every possible method of communication under the guise of national security. Plus, we now know it can hack other countries' nuclear arsenals. If you control the satellite, you control the world—end of story."

Raynor removes his hat and lays it on the table. He then removes his sling, slowly stretching his right arm and gently massaging his shoulder where Clara's bullet hit him.

"So, we're assuming the bad guys wanna take over the world using this Cerberus thing?" he asks.

"Pretty much," says Josh. "Bit stereotypical if you ask me, but these bastards seem determined all the same."

I massage my temples. My head hurts from trying to think about this monumentally screwed up situation. "Josh, you got any ideas where these ass-hats are hiding?"

He looks at Clark, who moves in front of the laptop, tapping away on the keys. "Actually, we have. As I've said, we've been doing our best to track their movements and narrow down their positions. We've had algorithms running to scan satellite feeds all over the world, as well as... ah, *borrowing* information from certain government systems... and I think we've got them."

He taps a few more keys, then spins the laptop around to show Raynor and me. On the screen is a topographical map of Eastern Europe, with a red circle placed on it. I look at it for a moment, trying to figure out the exact location.

"Ukraine?" I ask. "I thought you guys figured that much out already?"

"We did," confirms Clark. "But we've since been able to narrow it down to a more specific location." He leans over and points to the screen. "There's an underground medical research laboratory in Pripyat, about ten miles south of the river. Images from the region show recent activity. We think this is where Clara retreated to after she took Tori..."

I look closer at the screen. "Pripyat... isn't that—"

Josh nods. "That's the ghost town that was evacuated after the Chernobyl disaster in '86. Nearly fifty thousand people abandoned the city due to radiation levels. Even now, it's too polluted to live there. That's why we think they're underground, protected from any prolonged exposure to the surface radiation."

"How sure are we that it's Clara?"

"As sure as we can be," answers Clark.

I nod, processing the information and planning what comes next. It's the first time in a while that I've been able to focus on a single thing and picture the outcome.

"That's amazing work, guys—seriously. Especially given you're being forced to operate remotely, with limited access to your computers. How soon can we be ready to go in there?"

Josh and Clark exchange glances, which immediately worries me. Josh scratches the back of his head and looks away momentarily.

"Ah... we're not sure we can," he says reluctantly.

"I don't understand."

"Arranging transportation to get us into the country is going to be hard enough at the moment," he explains. "But assuming we *can* get there, we then have to navigate the city itself. While radiation levels have dropped below fatal thresholds, it's still not safe to spend prolonged periods of time unprotected in the city. We'd need special clothing and transportation, which isn't easy to get a hold of. And that's not considering any skirmish that might occur once we're there. It's bad enough without being under fire as well."

I turn and pace away slowly toward to the door and back again. I slam my fists down on the table, causing everyone to jump a little. "Damn it, Josh! This is Tori we're talking about! Fuck the terrorists and fuck the satellite. I'm only concerned about getting her back, and I fully intend to do just that. I'm not interested in what we can't do. I want to know what we *can* do!"

My outburst leaves them speechless, and I immediately feel bad. I'm just getting tied up in knots here. We're making zero progress, and every way I turn seems to result in a new problem. I hold my hands up to the three of them and take a deep breath.

"Look, I'm sorry. I just..."

"Adrian, it's fine," says Josh. "Listen, do you have the video message they left for you?"

I nod and retrieve the DVD from my bag. He takes it, puts it in his laptop, and plays it.

...

...

...

"Charming fella, ol' Hamaad, isn't he?" he says when it

finishes. "Somewhere, there's a straight-to-video horror movie missing its star. Let me see what we can do here..."

We all look on as Josh's hands become a blur over the keys. I catch a glimpse of Clark as he looks on. He's got that *Jesus, how does he do that?* expression on his face. That makes me feel bad because I know I gave him a hard time back in New York over, basically, not being Josh. Watching him work now will just hammer that point home even more.

Raynor's expression is on the other end of the spectrum. His jaw's open and his eyes are wide as he watches the screen move at a speed most normal people can't quite fathom.

"What in the hell are you doin'?" he asks, sounding probably the most Texan I've ever heard him sound.

Josh smiles. "To dumb it down for Adrian, I'm essentially scanning the background of the video and running software linked into one of the surveillance drones that GlobaTech still has operational. I'm trying to determine where it was filmed. I'll then cross-reference that with the digital time stamp in the metadata of the video file to see archived footage of the area at that specific time. Let's see if we can find where El-Zurak is hiding."

Raynor scratches his head and picks up his hat, putting it back on. "*That's* dumbing it down?"

Josh doesn't answer him, but I put a hand on his shoulder and smile. "You'll get used to it."

"And bing... oh," says Josh, sounding excited and almost immediately deflated.

"What's wrong?" asks Clark.

"I think I've found El-Zurak."

"Why's that a bad thing?" asks Raynor.

Josh looks at me. "He's in the middle of a mountain

range in Northern Afghanistan, close to the Tajikistan border."

I raise an eyebrow. "Not exactly the friendliest of places..."

Josh looks at Clark. "So, what's the play here?"

All eyes turn to Clark. He stands tall, puts his hands behind his head, and interlocks his fingers as he lets out a heavy sigh.

"If we're going to do this ourselves—and I don't see any other option right now—then we only have enough resources available to *maybe* hit one of these places. And that's a big maybe."

"So, what are you saying?" I ask. "We have to choose between going to Pripyat and rescuing Tori, or going to Afghanistan and attempting to take down a terrorist plotting world domination?"

The look on Clark's face is one of regretful stoicism. "That's about the size of it, yeah."

I turn and sit down on the edge of the table. I stare at the floor and sigh loudly. My head's spinning and my mind's all over the place.

Now what do I do?

23

"Adrian, I'm sorry, but there's only one logical answer here…" says Clark.

I stare him straight in the eye. I know what he's trying to say. Anyone with half a brain could see what the detached, unemotional, *logical* answer is. I see Josh hang his head and grimace at Clark's statement. It was absolutely not what I needed anyone to say right now.

I take a deep breath, trying really, really hard not to get angry but quickly failing. "Bob, right now, do I look fucking logical to you?"

My voice got louder with each word.

He holds his hands up defensively. "Hey, I'm just saying… we need to—"

"We need to get my girlfriend back!" I stand and face him properly. "I don't give a shit about anything else! Do you understand?"

I'm breathing heavy, teeth gritted, jaws muscles

clenched, eyes unblinking. I'm not looking at anyone anymore. I'm just angry at everything and everyone.

Why me? Why does all this shit have to happen to *me*? I just want this goddamn world to leave me alone...

Josh stands, looking at Raynor and Clark in turn. I think he appreciates that neither of them have ever seen me truly pissed off before, so he's assuming the role of diplomat.

"I think what Adrian's trying to say," he explains calmly, "is that Hussein will have gone to ground following the failed attempt to apprehend him in New York. Those Afghanistan mountains are impregnable, which means El-Zurak, Hussein, and whoever else is part of the Big Bad will be untouchable there until they decide to resurface. Any attempt to get to them would be a colossal waste of time and will likely get everyone involved killed."

He looks around the room. Raynor looks out of his depth. Clark looks like he feels really bad. And he should —asshole.

"On the other hand," continues Josh, "we probably *can* get to the underground facility in Pripyat. There will be a significant terrorist presence on site, including Clara Fox— someone we're justified in assuming is relatively high up in the food chain. We can take her out, deal a crippling blow to the organization, and maybe even delay their plans. Who knows? But we have a shot if we attack them in Ukraine. Plus, more importantly, there's an innocent civilian who means a great deal to someone who means a great deal to me, so the bottom line is: that's where we're going. Anyone got a problem with that?"

Clark shakes his head. Raynor simply shrugs, happy to go where we need to with no real opinion.

Josh looks at me and smiles. "How's that for logic?"

I visibly relax and stare at him with a look that says I'm

now angrier because he stopped me from being angry when I couldn't do it myself.

I shrug. "That's basically what I meant..."

He shakes his head and turns the laptop toward Clark. "Bob, can you start searching to see what operatives we have currently out in the field and where they are? I know they're in limbo at the moment, thanks to the NSA's sudden interest in us, but if we can get word to someone nearby, maybe they can help?"

He nods silently and gets to work. Josh looks back at me.

"Adrian, as soon as we can organize our limited assets, we'll get you into Ukraine. Then you can go do your thing and get Tori back, yeah?"

I nod but remain silent, still not yet fully trusting myself to open my mouth.

Josh moves next to Clark, and they quietly discuss whatever they're looking at on the laptop. Raynor sits on the edge of the table, staring at the floor. I can't imagine what's going through his head right now, the poor guy. But I sure as hell appreciate him having my back. He's a good man.

I have my shoulder bag open on the desk, and I sort through what I still have with me. My guns are at my back, which feels worryingly comfortable and reassuring to me.

There go those old habits again, dying hard as always...

I take out the camera and transmitter and place them on the table next to me. Then I take out two laser tripwire mines and a block of C4 and carefully put them down next to them.

"Jesus Christ!" says Raynor. "You walk around with bombs in your bag?"

I look up and smile. "I'd rather have it and not need it..."

We hear the sound of multiple car doors slamming shut

outside, followed by the heavy patter of boots on concrete. We all look up at each other simultaneously.

"What's that?" asks Clark.

I shrug. "Anyone else know we're here?"

Josh shakes his head. "No, we kept this location strictly between us..." His voice trails off. He looks down at the laptop like something's just occurred to him. "Oh, shit... they must've traced the signal when we connected to one of our satellites earlier! I thought I'd been quick enough logging in and out to avoid detection."

I quickly open the office door and look down to the warehouse floor below. Wave after wave of men dressed in black fatigues flood inside. There must be twenty of them, all armed with assault rifles and wearing tactical goggles.

"Fuck me..."

The air fills with the sound of many, many guns cocking and aiming in my direction. I spin around and shut the door behind me just as they all open fire.

"Get down!" I yell.

The four of us dive to the floor as the staccato roar of a thousand bullets hits the cabin, splintering the decayed walls around us. We all scurry to the back corner, keeping as low as possible. Josh has grabbed his laptop, thankfully. That's the only thing giving us half a chance at doing something about this mess. I tip the table up, offering slightly more cover for us than before.

"Does anyone have a gun besides me?" I shout over the endless onslaught from below us.

Raynor draws his weapon—a standard issue Glock 19. A nice, sturdy handgun with a fifteen-round magazine. It has a slightly smaller barrel than the Glock 17 and less recoil, making it more accurate and easier to control.

Josh and Clark shake their heads. I reach behind me and

un-holster one of my Berettas. I hand it to Josh, who nods as he takes it.

"Clark, take the laptop. Protect it at all costs. Stay behind the three of us."

He says nothing; he just takes the computer from Josh and stays low.

"Josh, John, stay behind me. Fire only on my instruction. Be ready to cover me."

"What are you hoping to do?" asks Raynor with genuine curiosity.

I check the magazine of my Beretta is full and work the slide, putting a bullet in the chamber.

"I'm going to do what I do best."

I dash over to the door, grabbing everything that slid off the table as I pass. I slam my back against the wall and take deep breaths, waiting for the right moment to return fire. I look over and see Josh tap Raynor on the shoulder, smiling.

"This is gonna be a sight to behold, my friend," he says to him.

You're goddamn right it is...

"Be ready to move!"

I take in a couple more deep breaths, slowing my heart rate down to the point where my body might as well be asleep. All noise fades away. Everything slows to a stop. There's nothing here but a bunch of people below me who no longer want to live, my gun, and me.

Above my head is a space where a window used to be. I hear a voice shout below, and after a few moments, the firing stops. I chance a quick peek over and down to the floor. There's a muddled group spread out across the expanse of the warehouse. I count twenty-two guys in total. I picture them in my mind's eye—the exact layout, where every man is, how they're standing... everything. I reach for one of the trip mines, adjust the settings, and prepare to arm it.

It's something GlobaTech designed in the last year or so —state of the art. Everybody uses them nowadays. They're the industry standard, I guess. The device is hexagonal and fits in the palm of my hand. It's maybe three inches thick. There's an inch-long round tube sticking out, where the infrared laser is housed. Inside is essentially all explosive with minimal technology making it work. Along the side are a few switches, which allow it to be armed and control how it will work. You can affix it to any vertical surface, flick the main switch, and it's on. If someone trips the laser, there's a timed delay before it explodes. The lethal blast radius is about twenty feet. Anything caught within that radius when it goes off has zero chance of surviving. Between twenty and forty feet, you're going to feel unwell afterward, but the chances of being killed by it drop by eighty-three percent.

I've set it so that once I arm it, there's a five-second pause before it's actually armed. I've also changed it to only delay for one second once tripped before it goes off.

Keeping the mental image of the layout below me, I take a breath and flick the switch to arm the device. Then I quickly throw it over my head and down to the floor.

If my aim and calculations are correct, we'll be safe from the blast, but most of the people down there will be eviscerated.

Time slows as I count in my head, waiting for the moment to start shooting. I look over at Josh and hold his gaze as the seconds tick down.

Five... four... three... two...

The explosive device makes a dull, hollow noise at it hits the floor.

One...

It's armed.

I hear everyone shout and freeze.

One...

The deafening explosion rips through the warehouse, drowning out the short screams of the lives it claims. The roar of the fire is loud, and the heat from the blast hits the office, taking our breath away.

In an instant, I stand and take aim. I glance down at the carnage I've caused below and see maybe five people still alive. Body parts are scattered around the place.

I quickly squeeze off a few rounds, taking advantage of their confusion. I hit all five remaining gunmen in the chest. I duck back down and rest against the wall, trying to slow my heart rate once more as an eerie silence descends on us.

Everyone slowly gets to their feet. Josh seems weirdly excited. Clark looks focused, like it's just another day at the office. Raynor appears to be in shock.

"What the hell just happened?" asks the sheriff, making his way over to the door.

"Adrian just happened," replies Josh. "Come on, let's get our shit together and get the hell outta here before reinforcements arrive."

Everyone files past me out of the office and down the stairs. I gather my things and follow them. As we reach the floor, we all stop and look around. The place looks like a slaughterhouse. There's a sea of blood on the floor, with severed limbs scattered all around us.

"Holy mother of God..." whispers Raynor.

I have to admit, even I'm a little shocked at the aftermath. It's been a long time since my Inner Satan was in a fight, and I've forgotten what it was like.

"Watch where you walk," says Josh. "No footprints in the

blood if you can help it. We need to minimize how much forensic evidence we leave."

We follow him across the room, navigating the human debris like it's a minefield. Eventually, we make it to the other side and head back out the fire exit to the parking lot. There are six blacked-out SUVs parked haphazardly by the doors. Thankfully, there are no more men. I head over to the nearest one and climb in behind the wheel. There's a console fitted on the dash, level with the gap between the two front seats. I tap the screen to bring up the HUD.

"What you got?" asks Josh, appearing beside me.

"It seems I just killed a whole bunch of NSA agents. Fuck!"

"NSA, CIA... this is real heavy, Adrian. What are you thinking?"

I look at him, fixing him with a determined stare. "We split up. We'll deactivate the tracking devices in two of these SUVs and head off in opposite directions. See if you can set up a secure line between the two vehicles, so we can keep in touch without giving our position away. From here on out, we're at our most paranoid. We stay off the grid until we figure out a way to get to Pripyat."

Josh nods and walks back over to Clark and Raynor, telling them the plan. I look back at the console. Let's see what the NSA have to say for themselves...

I click through a couple of basic screens. There are search functions for license plates and descriptions, as well as the ability to upload photos via Bluetooth. I type in GlobaTech and hit the search button. After a few moments, the screen fills with information. I feel my eyes go wide the more I read.

"Guys," I shout over. "You might want to take a look at this."

They all walk over to the vehicle. Clark stands next to the driver's door with Raynor just behind him. Josh climbs in next to me.

"I've searched for you guys on the NSA's database," I explain, "and it's come up with a whole lot of bullshit. According to this, the NSA thinks GlobaTech is funding terrorism. They've had orders handed down from their director to seize all of your assets as per Title 18 of the U.S. Code. I'm quoting here—'...all domestic employers are to be questioned, with priority focus on the following high-ranking employees and directors: Robert Clark, Josh Winters, and Ryan Schultz. These people are to be detained...' You boys are famous."

"This is bullshit," says Clark. "Who's running this investigation for the NSA? How can they think we're funding terrorism? We're working our asses off trying to stop it!"

"Well, somebody obviously forgot to tell *them* that. Forgive the potentially stupid question here, but why can't you just tell whoever cares that you're trying to help? Explain what we've learned and what we've been doing?"

"It's a nice idea, in theory," says Josh, rubbing his temples. "But at the end of the day, we've known since New York that there's more to this than just a terrorist group plotting an attack. We don't know who we can trust outside of our company. Schultz is running interference with the NSA, trying to clear our name without giving our game away. But now that we've just killed over twenty government agents, all of that is irrelevant. We're going to be one-through-four on everyone's Top Ten Most Wanted list in about half an hour."

"You guys didn't kill anyone," I say.

"We know that, Adrian, but we were there when you did, so as far as the law is concerned, we all pulled the trigger.

Besides, it doesn't matter who did what. We're all in this together."

I turn to Clark and Raynor. "You two, take a vehicle and get the hell out of here. Just pick a direction and drive. Contact us in six hours."

They both nod without another word, knowing it's the only option.

I turn to Josh. "Deactivate the tracking devices for us right away. Then we're gonna go in the opposite direction to these two."

He gets out of the vehicle and fiddles under the hood of our SUV, then the one nearest to us for a few minutes. Then he shakes Clark's hand and gets back in next to me. He looks at me with concern in his eyes.

"What are we going to do, Boss?" he asks.

I shake my head. "Long-term? I don't know. But right now, you just need to figure out how to get me into Pripyat. I'll take it from there."

He nods back at me. "Working on it. Now let's go. We need to stop off somewhere along the way."

"Where?" I ask as I start up and drive out of the parking lot. I turn left as Clark and Raynor turn right.

Josh simply smiles at me.

24

The stop-off he was referring to was in Kansas City, Missouri—roughly six hours north of Jonesboro. The weather changed many times on the journey, ranging from blinding sunshine to torrential rain. As we hit the city limits, it's somewhere in between the two—reasonably bright skies but raining lightly.

The trip passed quickly enough. We spent much of the first hour in silence, paying professional attention to our surroundings, on the lookout for any tails or government presence. Having not seen any, we came off the I-40 near Alma and hit the I-49, which we took all the way to Kansas. By the time we arrived, we were back into the old routine—banter, joking, blasting music, and generally catching up on the last two years since we parted company.

After navigating through the busy city following Josh's directions, I pull into a warehouse complex just outside the center, which houses long-term storage units. Three main buildings form a U-shape in front of us. The one directly ahead is wider than the ones on either side of us. There are large roller shutter doors on each unit, with a smaller door cut into each one. On the left and right, the buildings are narrower, with larger units.

"Here we are," says Josh as I pull over.

We both get out and stretch. I look around curiously. "What are we doing here?"

Josh sets off walking to the building on the right.

"Contingency plan," he shouts back over his shoulder. "Come on."

I follow him, confused and intrigued, up to the second roller door from the left. He produces a key from his pocket, removes the padlock, and then steps to the side, where a keypad is fixed to the wall.

Impressive security for a regular storage firm...

He enters his code and presses a button, and the shutters start to roll up automatically. He turns, smiling at me with a glint of excitement in his eye. The door disappears slowly upward, revealing what's inside. It doesn't take me long to realize what it is, and I fail to suppress a laugh of disbelief.

I look at the immaculate Winnebago standing before me. "You're kidding me?"

He shrugs. "Didn't have much use for it when I took the job with GlobaTech, but I knew I'd need it at some point, so I kept it here. No one knows about it but me, and I pay cash up front and in advance for the storage, so there are no electronic footprints for the payments."

I pat him on the shoulder, then walk inside the unit to inspect the vehicle. "You're something else, Josh."

It's an impressive vehicle. Much bigger and cleaner than the last one I saw. I'm glad he chose to upgrade using our newfound wealth.

He pushes past me and opens the side door. "Come on, I'll give you the tour."

I follow him on board, climbing the three steps that lead up and into the back. As with his old model, it's mostly open plan at the rear. The windows are tinted, so you can't see in from the outside. There's a long worktop running along the left-hand side, with various monitors, computers, and gadgets fastened in place. In the right corner, covering half of the back and right side, is a booth, with a brown leather, L-shaped sofa fitted in and a table in front of it. Next to that, finishing off the right side, is a workstation with a single computer on it. There's a narrow path linking the back area and the driver's cab, with the door on the left and a cupboard on the right.

"That's the generator," he says after seeing me look at it curiously. "It's an independent power source with an encrypted Wi-Fi connection for my toys. Saves the engine battery for running the vehicle."

"Nice," I say, genuinely impressed.

We both step through to the cab, which looks like the flight deck of the U.S.S. Enterprise. The seats are like armchairs, which would swivel around in their space. There's a center console separating the seats, filled with a variety of buttons and screens.

"Josh, this thing is unreal..."

He smiles like a proud father. "Isn't it? Not really taken it out on the road for any great distance. Figured now was as good a time as any for its maiden voyage."

He steps in behind the wheel and starts it up, then pulls out onto the main lot. I walk back to the SUV and drive it into the storage unit, replacing the Winnebago. I lock it back up again before climbing aboard. I place my bag on the seat at the back, then move through to sit beside Josh.

"So, what's the plan?" I ask him. "How are we going to get to Pripyat? We have less than three days before Clara said the Initiative's plans will come to fruition and she'll kill Tori. We're cutting it fine as it is."

"I know..." he replies, sounding worried. "Just let me speak to Clark, see if he's been able to round up any troops."

We turn out of the complex and head east. As soon as we hit the interstate, Josh dials Clark on a secure line via speakerphone. He picks up on the sixth ring.

"Yeah?" says Clark.

"It's me," replies Josh. "How are you guys doing?"

"We're good. The sheriff's driving. We're currently heading toward Colorado. Where are you guys?"

"Heading east toward St. Louis. We're in my Winnebago, so we're tooled up and secure. No acronym in the country can track me in this. What assets have you managed to find?"

"Not many, to be honest," he says regretfully. "Most currently on missions overseas have gone dark. Schultz will have sent an emergency communiqué out before he went along with the NSA, warning that we've been compromised, so they'll be following protocol."

"Shit. Understandable, but it doesn't help us. You got anything we can go on?"

"Hang on... you say you're heading for St. Louis?"

"Yeah, for now. Just trying to stay mobile. What are you thinking?"

There's a silent pause on the line, except for the tapping of keys on a laptop.

"If you head for Nashville, Tennessee, I might be able to hit up a contact for a private flight out of the States," says Clark. "He's not a GlobaTech asset, so there's no reason for the NSA to keep tabs on him. There's a small airfield just outside of Pleasant View. You'll take off from there."

"And where will we be heading?" I ask.

"I've got a guy in Gomel—a small town in Belarus. He's over there working security for a Russian diplomat. If you can get there, he'll get you over the border into Ukraine. Pripyat is maybe three hours' drive, all told."

Josh looks at me, silently asking for my approval of the plan. I simply shrug and nod. It's time-consuming, but it's all we have, so we have to take it and make it work.

"Bob, that's some fine work. Make the call and get the flight arranged. We're on the I-70 right now, maybe five hours out."

"Will do."

"Bob," I say, "you and John keep your head's down, okay? No unnecessary risks."

"We will, Adrian," he replies. "Don't worry about us. Just focus on getting your girl back."

"Thanks, Bob."

Josh hangs up the call and looks over. "Well, we have a plan, which is a lot more than we had five minutes ago. You all right?"

I sigh heavily, momentarily drifting as I watch the world whizz by through the window. "I'm tired. It feels like a lifetime since I slept properly."

Josh smiles sympathetically. "Get your head down for a bit. I don't mind driving. I want to give this beast a good run anyway. You can get a few hours, at least."

"Thanks, man."

I lean back in my seat—which, it turns out, reclines as well as swivels. Fancy! I close my eyes but don't think I'll get any rest, what with everything that's...

· · ·

22:42 CDT

"Wakey wakey! Hands off cocks, hands on socks!"

I snap awake in my chair, bolting upright with my hands gripping the arms. My eyes are stinging, not yet ready to look at the world after a deep sleep I didn't expect.

I look over at Josh. "Where are we?"

He's laughing. "We're about ten minutes from this airfield in Pleasant View. You've been out for almost the whole journey. Feel better?"

I rub my eyes and relax back in my seat, blinking to clear the fog. "Yeah, a little bit. You good?"

"Yeah, no drama. Bob called just to confirm the flight has been arranged. He and the good sheriff are lying low in a motel in Denver."

"Okay."

It doesn't seem like two minutes before we turn into a large field, hidden away behind a large cluster of trees. It's a dirt track, carved through long grass over the years. After a few minutes, we see a wooden signpost on the right, saying OLDE TOWNE AIRFIELD.

I point to it. "Hey, look. They spell things like you people used to back in the day... badly."

I smile as Josh gives me the finger.

We carry on down the track, which eventually opens up to a small, makeshift parking lot in front of a large hangar. The doors are open, and the plane stands there with a fuel tank next to it, connected via a pipe. There's a guy standing with it, checking the gauges as it refuels. It's a Cessna Citation 500—not a bad plane at all. It will have seen far more commercial use than military over the years. It looks a few years old, and the paint is worn in places, but it doesn't look like it will fall out of the sky.

I turn to Josh. "I want you to stay here."

"And I want to wake up next to a Playboy bunny every morning, but that's not going to happen either," he replies, looking slightly offended.

"Josh, I need you here. Bob and John are doing all they can, and I appreciate that, but you're the only one I trust to be here running things while I'm over there shooting things. I need you to keep your head down, guide me to Clara Fox, and then help me get out of there. You need to be here for that."

"Adrian, I can't let you go over there alone against armed terrorists—not to mention that bitch holding a gun to Tori's head. We both know you're gonna struggle thinking straight going against her. You need me with you."

I smile, genuinely touched by his passion and his unique insight into my state of mind.

"It'll be fine, Josh. I promise. I'm not the person I used to be."

"That's what I'm worried about," he says, like he didn't really want to say it but had no choice. "You've been out of the game for so long, I'm concerned you won't know how to handle something so personal."

"I think the remains of twenty NSA agents would disagree..."

"That wasn't personal. That was business. You weren't emotionally involved in that situation, so you just reverted to your instincts. Clara's the only one left on your shit list, and she's kidnapped the woman you love. I'll bet every penny of your fortune that when you see that with your own eyes, you're going to struggle. And we all know hesitation will get you killed, Adrian."

We fall silent. I know what he's trying to say, and I appreciate the concern. But he's wrong. Despite spending this road trip catching up, he ultimately missed over two years of my life. I'm not angry about that, but it's a fact. He hasn't seen me since Pittsburgh. He's basing his assumption about my state of mind on the person he knew two years ago. I don't want to offend him, but I absolutely need him here, coordinating my efforts.

I stand and walk to the back. I open my bag and place my guns inside, then close it again and sling it over my shoulder. Then I turn and hover by the door for a moment, looking at him.

"I need you here," I say matter-of-factly. "I've got a phone, so I'll call you when I meet your operative in Belarus. In the meantime, keep in touch with Clark and see how much of this puzzle you can put together while I'm gone."

He sighs heavily, then silently waves his hand at me, acknowledging what I've said even though he disagrees. Without another word, I step out of the Winnebago and walk across to the hangar. Halfway toward the plane, I hear the engine start up and him drive away.

I approach the hangar, and a guy appears from around the other side of the plane.

"You must be Adrian?" he says, extending his hand and smiling. "Jim Daniels. Nice to meet ya."

I quickly look him up and down. He doesn't look much like a pilot. He's probably around five-eight or five-nine, with a large stomach resting on a broad frame. His face is round and red, with an overly bulbous nose. I'd put him somewhere north of fifty-five.

I shake his hand, smiling politely. "Any relation to Jack?"

He laughs, which is deep and booming and comes from

the bottom of his sizeable gut. "I wish! I'd be earning a helluva lot more than I do flying this thing." He gestures to the jet with his thumb.

I look at the plane with little interest. "You know where we're going?"

Daniels nods. "Mr. Clark rang ahead and gave me the details. You just need to get comfortable and enjoy the flight."

I smile again and walk over to the door, which is halfway along the right side of the fuselage, opened and revealing stairs. As I step onto them, I glance to my right, out the other side of the hangar at the long runway.

"You a nervous flier?" asks Daniels.

I shake my head. "Not at all. Just looking around. Can't be too careful nowadays."

He frowns, confused, but then he smiles politely and walks off around the other side of the plane. On my left, the man with the fuel disconnects the piping, gives the plane a final check, and then climbs aboard the small truck with the tank on it.

"Everything's good to go, Mr. D," he shouts.

"Thanks, Al."

He drives off without a word, and I board the plane without another thought. Inside is much narrower than the Leah jets I've been on recently, but the seats still look comfortable and spacious. The white leather has been well looked after. I sit down on the first seat on the right side, resting my bag at my feet.

Compared to the paint job on the outside, the interior is definitely in better condition. There's not much in the way of luxuries, but I only need it to get me from A to B, and for that, I'm sure it will do just fine.

After a couple of minutes, Daniels climbs aboard. He closes the door behind him and locks it in place.

"Just be another few minutes, then we'll be in the air," he announces.

I nod. "Thanks, Jim."

I sit back and relax as best I can. I feel good about this. It's a positive step toward sticking it to the bad guys—the first for a good while. I just want to get Tori back. That's more important to me than killing Clara. I know there's still a terrorist threat to worry about, but I'll deal with that later.

True to his word, just over five minutes later, we're screaming down the runway, about to takeoff for Belarus.

"Here we go…" I mutter to myself.

25

So, let me explain to you why I no longer like flying.

In the past week or so, I've been on more planes than I have in the ten years before that combined. I've never traveled via private jet before all this, and I'll admit they are nice and comfortable. In another life, I could afford to buy ten of the damn things if I wanted. But the first plane I went on took me to New York, where I ended up jumping out of a window with terrorists shooting at me. Not the flight's fault, I know, but the circumstances surrounding why I had to get on the plane led to me having a bad experience, so it's all relative.

A CIA black ops squad hijacked the second plane, and I was taken to Colombia, where I was almost killed. Twice. Once by the CIA and once by a cartel.

The third plane, I'll admit, wasn't actually too bad. It got me home in one piece, but after the first two, I think I could be forgiven for thinking flying wasn't really the way to go.

Which brings us to my most recent flight... a private charter flown by Jim Daniels—someone GlobaTech has used for trips they don't want to keep a record of.

We left a small airstrip in Pleasant View, Tennessee and flew for around ten hours until we passed over Minsk, the capital city of Belarus. At that point, the delightful Mr. Daniels announced we were about twenty minutes away from Gomel, which was where I was to meet the GlobaTech operative who would take me over the border into Ukraine.

In keeping with the tradition of everything going against me nowadays, at that exact moment, the cockpit of the Cessna Citation 500 exploded. No warning. No explanation. Just... gone. We were at a decent altitude, so I had a little bit of thinking time, but I admit, it was a shock.

The plane was blown in half and began plummeting vertically, and I did everything I could not to get sucked out of the damaged fuselage. I managed to slide my bag over my arms and shoulders, at the front, against my chest. Then I got the parachute out of the security compartment, just outside of where the cockpit used to be, and put it over my shoulders and onto my back. After a moment to compose myself and think about just how shitty my life had become, I crawled over to where the door used to be and rolled myself out of the flaming wreck that was once my airplane—something I hadn't not done for many years, and even then, only a handful of times. Luckily, there's not much skill to it. You quite literally step out of the airplane. Or, in this case, kind of flop out of it. Ideally, with a parachute attached to you.

Freefalling through the air, I counted to six and pulled the cord, deploying my 'chute. Then I settled into a nice, almost peaceful glide.

And so, here I am. I'm currently... I don't know, maybe four thousand feet above the ground, making my way slowly down to Earth via a parachute, thinking about how much I hate flying.

I hate terrorists and I hate flying.

I hate not knowing what the hell is going on. I hate terrorists, and I hate fucking flying!

26

17:31 FET

I'm lying on the ground, looking up at the sky and watching the fireball that used to be my plane descend out of sight. The parachute is covering me almost completely—just my head and left arm are exposed. I'm aching all over, and I have no issue admitting I'm a little shaken up after the experience of jumping out of a plane.

You know how, in the movies, the hero always lands in a field? Somewhere out of the way? Well, that's bullshit. In real life—in *my* real, shitty life—you land in the middle of a busy street, surrounded by people and cars.

I take a few moments to compose myself, then prop myself up on my elbows and take a look around. Horns are sounding from angry drivers, and there's a small crowd of people gathered around me, curiously looking at me as I lie in the center of the road.

I slide my bag off my chest and rest it next to me. I run through a quick mental check of my vital limbs and organs.

I'm still in one piece. I scramble to my feet, shake the parachute off my back, and pick up my bag. I jog to the sidewalk, dragging the 'chute behind me. I hold my hand up in silent apology to the cars that have been delayed as a result of my unexpected appearance.

I take a proper look around as people start to go back about their business. I'm on a busy street in a one-story high, industrial-looking city. There are no tall buildings, no designer outlets, no modern or expensive cars on the road. The whole place seems to have a perpetually gray hue to it. I could be anywhere east of Germany. But I know we passed Minsk before the plane blew up, so I'm hoping I'm somewhere near where I need to be.

I step into a doorway and crouch down, open my bag, and put my holster on. I'll definitely feel better with my babies at my back. I take out the phone and put it in my pocket. I'll call Josh in a minute, once I've figured out where I am.

I carry on down the street, trying to look like I know where I'm going. But I come to a crossroads and stop on the corner, searching around for a clue as to which direction is best.

Yeah, I have no fucking idea where I am.

I step to the side and take the phone out of my pocket. I dial Josh's number, hoping he's done something technical so that no one knows I'm using it.

"It's me," I say when he answers.

"Have you made contact with our operative yet?" he asks.

"Not exactly. There was a slight problem on the way here that delayed me."

"What happened?"

"The plane exploded."

"What?" he exclaims. "Your plane blew up?"

I let out a heavy sigh. "Yeah. Just the cockpit, and it was ten hours into the flight, so I'm pretty certain it was sabotage. If I were to guess, I would say it was the guy who was refueling the plane when we arrived."

"Jesus... Adrian, this means the bad guys must know you're there. Watch your back."

"Copy that. And I'm fine, by the way..."

"Sorry. Yeah, I mean... I figured, so I didn't... y'know?"

"It's fine. The main problem is, *which* bad guys are after me? The terrorists? The CIA? The NSA? It could be anyone."

"I think we can rule out the NSA for this. Not really their thing. Could feasibly be the CIA, but I don't see the logic."

"No, me neither. Plus, they'd have sent the D.E.A.D. unit after me again, and I'd never seen the guy at the airfield before, so I think the safe bet is El-Zurak's band of merry men are coming my way."

"I guess they figured you'd work out Tori was in Pripyat with Clara and head there?"

"Sound thinking, but how did they know where I'd be flying from? Even though we were hacked by the NSA back in Arkansas, that doesn't explain how the Armageddon Initiative found out about the flight."

"Still no clue on that one, but we'll get there. You just focus on getting Tori back, okay?"

"I will. Which reminds me, where the hell am I? I jumped out of the plane and landed in the street, but I don't know how far I am from the rendezvous point, and there are no signs."

"Let me ping your signal from the nearest cell tower and pinpoint the location of your phone..."

There's a moment or two of silence while he works his magic. As I stand there, holding the phone to my ear and absently gazing at my surroundings, I feel a sharp prod in my back. Without reacting, I casually look over my shoulder and see a man standing behind me, holding a gun two-handed, leveled at the center of my back. He's a rough-looking guy, with dark stubble and tired eyes beneath a baseball cap. He's about my height, dressed in scruffy jogging pants and a sweater with a sleeveless jacket over the top. My initial thought is that he's a terrorist, but I dismiss it almost as quickly. There's no way they'd send *one* guy after me.

"Adrian?" he asks. His voice is deep and coarse, like he's smoked twenty a day for the last decade.

Keeping the phone to my ear, I slowly turn around and face him, raising a quizzical eyebrow. I glance at the gun, then back at him. I look at his professional, trained stance, his body language, the confidence... definitely not a terrorist.

"Ah, Josh? What's the name of the operative I'm meant to be meeting?"

"His name's Collins. Ray Collins," he replies.

"Thanks." I put the phone against my shoulder and look back at the man with the gun. "Ray Collins?"

He regards me for a moment, then slowly holsters his gun and extends his hand. I nod and put the phone back to my ear. "Josh, never mind. He's just found me. Call me if you find anything more out."

"Oh, good. Yeah, I will. Watch your back, Boss."

I smile and hang up, put the phone back in my pocket, then shake Collins's hand. "How'd you know where I'd be? *I* don't even know where I am."

"Ya fell from the sky in a ball of fire," he replies casually. "Ya weren't exactly hard to fuckin' miss."

I shrug. "Fair point. Where are we?"

"This... is Gomel," he says, gesturing around us at nothing in particular. "Ya were lucky. The wind must've carried ya farther south, so ya landed just a couple of miles short of our rendezvous point."

"First bit of luck I've had in a while," I say with a humorless smile. "So, how quickly can we get over the border?"

"Follow me. My car's nearby."

He walks past me and crosses the street. I follow him, taking a quick look around out of habit. We walk for a few minutes before turning right onto a side street, where a battered, rusted European sedan last sold in the '80s is parked against the curb. Collins walks round to the driver's door and climbs in. Somewhat skeptical of traveling in this thing, I climb in the passenger side.

Without a word, he drives off, then turns right at the end of the street.

"In the glove compartment are fake papers for the border patrol," he says. "If ya reach behind ya, the back seat will lift up. Use the space to hide your bag. They'll check it otherwise, and I'm guessing ya don't want what's in there being seen?"

I look behind me, then do as he says. I put my guns and holster in my bag and hide it in the seat.

"You done this before, Ray?"

He smiles. "Once or twice, yeah."

"Where are you from? Your accent is distinctive."

"I was born in Northern Ireland, but I've lived between the U.S. and Eastern Europe for the last thirty years, so my twang has faded a little."

"A good friend of mine is from London. He always corrects me on my allegedly poor use of the language."

He laughs. "Yeah, you Yanks sure ruined that over the years!"

"Oh, Christ. Don't *you* start..."

We follow the M-10 road for about half an hour, then turn left onto the P-33. It's another forty minutes of fairly straight, unadventurous road before we veer left onto the P-35.

"Okay, it's about an hour's drive along here 'til we hit the P-56," says Collins. "That's the road that will take us over the border and into Pripyat. Once we cross, it's about thirty klicks into the city itself. If ya wanna rest up, now's the time."

I shake my head. "I've slept enough."

I stare out the window at the foreign land passing us by. It always feels strange, being somewhere new. I forget I'm still on the same planet as home sometimes. The landscape looks and feels so different from Texas. Even the sun is colder here; the heat doesn't quite reach as far as the light. Fields and trees run off to the horizon in every direction. It's a beautiful place. Just a shame I'm here under such ugly circumstances.

"What exactly do ya plan on doing in Pripyat?" asks Collins after a few miles of silence.

"I'm going to kill the person who's kidnapped my girl-friend," I reply matter-of-factly. "And with some luck, I might take out a terrorist or three along the way."

Collins lets out a whistle. "Sounds heavy. I guess the rumors are true."

I turn to look at him. "Rumors?"

"About you. Most guys who work for GlobaTech's private security division have heard of ya because that best friend of yours is one of our top boys now. A lot of what people say about ya, I've dismissed as campfire stories, but looking at ya, seeing how ya got here and the belief ya have in what you're gonna do next... maybe there's something to those stories after all. I'm glad you're on our side."

"I'm not on anyone's side. I just want to do what's right. I hung up my guns a couple of years back, but some radical pricks tried to lure me out of retirement. So, now I'm balls deep in God knows what, trying to outrun the U.S. Government and stop a bunch of terrorists from doing something bad with a satellite that no one's meant to know about."

"I've only got a few hours before I have to get back to my assignment," he says regrettably. "Otherwise, I'd offer to help. Sounds like ya need it."

"Thanks, but you'd just get in the way."

He laughs and shakes his head. Silence falls inside the car once more.

19:56 FET

It doesn't take long to reach the border to Ukraine. We slow to a stop as we join a short queue of traffic waiting to get through the checkpoint. The sun is disappearing behind the trees that line either side of the narrow strip of road. The surrounding terrain couldn't be traversed in any vehicle, and if you approach on foot, you'll be picked up anywhere within five miles in a matter of minutes. It's a pretty secure checkpoint—one road in or out of the country.

There's a low concrete wall running away to the sides, with a large barrier covering the only gap in it that I can see from the car. A guard's hut to the right houses three men in military fatigues—all armed. There are two more men on either side of the barrier and at least four patrolling the queue of cars on the road.

One of the men signals the car in front to move forward. It does, stopping level with the hut. There's a guy behind bulletproof glass looking at screens inside. I'm guessing there's some kind of electronic pad underneath the ground measuring weight, or maybe even producing an infra-red scan of the vehicle.

Another man comes out and approaches the vehicle. The driver's hand appears through the window, passing over his papers for inspection. I can see a muted conversation— short, no pleasantries. The guard makes a quick lap of the car and hands the papers back. He signals to the men by the barrier, and between them, they manually raise it and usher the car through.

The guard from the hut turns to us and gestures for us to drive forward.

"Play it cool," murmurs Collins. "Don't say anything ya don't have to. We're two guys on a road trip. No business."

The guard taps on my window, and another appears and does the same on Collins's side.

He says something that I don't understand, and I look at him like a confused tourist. Seeing my reaction, he sighs impatiently.

"English?" he asks.

I smile. "American."

He rolls his eyes. "Papers."

I hand them over and look around casually as he checks them. Next to me, Collins is doing the same, but he's showing off and speaking in Russian.

"What is business in Ukraine?" asks the guard.

"Just on a road trip."

He eyes me wearily, but I don't think he's suspicious. I think it's just professional boredom from his mundane job. He glances back at the hut, at the guy looking at the screens.

He gives an almost imperceptible nod, which the guard acknowledges before turning back to me. He then looks over the car at the guy on Collins's side. They start talking in Russian.

"What's going on?" I whisper to Collins, a little worried now.

He shakes his head. "I don't know. Something about the car."

My door opens, taking me by surprise, and the guard leans in. "American—out of the car, now."

There's a non-confrontational urgency in his voice, and I comply without resistance. Collins does the same.

"Turn and lean on the car," he says to me.

I do, and he starts patting me down. I look across at Collins, who's going through the same thing. I raise an eyebrow, asking a silent question. He replies with a subtle shrug.

Great.

I look down at the ground as the guy moves his hands up and down my legs. I see a large metal sheet in the dirt, directly underneath the car.

Looks like a scale. Thought so. They'll measure the weight of the car and passengers. Standard security, I suppose.

I frown.

I wonder if they've weighed the car and thought it's too heavy for just Collins and me? If they search it, they might find my bag... and that would certainly prompt a few more questions, which I don't really want to answer. I look up again at Collins, concern flashing into my eyes. He shakes his head slightly, as if to say there's nothing to worry about, and I absolutely shouldn't kill every guard here.

I'm not panicking. Panic suggests fear, and I'm not afraid

of anything. What I *am* doing, however, is expressing concern over the possibility of wasting more of my valuable time. I reckon I've got less than twelve hours before Clara puts a bullet in Tori's head. I can't afford to stand here any longer flirting with these *Police Academy* rejects.

The look in my eyes tells Collins I'm losing patience. He responds with a look that pleads with me to ride things out. Against my better judgment, I stand still and let a random Communist continue to feel my legs.

A few more moments pass, and the guard finishes frisking me. He stands and signals to his friend by Collins to join him. They huddle together over by the security hut without a word to us. We both remain where we are, exchanging silent questions. Then my guard walks back over to us.

"Here are your papers," he says, handing my documents to me. "Enjoy your trip to Ukraine."

He spins on his heels and steps away to the side, looking at the vehicle behind, waiting to gesture them forward. The other guy hands Collins his papers without a word, and we both get back in the car.

"Heh... that was tense!" he says as he starts it up and drives slowly toward the barrier.

"I'm not sure those guards realize how close they were to being killed just then."

The barrier lifts for us. Collins eases through and builds up speed on the other side.

"So, this is it," says Collins. "The home stretch. Ya have any idea what's waiting for ya in Pripyat?"

I shake my head. I honestly don't know what kind of presence the Armageddon Initiative has in the deserted city, but I know I'll find out soon enough.

27

I hear a faint ringing noise and realize my cell is in my bag, still hidden away under the back seat. I reach behind and retrieve it, dragging it back through to the front. I open it, take out the phone, and answer it.

"Yeah?"

"Adrian, it's me," says Josh. "Where are you up to?"

I look over at Collins as I place the phone on speaker. "Where are we?"

"We're about eighteen klicks out from Pripyat, traveling along the P-56," he announces.

"You're making good time," observes Josh. "And hi, Collins."

"Mr. Winters," he replies professionally.

I raise an eyebrow. "Mr. Winters?"

Josh is laughing on the line. "Shut your face. Listen, I've got someone on the other line who wants to speak to you."

"Who is it?"

223

"He's an FBI agent."

My spider sense immediately starts to tingle. "How'd he get your number? What have you told him?"

"Relax," says Josh, recognizing my concern. "Bob put them in touch with me. *They* reached out to *him*. Look, I'll let the guy explain, but I'm inclined to trust him."

"Whatever," I say, choosing to remain skeptical following recent events. "Put him on."

The line falls silent for a moment, then another voice speaks. "Adrian?"

I frown. I know that voice. I scratch my head, trying to remember where from.

"Adrian, it's Special Agent Tom Wallis, FBI."

There it is!

"Tom?" I say, unable to hide the surprise in my voice. "Jesus! How are you doing? It's been a long time."

Close to three years, to be exact. I worked with Agent Wallis when I agreed to help the FBI back in San Francisco, when I had that thing with Danny Pellaggio. My God, that was a lifetime ago...

"I'm good, considering. You're a hard man to get a hold of."

"I know. What can I do for you?"

"I'll cut straight to it," he says. "A couple of local agents came to see you over a week ago about the murders of three men who were found in a car near where you live in Texas."

"That's right..."

"Adrian, I'm now working on a counterterrorism task-force for the FBI. As part of my job, I have to liaise with other agencies regarding any issue pertaining to suspected terrorist activity. As I'm sure you can understand, I've been hearing your name a lot recently."

I shrug. "Is there such a thing as bad publicity?"

He chuckles, then falls silent. "Is there anything you want to tell me?"

"Not really."

"Are you sure?"

"Yes."

"You mind if I ask why?"

"No, I don't mind. Me and you go back, Tom, and I'll admit I think you're a good guy. At least you were when I knew you. But in the current climate, I hope you won't take offense if I tell you that I don't trust you as far as I can throw you."

"No offense taken," he says. "In fact, that's exactly the reaction I was hoping for. I'd be worried if you trusted me, given what I know."

I shift in my seat. "You have my attention..."

"Josh, are you still on the line?" asks Wallis.

"Yeah," he replies.

"Okay. So, Adrian's currently sitting atop the CIA's most wanted list, and GlobaTech are the only focus of the NSA right now... anybody wanna confirm why?"

"I would if I knew," I say. "A lot of things don't make much sense now, if I'm honest."

"I'm gonna level with you," says Wallis. "I've got a good idea what you and GlobaTech have been doing. While it's not a matter a private military contractor has any jurisdiction over, that's not to say we're not glad to have the help. In fact, on behalf of a government agency who is essentially trying to do the same thing, I want to thank you for your efforts so far."

"You're welcome," says Josh. "Just a shame no one else seems to be so grateful."

"And why is that?"

"No idea," I say. "But it's getting old, real fast. I'm

JAMES P. SUMNER

involved in this whether I like it or not. It just so happens that GlobaTech has had an eye on things for a while, so I decided to help them out where I can."

"I wanted to get in touch with you to propose the same thing."

"What, you want my help?"

"I'd like to compare notes, yeah."

"Remember when I said I didn't trust you?"

"Yeah..."

"I still don't. Everyone else is trying to kill me. What makes you think I'll believe you aren't too?"

"They're not trying to kill you, Adrian. They're just trying to stop you from interfering in an inter-agency investigation."

I glance at Collins, who is driving quietly and now looking a little confused.

"Is that what they told you? I'm no expert, but I'm pretty sure they're trying to kill me, Tom. In fact, scratch that—I *am* an expert, remember? My first clue was the special ops team that the CIA sent to hijack and blow up my plane..."

Wallis says nothing.

"Then there was the twenty-man NSA squad, all armed to the teeth, who stormed a GlobaTech safe house and opened fire on me without any provocation."

Still nothing.

"Tom, if they want me to stop, they just need to ask. I'll gladly step away from all this if they're willing to take over. But I don't think they are. I think, for whatever reason, GlobaTech and I are being set up. Whether the acronyms are being fed bullshit information or running the show themselves, I dunno. But what I *do* know is that it's me against them, whether I like it or not. And I'm sure you can't blame me for assuming your acronym isn't any different."

I hear Wallis sigh heavily on the line. "Just out of interest, what happened to all these men who were sent to kill you?"

I massage my forehead and stare out of the window at the desolate landscape passing by.

"Don't ask questions you don't wanna know the answers to, Agent Wallis."

He sighs again. "Shit. Okay... I've made contact and asked for your help, so my job's done. After everything you and I went through back in 'Frisco, I hope you can see past whatever's going on here and trust me long enough to accept my help. I'm not asking you to trust the FBI. I'm asking you to trust *me*. Josh has my number if you change your mind."

He hangs up, leaving Josh and I on the line.

"What do you think?" he asks me.

"I think I'm about twenty minutes from Pripyat and need to focus on getting Tori back. You?"

"I think we should trust him. He stuck by you back in the day, despite everything they knew about you. Forget who he works for. I don't think he'd have contacted you to set you up."

I shrug. "Fair point. Okay, you have my blessing to call him back and give him as much or as little information as you see fit. If it helps us or them, then that's a good thing."

"Agreed. Listen, keep your earpiece in and the line open. I'm watching you via satellite, and I'm here if you need anything."

"Thanks."

"Watch your back, don't do anything unnecessarily stupid, and get your girl back, okay?"

"Fuckin' A."

He hangs up, and I look at Collins. "What do you think? Should we trust the FBI?"

He glances at me briefly. "Man, I don't trust anybody."

"Good answer. How far out are we?"

"It's a little over quarter of an hour before we reach the city limits. I've got a face mask you can use in the trunk. It covers your nose and mouth. It'll give you that extra bit of protection against the low-level radiation, just while you're finding your way around."

"Thanks, Collins. You're a good man."

He smiles and shakes his head. "I'm many things, Adrian, but I'm not a good man."

"Well, you're helpful. Sure you won't join me? There'll be lots of terrorist types to kill... it'll be fun."

"Ya really are fuckin' crazy, aren't ya?"

"Insanity is a matter of opinion. I'd say I'm... driven."

He laughs. "Wait 'til I tell the boys about this one! No, as soon as your ass is outta my car, I'm heading back over the border. I've got a job to do."

"Understood."

We cover the rest of the journey in silence. I try to steel my mind, focus on the task at hand, and forget about the million things that could go wrong. I've got my Berettas, which are all I need. I'm trying hard not to keep thinking about Clara Fox too. I buried Adrian Hell, along with his demons and his shit list, when I left Pittsburgh. Thanks to her, they've all been dug up, and I've made a conscious effort not to let them take control of me again. But as I look out the window and see the haunting skyline of the abandoned city of Pripyat, I can't help but think I could probably do with a little controlling right now...

We enter the city limits and blast through the empty streets. It's a strange feeling, driving through a completely deserted city that used to be home to nearly fifty thousand people. When Chernobyl happened back in '86, the entire city was evacuated within a couple of days. Radiation levels have dropped way below fatal in the thirty-one years since then, but it's still uninhabitable long-term.

"Slow down a bit," I say to Collins. "Stick to a speed limit or something. We don't want to attract any attention."

"Okay," he replies, slowing to a steady cruise at forty.

I look around and see the decaying buildings, the occasional abandoned car, and broken windows in storefronts along each side of the street.

"Welcome to Terroristville..." I mutter quietly.

"Ya think they've got eyes all over the city?" asks Collins.

"It wouldn't surprise me, but I doubt it. Not practical or necessary. They'll have set up a perimeter around their underground lab, but that'll be it. The place is a ghost town. They'll see or hear people coming from miles away."

Almost subconsciously, he slows to thirty as we take a left, passing by a school on the right-hand side. I reach in my bag and retrieve my earpiece. I sync it with my phone and put it on, dialing Josh.

"We're here," I say as he answers.

"I've got you," replies Josh. "Tell Collins to take the next right and pull over."

I do and he does.

"The underground facility is a couple of klicks east of your location," he says. "You're better off on foot from here."

"Copy that," I say, grabbing my bag and getting out of the car. Collins follows suit.

"End of the road," I say to him as we stand side by side at the trunk. I extend my hand. "Thanks for the ride."

He shakes it.

"It was an honor." He pops the trunk and gestures inside. "A parting gift."

He leans in and lifts up the floor, revealing another hidden compartment underneath. He takes out the mask he told me about and hands it to me. It's a wraparound that covers the bottom half of the head. It's black and elasticized, with hard plastic at the front to cover the nose and mouth. On the front of it is the bottom half of a skull, crudely painted on. I smile, feeling my Inner Satan stretching and cracking his knuckles, like a beast awakening from his hibernation.

"*This* is cool as fuck, man. Thanks."

He smiles. "Thought ya might like it. There's this too."

He hands me a body harness, designed for tactical operatives to carry their weapons and tech in the lightest, most maneuverable way possible. I rest my bag at my feet and then put my arms through it, fastening the clasps down my side. The front and back has holsters and pockets. The straps are a thin, flexible carbon fiber, running vertical over each shoulder and down to another strap that fits around the waist. There are two more diagonally across the front and one horizontally across the back. After some minor readjusting for comfort, I stretch and quickly get accustomed to it.

"You'll need this to go at your back," he continues, handing me a pump-action Ithaca shotgun. I take it in my right hand, feeling the weight. It's an impressive weapon. Good for crowd control and close quarters combat.

I suspect I'm about to see quite a lot of that...

"Jesus... this is like Christmas. Thanks, Collins. If I get out of here alive, I definitely owe you one."

He smiles. "I'll hold ya to that. Good luck."

He turns and gets back in the car, reverses down the

street, and then turns back the way we came. I watch him go for a moment, then re-focus. I take my holster out of the shoulder bag and strap it to my back. I slide both Berettas in place and store every spare mag I have in the various compartments of my harness. I slide the Ithaca over my shoulder and down my back, slotting it in place. Finally, I take the remaining proximity mine from my shoulder bag and clip it to my hip. I then throw the empty bag to the side of the street and take a deep breath, then slide the mask over my head, adjusting the front so that it fits comfortably over my nose and mouth.

"You totally think you're Rambo right now, don't you?" says Josh in my ear.

I smile. "I feel like him."

"You *look* like him!"

"How do you know? Your satellite feed isn't *that* good, is it?"

"GlobaTech's is close to it, but I'm in the Winnebago, and my shit's better. It's a high definition, grayscale, real-time feed of your exact location. Look up and wave, honeybunch!"

I frown for a moment and then gaze upward, flipping my middle finger to the clouds.

"Asshole."

"Love you too, man."

"So, where am I heading?"

"At the end of the street, take a left, then a right. You should see a hospital in front of you."

"Copy that."

I set off in a light jog, taking the directions Josh is relaying to me on comms.

"I see the hospital," I confirm after a couple of minutes.

"Good. On the other side of that building, half a klick

northeast, is a medical research facility. That's where the underground lab is."

"What's the best approach? I must admit, I'm feeling skeptical about just walking up to the front door and knocking..."

"That's not like you," says Josh. "You're normally about as subtle as a—"

I turn right and see a parking garage next to the hospital. It has three levels. I stare across the street at the structure.

"Tank?"

"Yeah... that's you, all right."

"No, Josh... I can see a tank."

"Are you sure?"

I frown with slight frustration. "What kind of a question is that? Of course, I'm fucking sure. It's a tank!"

There's silence on the line for a moment. "Where is it?"

"It's inside a parking garage, ground level."

"Hmm..."

"What?"

"Oh, shit!"

"What, Josh?"

"I just completed a sweep of the area and came back with nothing. No signs of life anywhere. Then I thought, they know you're coming, so they can probably hazard a guess as to the kind of support you have. They would've parked the tank under the cover of the garage to remain out of sight from any satellites or drones."

I step back around the corner and drop to a crouch. "Well, that's just cheating. Any signs of life nearby?"

"I couldn't see anything initially, but then I did a second sweep, looking at buildings and structures nearby."

"And?"

"And... there are four bus shelters near the entrance to

the facility. Except they *aren't* bus shelters—they're just made to look like they are, so someone like me wouldn't think twice while looking down from a satellite feed."

"So, what are they?"

"My guess is they're makeshift tents or covered guard posts. They're about twenty feet long, maybe six feet wide. You could easily stand five guys under each one, side by side, and be hidden from view. There's no way you're getting inside that facility through the front door, Adrian. They're too well prepared for you coming. This is really bad."

"No shit, Einstein."

"Sherlock."

"What?"

"The saying is: *no shit, Sherlock.*"

I sigh. "You can be a real pedantic sonofabitch when you want to be. You know that?"

"Yup!"

I take a moment to think. I don't have eyes on any patrols or sentries, so I'm confident they don't yet know I'm here.

"Any other way into the facility?"

"Not unless you can find a way to the roof without being seen," he replies.

"Shit."

I instinctively look around, second-guessing myself. Maybe I'm surrounded and just haven't noticed. My gaze rests on the tank. It's a state-of-the-art combat vehicle, green and black. It's only been in circulation twelve months. The sides and back consist of several thick, angular, metal plates that are welded to the basic frame, providing unrivaled protection on three sides. It's concerning that a relatively new and unknown terrorist network has tech like this.

I can't see the head and long barrel of the attached cannon, but I'm pretty sure I know which model it is, so I know what the gun will look like. There'll be a hatch on the top with two men inside.

After a few moments, I've figured out how I'm going to get Tori back.

"Josh, I take it you already have schematics of this place?"

"Of course!" he scoffs, as if insulted.

"Good. Work on finding the quickest way inside the facility and to the underground labs."

"And what are *you* gonna be doing?" he asks.

I look across at the tank and smile. "I'm gonna go work on my subtlety."

28

Keeping low, I dash over to the garage, approaching the tank from behind. It's a Goliath-class assault vehicle, which I know uses a system of cameras to offer the two-man crew inside a three-sixty view of the surrounding area. It's pretty hard to sneak up on someone that basically has eyes in the back and sides of their head, but if I can get close enough without anyone seeing me, I can rush the tank before they can react. It's a big and powerful machine, but it's slow and currently in a confined space, so that's an advantage to *me*.

Careful not to get too close to the parking garage, I cross the street and plant my back against the wall of the building next to it, in a small alcove. I lean against the side and slowly edge forward, just enough to glimpse up and down the street.

"Adrian, I can see what you're doing, you crazy bastard," says Josh.

I don't reply, focusing on the task ahead of me. I try to

make a move for the tank, but for a moment, it feels like I'm standing in quicksand. I stop myself.

I grimace, angry at myself.

"I saw that," says Josh. "Hesitation will get you killed. If you intend to do what I think you are, then for crying out loud, just fucking *do* it. Don't piss about, worrying about being seen. They know you're there, so go and kill them already!"

I take a deep breath. I'm annoyed at myself for that split-second of doubt. He's right, as always.

Don't tell him I said that.

I close my eyes, reach behind me, and draw one of my Berettas. I take another deep breath and open my eyes again. When I do, I feel all traces of humanity leaving me. My heart rate increases as the adrenaline starts to kick in. I feel the buzz, the excitement—everything I gave up nearly three years ago.

My Inner Satan slides behind the wheel and starts the engine.

Showtime.

"Just find me a way inside," I say to Josh.

I step out and run at the tank, heading inside the parking garage and approaching it from the left rear side. In one movement, I jump up on the back of it and make my way up onto the head. I place my left hand on the hatch and yank it open. Two startled men in military fatigues look up at me with a vacant stare. As I hoped, they didn't see me approach.

Without a word, I fire twice, putting a bullet in each of their heads and killing them instantly. I holster my gun and climb inside, shutting the hatch behind me. The whole area is maybe seven by seven. I'd find it a tight squeeze without the two dead terrorists in here with me. I drag the guy at the front off of his chair to the floor, then step on him to climb into the seat and take control.

In front of me are three monitors, with two consoles side by side on the small work surface. On the left and right screens, a single horizontal line down the middle of the screen splits the view. On the outside of the feeds is a view of the left and right sides. On the inside feeds are images from behind the tank, to the left and right.

The middle screen shows what's ahead of me, essentially through the eyes of the cannon.

These new tanks really don't mess about when it comes to warfare. They're as close as you can get with a tank to semi-automatic and fire large incendiary shells.

I know how to drive a tank. I mean, I did it a couple of times about twenty-five years ago, so I wouldn't call myself an expert, but I reckon I can figure it out.

There are three joysticks built into the console area, which is a little different from what I remember. Why the hell do I need three?

"Josh, you there?" I ask, tapping my earpiece.

"I'm here," he says. "Let me guess... your grand plan has hit its first stumbling block because you can't drive the fucking tank you just commandeered. Am I right?"

"Now isn't the time for rights and wrongs," I say dismissively. "Just tell me how to move the damn thing."

"The Goliath-class is slow but powerful. You need to keep it as straight as you can. The right-hand stick gives you throttle and brakes. The left hand one is your steering. The middle one—"

"Blows shit up?"

"Exactly."

"Why do they need two guys to run this thing, then?"

"It's much easier if you have one person navigating and

one person shooting. There'll be a secondary control system for the gun that the other guy can use."

There's no denying this thing is a beast, but it also looks like something off *Star Trek*, and I'm not a hundred percent confident I won't kill myself using it.

"Hey, Josh, they have a PA system built into it..."

"Yeah, they'll use that for crowd control, I suspect."

I smile to myself.

I've just had the *best* idea...

I take my phone out and place it on the console in front of me, next to the microphone.

"Josh, can you send a song to the phone I'm using?"

"Erm, yeah. Technically, I could. Why?"

"I'm thinking I might go *Apocalypse Now* on these assholes!"

He laughs. "One second..." My phone beeps. "There you go. File sent. There'll be a micro-USB port in the console. Stand your phone in it and play the file."

I do as he says.

I move the right stick forward, and the machine rumbles to life, juddering slowly out of the garage. I flick the switch so that I'm broadcasting, then crank the volume all the way up just as the opening of *Black Betty* by Ram Jam starts.

I carefully turn right, then left, lining myself up and approaching the facility head-on. Looking through the monitors, I see Josh was exactly right. There are twenty guys spread around the main entrance, under cover from satellite detection.

The music blasts as every single terrorist aims their weapons and fires at me. The high-pitched whizzing sound of bullets bouncing off the tank rings out but ultimately does nothing to deter me from unleashing Hell itself on these pieces of shit.

I take control of the middle stick, line up my shot, and fire once. The *ka-boom* is deafening, and the whole tank shudders as the ground to the left of the entrance explodes in a cloud of smoke and rubble and body parts.

I aim over to the right and do the same.

Ka-boom!

Another cloud of smoke and terrorists. I slow down as I approach the sidewalk that leads to the main entrance of the facility. I use the cannon to look around. The building is in a state of decay; the brick has crumbled and cracked, falling away in some places. It's borderline derelict, but I'm assuming the underground section is much better preserved.

"How far down are they?" I ask Josh, tapping the earpiece a couple of times when I get some static feedback.

"Based on the thermal imaging scans, I reckon about three floors," he replies. "I've got the layout up on my screen now."

I aim the cannon at the main door and the last handful of terrorists who have so far evaded my wrath. I line up the shot and fire, blowing the entire front wall to pieces.

"Knock, knock, assholes."

I grab my phone and climb out of the tank. I drop down to the street and draw one of my Berettas, attaching the suppressor as I make a quick sweep. The entire area looks like a warzone. There are *bits* of people all over the place. Dark stains of blood cover the streets as I walk toward the hole that used to be the main entrance. I re-holster my gun and pick up one of the dead men's assault rifles as I walk past. It's an AK-47. Not ideal, but it's in one piece, so it'll do. I'd rather save *my* ammunition for when it counts. I scoop up a couple of mags as I walk on and slide them into a spare pocket on my body harness, then check the weapon's locked and loaded.

I walk inside the building, checking every angle for signs of life. It's a large, open-plan foyer—the right wall was once glass, floor to ceiling, but now the slight breeze quietly whistles through the place as I walk on. There's a large front desk on the left, and beyond that are elevators and stairs which lead both up and down.

I walk by some upturned chairs and tables. I catch one of the chairs with my right leg, and it scrapes on the floor, which sounds loud in the surrounding silence. I quickly drop to one knee, raise the gun, and prepare for any movement. I wait a few moments, but there's still no sign of life.

Happy I'm under no immediate threat, I continue on to the stairs in front of me.

"All quiet here," I whisper into my earpiece.

"The surrounding area's quiet too," replies Josh. "Looks like you took out the bulk of the security perimeter."

I reach the stairs and lean over the railings, looking up and down and checking for movement. "Looks clear. I'm heading down. You say it was three floors?"

"Yeah. We might lose comms, so stay sharp, okay? Don't focus too much on Clara."

"Copy that."

I take a deep breath and head downstairs slowly, checking the angles and pausing at the bottom of each flight. As I approach the stairs down to the third sub-level, I hear the first signs of life.

"Josh, you there?" I whisper, but the line's dead. I check my phone and see there's no service. I take the earpiece out. No need to wear it if I can't use it.

I climb down the last staircase and come out in a small, tiled lobby. The walls show signs of damp and decay, but the lighting works fine, and the floors look clean. It certainly doesn't look abandoned, like everything else around here.

The lobby seems like a sort of hub. The stairs descend into the middle, with corridors and rooms off in every direction. I stand still, holding my breath and listening for any clue as to which way I need to go. With my back to the stairs, the corridor ahead of me is dark. I glance left and right. Both corridors are bathed in fluorescent light from fixtures quietly buzzing overhead.

I step forward slowly, turning right and checking behind me. That's well lit too, but I hear something from the right that makes me turn. Just a faint sound of movement. I look at the sign on the wall, which says LEVEL 3—RESEARCH LABS beneath what I assume is the Russian translation. I take a step down the corridor but stop when I hear more movement from behind me. I look over my shoulder, at the corridor facing the back of the stairs, and see two men walking toward me. They're unarmed and appear to be deep in conversation, so I don't think they've seen me. I press my back against the wall and listen.

"He'll be here soon," says one of them. "The Fox said he's already in the building."

The Fox? Really?

Well, they know I'm here... or at least, that I'm on my way. I crouch and carefully rest the AK-47 on the floor, keeping my eyes on the two men the whole time. They haven't seen me, and they're drawing level with me now. It's amazing how invisible you can be when no one's looking for you. They know I'm heading this way, but because they don't think I'm here yet. It doesn't enter their heads to look around, so even though I'm likely in their peripheral vision, they haven't registered my presence. This is good news for me and, frankly, fatally bad luck for them.

I slowly draw a silenced Beretta with my right hand. I wait for them to pass the stairs and me. They're heading for the darkened corridor. I step out and silently fall in behind them. I need to play this smart. I should find out what I can about what I'm walking into.

I raise my gun and fire once at the man on the right, putting a bullet in the back of his head, just above the neck. He dies instantly and hits the floor at roughly the same time the spray of blood and brain matter does.

Shocked and unprepared, the remaining man spins around, but in the time it's taken him to do that, I'm already moving toward him, so he turns just as my left elbow is swinging in. It meets his jaw as he looks around and catches it full force. He spins away from me and drops to the floor, landing on his back. I'm on him right away, dropping down and pressing my right knee hard into his chest. I push the barrel of my gun into his right temple and place my left hand over his mouth.

"Do you know who I am?" I ask him, my voice muffled slightly through the mask.

His eyes are wide with surprise and fear, and he nods vigorously.

"Good. That saves me some time. Does Clara know I'm here?"

He nods again, slower this time, like he's really thinking about the answer.

"Okay. I'm going to remove my hand from your mouth now. Just in case you get any funny ideas about making any noise, I want you to remember two things: my gun is still pressed against your head, and bits of your friend's brain are scattered across the floor next to us."

I slowly remove my hand. He remains silent.

"Excellent. Now where is everyone, and how many of

you are there?"

His breathing is rapid, and his eyes are darting in every direction, as if looking for a way out.

"B-back there," he says in a Scandinavian accent. "There are m-m-maybe fifteen men."

"And where's the woman they've kidnapped?" I press my gun harder against his temple. "Don't lie to me."

He closes his eyes and grimaces as panic and fear set in. "P-please... I'm just a tech guy. I'm not a soldier!"

I jab him hard in the stomach with my left hand. "I didn't ask who you were, did I?"

He tries to sigh, but he's breathing too quickly to do it effectively. "She's t-tied up in one of the labs. Please... I have a f-family."

I look at him for a moment, searching for an ounce of humanity so that I could give a shit. Unfortunately for him, I left all that back in Tennessee with Josh. The only thing I can think of right now is vengeance.

"Lucky you," I say to him. "At least you'll have people to plan your funeral. Next time, maybe think twice before working for a bunch of terrorists, yeah?"

I pull the trigger, sending a conical spray of dark blood across the floor. I stand and look over my shoulder, at the corridor where these two came from. Then I look left and right.

I wonder if this floor is connected in some way, like a network? If I go left, would that bring me out on the other side of the area where Clara is?

It's a big gamble. I'm running out of time, and I can't afford any mistakes. No, screw it. I know that they're straight ahead, so that's where I'm going.

I draw my other Beretta and stride quickly and purpose-fully toward the corridor at the opposite end, toward Tori.

29

The end of the corridor doglegs to the right and out into a large area. It's separated by temporary partitions all the way around the edge, with an open area in the center.

I stand in the doorway momentarily, getting a good look at the room and planning my attack. There are a couple of men patrolling the perimeter, but the majority of the forces are in the center, which is where I assume Clara and Tori are.

I crouch and head right. The partitions are thick, painted wood up to about waist height, then glass up to the ceiling. They're capped off with a thin border of wood again, leaving a gap between the top and the ceiling. I look up and see piping and air vents all around. It's definitely some sort of old lab, but the tech seems new. They must've been reno-vating the place for months.

Keeping low, I follow the room around and start to veer left, coming to a gap in the partitions. To my left is a

244

pathway that leads into the middle of the hub. Straight ahead is more cover. I glance behind me, then peer around the corner. I have a direct view into the middle, and I see a large group of men standing around. They all have hand-guns, which, thankfully, are holstered at their sides. They're congregating around a large monitor, but the next partition obscures my view.

What did that guy say before? Tori's tied up in one of the labs? I'm guessing he meant they're holding her in one of the partitioned lab areas, away from the main group. If I can find her, I might be able to get her out of here before drawing any attention to—

I feel the cold metal of a gun barrel rest gently against the back of my head. I close my eyes and sigh.

Shit.

"Get up," says the voice. "Drop the guns."

I stand, leaving my Berettas on the floor at my feet. I feel a hand unsheathe the Ithaca from my back and toss that to the side as well.

"Move," he says, jabbing me with the gun.

I turn left and head toward the group in the middle. As I approach, more of the scene becomes visible to me, until I'm standing in the middle of the space, surrounded by the huddle of terrorists. There are some tables and chairs on the left, with two small glass labs behind them. The doors are closed. I count ten guys all sitting around, looking at me curiously and smiling.

On the opposite side to me is another glass lab, with pathways on either side. The door's closed, and there's a man standing outside it. I look through the glass and see Tori. Despite the circumstances, I still breathe a sigh of relief, happy to know that she's still alive.

She's sitting down, looking straight ahead. I'm on her

right side, so she hasn't seen me yet. Her hair is matted and she looks tired, but other than that, she looks as beautiful as I remember. It feels like a lifetime since I've laid eyes on her. I feel a sudden wave of guilt. I blame myself entirely for her being here. I should've protected her. I should've—

"Hey! Are you paying attention?"

A strong, female voice interrupts my train of thought. I look to my right and see the large screen in full for the first time. There's a table next to it, with papers laid out across it and a laptop on the right. Standing in front of the screen, staring at me with an evil bemusement, is Clara Fox.

As seen on the DVD she left me, she has shoulder-length, jet-black hair and dark make-up. She reminds me a little of that Salikov woman I killed back in Heaven's Valley. She strides purposefully toward me and snatches the mask off my head, discarding it to the floor.

"Adrian Hell..." she says. "You took your time."

I shrug. "Sorry to keep you waiting. I was too busy killing all your men up on the street."

She laughs. "You think that bothers me? This is the end of the line for you and the beginning of the Armageddon Initiative's plans to reset the world!"

She sounds like a Bond villain.

"Wow... you are seriously fucked in the head, aren't you? I guess watching me beat your old man to death has left you with a few issues."

Her smile fades. Her eyes go dead, staring at me like she isn't human. She holds my gaze for a moment, then looks at one of the men and nods. He stands and walks over to the lab opposite. The man behind me pushes me forward with his gun, and I step farther into the middle of the area, standing directly in front of Clara.

A moment later, the guy reappears, escorting Tori by her

arm. Her hands are behind her, presumably bound together, and her eyes are red from crying.

"Oh my God, Adrian!" she shouts.

She goes to run toward me, but the guy restrains her, and she struggles in his grip.

"Let *go* of me, asshole!" she yells at him.

I fail to suppress a small smile. That's my girl, defiant to the last.

"Tori, are you okay?" I ask her, trying to remain as calm as possible. "Are you hurt?"

Before she can reply, Clara steps forward. Without a word of warning, she leaps toward me and unleashes a right knee into my side. I didn't see it coming. I wince at the impact, double over, and drop to one knee. She smashes her left elbow across my face, catching me on my cheek. It hurt likes hell, but I do everything I can not to register it. I stay still, staring at the floor and breathing hard through gritted teeth, absorbing the pain and using it to fuel my growing anger.

I look up at her for a moment, then slowly get to my feet. "You've gotten brave in your old age. Makes such a difference being surrounded by all your friends, doesn't it?"

She strolls over to Tori and strokes her hair, twirling it in her finger. She's taunting me. "I see nothing changes, Adrian. You're still blind to the truth that is so clearly laid out in front of you. What's happening is inevitable. Times have changed and left you behind. You cannot stop what's now in motion."

She turns to Tori and grabs both her cheeks in her hand, then kisses her lips, forcing herself onto her with no emotion. As she moves away, Tori spits on the floor.

Clara looks at me and smiles. "I've worked closely with Hamaad El-Zurak to make this organization what it is. Yalafi

Hussein is an idealist, but he's naïve. He still thinks you can impose your will upon people by using archaic methods of terrorism. El-Zurak is a great man, and his vision for a new world is... extraordinary."

I tune her voice out and focus on the environment around me. I've been so concerned with getting Tori back, I think I've lost sight of the bigger picture. Not since back in New York, when I took Hussein's laptop, have I really thought about what's at stake.

I look around the room and start to see things that I hadn't noticed before. Time slows to a stop as I take in every single detail. It's almost like an epiphany. Speaking to Clara has made me see that I don't actually *care* that she managed to get away from me years ago. She's not Wilson Trent. She hurt my pride more than anything, which is the only reason I held a grudge. But I don't anymore.

There are ten guys to my left and one behind me, who has a gun to my head. But the group of ten all have their guns in their holsters. The average time for someone to draw their weapon and effectively take aim is three seconds. It'll only take me two to disarm the guy behind me and fire at least four bullets...

The screen behind her has a technical diagram of a satellite, which I can only assume is Cerberus. The setup of this scene is like a lecture. That says that she knows a decent amount about what Cerberus does, which validates her claim that she was close to El-Zurak.

The table on my right is covered by papers and a laptop... those papers are confidential documents. I've seen enough in my time to recognize material that should be redacted. If I were to hazard a guess, I'd say CIA. I can't think of any way someone like Clara would've been able to get their hands on classified files like that without at least having an inside man. But the CIA isn't the kind of place where you can bribe people...

Slowly but surely, the pieces of this puzzle start to slot into place. Now I just need to get out of here and tell Josh I've solved things all on my own for once.

Clara slaps me hard across the face, speeding time back to normal and bringing me back to the real world.

"Are you even listening to me?" she screams.

I look at her with the most neutral poker face I have and shrug. "Not in the slightest. Sorry." I look across at Tori. "Baby, we're gonna get out of here, okay? Just trust me."

She nods. Clara slaps me again. "You arrogant bastard! You've always been so full of yourself, and why? You're outnumbered and on the losing side of a war your country doesn't even know it's fighting!"

I sigh and look at her with feigned sympathy. "I feel bad for you, Clara. I imagine you've spent the last few years harboring a grudge against me. It's slowly consumed you to the point where you probably don't even care about El-Zurak's plans for Cerberus. All you care about is getting back at me. Am I right? I mean, you were the one who told these extremist pricks about me in the first place. You would've known then that I wouldn't have come and worked for you. I think you did it knowing it would prompt me to come looking specifically for you, so you could make some half-assed attempt at getting revenge."

She's taken aback but quickly recovers.

"Well, you're here, aren't you?" she says, like a petulant child. "So, you're just as stupid as you've always been, walking right into a situation you knew was a trap."

"Yeah, but I'm not here for *you*, Clara. I'm here for her." I nod at Tori. "I couldn't give a shit about you. Don't you get that? I stopped holding a grudge against you a long time ago. You've been building yourself up to this fantastic show-down between us, and the fact of the matter is, I simply don't care."

Okay, so that was a small lie. I *do* care. I'd happily snap that psychopathic bitch's neck right now. Forgetting the betrayal years ago, she kidnapped my girlfriend. That alone signed her death warrant. But she doesn't need to know that. It's more fun to make her think she's insignificant and watch her fester until she bursts.

I look over at Tori who, bless her, is trying not to smile. I wink at her and see her swell up as she takes a deep breath, full of pride for her action hero who's about to save her.

Those are her words, by the way.

I slide my left foot subtly out to the side, just a couple of inches, widening my stance a little. Then, in one movement, I flick my right heel up behind me, catching the guy behind me in his balls. At the same time, I duck to the left to avoid the potential stray bullet. Luckily, there isn't one. Sensing him bend forward, I spin around, push him over, and snatch the gun out of his hand in one motion. As I complete my turn, the room slows down once more. I look past Clara and go straight for the guy standing by Tori. Mid-turn, I fire once and put a bullet between his eyes. He falls backward, and Tori jumps in shock, putting her hands over her mouth to suppress a scream.

I continue the turn, coming around to face the bunch of ten. I know I'm only going to get a couple of shots off before they start to react, so I fire three bullets at the guys nearest to Tori. I hit two in the chest, killing them instantly, but only wound the third by catching him in the arm.

Time resumes its normal speed. Without thinking, I run at Tori, scooping her up in my left arm as I dash past her to find cover.

"Come on, baby. We're leaving!"

She shrieks in shock as I sweep her off her feet, whizzing her around and grabbing her arm, helping her run while still tied up.

"What the fuck?" yells Clara behind me. "Don't just stand there, you idiots! Shoot him!"

We're on the opposite side of the room to where they caught me, so I know my guns aren't close by. We're crouching down around the corner of a partition.

I glance at Tori. "Are you all right?"

She nods but doesn't respond. I look behind her at her wrists, still bound in standard-issue law enforcement handcuffs.

"Pull your hands apart as much as you can."

She frowns and does it, tightening the chain. I take aim and fire once, making her scream. Before she can say anything, I lean around the corner and fire off a few more rounds, hitting another two men. So, that's four down, one wounded... which leaves six, plus Clara and two stragglers. This isn't going to be easy. While I have cover right now from anyone in front of me, it's ultimately a large, open, circular room, so they can come at me from either side as well.

With no real option for long-term protection, I need to take the fight to these assholes.

"Tori, we need—"

She interrupts me by kissing my lips, quickly and with as much urgency and love as anyone can give. "Just get me out of here."

I smile and nod. It's a weird feeling... my Inner Satan is in full-on survival mode right now, but the usual thirst for violence that goes with that isn't there. I just feel a need to do what I have to, nothing more. It's quite liberating.

I put my gun in her hand. "Wait here. If anyone comes near you, shoot them."

Her eyes are wide, betraying a mixture of fear and lack of understanding. It's a lot to ask someone who's normal to take a life. I look her in the eye, so she can feel reassured and safe—so she can believe that it'll be okay.

She purses her lips and nods rapidly.

I smile. "That's my girl."

I stand and run to the right, keeping low. The remaining men are spread out and taking cover behind partitions and desks. I doubt the idea of me being unarmed at any point would've crossed their minds, which buys me some breathing space. But I know the guys on the perimeter will still be there, covering the exits, and they'll see immediately that I don't have my gun. I need to act quickly.

I make my way around the outer wall of partitions, counterclockwise, and soon meet the first two guys, who are guarding the way I came in. They have their guns drawn but aren't expecting me to run at them. They're standing quite relaxed and facing forward, into the middle of the room.

I reach them and deliver a kick to the first guy's gut at full speed, sending him flying backward. I use the impact to take away my momentum, stopping to throw three punches in quick succession at the second guy—one to the gut, one to the side of the ribs, and a third to the jaw. He crumples to the floor and drops his gun, which I pick up in time to fire at the first guy, who's back on his feet and taking aim at me. I hit him twice in the chest and then immediately duck back down as someone in the middle shoots at me.

I wait a moment, then put a bullet in the second guy's head, who's lying at my feet. I quickly continue my circuit, firing into the middle every time I come up to a gap in the walls. I don't have eyes on Clara from my position anymore, but I can still spot where most of the men from the group are.

I see an opportunity for a shot, so I step inside the first layer of wall and crouch by a desk. I line up my shot and fire twice, hitting one of the guys in the neck, despite his cover.

I carry on and see my weapons just ahead of me. Keeping my gun aimed ahead, I slow down and crouch, eager to get ahold of some real firepower. I reach my Berettas, but bullets immediately pepper the ground around me, forcing me to duck back behind cover.

I look at my babies as the wooden partitions splinter around me, desperate to feel their comforting weight in my hands once more. I'm biding my time, waiting for a pause in the onslaught before I can make a dash for them again.

After a few moments, the firing stops and I seize the opportunity.

Got them!

I scoop them up and take cover on the opposite side of the gap. I put both Berettas in my holster and pick up the Ithaca. I chamber a round and hear the comforting double-crunch of a shotgun ready to fire.

I take a breath and close my eyes.

Showtime.

I spin around the corner and stride purposefully toward the center, the Ithaca aimed straight and low. I see movement in the corner of my eye on the left, so I turn sharply and fire.

The great thing about a shotgun is the damage it's capable of. The buckshot sprays out in a conical arc in front of me when I fire, and the closer the target is, the more chance of them being blown in half. Right now, at this range, I don't even need to be accurate. If someone's within ten feet of me, I can aim loosely in their direction and they're dead.

The shot cuts through the table and hits the man hiding behind it in the chest. Just behind him, another man appears, and I fire again. He flies backward from the impact, dead before he hits the floor. I flick to the right in time to see another man peek around the side of a partition. A shot in his direction blasts through the wall and rips through his torso.

That's three more down... can't be many left now, surely?

I reach the middle, where the original group is standing with Clara. I can't see her anywhere. I do a slow circle, turning clockwise. The trick is to point the gun in front of where you're looking, so the weapon completes the turn before you do. That way, when you see something move, you can take it out straight away, instead of having to readjust your angle first, which would cost you valuable seconds.

I look past the large monitor and see two men side by side, who must've been following me. As I see them in my peripheral, I fire on instinct, knowing the barrel of the shotgun is aiming in the right place. I catch them both in the stomach with one shot.

I hear movement behind me, so I spin faster and drop to a crouch, lining up the shot. However, as I look around, I freeze. In the gap is the last remaining man, aiming his gun at me. Next to him is Clara Fox. She's got a gun in her hand too, and it's pointing at Tori.

I let out a heavy sigh.

Shit...

30

"Drop it," says Clara, slightly out of breath. "Or I drop your girlfriend."

Man, she looks *really* pissed off. I must've done a good job winding her up before. It's worrying that she appears so unstable, given she's holding Tori, but at least I know she's unlikely to be thinking clearly. I'll use that to my advantage when the time's right. For now, I'll do as she says. I toss the shotgun to the floor.

She nods at me, looking at my body harness. "And those custom pieces of shit you're in love with."

Reluctantly, I remove both Berettas from their holster and drop them next to the shotgun.

She leans toward the man next to her. "Go and secure him. But be careful."

I look at Tori. I hold her gaze so that she can see into my eyes and see the confidence in them. I want her to believe this will all be okay because it will be. I've already won.

255

Clara has messed up, and it'll cost her life. She just hasn't realized it yet.

But she will.

The guy approaches me on my left side. He's tall, maybe my height. He looks like he works out; he has a big frame, but he's an amateur. The guy's arms are fully extended, meaning his gun will be within reach of me long before his body. I almost feel bad. It's *that* easy...

With a quick movement, I grab his gun hand by the wrist with my left hand, pushing his palm toward him with my thumb. This puts a strain on the tendons, causing an involuntary reflex that straightens the fingers, which consequently forces him to loosen his grip on the weapon. As it falls from his hand, I lean left and catch it with my right. Then I turn his wrist away from him, forcing him to follow it with his body to relieve the pressure. As he does, I whip my left leg across and kick him hard in his right knee. With his body going left and now his legs going right, he quickly falls to the floor.

In the same motion, I raise the gun and point it at Clara. "Step the fuck away from her, now!"

"One more move and she's dead!" she screams back at me.

I smile and shake my head. "No, she's not. You're a mercenary, Clara, not an extremist. You're not willing to die for this cause, and right now she's the only thing keeping you alive. You're not going to kill her, no matter what I do. Not until you've gotten out of here. Which isn't happening, by the way."

I casually lower the gun and aim left, firing three times at the guy on the floor without looking. All three bullets hit him in the chest. His body jerks from the impact and then slackens in death. I re-aim at Clara.

"See?"

I look in her eyes. Panic is setting in. It's just her and me now. Yes, she has a hostage, but she knows me. She knows there's no way out of this that doesn't involve her dying. Is she spiteful enough to kill Tori anyway, knowing she's as good as dead, just to make sure her final act is to make me suffer?

Of course, she is.

But that doesn't mean she will. The Armageddon Initiative will have paid her a significant sum of money for helping them put this attack together. She won't want to risk losing that if there's a chance she can get out of here, no matter how small the odds.

"It's over, Clara," I say, more calmly now. "Let her go, and maybe you can get out of here."

"How's that?" she snaps back. Her gaze darts around the room, as if looking for a new solution.

"You help me get to El-Zurak and stop the hijacking of the Cerberus satellite, and I'll do what I can to make sure your help is taken into account when this is all handed over to the FBI."

She laughs loudly, exaggerating it to show she's actually insulted. "Fuck you, Adrian. Fuck... *you*! Do you think anyone would be lenient with me if all this failed?"

"Honestly? No. I think they'd give you the chair. But I said I'd do what I could for you, and I mean that. Just let Tori go."

She glances at Tori and smiles that sick, evil, emotionless smile I remember seeing years ago. I clench my jaw muscles as I sense what's about to happen.

"So, explain to me how the brooding, tormented soul of the legendary *Adrian Hell* has found it within him to get himself a girl," she says. "What about your dead wife? Huh?"

There it is.

Bitch!

The *Try to Make Tori Hate Me* card.

And not only that, but she said my name like she was air-quoting it, which is infuriating on a whole other level.

Tori's eyes widen, then narrow as she frowns with confusion. She stares at me in silent inquiry, then turns to look at Clara scornfully.

"Oh, did you not know?" asks Clara with feigned innocence. She looks over at me and smiles. "Adrian, does she not know *anything* about you?"

I feel my finger involuntarily tighten on the trigger. I fight the urge to risk shooting her while Tori's so close.

"She knows everything about who I am," I say, feeling the need to justify myself. "She doesn't need or want to know anything about who I *was*."

"It looks to me like she's curious..."

With the gun in her right hand, aimed at Tori's body, she puts her arm around her and pulls her close like an old friend.

"How about us girls have a nice talk about our man over there? Eh?"

Tori turns to her and looks her dead in the eye. "Go to Hell."

"Ooh, feisty!" She turns to me. "I can see why you like her. But seriously, Tori, there's so much you should know about Adrian. Like, for example, did you know he's one of the greatest assassins ever to pull a trigger? Did you know he killed my father?"

Tori's livid with Clara, staring a hole through her with wild eyes, and she must be frustrated knowing there's little she can do to stop her. But to be honest, I wouldn't want her to try. Clara's a trained killer and capable of hurting her—or worse. I'm just grateful Tori and I have already had the conversation, and she said she understands why I don't want to talk about it and accepts that. She always said she loves me for who I am, so anything Clara says won't have the intended effect on us. It'll just make me want to shoot her more.

"And another thing," continues Clara, oblivious to Tori's stare. "The thing that made Adrian tick all those years he spent alone was the guilt of being to blame for the death of his wife and daughter."

That makes Tori look at me. Her eyes ask me a thousand questions all at once. I look at her apologetically, genuinely sorry she has to go through all this. But I take exception to Clara's statement.

"Hey, I wasn't to blame for their deaths, and I've since killed the guy who was! Don't—"

I stop myself as I see the sick smile creep across her face. She just suckered me into that exchange and got a reaction out of me that I shouldn't have allowed. The look on Tori's face confirms it.

Shit.

Josh was right. I allow myself to get too emotionally involved, and it sometimes clouds my judgment. That wouldn't have happened if he'd been here.

Let's not mention it, though, eh?

"Well played," I say, trying to recover gracefully. "I know what you're trying to do, Clara, and it won't work." I look at Tori. "Sweetheart, if you have any doubts or concerns about me after this, I completely understand. I swear to you, I'll tell you whatever you want to know. But can I please ask that, for now, you trust me and let me get us out of here?"

If ever I needed more proof that Tori is my ideal woman, she struggles to suppress a smile and winks at me.

"Lead the way, Action Man!"

Clara's face contorts with disgust. "Oh my God, really? I think I just threw up in my mouth."

Still holding Tori with her left hand, she points her gun at her mouth and makes the vomiting gesture, doing her best to ridicule us both and get more of a reaction out of me.

I'll give her a fucking reaction...

Without thinking, I whip the gun up and fire in one movement. The bullet catches Clara at the bottom of her neck on the left, where it meets the trapezius muscle. Tori jumps out of her skin in surprise as a thin spray of blood hits her face. Clara is equally caught off-guard. She claws at thin air with both hands as she tries to stop herself from falling backward. Not wasting the opportunity, Tori quickly puts some distance between them. I dash over and kick the gun out of Clara's hand the second she hits the floor, then take aim and cover her.

"Put pressure on the wound so that you don't bleed out. Both hands. Now!"

She does, probably more because of her own survival instincts than because of my order, but the outcome's the same. She's lying on her back, staring up at the ceiling and breathing fast and shallow.

I kick her foot. "I'm a good shot. You won't lose too much blood if you keep your hands on the wound. You need to stay alive long enough to help me."

"What makes you think I'll help you with anything?" she says, coughing and struggling to get her words out.

"Because you hate me. I think you'll want to tell me the full extent of what I'm up against, so you can watch me realize I'm doomed to fail. I think you'll get some twisted level of satisfaction from it."

She smiles weakly as more blood starts to spill from her wound. I quickly look at it. There's a chance I might've nicked an artery with the bullet, which means she doesn't have long. I need to act fast.

I turn and point to all the documents laid out on the table behind us, looking at Tori. "Babe, gather up everything over there. We'll take it with us. Hopefully, there will be something useful."

I look back at Clara. She's given up putting pressure on her wound. I see the last sliver of defiance in her eyes. "Clara, listen to me. What can you tell me about El-Zurak? How can I get to him in Afghanistan to stop him controlling Cerberus?"

She moves only her eyes and looks at me with a mixture of loathing and defeat and confusion.

"Who... who said he was in Afghanis... tan?" she asks weakly.

I frown. "We tracked him there via satellite. We found you here and saw him and Yalafi Hussein in the Afghan mountains. We figured he'd be untouchable there and impossible to find, so I came after you to rescue Tori."

She struggles to laugh, instead letting out a sickly wheeze, followed by a cough and a wince. More blood oozes from her neck and pools around her on the floor.

"You might want... to check your intel. Hamaad...El-Zurak is... is in the States. You're too... late."

I can't hide my surprise or anger. I don't know if she's telling the truth or just trying to wind me up. I suppose there's little reason for her to lie at this stage...

I turn to Tori, who's standing by the table with a handful of papers and folders. "Got everything?"

She nods.

I bend down, dropping the gun I had, and pick up my Berettas and the Ithaca. I holster each one on my harness. "Let's get out of here."

We set off walking toward the corridor I came down initially.

"Adrian... wait," says Clara weakly. I stop and turn, staring at her impassively. She looks at the gun I left on the floor, then back at me. "P-please..."

I know what she's asking. She doesn't want to lie on the floor and bleed to death. She wants the honor of going out on her terms. I regard her for a moment and ask myself if I hate her enough to deny her the opportunity to have a warrior's death. And do you know what? I honestly don't. My initial anger toward her, when I first found out she was involved, only stayed because she'd kidnapped Tori. I'd have hated anyone who tried to hurt the woman I love. I realize now that the fact it was Clara was irrelevant. I'm actually surprised at myself for being so rational about it, but under the circumstances, holding a grudge against someone who turned their back on me over four years ago seems kind of... petty. There are much bigger things going on for me to worry about.

I nod and take a step toward her, but Tori grabs my arm. "Adrian, what are you doing?"

"It's okay," I say, looking at her and placing my hand on hers. "This won't take a minute."

She doesn't understand, but she trusts me and lets me go. I walk over to the gun, take the magazine out, and leave one in the chamber. Holding the barrel, I crouch down next to Clara and place the butt in her hand. She's barely breathing now, but her eyes look at me, and for the first time ever, I see honesty in them.

"Th-thank you..." she whispers.

I smile. "You're still a bitch."

She smiles a smile that offers no apologies but nevertheless calls a truce between two people who have lived on different sides of the same coin.

I stand and walk back over to Tori. "Come on," I say, leading her with my arm around her shoulder down the corridor and toward the stairs that lead back up to the street.

"What was that about?" she asks, genuinely curious.

Before I can answer, we both hear a single gunshot from inside the lab. We look at each other. Tori has surprise in her eyes, while I'm trying to look sympathetic.

"Nothing," I say as we climb the stairs. "Now let's get out of here."

31

We reached the street, and I contacted Josh. I told him Clara was dead, Tori was safe, and we needed a ride home. Within an hour, a helicopter arrived and flew us to Chernigov airport. Despite being closed for the last fifteen years, the runway was still accessible. There was a private jet waiting for us there, which had us in the air almost straight away.

We didn't say much for the first few minutes. Tori looked around in amazement at how the other half lives—the nice leather reclining seats, the plush carpet, and the stewardess who needed absolutely no prompting to bring us both an ice-cold beer.

She's sitting opposite me now, leaning back and staring at the ceiling with the bottle in her hand. She takes a deep breath and a grateful swig of the beer, then looks at me. I've been sitting patiently, sipping my drink and waiting for the inevitable onslaught of questions.

"Adrian, I owe you my life," she says. "How did you ever find me?"

I raise an eyebrow, surprised. I shrug casually and smile. "I had a little help."

Before I can say anything else, she stands and moves over to me, straddles my lap, and kisses me like it's our last day on Earth. I wrap my arms around her waist and hold her close to me, savoring her smell, her taste, and her warmth. We part after a minute or so, short of breath, with our hearts beating slightly quicker than before. I look over at the stewardess, who is respectfully looking at the floor and smiling to herself. Tori kisses my nose and rests her forehead against mine for a moment, then sits back in her seat and takes another pull of her beer.

"Adrian, I... I have to ask you a couple of things."

Oh boy. Here we go.

"Sure. I'll tell you whatever you want to know. I promise."

"Okay..."

She composes herself, seemingly struggling to find the words.

"Take your time," I say. "You've been through a lot—more than anyone should have to."

She smiles and tries to remain strong, as if she's trying to prove something to me or to herself. "Why did you come for me?"

I frown with slight disbelief. "What do you mean? I was prepared to tear this world apart to find you, Tori. I—"

"You told that woman you only came after her because you couldn't go after the other guy. Should you have done something else besides rescue me?"

"Babe, no—of course not. You're more important to me than anything."

"I know," she says, smiling briefly. "But you agreed to help your friends stop those terrorists who attacked us at your bar. Be honest with me, Adrian. Was there something else you should've done besides coming after me?"

I take a breath and stare at the floor. I need to choose my words carefully here, and this kind of thing isn't my strong suit.

"I'll tell you everything I know about what's happening another time. But to summarize, there's a guy called Hamaad El-Zurak, who's planning a large-scale attack on, I suspect, most of the Western world. Our intel told us he fled to a mountain range in Afghanistan, essentially making him untouchable. The ideal play was to go after him—cut the head off the snake, so to speak. But we also knew that Clara had come to Ukraine and that she had you. I immediately said I was coming for you, but other people pointed out that the right thing to do was go after El-Zurak because of the threat he poses. We argued, and I came close to shooting people out of frustration, but... Josh stepped in and pointed out that going after you *was* the better move because there was a higher chance of success, and it would still be a massive blow to the terrorist organization."

She nods. "So, there was no way you could've gone after the other guy?"

I shake my head. "Not without being killed, no."

She nods slowly. "Okay."

"You sure? It seems like something's bothering you about it."

"I just..." she sighs. "I wouldn't have forgiven myself—or you—if coming to save me meant innocent people suffered and died at the hands of some lunatic extremist."

I smile. I love her.

"Babe, I'll do whatever I can to stop these assholes, but

there's no way I'd want to save the world if you weren't gonna be in it. End of story."

She's quiet for a moment, then the smile creeps across her face. "Adrian, you're an... impressive man. And I love you."

I feel my cheeks flush slightly, which I'm glad Josh isn't around to see.

"I love you too."

"Right, now what was that crazy bitch going on about before?" she asks, her mood changing in the blink of an eye. "You killed her *father*?"

I sigh. "Yeah, I did."

"Why?"

"Because he was a terrorist who was trying to detonate a nuclear weapon in Nevada."

"Oh, well... wait—wasn't there something in the news a few years back about a bomb going off in Nevada?"

"The Nevada Incident? Heaven's Valley?"

"Yeah, that's right!"

I nod. "Yeah, that was me."

"Holy shit! So, that thing she said about you being an assassin... is that for real?"

"It is. Or it was. I retired. But that's why those men originally came to the bar. They wanted to recruit me because they knew who I used to be."

"And who did you used to be?"

"Adrian Hell."

She's silent for a moment, then she bursts out laughing. It's a real belly laugh. She laughs so hard that she stops breathing. Then she starts shaking and doubles over, wafting herself with her hand. "Oh... my... God! Adrian *Hell*? Really? Who thought up *that* name?"

I shift uncomfortably in my seat, unsure how to react. I think my feelings are hurt...

"Well, the name was kinda given to me, but I liked it, so it stuck. What's wrong with it?"

"You sound like a villain in those comic books!"

"Hey! I was—and still am—the most feared killer who ever lived, I'll have you know."

"That may be so, but to me, you're simply Adrian. You own a bar, and while you're strong and tough, you're the most loving man I know. I can't imagine you being a... contract killer."

"To be fair, I did just kill, like, thirty guys to rescue you. I hijacked a *tank*, Tori."

"Like I said, tough and strong!"

She smiles. I honestly don't understand why she has no issue with my past.

"One more thing, then I'll go back to kissing you."

"Shoot."

"What happened to your wife and child?"

I take a deep breath. "Tori, I... that's a long story. And to be honest, now isn't the time. Do you mind?"

"I understand," she says with a smile. "But I do want to know, okay?"

"Okay."

The stewardess walks over and politely clears her throat. "Sir, I'm sorry to interrupt, but there's a call for you."

She hands me a cell phone, which I put it on speaker.

"Yeah?"

"Adrian," says Josh. "You all right?"

"Yeah. Thanks for the plane."

"No worries. Tori, are you there? How are you holdin' up?"

"Hey, Josh," she says. "I'm fine. Thank you."

"Good. Both relieved Clara's dead?"

"Honestly?" I say. "I can't say I'm bothered either way."

"Check it out—my boy's all grown up!"

Tori smiles at me. I roll my eyes.

Josh continues. "Listen, I radioed the pilot and got him to re-direct your flight. We'll meet you at Fort Worth."

"Texas? What's happening?"

"Tell you when you get here," he says cryptically. "Get some rest."

"Okay, see you soon." I hang up and look at Tori. "Something's not right."

"What makes you say that?" she asks.

"I dunno, exactly, but my spider sense is tingling."

"Your what?"

"My spider sense..."

She shakes her head and laughs. "My God, I got rescued by a cartoon character!"

I finish my beer, trying really hard not to take offense. "Try to get some sleep. You've been through a lot, and it's a long flight. You need to get some rest."

"So do you," she says. She curls up in her chair, tucks her legs underneath her, and leans back.

"I don't have time to sleep." I pick up the pile of papers and files that we took from the underground lab. "I need to prepare for when we land."

21:35 CDT

Tori snaps awake as the pilot's voice comes on over the speaker system to announce we're half an hour out from

Fort Worth. I look up from the papers, which have kept me distracted for the best part of six hours, and smile at her. "Feel better?"

She nods and smiles back, looking half-asleep still. I gather up the papers I had strewn across the table next to me and massage my temples. My head hurts. These files contain a lot of information. Some of it is classified but irrelevant. Some of it relevant and a little disturbing. But mostly, they served to help me piece together this whole mess and figure out who's doing what and why. And *that's* why my head is hurting. I'm pretty sure I'm right about my conclusions, but I really don't want to be.

"You manage to get any rest?" she asks me.

I shake my head. She looks at me, full of sympathy.

"Honey, you really need to sleep. What's it been? Twenty-four hours?"

"At least."

"You're going to be no use to anyone if you're walking around half-dead. When we land, you're getting some rest before we do anything else. No arguing."

"Tori, I can't. This whole thing—"

"This whole thing can wait," she says, interrupting me before I can protest further. "GlobaTech can handle it, or they can hand it over to the authorities and let them handle it. The whole world isn't resting on your shoulders, Adrian, no matter how much you think otherwise."

I try to smile, but I don't manage it. "Tori, that's just it. Right now, this whole thing *is* on my shoulders. GlobaTech basically doesn't exist at the moment. Josh and Bob Clark are on the run because the NSA closed them down. The CIA has been trying to kill me for the last week. The government is convinced it's me behind all this, working with the bad guys, and I've been trying to figure out why their intel is so off. And thanks to all these…" I point to the papers next to me. "Now I know why. And we can't trust the authorities. We can't trust anyone."

"Adrian, what the hell's going on?"

"I'll tell you when we're all together."

The pilot comes back on to tell us we're making our final descent and will be landing in a few moments. We both sit back and strap in.

By the time the wheels touch the ground, I've played out every outcome I can think of in my head and decided on the best course of action. What I'm about to go up against is unprecedented—not just for me but for everyone. I can't do it on my own, but I've never asked anyone to willingly fight alongside me before. I don't need to ask Josh because I know *he* will, whether I want him to or not, but involving people in my fights isn't something I've ever been comfortable doing. Sadly, what I know now is about to change everything.

We taxi to a stop, and the stewardess opens the door for us. I thank her and the pilots, then step off the plane. I see Josh waiting for me. The weather is welcoming and warm, despite the late hour—a nice change from the harsh winds and perpetual dullness of Eastern Europe. We shake hands, and he hugs Tori before saying anything.

"The rest of us are inside," he announces. "I took the liberty of speaking to Agent Wallis and inviting him to the party. I trust him, Adrian, and we need all the help we can get."

I nod gravely. "I know we do."

He sees the look and becomes instantly concerned. "What's wrong?"

I hand him the pile of papers and files. "We took these from the underground lab in Pripyat. Clara had them, along with a slideshow of the Cerberus blueprints."

"What are they?" he asks, briefly skimming through them.

"They're classified CIA documents, mostly."

His eyes widen. "Clara had these?"

"She did. But more importantly, the Armageddon Initiative had these. Let's get inside. I don't care who's in the room with us anymore, Josh. I know enough to make an educated guess what's really going on here, and if I'm right—and I hope I'm not—then we've got a helluva fight on our hands."

There's a Jeep waiting for us at the end of the runway with an MP in the driver's seat. Josh climbs in next to him, and I help Tori up into the back before stepping in next to her. He drives us across the base, following the road system past the barracks and training grounds. There's a small presence of troops doing exercises and marching, but they ignore us.

"Are we safe here?" I ask Josh.

He looks over his shoulder to reply. "As far as I know, the military don't give a shit about what the government-funded acronyms are doing. I don't think they're on our side, but they definitely aren't on theirs, so this is neutral ground and safe enough."

The driver stops outside the main office building in the center of the compound, and we all get out of the Jeep without a word. The building is low and wide—only two stories high, but it takes up most of the road. It's a basic, low-cost structure, which is typical for the Army. Cheap, simple, effective—should be their motto.

We follow Josh inside. He leads us down a corridor, past the guard at the front desk on the right-hand side, and into a conference room, which is the last door on the left. Inside, sitting around a rectangular table, is Sheriff Raynor, Bob Clark, and Agent Tom Wallis of the FBI. They all stand as we enter. Raynor's the first to approach us. Tori throws her arms around him, giving him no choice but to awkwardly pat her back.

"I'm glad you're safe," he says. She lets him go and steps aside, and he extends his hand to me, which I shake gladly. "Glad you're home safe too."

"Thanks, John. I'm sorry I've roped you into all this."

He waves his hand dismissively. "I'm about due for some action. Nothing's happened in Devil's Spring for ten years, not since someone stole Hoops's sign from outside his shop."

I smile regretfully. "Well, taking out the NSA is one thing..." I turn to the rest of the room. "But what we're up against now is something else entirely. You might wanna sit down for this."

Everyone exchanges looks of concern and takes their seats, except Wallis, who walks over to me. He's looking good in a new suit. He has a slightly more weathered complexion than the last time I saw him, but I do tend to have that effect on people. Life's always a bit more stressful after I've been in town, sadly.

"I know you're reluctant about my involvement," he says. "But I can help you, and Josh trusts me, so I hope you will too."

I nod and pat his arm. "It's good to see you, Tom. And yes, I trust you. Frankly, right now, I need all the help I can get."

He nods back and takes his seat. I walk to the head of the table on the left of the room and look at everyone. Josh and Clark are on my left; Raynor and Wallis are on my right. Tori is at the opposite end to me, looking out of place.

I drop the files I took from Clara on the table in front of me.

"Guys, we have a big fucking problem."

32

The room is silent with anticipation and a morbid curiosity to know the full extent of the threat we face. I gesture to the documents in front of me. "I took these from the underground facility in Pripyat. Clara Fox had them in her possession. She also had a detailed presentation on a big screen showing blueprints of the Cerberus satellite. Tom, are you up to speed on what we all know so far?"

Wallis nods. "Pretty much. I wasn't really any help. You guys knew everything I did and filled in most of my blanks for me."

"I thought that might be the case. But I'm grateful for your help here. Having a government agency on our side is a luxury we didn't expect to have, and it'll make a big difference if you can make sure your people understand that everyone in this room is trying to help."

"We do," he says, nodding.

"Good. So, here's the story so far: back in New York,

when I first took Yalafi Hussein's laptop, he was meeting someone dressed in a four-star general's uniform who had protection from guys in dark glasses and earpieces. He was almost certainly American but remained an unknown factor. My flight out of New York was hijacked by a CIA black ops unit called D.E.A.D., who re-directed my plane to Colombia and tried to kill me. I escaped and linked up with a local outfit that turned out to be a cartel, run by one Carlos Vega. In keeping with tradition, after an hour or so in my company, they tried to kill me too. I escaped again but not before torturing Vega and getting some information out of him."

"Hang on. I thought the cartels were extinct?" asks Wallis. "Since President Cunningham's reforms on the world drug trade, they can't make any money."

I nod. "It turns out he was running guns for someone in the U.S. who uses the codename Ares. He shipped weapons all over the world for him in return for a large paycheck. We already knew from GlobaTech's investigations that this Armageddon Initiative was on a recruitment drive. We then found out their interest in the Cerberus satellite from the laptop I stole. Hamaad El-Zurak is the guy running things. We found out Clara Fox took Tori and tracked them to a base in Ukraine. Our intel also said Hussein and El-Zurak had fled to Afghanistan, following my intervention in New York. With me so far?"

Everyone nods and mutters, so I continue.

"But then we have the CIA black ops unit trying to kill me, saying the laptop I stole was government property. And we have the NSA raiding GlobaTech, then my bar, before sending a team in to kill us at a safe house in Arkansas."

"This is the worrying thing," adds Josh. "We know the information these guys have is bogus because we're not the

bad guys. We can only assume that the terrorists have operatives inside these organizations, controlling what intel is
distributed and making it look like we're the enemy."

"Exactly," I continue. "But thanks to these papers, I think
I've got the missing links. The only things we need to find
out now, assuming I'm right, are the reasons *why* and what
the endgame really is."

I sort through the papers and pull out two files. One is a
classified file outlining the proposal for the Cerberus
project. The other is a redacted personnel file. I throw them
to the center of the table.

"The first shows the initial outline of what Cerberus was
to be used for. The White House submitted the proposal to a
Senate subcommittee three months after Cunningham took
office. It mentions everything GlobaTech eventually did to
it. The plan was to advertise it to the public as a weapon
against terrorism, to be used to safeguard our own nuclear
arsenal and state secrets. The subcommittee's response is
also there. It details how they rejected the idea, saying it was
too open to corruption and that the methods intended were
a violation of the public's right to privacy."

Wallis takes the file and skims through it. Raynor frowns
and looks at me. "Forgive the stupid question, but if this
satellite still does all of those things, how did they get the
Senate to approve it?"

"That's a perfectly fair question, John, and I haven't
figured it out yet."

I turn to Josh, who's already produced his laptop and is
looking at me, smiling. "On it, Boss."

He buries himself in the keyboard and starts tapping
away.

"So, what's in the personnel file?" asks Clark, who's been
silent so far.

I let out a heavy sigh. "That would be our mystery four-star general from New York."

Josh looks up from his work. The tension in the room heightens as people hold their breath. I lean over and open the file, revealing a large color picture of the man I saw in Hussein's apartment.

"Folks, meet General Thomas Jack Matthews."

Everyone frowns at the anti-climax—except Wallis, which is what I expected.

"You must mean another General Matthews, right?" he asks.

"Another?" queries Tori. "Who's the first one?"

Wallis looks at me, and I raise an eyebrow and sigh. "I'm afraid not, Tom. There's only one, and he's currently the director of the CIA."

The heavy silence that descends is palpable. No one knows what to say or where to look. The man in charge of the Central Intelligence Agency was meeting with a known terrorist, discussing a top-secret government satellite that can control the world's nuclear arsenal. There are so many things that aren't right about that, I don't know where to start.

Josh stands and begins pacing up and down the left side of the room. I find myself doing the same thing on the opposite side. Now that every piece of information we have is out in the open, we need to fit them together.

I glance over at Josh, who is muttering to himself, working through every theory he comes up with. Working at GlobaTech, away from me, has been good for him. It's given him a renewed purpose, a fresh challenge to apply himself to—which is exactly what he needed after watching my back for half his life. But looking at him now, I see him step back into his old role so easily, it's like he never stopped.

"So, we all think Matthews is Ares, right?" he says.

Everyone at the table exchanges a look that says not one of them has thought about it yet.

"Yes," I reply.

"So, it's fairly safe to assume that he's the one behind the CIA's attempt to kill you in Colombia, as well as the source of information that the NSA's been working with..."

"I agree."

"But why?"

"I don't know. That's one of the problems we have—finding out what all this leads to."

"What's the other problem?" asks Raynor.

"Stopping them when we've got the entire CIA trying to kill us."

He sighs. "Yeah, that'll do it..."

I look at Clark. "Bob, get on Josh's laptop. Do a background check on Matthews. Look for any history of extremist beliefs—anything that could explain why he'd work with the Armageddon Initiative and betray his country."

"On it," he says. He slides into Josh's seat and taps away on the keyboard.

"Josh, tell me how El-Zurak is going to take control of Cerberus."

He shrugs. "I don't see how he can. Even if he had some tech out in the mountains, there's no way he'll have anything sophisticated enough to hack a government satellite from there."

I click my fingers, remembering the one piece of information I've not told them.

Whoops.

"Oh, shit. Yeah... he's not in Afghanistan. Hussein and El-Zurak are in the U.S. Clara told me."

"And you believe her?" questions Wallis.

I look over at him and nod. "Yes, I do."

"So, where is he?" asks Josh.

"I don't know, but I know how to find him."

"How?"

"Tell me how he'd take control of Cerberus."

He nods slowly, seeing what I'm getting at. If we know *how* they'd do it, then there's a good chance we'll be able to figure out *where* they need to be to do it. I imagine there aren't too many locations with the hardware capable of taking down a satellite.

"They'd need to access the servers first," explains Josh. "They'd need to hack in past the firewalls and then upload codes to give them control over each function."

"Let's assume they won't be content with just our nukes. How easily could they steal other peoples' nukes?"

"End of the day, that's what Cerberus was built for," he says with a shrug. "I obviously wasn't involved in designing that particular feature, but there would almost certainly be an interface for doing it."

"Where do these codes come from? Are they military?"

"Do you mean, can the CIA provide them? No, I don't think they can."

"So, they have to hack those codes, presumably? Is that easy?"

Josh shakes his head. "It's virtually impossible. It's beyond my capabilities, certainly."

"Do you know anyone who could do it?"

"That would be a short list... but no, I can't think of anyone."

"So, could El-Zurak have someone who could do that?"

"It's possible but unlikely."

"Okay, so that means he already has access to the codes.

If he didn't get them from Matthews, we need to find out how he got them and fast. With Clara dead, they won't be hanging around."

Clark interrupts us by slamming his fist on the desk. "Goddammit!"

"What?" I ask.

"Nothing on General Matthews. The guy's a Boy Scout. A patriot, through and through. He had a decorated military career and worked as a consultant for years before being given the position of CIA director by President Cunningham. If I weren't involved in this mess, I'd swear blind there's no way he'd be working against his country with terrorists."

"Okay, so that's not the way to go. Josh, keep working the Cerberus angle. Where would El-Zurak need to be to hijack the satellite?"

He resumes his pacing, and I let the room fall silent. I walk over to Tori and sit on the desk in front of her. She smiles at me.

"How are you doing?" she asks.

"I'm all right. Just tired of not knowing what we're meant to be doing, y'know?"

"You'll sort it. Don't worry."

"How are you, anyway? You've been through some crazy shit recently. How are you holdin' up?"

She throws me a salute and winks. "I can deal. It's fine."

I know she's lying. I see in her eyes that she's accepting everything that's happening because her mind isn't allowing her to believe it's all real. When all this is over, it'll hit her like a freight train, and she'll really struggle. And when that happens, I'll wrap my arms around her and tell her it'll all be okay. But for now, I'm happy to let her show me she's strong.

What's that saying? *Fake it 'til you make it...*

"Sonofabitch!" yells Josh behind me. I turn and everyone else looks up at him.

"What?" I ask.

"I'm an idiot! I'm really sorry, Boss. It didn't occur to me before. Cerberus, like any other satellite, has to be monitored from the ground. Most things like this are run from NASA. We have our own site in Santa Clarita that tracks the satellite network we run. Cerberus is a NASA-funded project but was outsourced to a few different companies—including GlobaTech. Consequently, the main servers and control hub were housed in an outsourced location."

I stand, hoping I know where this is going and failing to contain my excitement. "Where, Josh?"

He ushers Clark out of his seat and takes his place in front of his laptop once more. A few moments later, he spins the screen around to show the room.

"ComForce Securities. They specialize in protecting companies worth lots of money who are happy to pay to outsource their security. They have a good reputation in the industry and handle many large contracts—like the Cerberus gig with NASA. The servers are housed inside their Atlanta office. ComForce own the building, so it'll be protected by their own security personnel, but the people who work there are likely NASA. They won't have the codes, but they process the data and feed it back to the CIA if something is flagged as a potential threat to national security."

"That's where El-Zurak is going to hijack the satellite from." I turn to Wallis. "Tom, take all this information and give it to your superior—someone you trust."

He's already on his feet, gathering the files together. "I'm on it."

"And Tom, make sure you *can* trust them. I'm not suggesting this is the case, but if the director of the CIA is involved, and he's been leading the NSA astray to help him assist the terrorists and take us out, there's no reason why he can't have compromised another agency as well. Just watch your back."

He nods. "I've got to make some calls, right away."

He heads out of the room, closing the door behind him. Raynor looks at me. "Do you trust him?"

I nod. "Yeah, I do. He had my back before, and I see no reason why he wouldn't again."

Raynor nods and stands, pacing slowly around the room. I recognize the look on his face. He's trying to wrap his head around something and can't, and he's frustrated by it.

I turn to Josh. "That's good work, man. How quickly can you get me on the road to Atlanta?"

Tori stands and grabs my arm. Her eyes are full of concern. "Ady, you can't go there alone. Let the FBI handle it now. What more can you possibly do?"

I sigh and massage my temples. I'm running on empty, and my mind won't switch off long enough for my eyes to close for five minutes. But I can't stop. Not now. Not so close to the end.

"Babe, I have to. I have to see this through to the end. We've all been through so much, and they've attacked me too many times for me to just walk away now."

She punches my arm in frustration, raising her voice. "Adrian! I know I wanted you to fix this, but everything you just said is beyond any one man—even you! You've just given all the information to the FBI. They're going to have teams of men equipped to handle this. Why can't you just walk away from it? You're not the comic book character you used to be! I don't want to lose you!"

Her eyes fill with tears. Behind me, I hear everyone holding their breath, unsure whether I'm going to respect the pleas of my girlfriend.

"Tori, you can make all the jokes you want about me, my name, or the fact that I don't look like a killer to you. But the bottom line is this: I'm probably the deadliest man alive. I say that with no ego. I'm simply stating a fact. I was a successful and highly coveted hitman for a long time. Gangsters, terrorists, drug lords... they would crap themselves at the mention of my name. Everybody wanted to hire me, and nobody wanted me coming after them."

I pause, debating whether to continue, but I figure there's no point in stopping now.

"I used to lie to my wife and daughter about what I did for a living. I thought it would protect them. One day, I took a contract that incurred the wrath of someone too big for me to handle at the time. They came after me, and when I wasn't there, they slaughtered my family. I found them, I panicked, and I ran. I ran for nine years with Josh at my side. I went through some dark times. You hear people talk about their demons... I used my demons to help me become a more effective killer. They made me who I was. If anyone tried to push open my door, what was waiting behind it would annihilate them. That was my life until I decided I couldn't live with the guilt anymore. With Josh's help, I went back and destroyed the person who took my family away from me. I took everything he had and killed him with my bare hands."

Tori's shaking, staring at me as if I'm a stranger standing in her home. But I continue anyway.

"These bastards have spent the last week trying to kill

me. They kidnapped you, they destroyed my bar, and they've managed to turn every government agency in the country against me and my friends—all because we tried to help. I can't let that stand, Tori. I don't know how to just forget about this and walk away, to let someone else finish *my* fight. I'm gonna find Hamaad El-Zurak, and I'm gonna look him in the eye before I put a bullet in his head. That's what's gonna happen next, okay?"

She takes a moment but seems to unfreeze. She nods and sits down silently. I take a breath, realizing I might've overstepped the mark a little. But I'm tired... no, I'm *exhausted*... and more than a little on edge because of what comes next.

I turn back to Josh, who is looking at the laptop again. He's been around me long enough to know that if I have an outburst like that, it's best to not say anything until I do.

"Josh, how quickly can we get to Atlanta?" I ask him, calmer now.

"The drive is a little over eleven hours, east along the I-20. If we set off now, we'll make it by morning."

"Borrow two vehicles from here if you can. We need to leave in the next fifteen minutes. You'll come with me and Tori. Bob, you'll go with the good sheriff and Wallis."

"What's the plan when we get there?" asks Clark.

I shrug. "Tell you when we get there."

Josh smiles and packs up his laptop. Everyone stands, and we file out of the room. I wait for Tori, who walks out without looking at me. I follow her out, turning the light off in the room and closing the door.

One way or the other, Atlanta will be where all this ends. I just hope we can get to El-Zurak before he takes control of Cerberus.

33

The eleven hours flew by for me—mostly because I slept for a good portion of them. We managed to borrow two military-issue sedans. Josh was happy driving, so I sat in the back with Tori. We talked about her concerns and the things she didn't understand. I told her the full story about my family and Wilson Trent, and we fell silent. Soon after, we fell asleep.

I slept like the dead.

I've just woken up. Tori is lying on me, still snoring. I smile at her and look up, catching Josh's eye in the rearview mirror.

"It's alive!" he says. "Feel better?"

"Much—thanks. Sorry I left you to do all the driving."

"You've been leaving me to do the driving for fourteen years. Why should today be any different?"

He smiles. I give him the finger before smiling back. "Where are we up to?"

"We're maybe fifteen minutes away from the ComForce site. I've just spoken to Bob. They're about a mile behind us."

"Okay. Has Wallis heard anything back from the FBI?"

"He said we've got a counterterrorism squad en route to rendezvous with us here. That will help dramatically. He did say he had to take point once we're there, though. It'll be the FBI's show. We're just concerned citizens."

"Whatever. As long as they get the job done, I don't care who thinks they're in charge."

I look out the window as we reach the outskirts of Atlanta. The cold morning sun lights up the gray skyline. The flow of traffic slows as we reach the city, which I guess is expected. There are almost half a million people living in the state capital, so mid-morning will be busy.

The ComForce office we're looking for is on John Portman Boulevard, not far from the Georgia Dome. Josh seems to think this is a good security measure. There's little chance of people looking for the servers in a civilian building.

I see the Dome up ahead on the left, looming across the sky as we head east along Mitchell Street. Next to me, Tori stirs and sits up straight, rubbing her eyes.

"Are we there yet?" she asks groggily.

"Yeah, just a few minutes out. When we get there, I want you and Josh to wait in the car, okay?"

"I don't think so!" shouts Josh from the front before she can say anything.

"Not up for debate, man. You're staying here for two reasons. One, you're going to protect Tori at all costs. Two, I want you on your laptop, doing whatever you can to stop anyone else from hacking into the building to try and stop us. I'm sure there's something you can do along those lines?"

He goes to argue but stops himself, realizing there's little point. He lets out a heavy sigh and nods. "Yeah, I can do a few things that might delay anyone trying to hack the servers. I can remotely block the Wi-Fi signal for a start, which will make life difficult."

"Good, then you can do that from here. I'll leave you one of my Berettas. If anyone you don't know comes within twenty feet of the car, put a bullet in them."

He sighs again. "Got it."

I turn to Tori, who looks upset. "Listen, I know you don't want me going in there, but I have to finish this. I need you to understand that."

"What if... I don't want anything to happen to you," she says, her voice cracking.

Josh glances around in his seat. "Tori, sweetheart, I've seen this guy break into a house full of armed mafia goons and take them all out on his own. We're talking thirty-plus guys, easy. Just a couple of days ago, he took out twenty NSA agents sent to kill us. Like it or not, he's a dangerous bastard when he wants to be. And when his little Inner Satan gets pissed enough, he will literally raise Hell. How do you think he got his name?"

She looks at me with bemusement. "So, you really *are* this big, scary badass? Not just a soldier with a comic book fetish?"

The car swerves as Josh laughs so hard that he loses control temporarily. I throw him a look, which he sees in the mirror, and he holds his hands up in silent apology.

I turn back to Tori. "It's things like this that make me love you more. But yes, I am *that* scary and badass. And if El-Zurak shows his face here tonight, I'm gonna make sure he knows exactly who I am before he dies."

We pull over across the street from the offices, and Josh kills the engine.

"Then what are you waiting for?" she says with some initial reluctance. "Go be a badass."

She leans over and kisses me, then I get out of the car. I stand on the sidewalk and stretch my entire body. Then I walk around the car, open the trunk, and take out one of my Berettas, which I tuck into the back of my waistband. I take the other by the barrel and discreetly pass it to Josh through his open window. "Be good to it..."

"I know, I know," he replies as he takes it. "...and it'll be good to me."

I smile and walk back around the car to stand on the sidewalk. I look across at the building. It takes up most of the block and towers a good twenty stories over the city. A fluorescent glow bathes the lobby, where a front desk takes up half the floor space. There are three guards behind it and a gateway metal detector to the left of it.

I look up and down the street, trying to figure out how many people are going to storm this building, where they're going to come from, and when. I have to assume that since El-Zurak faked being in Afghanistan, he knew about this place before we did. But it can't be easy planning an assault in the middle of a large American city without attracting too much attention too soon—even if the CIA is helping him.

It's got to be imminent. It'll be any time in the next twelve hours, I expect. It looks like we've got here first, which gives us chance to do this right and warn people beforehand. Once the FBI arrive, if the Armageddon Initiative *do* attack the building, not even the CIA would risk a public confrontation where they could be seen fighting against the people trying to stop the terrorists. The more public this gets, the better it is for us.

We can prove we've done nothing wrong—if you don't count the multiple NSA agents I've killed. Any publicity will only serve to highlight the wrongdoings of the people involved who are fighting on the wrong side, and that works for me.

I look left and see the other sedan approaching. It pulls up behind us, and everyone climbs out. Josh and Tori join us on the sidewalk, and we stand huddled in silence for a moment.

"Wallis, what's the latest?" I ask when they approach.

"The Special Agent-In-Charge of my Counterterrorism Task Force has all the information and theories we have. A team is on its way; they're about ten minutes out. He said to sit tight, wait for them, and then we'll approach the building. They'll set up the perimeter, and you guys can come in with me. I'll speak with whoever's in charge in there and get them to tighten their security presence on site, and we'll see what happens."

I nod. Then I turn to Josh and gesture with my head for us to step away from the group. He follows me, and we sit on the hood of our car, just out of earshot. I keep my voice low anyway.

"I don't like it."

"Which part?"

"The *waiting for the FBI to arrive* part. Doesn't feel right."

"You think it's a set-up?"

I shrug. "Maybe. But it might just be paranoia."

"Always go with your gut," he says reassuringly. "You taught me that."

I smile.

"You think Wallis is in on this?" he asks.

I shake my head. "Nah, my gut says Wallis is with us. I'm just not convinced his boss is."

I stand and Josh follows.

"It's not paranoia if the bastards are really after you..." he mutters.

We walk back to the group.

"I think we should go in now," I announce. "We'll wait for the back-up from inside."

"Negative, Adrian," says Wallis. "We wait for FBI support."

I shake my head. "We don't need support right now. We'll need it once the bad guys turn up. Right now, we're just wasting time when we could be establishing ourselves inside and preparing for an attack. We need to give these ComForce guys all the notice we can, not stand outside for ten minutes jerking off."

I study his body language. He's frustrated with me—or maybe just frustrated in general, which would be understandable. His shoulders are slumped slightly forward, which signifies defeat. I'm assuming he knows I have a valid point, and at least part of him agrees with it.

Now to sway his decision.

"Tom, I'm going in anyway, right now. It'll go a lot smoother if you flash your credentials for me, but they're not essential."

"Ah, shit," he mutters. Then he lets out a heavy sigh. "Fine."

I smile. "Good man! Right, Bob, establish a comms link with Josh. He's going to run point on the tech side of things from out here. Tori will be with him. You'll be my tech on the inside. Sheriff, any law enforcement muscle you can lend will be gratefully appreciated. Tom, you can take lead on it. Flash your badge and say whatever you've got to say to get them to believe us."

Everyone mutters their understanding.

Wallis nods. "And why are you there again?"

I shrug. "In case things go wrong and some people need to be shot."

"Figured…"

I turn to Josh and we bump fists.

"Good luck," he says.

I nod. "You too. Keep her safe." I turn to Tori, wrap one arm around her waist, and hold her close. I kiss her forehead. "Do whatever Josh says, okay?"

She squeezes me tightly with both arms and buries her head in my chest, nodding against it.

We part, and I look up and down the street one last time. I see nothing that raises a red flag, so I cross over. Raynor, Wallis, and Clark follow me. I walk up to the main doors and pull them open. We step inside, and one of the guards walks over to greet us. Wallis flashes his badge straight away, to minimize any resistance or delays. The other two guards come from around the desk and join their colleague, looking curious and excited.

"Fellas, I'm Special Agent Tom Wallis with the FBI Counterterrorism Task Force. We have reason to believe there's an imminent threat to this facility, and we need your assistance."

The guard on the left—a tall man with a short, unkempt beard and red hair—shakes his head. "There must be some mistake. We're just a security firm. What kind of threat is it?"

"Are you aware of what's stored in this building?"

The first guard shrugs. "Nothing. It's just an office. We've got our accounting department on the twelfth floor, and the directors have been in this week for their bi-monthly board meetings, but that's it, really. It's mostly a service center."

Wallis glances at me questioningly. I discreetly nod in response. I believe him. He's just a security guard. There's no reason to trust him with confidential information.

"Sir, there is extremely sensitive... *material* on site belonging to one of your largest clients, and some really bad people intend to steal it. This is a threat to national security, and I'm going to need your help securing this building. I've got a team on the way to set up a perimeter and—"

The guard on the right holds up his hand, interrupting Wallis mid-speech. He's a smaller, more rotund individual. I doubt he's seen his belt buckle in twenty years.

"Wait a minute. You can't just waltz in here and tell us how to do our jobs. We're a goddamn security firm! You're gonna need to speak to our supervisor before you take one more step inside this building. Do you understand?"

Wallis goes to respond but stops himself, perhaps realizing that further discussions with this guy will only delay matters even more. He steps to one side and turns to me with a somewhat begrudging look on his face. I graciously nod and step forward.

I look the guard up and down. "What's your name?"

"Dixon," he replies.

"Okay, Mr. Dixon, let me clear a couple of things up for you. See my friend's shiny little badge? That outranks any supervisor you've got, so their input is irrelevant. My friend also told you this is a matter of national security. Those two words mean no one cares about your procedures. You've got, I'm guessing, at least one entire floor of this building dedicated to running a computer system for one of your clients. Your client has its own employees working here around the clock. You must have some idea what I'm talking about if you sit behind that front desk all day. What floor are the non-ComForce personnel working on right now?"

He looks me up and down, just as I did a moment ago. He seems apprehensive, maybe even a little intimidated, but unsure why. I figure him for the most senior of the three, so he'll want to try and exert some authority over me.

"And just who might you be? I ain't seen no badge from you."

"I'm a consultant. I don't need a badge. I just need the FBI guy to vouch for me. Which he does, by the way. Now Mr. Dixon, I won't lie—I'm not big on wasting time, and my patience isn't what it used to be, so just tell us which floor and we'll be on our way."

As he's about to speak, five black SUVs pull up outside with blue lights silently flashing. Each one has the FBI logo emblazoned along the side in large, white lettering. I look at Wallis, who nods and makes for the door to meet them.

I look at Dixon. "And these guys *definitely* aren't big on wasting time..."

His eyes go wide. He's probably never seen anything like this other than on TV shows. "F-f-floor sixteen. Bunch of guys work there twenty-four-seven. They're not our people, but we check them in and out. N-nice fellas."

"Thanks, Dixon. You're a good man."

I turn to Clark, who nods and sets off across the lobby. Raynor and I start to follow him, but we all stop in our tracks as the front doors burst open behind us. We turn and see Wallis hurriedly walking alongside an FBI agent, whom I assume is in charge of the men outside. Behind them, four of the agents from outside are marching, kitted out in full riot gear, with their MP5 submachine guns locked, loaded, and aimed forward.

"This is *not* why you're here!" says Wallis, imploring the agent in charge to listen to him. The agent ignores him and strides purposefully over to us.

"Adrian Hughes?" he asks me as he stops in front of us. His voice is deep and gravelly, like he smokes forty a day. His eyes are deep-set and dark, and his tanned complexion makes him look Mediterranean.

I shake my head. "Nope."

His eyes narrow, and he squares up to me. "Don't fuck me around, asshole."

I smile. "I could say the same to you. Thought you were here to help?"

"I'm here to detain a small group of known terrorists until people arrive to take them away."

"Good. So am I."

"Are you fucking with me? Or are you genuinely this stupid?"

I smile again. "Bit of both, probably. But we're on the same side. You should listen to Agent Wallis."

The agent glances back at Wallis, who's looking apologetically at me. Then the armed unit moves to surround us.

"Check them for weapons," he says.

I take a step back as the first man from the unit makes a move. I raise my right hand and point my finger at him. "I swear to God, if you touch me, I'm gonna shove that gun so far down your throat, you'll be shitting bullets. I won't tell you again."

The guy stops. He isn't intimidated, but I put that down to sheer ignorance. Nevertheless, he stops and makes a point of readjusting his grip on his MP5.

Raynor steps in between the armed unit and me, his hands held out to the sides. He looks at the man in charge. "Agent, I'm Sheriff John Raynor from Devil's Spring in Texas. As a fellow lawman, I'm asking you to listen to what we have to say. We're not—"

"Texas?" he says, cutting him off. He looks him over with something akin to disgust, lingering a moment longer on Raynor's hat. "I never would've guessed. Listen, Sheriff, you're so far out of your jurisdiction, you need a passport to take a piss. As far as I'm concerned, you're a civilian, and you will do as you're told or face being detained along with your boy here." He puts his hand on the left shoulder of the first guy in the unit. "Search them and confiscate everything. If any of them resist, shoot them in the leg."

He turns and walks off, brushing past Wallis, who looks at me again before following the agent out of the building.

"You heard the man," says the guy. "Search 'em."

The unit steps in toward us, letting their weapons hang loose while the first guy covers us. They take Clark's laptop and phone, and then Raynor's gun, before pushing them both off to the side. One of the guys walks off with the items and another aims his gun at them. The remaining two look at me.

"Now you," says the first guy. "Hands to the sides, feet shoulder-width apart. No sudden movements."

I clench my jaws muscles and reluctantly obey. I have no doubt he'll shoot me, and now isn't the time to make any *more* enemies than I already have. He pats me down and takes my Beretta from my back.

"Now what?" I ask as they step back.

"Outside," he replies, gesturing with this gun.

We all file outside. I see Josh and Tori waiting for us on the sidewalk, surrounded by more FBI agents in riot gear.

"What the hell's going on?" asks Josh when I walk over.

I shrug. "I have no idea."

"Wallis?"

I shake my head. "No idea either. This isn't him."

The agent in charge walks over to us, with Wallis just behind him. "The five of you are being transported out of here in a few minutes."

I raise an eyebrow. "Not by the FBI, I'm guessing?"

His eyes narrow again. "No, another team is on its way." He turns to Wallis. "Good work, Agent."

Wallis simply hangs his head, knowing someone has played the game better than him.

"What's your name?" I ask.

The guy stares at Wallis a moment longer, then looks back at me. "I'm Special Agent-in-Charge David Freeman. Why?"

"When all this is over, and the world's gone to shit, and the American people are looking for someone to blame, I want to know whose name to give them. Now I do."

He holds my gaze momentarily, then turns on his heels, striding off toward the huddle of armed men. The unit of four spreads out in a semi-circle around us, guns trained in our direction.

I look at Wallis. "What happens now?"

"I don't know," he replies. "I'm sorry, Adrian. I thought I could trust him. I thought they were here to help."

"It's not your fault. They probably *were* here to help. I suspect they got a call on their way here with new orders."

He frowns. "From whom?"

A large black transit van approaches and screeches to a halt nearby, with a matching black sedan behind it. The side doors slide open, and three men jump out. They're dressed in black with no marking on their uniform. Freeman moves to meet them, but they barge past him, heading straight for us. They frog-march us to the van and line us up. Tori looks at me with fear in her eyes.

"It's all right, babe," I say, trying to reassure her. "We'll be fine."

In truth, I'm not sure we will be.

Before any of us can react, they secure our hands behind our backs using zip ties, and bags are placed over our heads.

We're ushered into the back of the van, and in the darkness, I hear the door slide shut. I hear the scuffling as we all re-position ourselves so that we're sitting upright against the sides.

"Adrian, I'm scared," whispers Tori. Her voice cracks with emotion.

"Don't be. We've got rights. They can't hurt us. Just lawyer up and plead ignorance. You'll be out of this in an hour."

"What about you?"

I sigh. "I... might have a bit more explaining to do."

34

The bag is whipped off my head, and my eyes sting in the bright lights. I squint until they adjust. It's disorienting to travel with your eyes covered. I have no idea how long we were on the road, nor where we went.

I blink a few times and look around me. I'm in a small room, no bigger than ten by ten. There's a mirror along the wall to my left. There's a table in front of me and a chair opposite. I'm sitting with my hands still bound behind me and my arms resting over the back of my chair. There's a constant, low buzz from the lights above me and a faint smell of disinfectant in the air. The door's on my right in the far corner.

And that's it.

I turn and look at the mirror. It has to be a two-way. I wonder who's behind it, watching me...

I hope everyone else is all right. I suspect they're all in

similar rooms. I'm not concerned about Tori. She has nothing to do with this. She's a victim, plain and simple. Whoever took us doesn't have any grounds for holding her.

It's Josh and Clark I'm worried about. GlobaTech is on the NSA's radar, and they've been heavily involved in tracking the Armageddon Initiative and running missions to stop them. Even before I got dragged into all this, they were elbow-deep in terrorists. They're going to get both barrels here.

The door opens and a man walks in. He's wearing a black suit and a bright white shirt with the top button unfastened. His red and brown striped tie is loosened slightly around his neck. He looks young—compared to me, at least. Clean-cut and clean-shaven. Full of self-importance.

CIA.

I smile at him as he sits down opposite me. He flashes a sideways glance at the mirror, then clasps his hands on the desk and leans forward.

"Who do you work for?" he says.

I tilt my head slightly, over-emphasizing that I'm weighing him up. "Aren't you meant to introduce yourself? Tell me this conversation's being recorded? Read me my rights?"

He remains silent.

"Oh, I see. Let me guess: your name's Smith, this isn't being recorded, and I have no rights anymore?"

Silence.

"I'll take that as a yes. Don't worry... I used to be a *Smith* as well."

He takes a slow, relaxed breath. "Who do you work for?"

"Myself."

"Who do you work for?"

I raise an eyebrow. "Are you deaf?"

Silence.

"I own a bar in Texas called The Ferryman. It's due for some renovation work, but it's a nice place. You should come in for a drink."

This guy should be a poker player. His face betrays nothing. But I'm just getting started...

"What were you doing in Atlanta?" he asks.

He said that in the past tense, so I'm guessing wherever I am right now, it isn't Atlanta.

I shrug. "Just trying to help."

"Who do you work for?"

I sigh. "Look, I used to sit where you are, back in the day. I know the techniques. Ask the same question over and over again until it angers the prisoner enough that they lose their temper and let slip the answer you suspect they're lying about. That won't work, and I'll tell you why. I'm not lying. I'm not a bad guy. I'm not a terrorist. I don't work for anyone. Ask me what I've been doing for the last two weeks."

He glances at the mirror again.

"Are you allowed to ask me anything other than *who do I work for*?"

"Tell me your story."

I nod. "Okay. Okay... now we're getting somewhere. One question before I start. Do you know who I am?"

He's silent again.

"I'll take that as a yes. Okay, a couple of weeks ago, three guys walked into my bar. I know that sounds like the start of a joke, but..."

He remains silent and expressionless.

My smile fades. I shrug. "Forgot you guys don't have a sense of humor. Anyway, they asked to speak to me in private, and they told me a man called Yalafi Hussein sent them to offer me a job. I told them I was retired and not in the least bit interested in working for them or their cause. They didn't like being told no, so we discussed it further, and I threw them out of my bar with a few broken bones."

His expression remains deadpan. He's unimpressed and doesn't believe me. He simply gestures with his hands for me to continue.

"Terrorists from all over the world then flocked to my bar and turned it into Swiss cheese in an effort to kill me. I took them out, and that's when GlobaTech made contact."

The guy shifts in his seat a little. "GlobaTech are known terrorists. Are you admitting your involvement in their activities?"

I sigh. "They're not terrorists. They're a private military contractor who were approached by the bad guys over twelve months ago. They rejected their offer back then and have been tracking them ever since, gathering intel to share with government agencies in an effort to stop a potential threat."

"We have evidence to the contrary," he replies nonchalantly.

"Show me."

"No."

"Why not?"

"Because I don't have to prove anything to you. You're the one being interrogated here."

"So, do you guys just believe the first thing you're told nowadays? Back when I was on your books, we'd have to verify intel before acting based on it."

"Back in your day, you must've had questionable sources."

He immediately falls silent. His face—more specifically, his left eye—betrays him for a split-second. He squints with his eye, which I spot as his tell for when he's made a mistake or is losing his composure.

Got you.

"What makes your source so damn good that no one questions it?"

"Who says we don't question it?"

"You just did. You were told by someone that GlobaTech are the bad guys, as is anyone who's helping them, and you're blindly acting on their word. Can I guess who?"

Silence.

"A CIA unit that I used to run hijacked my plane and took me to Colombia, where they accused me of stealing government property before trying to kill me. They then shot their own commander. Care to explain that?"

He shrugs. "Seems to explain itself, doesn't it?"

"Well, I *did* steal a laptop…"

"And the orders were to retrieve it from you."

"Except I didn't steal it from a government employee. At least, I hope I didn't."

He's silent for a moment, but I can see him wanting to bite.

"What do you mean?" he asks.

And… reel him in!

"I will go on record right now—assuming there *is* a record?—and say that I stole a laptop from an apartment in New York. That apartment wasn't empty. The man in possession of the laptop at the time was Yalafi Hussein, the known terrorist who masterminded the assault on my bar. He had armed men with him. Want to know whom he was meeting when I broke in?"

I see a flicker of doubt. I know this guy will have had extensive training in the art of interrogation. Probably torture too. He'll be an expert in determining whether someone is lying or not. I know I'm telling the truth, and so does he. That confuses him because someone who's telling the truth is giving him information that directly conflicts with what he's been told by his superiors. Hence the doubt now clouding his mind.

"Enough," he says. "You've had your chance to explain your actions. If you continue to lie, you will be treated as a traitor to this country and prosecuted as such."

I chuckle. "Son, we both know I'm not lying. Go on. Go outside and ask your boss to disprove what I'm saying. I bet you my considerable fortune he gives you the brush-off, just like you've given me."

He goes to stand but hesitates.

"Go on," I urge. "I've got all day."

He waits a moment before standing, to make it seem like it was his choice and not because I told him to. Then he walks over to the door, opens it, and leaves, slamming it closed behind him.

I sigh heavily and relax. Round one to me there, I think. Now I just have to wait for someone else to walk in who outranks the first guy, and we get to dance all over again.

??:??

I reckon they've left me a good twenty minutes. Maybe half an hour but no more. They'll be in here any minute. I know as well as they do that time isn't on their side, so they can't afford to give me the full psychological work-over and leave me here for a few hours.

The door swings open a moment later.

Told you.

General Thomas Matthews, the director of the CIA, is standing before me, wearing his suit and medals with pride. I wasn't expecting to see him here, and I admit it catches me off-guard for a moment. But I recover quickly.

"Hey, General. I've not seen you since New York. How've you been?"

He remains silent, standing firm and regarding me with distaste.

"Come on, you must remember me?" I continue. "I'm the guy who barged in on your meeting with Yalafi Hussein, stole his laptop, and jumped out of a window. Say, what were you two talking about? He's not a nice guy, y'know. Strange, someone of your social standing cavorting with the likes of him..."

"Boy, I've never seen you before in my life," he says finally. His voice is powerful and suits his tall, broad frame. "Now tell me everything about the terrorist attacks you've been planning."

"Wow... okay. Where shall I start? First of all, you're a terrible liar. That first guy was better. Second, going from a lowly interrogator straight to the director is unheard of and is pretty much an admission of guilt on your part. You might as well set up a large neon sign on the roof saying, 'Free Conspiracy with Every Purchase!' The fact you're here shows you're panicking and desperate. You know exactly what I know, and I know everything about your involvement in all this... *Ares*."

His eyes betray him. He mustn't have figured we'd make the connection between him and the cartel, but after what I learned from Clara, it was *obvious* to the point where it's insulting.

He remains stubborn and steadfast in his act. "I don't know what you think you know, Adrian Hell, but you have no concept of what's at stake."

"I have a rough idea."

"You really don't, soldier. This world is a shitty place, and sometimes you gotta do things you don't agree with to get the result you want. Now tell me what you know about the terrorist attack!"

I frown.

That was an odd thing to say... and all of a sudden, it's not *my* terrorist attack anymore.

"You tell me, General. I'm still trying to figure this whole thing out. But I've been busting my ass for two weeks to stop the attacks myself. We're on the same side in this."

The general smiles. "No, we're not."

I shrug. "Yeah, you might be right there, actually."

We're both silent for a couple of minutes. Then the general opens the door and lets the first guy back in.

"Take him to a holding cell," he orders. "Once they're all together, they'll be shipped out to GitMo."

What? Guantanamo Bay?

I shake my head. "Are you fucking kidding me? That place is closed!"

The general turns to me and smiles. "Says who?"

"The president!"

He laughs. "Not *this* president."

The first guy lifts me by my arm to my feet and marches me out of the room. As I pass Matthews, I stop. "This ain't over, General. Not by a long shot."

He ignores me and looks at the guy escorting me. "Get this sonofabitch out of here."

He pushes me out of the room and leads me right, down a long corridor. The walls are plain and dirty cream. The floor is thirty-year-old linoleum. At the end, we turn left and go down some narrow stairs that lead into an underground parking lot. It's mostly empty, save for a large truck over in the far right corner.

He marches me over and opens the back of it. Inside, Clark, Josh, the sheriff, and Tori are all sitting on small benches, two on either side. Their hands are cuffed in front of them and linked via a chain to metal hoops in the floor. He pushes me up the steps and sits me down on a bench of my own, facing the door. Reaching behind me, he removes the plastic ties, then pulls out a pair of cuffs and secures me in the same way as the others.

I wait for the door to close.

"Everyone all right?" I ask.

They all nod.

I look at Tori. "Are you okay, babe? Did they hurt you?"

She shakes her head. "I'm fine. They didn't touch me."

"Any idea what's happening now?" asks Josh.

I nod. "I had a chat with General Matthews. He told me where they intend to take us, but it doesn't matter. We're getting out of here and stopping El-Zurak from taking over Cerberus. End of story."

Clark looks around the interior of the truck and pulls on his chain. "Doesn't look good, Adrian. So, where are they going to take us?"

I sigh. "Guantanamo Bay."

"Oh, shit..." says Josh.

"This is bad, isn't it?" asks Tori.

I nod. "It was meant to have been closed years ago, but apparently, it's been re-opened. And yes, it's pretty bad."

"It's where terrorists are taken to disappear," adds Josh.

"But we're not terrorists!" shouts Tori, panicking.

The truck starts up, and we move off.

I shrug with defeat. "That doesn't seem to matter anymore."

I lean back against the side of the truck and close my eyes.

Now what do I do?

35

Why is the CIA so bothered about me? And GlobaTech, for that matter. There's no way they can seriously think we're terrorists. It's obvious we've been trying to help all along. And they *must* know about the genuine threat, so why ignore it?

I'm sitting in the back of a truck with everyone in this world that I trust, secured to the floor by my wrists, as we're driven to a place where the U.S. government absolutely does *not* torture terrorists for the rest of their lives...

I've been in worse situations.

Can't think of any right now, granted, but I'm sure I have been at some point.

I look over at Josh, who's leaning back and staring at the roof. I recognize the look on his face. He's thinking of a way out of here.

Next to him, Bob Clark is staring at the floor. He's a corporate guy. Smart, loyal... a little stupid sometimes, but he's been there to help me when I've needed it, and I can't forget that. But he's not cut out for this. In a board meeting, he would be deadly. But in the line of fire, he's useless. And I don't mean that in a bad way. I just mean that he will start to panic and shut down, rendering him incapable of doing anything useful. So, by definition, he's useless.

Opposite him is John Raynor, my local sheriff and one of the most honorable men I've ever known. He's a good man and a good friend. He's stuck by me simply because I live in his town, and he sees me as his responsibility, which is nice. But I feel bad for dragging him into this. He should've cut and run after Arkansas when we ditched the NSA.

I say ditched... I mean when I killed them all.

In between him and me is Tori Watson, my girlfriend. The only woman on this planet I've ever loved besides my wife. She never knew the old me. She never knew Adrian Hell. She fell in love with the person I became when that part of me died. Clara Fox kidnapped her so that I'd go looking for her—part of a plan for her to satisfy her twisted quest for revenge against me that she'd harbored for years. When it boiled down to it, I realized she'd become irrelevant to me. But Tori went through a lot, and now she's here, backing me up unquestioningly.

These people are risking their lives to help me. The least I can do is make sure they don't have to sacrifice them as well. I need to find a way...

What's that noise?

I sit up, straining over the mechanical rumbling of the noisy engine.

That sounds like...

"What is it?" asks Josh.

I shush him and hold my hand up so that everyone knows to stay quiet.

Is that…

The noise gets louder, and the others hear it too.

Clark looks up. "Is that…"

I nod. "I reckon so."

"What is it?" asks Tori.

I point to the roof. "There's a helicopter approaching. How long have we been on the road? Anyone?"

"I'd say no longer than fifteen minutes," offers Josh.

"This type of truck is designed for long-haul transfers. If we were only going a few miles, we'd have been moved in the same type of van we were brought in."

"What does this mean?" asks Raynor.

"I doubt we're being switched to a helicopter this far into the journey. It's getting closer, so it makes sense to think it's on an intercept course with us, but whoever it is isn't here to move us anywhere."

"So, what do they want?" asks Clark.

I shrug. "I imagine we'll find out soon enough."

I sit back and try to relax. After a couple of minutes, the truck brakes sharply, and we screech to a halt. I hear both doors of the cab open and boots drop to the ground, followed by raised voices over the loud whirring of helicopter blades.

There's nothing for a few moments, then the whirring gets louder as the chopper takes off and flies away. Silence descends, and everyone exchanges concerned glances.

Then the back door unlocks and opens. Special Agent Tom Wallis is standing there, holding a set of keys. "I swear to God, this is the dumbest thing I've ever done!"

He steps inside and starts unlocking our cuffs.

"What the hell?" asks Josh.

"Long story. I asked Freeman to contact the CIA office that you were taken to and make sure you were okay. They told him you'd been questioned, admitted your guilt, and were en route to a secure facility to be processed."

"That's bullshit," I say.

"I figured. I got an FBI chopper to fly me to the CIA building, and from there, we covered a ten-mile radius until we found you."

"What happened to the driver?" asks Tori.

"He and his friend are outside on the ground, knocked out."

He frees the last of us, and we pile out onto the street.

"Where are we?" I ask.

"Just outside of Jacksonville, Florida," says Wallis.

I look around. The sun's rising, and there's already a warm breeze blowing.

"How long since we were taken from ComForce's building?"

Wallis frowns at the question.

"It's been a disorienting few hours..."

"Ah, right." He checks his watch. "Maybe eighteen hours."

I look at Josh. "We're... what? Five hours from Atlanta?"

He nods. "Easily."

"Shit. Okay, first two cars we see, we take—no questions asked. Wallis, I'm really grateful for you sticking your neck out for us like this. I can't ask you to do it anymore. I don't expect you to come with us..."

He waves his hand to dismiss my concerns. "I'm already in way over my head. If I go back now, I'll definitely lose my badge and probably my freedom. At least with you guys, I can do something good before that happens. I'm in."

I stare down the road and see a car approaching.

"Well, you've not lost that badge yet." I point to the car. "Use it."

Wallis flags the car down and feeds the poor driver the standard line about it being official government business and the FBI appreciating his cooperation. He then holds the driver's door open as he climbs out and looks at me. "You take this one. I'll flag another for the rest of us."

I nod. "Okay. Tori, John, you're with me. Get in." Raynor slides in behind the wheel, and Tori climbs in the back. I turn to the owner of the car. "Sorry, but I need your cell phone."

The guy hesitates for a second, then takes another look at the FBI badge and sighs. He hands it over. I turn to Josh. "I'll call you on Wallis's cell if I need you. I doubt you'll be too far behind us, anyway. You and Clark figure out a way to stop Cerberus being hacked. Let Wallis do the driving."

He holds his hand out and I shake it. "This time, Adrian."

I nod. "This time."

I turn and get into the passenger side of our newly acquired four-door sedan. Raynor guns the engine and spins us around. We speed off toward Atlanta and the ComForce building for the second time in twenty-four hours. The CIA will soon get word we've escaped, so they won't be far behind. The FBI will be on the hunt for Wallis, so they'll be on our tail as well. We need to be quick and lucky if we're to get there in time.

"So, what's the plan, assuming we reach Atlanta without being arrested again?" asks Raynor.

"I'll tell you when we get to Atlanta," I say.

April 17, 2017 — 07:30 EDT

. . .

Truth is, I actually *do* have a plan this time. Or at least, the beginnings of one, which is a lot more than I normally have when I'm preparing for a fight. But I don't want to share it in case we get caught. Plausible deniability, I think the politicians call it. If anyone asks, they can tell the truth and say they had no idea why we were heading to Atlanta. It's better for them.

The problem I have now is that I have no weapons. I've lost both my Berettas, which I'm pissed about, and Raynor's lost his gun too, so we're unarmed and driving full-speed to launch an arguably futile attack on a terrorist network.

Retirement's more stressful than when I was an assassin.

I place the borrowed cell phone into the hands-free kit and dial Josh's number. Unfortunately, I'm not the best when it comes to technology. I thought I pressed dial, but for some reason, I've managed to turn the radio on.

"For God's sake," I mutter. I move to turn it off again, but Raynor stops me.

"Hold on," he says, turning it up.

It's in the middle of a live news report.

"...have been here for several hours. So far, there are no casualties or demands, but a video has been transmitted to local stations showing hostages on the sixteenth floor. For those of you just joining us, we are now in the sixth hour of a siege at an office building in downtown Atlanta, where an unknown number of suspected terrorists have taken control of the ComForce Securities office. Their motivation is unclear, and so far, they have made no demands. Local police have set up a perimeter around the building, and an FBI negotiator and SWAT team arrived on the scene a couple of hours ago. More on this breaking news story as it happens."

Raynor flicks the radio off and looks at me. "We're too late. They've taken the building."

Overcome by an inexplicable rage that I've not felt in a long time, I let out a guttural scream and thump my fist on the dashboard. "Fuck!"

Behind me, Tori squeals and jumps in shock. Raynor raises an eyebrow and looks ahead, leaving me to my frustration. It subsides as quickly as it came, and I start thinking rationally again. "No way is this over, not after everything we've been through."

I try calling Josh again, and it works this time. The ringing sounds out over the speaker system in the car.

"Have you heard the news report?" I ask when the call's answered.

"No. What's happened?" replies Josh.

"They've taken the ComForce building as of six hours ago."

"Shit!"

"We're easily three hours out still. How long would it take them to gain control of the satellite?"

"Jesus... I don't know, Adrian. They've got to get access, then use it to control our nukes, then launch them... assuming that's what they want to do. If they're trying to hack someone else's, it'll take longer, but—"

"Best guess?"

He sighs. "Best case, twelve hours. Worst case, they already have control of our nuclear arsenal."

"Fuck. Right, well, we'll assume they haven't cracked it yet. The news reporter said there haven't been any demands. We just gotta hope we reach them in time to stop them."

"What's the plan once we get there?" he asks.

"I'll tell you when we get there."

36

The drive seemed to drag, probably because I was clock-watching the whole way. I feel a sense of urgency—a physical need to be somewhere I'm not, and the fact I can't travel to where I need to be instantly is infuriating. I have little patience at the best of times but knowing a bunch of insane assholes are trying to start a third World War in the middle of Atlanta has shredded every last ounce of it. Now I'm just angry.

Raynor turns right on East Mitchell Street. As I see the Georgia Dome loom into view, a sense of *déjà vu* hits me.

"Let's try this again..." I mutter to myself.

Up ahead, I see the ComForce building on the left. There's a full-blown media circus out front, starting from the middle of the road and heading away from the building in every direction. On the sidewalk out front are at least four large Hummers, painted a faded dark green. They're parked at haphazard angles, and all the doors are open.

I turn to Raynor. "Take the next left. See if we can work our way around back."

He nods and turns onto Spring Street just before we hit the outer rim of the police cordon.

"Should we tell Josh to do the same thing?" asks Tori from the back.

I shake my head. "I know Josh. He'll think exactly like I did."

The street isn't busy, although I imagine they're treating the ComForce building as toxic. The cordon around it will probably stretch quite far.

"Keep going, John. Take the second right, not the first. Keep an eye out for any local law enforcement."

Sure enough, as we pass the first right turn, I see a small patrol—two squad cars, four cops—parked across the width of the road.

"How are we actually gonna get near the damn place?" asks Raynor.

"We'll wait for the others and approach on foot."

We carry on and take the next right on Simpson Street, which has no police or media presence visible.

"Pull over on the left here."

We do, and Raynor kills the engine. "What now?"

I sigh. "We wait."

Ten minutes pass in tense silence. Tori shifts nervously behind me. Then a car turns onto the street and stops behind us.

I check it in the rearview. "They're here. Let's go."

We get out and walk to meet the others. They all get out and slam their doors shut. Josh stands opposite me on the sidewalk. Clark and Wallis appear at his side; Tori and Raynor appear at mine. We form a close circle and regard each other for a moment.

I look at Josh and nod a curt, urgent greeting.

"So, what's the plan, Boss?" he asks.

I clench my jaw muscles and take a deep breath, looking at everyone in turn. "There is no plan. Not this time."

Josh nods. Everyone else exchanges confused glances. I feel Tori's hand on my arm. "Adrian, you need to tell us what to do..."

I look at her and smile weakly. I haven't got the mental capacity to be nice at the moment, but I'm trying really hard for her benefit. She didn't ask for any of this. She's not here by choice, and she's so far out of her depth, she probably can't comprehend the gravity of the situation or what's at stake.

"We know what to do, Tori." I address the group. "Look, this is it. Whatever the fuck is happening ends right now— one way or the other. We know who's in there, and we know what they're trying to do. We're all smart, capable people. We have to stop them; it's that simple. I don't know the best way of doing that. I just know that we have to do it, and we're probably gonna need to kill a lot of people before we can. This isn't gonna be easy, but I need you to stay close, trust me, and do what I say."

They're silent, which I take as a sign they're on board.

I look at Josh. "I need you to stay here with Tori and do what you can to stop—or at least delay—those assholes from taking control of Cerberus."

He nods. "Sure thing, man. There are media and FBI trucks all over the place. I'll find one I can use and talk my way inside."

"Good idea. Sheriff, Clark, Wallis... you guys are with me. You see somebody you don't know, put a bullet in them. Hesitate for even a second, and you're dead. We know they'll be on the sixteenth floor, so that's where we're heading. We'll figure the rest out once we're up there. Questions?"

"We don't have any weapons," says Clark.

I grimace. "There are four cops on the next street over. They'll be armed, and I'm sure they won't mind if we borrow their guns."

Clark looks at the ground. "Sorry I spoke..."

I see a half-smile flicker across Josh's face.

"Everyone ready?" I ask.

They nod. I turn to Tori and place my hands on her shoulders. "Stay with Josh. Listen to him. Trust him. I'll be back before you know it."

She goes to speak, but I kiss her lips. When we part, I smile and wink at her, and the tension relaxes. The doubt leaves her eyes.

"Go get 'em," she says with a brave smile.

Without another word, I turn and move quickly across the street. I hear everyone else follow me. We head past a park on our left and through the courtyard of a plaza, approaching the corner of Baker and Peachtree. I drop to a crouch, gesturing with my hand behind me for everyone to do the same. I peek around and spot the four cops halfway down Baker Street. We'll be coming at them from behind, but we need to be quick and quiet if we're to take them out without raising an alarm.

I look behind me. "Once these guys are down, we won't have long before someone checks in with them and finds they can't answer. Once that happens, the alarm will be raised, and any advantage we have will be gone."

I look back up the street. There are rows of shops on either side. Some have bigger doorways than others, which will have to make do for cover.

"Split up, keep low, and stick to the doorways. Stay out of sight. I'll get the weapons."

I feel a hand on my shoulder. I turn to see Wallis with a look of concern on his face. "Adrian, you'll need help disarming them. There are four guys, and—"

I shake my head. "I do it alone. If they see four guys, they'll report four guys when they come to. If they only see me, no one will know you three are here, which might just help keep our advantage a bit longer."

He sighs. "But..."

He trails off as Raynor puts his hand on his shoulder.

"I think Adrian will manage just fine," he says, then looks at me and smiles.

I nod and set off around the corner. I move quickly and duck into the first doorway on my right. I press myself against the door, keeping out of sight from the cops ahead of me. I look behind me and see the guys moving one at a time down the street, occupying doorways across from me.

I wait until everyone's in place and hidden before peering out again. The cops still have their backs to us. I look across the street and see the next vacant doorway that would provide adequate cover. It's close enough that, from there, my next move will be to take out the cops.

I look at them more closely now that I'm nearer to them. The four of them all look the same—like they've come off a production line. All are white males and look a little heavy around the mid-section. Their body language screams complacency and routine boredom.

I almost feel sorry for them.

I wait until I'm sure they're preoccupied among themselves, then make my move across the street. I keep low and move a little faster than a walk, holding my arms out and my palms facing outward, signaling to everyone to stay where they are. I reach the doorway opposite, slightly further along the street, and press my back against it. I pause to slow my breathing down and compose myself.

I look around at the cops again. As I expected, they haven't seen me. I step out and walk toward them. The two squad cars are at an angle with their hoods close together, like an arrowhead in front of me. The four cops are on the other side of them, facing Spring Street.

Time to act stupid.

I change pace and walk nonchalantly toward them, staring at the sidewalk as if I'm minding my own business and going about my day. I get level with the car on the left before I attract their attention.

"Hey," shouts one of them. "You shouldn't be here. This street's closed."

I look up, feigning surprise and confusion. "Hmm? Sorry... me?" I ask absently, pointing to myself.

"Yeah, you. Street's closed. Go back the way you came."

I frown. "What's going on? Is this a crime scene?"

Another cop, looking slightly irritated, takes a step toward me. "We got a situation, and it's not safe to be here." He points back toward the Plaza. "Take a walk, all right?"

"But I need to get to my office, which is this way..."

The second cop takes another step toward me, and a third speaks up from the group. "Hey, asshole—today isn't the day, all right? Take the long way to work. Now fuck off before you get yourself arrested."

I'm standing just in front of the cars, level with the four of them. One guy is about ten feet away from me. I need to get the rest of them closer...

"The long way? That's not fair! I pay my taxes, all right? You can't talk to me like that! What's your badge number? I'm going to report this!"

The other three join the first one and move closer still, putting them in a line about seven feet from me. The first guy that spoke puts his right hand up, moving his left to rest on his belt. "Sir, you need to go back the way you came. It's not safe here."

I smile. "You got that right..."

I step forward and grab his right wrist with my left hand, pulling him toward me. He loses his balance, having not suspected the attack. As he stumbles toward me, I whip my left leg forward, keeping it low, and sweep his right knee out from under him. He goes down, and I take two quick steps into the line of cops, striding over him and putting myself second from the left out of the four.

I crouch and smash a straight left into the stomach of the guy to my right. As he creases forward, I stand and slash my right elbow behind me, catching the guy to my left on the jaw, sending him down.

I look forward again and bring my right knee up to meet the jaw of the guy I hit in the stomach. It connects flush on the side of his chin, and he drops to the ground, unconscious.

I sidestep quickly and lunge for the fourth guy, who's furthest from me. I grab his collar and swing him counter-clockwise, lining him up with the first guy, who's just getting to his feet. I push hard, sending one into the other. They fall like dominoes. I dash over them, crouch, and deliver a short, sharp right punch to both of their noses. They jerk and twitch before going to sleep.

I stand and survey the scene, making sure I incapacitated all four of them. "Okay, guys, we're good. Hurry up and pick a weapon."

They jog toward me. I crouch back down and take the gun from the last guy I hit. It's a Glock 22, which is a semi-automatic with a black chamber on an olive frame. He has two spare mags with him, each of which holds twenty-two .40 caliber Smith and Wesson rounds. It's a good handgun —lightweight and accurate, due to the muzzle break on the later models that reduces recoil.

I stand and tuck the gun in the back of my waistband. "Come on. Tick-tock, gentlemen!"

I watch as they gather the weapons, then set off back the way we came. I hear them behind me.

I pause at the corner and look back at them. "Everyone good?"

They all nod.

I glance around the corner and look down Peachtree Street. At the far end, I see lights, the hustle of the media, and the police. The ComForce building takes up most of the block, with just a few small stores on this side. I quickly glance at my watch. I bet the stores have closed up because of everything that's happening. There may still be people inside, though...

"Okay, we go in one of these stores. There must be a back way out that'll lead us to the back of the ComForce building."

"Hold up," says Wallis. "If you're right, and we *can* gain access to the rear of the building, we'll be pinning ourselves inside the alleys behind these stores. If they have people covering that side, we'll be sitting ducks."

I shrug. "You got any better ideas?"

"Let's look for roof access first. There might be a fire escape, but even if there's not, we'll be able to see any alleys or service entrances before we approach them on the ground."

"If you wanna waste time scouting around while terror-ists blow up the planet, go right ahead. Personally, I'm getting inside that building as quickly as I can. If I see anyone, I'll shoot them."

Wallis looks to Clark and Raynor for support. Clark holds his hands up in a *keep me out of it* gesture. Raynor just shrugs. "Time's against us." He turns to me. "But that said, it don't matter how quickly we get inside if we're shot down the moment we do."

I sigh. "Fine. Come on."

I keep low and head to the entrance of the first store, which is a local coffee shop. I try the door, but it's locked. Inside, I see members of staff cleaning. I tap on the window, and one of them looks over. I point to the door, and they shake their head, mouthing to me that they're closed. I look at Wallis, who steps up without a word and places his FBI badge to the glass. The worker's eyes widen slightly, and they turn to say something to their colleague. The two of them stand looking at us, then walk over and open the door.

"FBI," says Wallis, taking point and pushing past them into the shop. "Do you have a rear entrance or roof access to the property?"

The taller of the two workers steps forward, taking charge. He's a skinny guy, probably younger than he looks, with fair hair and bad skin. "Just the service entrance. There's an alley out back where we keep the trash."

Wallis looks at me and raises an eyebrow.

I nod. "Perfect."

He turns back to the work. "Thank you for your help. Now lock the front door behind us, and don't open it for anyone else, understand?"

The guy nods eagerly. "Hey, is... does this have anything to do with what's going on outside?"

Wallis flicks his eyes to me. "The less you know, the

better. Just keep your doors locked and stay put 'til you're told the area is safe."

The workers look at each other excitedly. I push past everyone and head through the back at the side of the service counter. It's a small kitchen, with another door leading to a larger storage area. A makeshift office space is in the right corner, consisting of a small desk with a chair behind it. Shelving units contain boxes of coffee and snacks. On the left wall is a double door with an EXIT sign above it.

I head for the doors. I draw my gun and hold it two-handed in front of me, ready. I lean against the left door and listen for a moment, then push it open and peer slowly around it. Seeing nothing, I step outside and quickly snap my gun level, checking all the angles. Behind me, Wallis and Raynor do the same, slotting in step with me to form a triangle. Clark comes out last, staying a few steps back and covering the rear.

The area outside is small and enclosed. Facing the doors is a wall belonging to another store. The right is a dead end too, leaving us with no option but left. This brings us to a miniature courtyard. Against the left wall and the wall behind us are large dumpsters surrounded by trash bags. Ahead of us is a narrow passageway that opens out on John Portman Boulevard, just to the left of the ComForce building. Off to the right is another alley leading farther into the courtyard. I head for it with the others covering. I look up and all around but see no movement.

So far, so quiet.

I press myself against the wall and peer around the corner. This alley leads along the back of the stores on Baker Street but opens up to the left about three hundred yards in front of me. I signal for everyone to stay where they are, and I push on, keeping low and pausing just before the left wall disappears. I scan the area and see a small patch of grass with a large tree in the center—easily fifteen feet high. All around it are old wooden benches, and beyond them is the back entrance to the ComForce building.

Much like the front, there's a security desk just inside the double doors on the right. There's a pad for scanning a swipe card next to some glass gates, which I assume open automatically when you produce a card.

The glass is tinted, and I can't see inside well. However, I see two men patrolling the perimeter—one on the other side of the tree, with his back to me, and one walking away from me to the right, along the width of the building. The second guy's holding a submachine gun close to his right hip. The strap is slung over his left shoulder.

I glance over my shoulder and motion for everyone to join me. They move quickly, forming a line next to me.

"Well?" whispers Wallis.

"Two guys are guarding the rear entrance. I can't see inside clearly."

"Silent takedown?"

I sigh and shake my head. "Too far away and too far apart."

There's no way inside without taking these two out. But there's no way of doing that without shooting them, which will make an awful lot of noise and attract unwanted attention.

I peek around the wall again. The guy by the tree hasn't moved, but the other one with the submachine gun is walking back across the building toward us.

He'll have to go first. I'll have a second, maybe two, after dropping him for the guy by the tree to react and turn around.

Plenty of time.

I look back down the line, catching everyone's eye in turn. "You know that element of surprise I've been so desperate to keep?"

They all nod.

"Well... fuck that."

I turn and move out, raise my gun, and fire. The bullet hits the guy with the submachine gun in his chest, high up just below his throat. As he falls backward from the impact, I snap left and fire again, catching the second guy in the side of his head as he steps out from behind the tree. His face disappears in a crimson flash, and his body slumps to the floor.

Screams from the street beyond fill the air. I look up at the building, expecting to see signs of commotion sixteen floors above me. There's no movement anywhere. I walk quickly over to the first guy, tucking the borrowed Glock 22 back in my waistband. I pick up his weapon—a Heckler and Koch MP7—feel the weight, and check the mag.

Time to end this.

37

I take position next to the door, with Wallis across from me. Raynor and Clark spread out, covering from a slight distance. I look across and nod. Wallis responds the same. I push the door open hard and dash in, then slide to a stop on one knee and sweep the area quickly for signs of life. Wallis appears next to me, and the others come in moments later.

The area isn't as spacious as the main reception area out front. There's a small station on the right side, currently unoccupied, with elevators in the far wall opposite us. On either side of them are double doors. The right side leads to a stairwell, according to the sign next to it. My guess is that it leads to the front of the building. In the center of the space is a mid-sized circular marble decoration, which contains some indoor plants at the base of a large palm tree.

I jump over the glass gates by the swipe pads and walk toward the elevators, gun ready. As I draw level with the plants, the door on the left bursts open. Three men rush through, screaming and firing carelessly in my direction. I spin away to my left and duck behind the tree. Wallis and Clark dive right, behind the desk, while Raynor crouches by the glass swing gates.

The three men fan out, firing at us relentlessly. I squeeze off a quick burst of blind fire off to the right, creating a momentary pause in their onslaught as they move for cover. In that split-second reprieve, I stand and fire at the man on my far left, dropping him with a controlled burst to the chest.

To my right, I hear multiple shots from Wallis, who's resting on the desk and taking aim at the remaining two gunmen. He kills one with a well-placed bullet to the head and wounds the other by catching his shoulder. As he stumbles from the gunshot, I let off another burst and hit him in the right side, pushing him away and into the door. He hits it hard and slides lifelessly to the floor.

"Everyone all right?" I shout over in the deafening silence that follows.

"We're good," replies Wallis. He walks out from behind the desk with Clark close behind.

Raynor steps over the glass gates and joins us. "So much for the quiet approach."

I shrug. "I've never been one for stealth. Now we need to get to the sixteenth floor. Elevators aren't an option."

Wallis nods. "Agreed."

"We'll split up. Raynor and I will go left. Wallis, you and Clark take those stairs on the right. Keep quiet, don't fire unless absolutely necessary, and we'll converge on the sixteenth."

"Won't those doors lead us to the front of the building?" asks Raynor.

I nod. "I assume so, yeah. We just need to keep our

heads down and be quick when taking anyone out. I know there's a door to some stairs in the left corner as you look from the front doors. My guess is we'll come out at the opposite end of a corridor to these two."

"That might work out well," adds Wallis. "If the media see you from outside shooting terrorists, the story will break that *we're* fighting back, which will put pressure on the people who *should* be and aren't."

I hadn't thought of it like that, and it certainly makes sense. But it makes me think about another factor.

"It's not going to be long before people turn up who don't want us here. The CIA will try to kill us. The FBI will try to arrest us. Either way, it doesn't end well. Bottom line is, El-Zurak's somewhere above us, and he needs to be shot —preferably *after* he tells us what this has to do with the director of the CIA."

"Agreed," says Wallis. "We need answers, ideally with evidence, before we shoot anyone important. Good luck, Adrian. See you up there."

I nod and look at Clark, who doesn't look so good. I'm guessing he has concerns about voluntarily walking into a gun battle. "Bob, relax. There are three MP7s over there, so everyone grab one. Let Wallis take point. You stay back and provide covering fire where necessary. Once we're up there, we need you to disable Cerberus."

"If I can..." he replies quietly.

"You can. I know you can. We'll buy you all the time you need to do it, okay?"

He nods. I turn to Raynor. "Ready?"

"When you are, Adrian."

The three of them move over to the dead terrorists and take a weapon, putting their handguns in the waistbands as

I have. We then pair off and head over to our respective doors.

"Thanks, Tom," I shout over. "Watch your back."

"Any time," he replies. "You too."

He heads through the doors on the right, reluctantly followed by Clark.

"You think they'll be okay?" asks Raynor.

"Don't worry about them. Worry about us."

I walk over and open the door to the left. I step to the side and prop it open with my foot. Raynor nods and walks through, stopping in a crouch and covering as I step through. I guide the door closed behind me with my hand to reduce the noise.

We're at one end of a long corridor. There's plush carpet underfoot, which I'm thankful for; it reduces the noise of our footsteps. Halfway along, on the left, is a fire exit. Just farther on from that, on the right, I can make out another door.

"Watch my back," I whisper.

We both set off down the corridor toward the main reception area ahead. We make it halfway, then the door on the right bursts open, and three men step out. I freeze and hold my breath, holding up a fist to signal to Raynor behind me.

They look in a hurry and, thankfully, don't look left. They practically run ahead and disappear out of sight.

I let out a heavy breath and hear Raynor do the same.

"That was close," he whispers.

I nod and set off again. I manage two steps before the same door bursts open again. Two men step out, but this time, they turn left and stop in their tracks when they see me. I'm frozen with a goofy, awkward smile on my face. The whole scene slows to a stop for a moment, with everyone caught off guard.

"Hey, fellas..."

Just as they resume normal speed and go to shout something, I squeeze the trigger twice with only a slight movement in between. Two bursts of fire hit them both in their chests, and they flail backward to the floor. I step to the side to allow Raynor a clear shot ahead.

"Wait a sec," I say to him.

Sure enough, the three from before head back around, guns aimed at us. I fire off a couple of bursts, as does Raynor. Between us, we drop them all before they have the chance to fire at us.

"So far, so good," he says.

"So far..."

We reach the end of the corridor, and I peer around the corner. I can hear a faint roar of commotion from outside, and the flashing of cameras through the doors momentarily blinds me.

Our little exchange was obviously overheard.

It looks clear, so I step out, checking the angles while Raynor covers my six. The door to the stairwell is on my right in the corner, as I remembered.

"We good?" I say without turning round.

"I reckon so," replies Raynor. "I assume most of their manpower will be upstairs."

"I'd imagine so."

I make it to the door and wait for Raynor to take up position across from me. I put one hand on the handle, ready to pull it open, but just as I do, I hear a noise behind me. I look around to the front doors and see objects being thrown, breaking through the glass, and skidding across the floor.

Oh shit...

"Tear gas!" I yell, bringing my left arm up across my face as the violent hiss of releasing gas fills the air. "Get through the doors!"

Raynor opens them and steps through. Gunfire erupts from the front doors, and I return blindly, coughing on the fumes. I dive through the doors and drop to my knees, struggling to breathe.

"You all right?" asks Raynor, crouching down beside me.

I nod and stand. I look through the glass door to see a four-man squad entering the building, dressed head to toe in black, wearing masks and tactical goggles and armed with assault rifles.

"Shit," I say, still choking. "The CIA's here."

"You sure?" asks Raynor.

"I recognize the outfit. They're not here to arrest us. We need to move."

We turn and start up the stairs, taking two at a time, not caring about who hears us. By now, everyone will know someone's here, even if they don't know it's us. I just hope Wallis and Clark are having better luck than we've had so far.

We make it up four floors before I hear any noise. Above us, a door slams open, and I hear the stamping of multiple pairs of boots on stairs. I take a chance and lean over the railing to look up. I quickly duck back as a hail of bullets spits down at me, followed by shouting.

"Company?" asks Raynor.

I nod. "Maybe three floors up and heading this way."

"Those CIA boys won't be far behind us, either."

We keep going, quickly reaching the fifth-floor stairwell. I stop by the door to catch my breath. "We'll dig in here, kill these bastards, and carry on."

More gunfire rings out in the stairwell, this time from below.

"You seem confident!" shouts Raynor over the noise of the gunfire.

"Confident... crazy—it's a fine line, I guess." I look at the door and back at the stairs, playing out every scenario I can think of in my head. "Okay, go back down the stairs. Just one flight—crouch down out of sight."

Raynor does so without a word. I wait near the door, listening for the men approaching. When they're only one flight away, I pull the door open hard so that it slams against the wall, then head back down the stairs, quickly and quietly, to join Raynor.

"What are you doing?" he hisses.

"Watch."

The men appear a second or two before the door slams shut. There are five of them. Instinctively, they open it and pile through.

Hook, line, and sinker, assholes.

"Come on!" I whisper to Raynor.

Swiftly, we run back up the stairs and through the door. We turn right to see the men filing through the office area in a blind rush. They all stop and fall over each other as they hear me enter, but I open fire before they can turn and react. Taking my lead, Raynor fires as well. With them huddled together and caught off guard, a few controlled bursts of gunfire drops them all with minimal fuss.

I know I could've let them go and snuck past, but that would mean five guys running around, who will ultimately head back to the sixteenth floor, and I could do with leveling the playing field as much as possible before I get up there myself.

"You're a devious son'bitch, you know that?" he says,

half-smiling but with an expression that betrays his concern.

I shrug. "Just doing what I need to. Come on. We're not done yet."

We move and stand on either side of the door just as the four CIA agents pass us. I look at Raynor and nod, which he acknowledges. As the last one draws level, I push the door open, hard, and hit him with it. I step out and crouch, emptying a burst of fire into the chest of the guy on the floor at close range. Behind me, Raynor fires over my head at the group of three, dropping two of them but missing the one who is already halfway up the next flight of stairs. I snap my gun up and fire, catching him in the leg, causing him to fall back down the stairs. As he lands, Raynor fires and finishes him off.

I smile. "There's hope for you yet, Sheriff."

He scoffs. "After a week in your life, I'm ready to retire. How the hell did you live like this?"

I shrug. "I'd say you get used to it, but I'd be lying. You just... learn to ignore the things any sane person would find an issue with."

We take a couple of moments to catch our breath, then set off up the stairs again, taking two at a time. We make it to the sixteenth floor without further conflict.

I listen at the door, hearing movement close by. I signal to Raynor to sit tight, and I adjust my grip on my gun, getting comfortable as I prepare for the next onslaught.

I don't know what's beyond this door, but I have to assume the Armageddon Initiative has come prepared. El-Zurak's here, so he'll make sure he's well protected. They'll also have hostages. The fifth floor looked empty, but I don't know about the rest. My guess is the majority of people got out during the initial takeover. I doubt anyone on the sixteenth floor would've been so lucky, though.

I have to play this smart and absolutely shouldn't kick the door down and start shooting... no matter how much I might want to.

I look at Raynor. By now, he has come to know me pretty well. He looks at me with a raised eyebrow and sighs heavily, as if sensing my struggle between what's smart and what's crazy.

I place a hand on the door and gently push it open a fraction, revealing a slim glimpse of the corridor running off to the right. I see a couple of offices on the left but can't see all the way to the other end.

"Looks clear," I whisper.

I push it open farther but stop when I hear footfalls away to the left. I hold the door still, not allowing it to close. Whoever's there might notice it's slightly open; they might not. But they would *definitely* notice it move, so I play the numbers game and sit tight, holding my breath.

Two men walk into view, striding purposefully away from me with guns held loosely by their side. I signal to Raynor, gesturing with my hands for him to follow me. I ease the door open enough to fit my head through and quickly look around to my left. A quick movement, just a glimpse.

There's no one there. I look right, to the end of the corridor, and see the door leading to the opposite stairwell. I hope Wallis and Clark have made it here unscathed. The two men stop at the far end, just in front of the door.

"Wait," I hear one of them say. He reaches for a radio clipped to his belt. He picks it up and holds it to his ear, listening intently. His body language changes, and he appears on edge, looking around and shifting on the spot.

"We're under attack!" he says to his friend. "Come on!"

They rush off to the left, out of sight, unblocking my view of the other door just as it opens a fraction. I see Wallis poke his head out, doing exactly what I've just done. Our eyes meet, and we give each other the OK gesture with our hand. I signal to him to head down the corridor to his right, after the two men. I'll head left with Raynor.

Keeping low, we all step out and check the immediate vicinity. Happy we're clear for now, I move off to the left with Raynor close behind me. They know we're coming, which makes things slightly harder, but it's not exactly unexpected. We'll deal with it as best we can.

At the end of the corridor is a right turn, with an office on the left taking up the corner. I stop with my back against the wall on the right and peer around it. The layout seems to be a square within a square. I suspect the majority of the personnel are based toward the center, with the outlying offices reserved for management.

I see no movement, so I make my way around the corner, keeping beneath the windows of the offices, out of sight. As I make my way along the left side with Raynor behind me, I realize exactly how big the office is. It feels like the goddamn TARDIS!

I hear movement close by and stop, signaling for Raynor to do the same. There's a low hum coming from up ahead, making it difficult to hear any footsteps. Just in front of us is an opening that leads inside the inner square, to the right. Must be another corridor running through the middle...

I edge slowly along the wall, keeping in a crouch, and stop at the intersection to take a quick peek. I feel my eyes widen at the sight before me. I was wrong about the layout. The inner square is open-plan, with a large bank of computers at the far end, in front of a huge display screen

JAMES P. SUMNER

that runs practically the full width of the wall. It looks like something out of a NASA launch control center—which would make sense, given this is where they run the Cerberus satellite.

In front of the console are three men and a woman, kneeling down with their hands behind their heads and their ankles crossed behind them. They're smartly dressed and look terrified. I count maybe sixteen armed men scattered around the area, all tense and alert with fingers on the triggers of their assault rifles.

At the console, with their backs to me, are three more men. They're all sitting, working feverishly away, pausing occasionally to look up at the big screen. Standing over them is Yalafi Hussein, leaning casually on the backs of their chairs, speaking in a language I can't make out. Off to the right, directly across from me, sitting in the shadows, is another man. I can't make out his face because of the lighting, but I can tell from the shape of him who it is.

Hamaad El-Zurak.

Every fiber of my being is screaming, urging me to jump up and put a bullet in him right now and end everything before any innocent life is lost. But there's something—I guess it's my voice of reason—telling me to wait because I'd be killed in the process and would never learn the truth behind everything that's happened.

This voice of reason is a strange thing. A bit boring compared to my Inner Satan, but it's undoubtedly smarter and will probably live longer.

Gunfire on the other side of the office space interrupts my train of thought. I peer around the corner again. A man across from me falls into view, landing dead at El-Zurak's feet. He screams something indecipherable and gestures to the nearest three guys on his left, who rush out and into the opposite corridor. I look on as more shouting and gunfire sounds out. Then Wallis and Clark walk in at gunpoint, unarmed.

Shit!

I look back at Raynor. I see a look of apology on his face, which I don't understand. But then I look up and see two men, one with his gun touching the back of Raynor's head and the other aiming at me.

Double shit...

38

One of the men shoves me in the back, jabbing me hard with the barrel of his gun to move me into the control center. I look over my shoulder at him. "Boy, if you touch me again, I'm gonna break you in half—we clear?"

He smirks at me but does nothing.

Everyone in the room turns to stare at the four of us as they position us into a line in front of El-Zurak. He's wearing white robes underneath a dark gray sleeveless body warmer. His beard is long and streaked with gray, and his dark skin is like old leather. He stands and walks down the line slowly with a look of disinterest on his face. He stops in front of me. Our faces are mere inches apart. He looks into my eyes, staring at me like I'm nothing. I regard him in much the same way.

I examine his features and think back to my first impressions of him on the DVD Clara left me. I don't know whether it was his eyepatch or just the circumstances at the time, but I remember feeling unnerved as I watched him on the screen. But now, after everything that's happened, I'm finally face to face with him, and I'm a bit underwhelmed. I've met a lot of bad people in my time. Most of them have paid me to kill someone, I admit, but it's almost like when you meet a celebrity. There's this expectation that they'll live up to their reputation.

This guy is the mastermind behind the largest terrorist plot in the history of mankind, but all I can think of is that I expected him to be taller. And that he looks a little like a pirate.

His right eye narrows at me. "How do you feel, Adrian Hell?" he asks, speaking slowly and deliberately.

I shrug. "I'm all right. Could do with a drink if I'm honest."

His lip curls slightly. In a flash, he hits me across the face with the back of his right hand. I didn't even see it coming. My head whips to the left, and I'm speechless for a moment. I look back at him, my body tensing as the anger rises inside me.

"Clara was like a daughter to me," he says.

"Well, I've already killed her biological father. Might as well kill her adopted one as well—complete the set."

"Your arrogance offends me. It is over, Adrian Hell. You have lost." He turns and moves toward the console, gesturing to the large screen. "Soon, we will use your own satellite against you to take control of the world's nuclear weapons and purge the West—"

I interrupt him by over-exaggerating a loud yawn. He glares at me.

"Oh, I'm sorry—weren't you finished?"

"Enough!" he yells. He turns his back on me and speaks to one of the men at the console in another language.

Next to me, Raynor leans close. "I'm real glad you ain't a politician, you crazy bastard."

I smile and look over at Wallis and Clark, who are both staring quietly at the floor.

"Hey, Hamaad. Can I ask you something?"

He turns, his face a picture of annoyance.

"I'm just wondering, why are you doing this? I mean, all this talk of purging is a little stereotypical, don't you think? What's the *Western world* ever done to you?"

Before he can talk, a deep voice speaks out from behind us.

"I'll answer that."

We all turn and look over as General Thomas Matthews walks in. He's accompanied by a ten-man squad of anonymous CIA operatives, dressed in the same black outfit as the guys we took out on the stairwell earlier. He strides confidently into the room and stands beside El-Zurak. He regards him for a moment and then extends his hand. El-Zurak looks down at it, as if hesitating, then shakes it.

"Congratulations on carrying out the mission, Hamaad." He turns to me. "Adrian Hell, you've been a colossal pain in my ass from day one."

I wink at him. "Thanks."

"That's not a compliment, you little prick!"

I smile but say nothing.

"You want to know why we're all here? It's like I said to you before—sometimes you gotta do things you don't agree with to get the result you want."

I shake my head in disbelief and confusion. "You're the director of the goddamn CIA! How did a piece of shit terrorist recruit *you*?"

Now Matthews looks confused. Then he laughs. "Son, he didn't recruit me... I recruited *him*."

And there it is.

His words hang in the air. The four of us exchange looks of shock and even more confusion as we piece everything together.

The CIA recruited El-Zurak to carry out this attack. That explains, well, pretty much everything. It explains why the Armageddon Initiative was able to get so big and stay so secret for so long. It explains why the whole world thought we were the bad guys—the CIA was feeding everyone false information. And who would question intel that came from the CIA, right?

I let out a heavy sigh, realizing that the world has been played. "Triple shit…"

Matthews is all smiles in front of me. His men remain emotionless at the back of the room, but the terrorists are laughing among themselves. "Don't feel bad, Adrian. You were never supposed to be involved in the first place, but even though you were, you were never going to win. This is bigger than you. Bigger than GlobaTech. Bigger than all of us."

I massage the bridge of my nose with my right hand. "Just explain it to me. If we're gonna die here, that's fine, but for my own peace of mind, can you just fill in the blanks using simple words, please? Why do this?"

The general paces over to the console and looks up at the big screen, then paces slowly back toward me. "President Cunningham has created a glorious nation. We now live in a time of prosperity unrivaled in the last fifty years. His larger vision is to use our great country as a blueprint for other nations on the planet so that they, too, can enjoy this new world we live in.

"But other global leaders don't have the same drive, the same dream, as our president. They merely look on with jealousy and resentment as we try to help them. They're seemingly content with their own miserable existences, yet still eager to have what we have. They want the thriving economy, the low crime rate, the high approval ratings, legal whores, and legal highs, but the narrow-minded sons of bitches want it all handed to them on a silver platter! They don't want to work for it. They want us to hand our wealth and decadence over to them, no questions asked, and that's not how the world works.

"President Cunningham is... disheartened, to say the least. I took it upon myself, as director of the world's most powerful intelligence agency, to do what needed to be done. If other people don't want to work with us voluntarily, then something needs to be done to *force* them, to make them see that our way of life is the only way that actually *works*. If everyone did things the way we have, this world would be a better place."

"You're fucking insane..." says Wallis. "This is just bat-shit crazy!"

Matthews looks over at him. "This isn't insanity, Agent Wallis. This is necessary. It's what needs to be done for the greater good. If people aren't willing to work at change, then it's our responsibility as the most powerful nation on this planet to reset those ways of life and help them rebuild from scratch."

I clear my throat. "Is it me, or does all this sound eerily familiar?"

Matthew looks at me, confused.

"I'm pretty sure a German guy tried something like this a few years back... and later, a group of people not dissimilar to ol' Hamaad here."

He scoffs. "They were narrow-minded idiots and dicta-tors. We're visionaries!"

"Wow... General, seriously—that's a thin fucking line you're walking there, buddy."

"This has to be done!"

"Says who? Who gave you the right to be judge, jury, and executioner for the entire world? You're nothing but a glorified office boy."

"I have the president's ear and enough experience fighting for this world to feel justified making this decision on behalf of it."

"So, why hide? Why not say everything you just said to me?"

"Because I've had enough years in politics to know how the public mind works. The masses are shortsighted and will only see the initial change, not the long-term benefits. There'll be an outcry, and it's much easier to give people someone to blame—someone to hate."

In a weird way, I'm actually impressed at how they managed to pull this off, even if I don't agree with it. But I still need to find a way to stop it. I'm hardly an advocate of diplomacy, but even I know that starting a third World War in the interest of peace on Earth is all kinds of fucked up.

And therein lies my problem. A CIA unit and a dozen armed terrorists surround me. I have no weapon, and I'm nowhere near the computer that can stop this. And let's be honest, even if I were standing next to the damn thing, I wouldn't know what to do with it.

For the first time in my life, I feel a genuine spark of fear inside me—not because I'm almost certainly going to die here but because I physically cannot make things right. I can't stop the people responsible, and I can't prevent the loss of any innocent life.

I'm helpless. It feels like drowning, and I don't like it. I think Matthews can see it in my eyes because that sick, twisted sonofabitch is smiling at me like he's already won.

I clench my jaw muscles to suppress the anger bubbling away inside me. "So, what now?"

He smirks back at me. "Now? Now we change the world."

He turns and walks over to the console, standing beside one of the men sitting in front of it. El-Zurak moves next to him, and Hussein joins them from across the room, where he's been watching the scene unfold in silence. "Execute Cerberus protocol Alpha-Zero-Niner. Authentication code Foxtrot, Zulu, Eight, Seven, Delta."

After a few moments tapping away, the man announces he's done as the general ordered. The large screen flickers, and trajectories start appearing all over a topographical map of the world.

There are a *lot* of trajectories.

"Holy shit..."

Raynor leans over to me again. "I hope Josh was able to do something clever down there."

I shake my head. "Honestly, John, I can't imagine he'd have been able to stop this. I mean, look at it. It's a fucking NASA control system. How can you hack that with a laptop in the backseat of a car?"

Wallis and Clark look over, silently imploring me to do something, *anything*, to stop this. But I don't know what. They'll gun me down in seconds if I move.

I need to stall him.

"There's still something I don't understand," I say to Matthews, who turns to look at me. "What was with all that *Ares* crap? Surely, you could've used any number of methods to move weapons around for these crazy bastards? Why illegally fund the only cartel left? Did you not think it'd raise too many questions?"

He glances at El-Zurak, nods discreetly, and then walks over to me with a look of regret on his face. Behind him, El-Zurak moves over to the console and leans forward, talking in a hushed voice to the operators.

"That was a bit of bad luck, I'll admit," Matthews says to me. "When we found out the extent of your involvement, we had to act quickly to get you out of the picture. We re-routed you to Colombia because I had a unit close by who could be ready on short notice to take you out. When you convinced one of my team to start questioning my orders, I was forced to take drastic measures, which, unfortunately, led to you being on the run. It was pure fluke that you stumbled across Vega's operation. Everyone knows the cartels don't exist anymore, which was why it was perfect to use one. No one would think to look for them. Vega moved guns and technology all over the world, wherever El-Zurak and Hussein needed it."

"Jesus..."

Clark takes a step forward, which surprises all of us. "What I don't understand, General, is that you went to all this trouble to hide America's involvement in this, only to have us blow the shit out of half the world, essentially admitting blame all along."

Matthews smiles and shakes his head. "Why, the United States isn't launching an attack on anyone, Mr. Clark. As you can see from the screen, it's China, North Korea, Russia, and Pakistan... *they're* the ones launching an attack. We're just the victims of a heinous act of terrorism."

Clark looks at me, wide-eyed, and I see the realization of defeat hit him as it did me moments earlier. This is what

Cerberus does—it protects our nuclear weapons while having the ability to steal everyone else's.

Matthews turns away and looks at the screen. "Prepare to launch, gentlemen."

Before any one of us can react, Clark lunges toward to the console. "No! You can't!"

Matthews and El-Zurak turn and watch Clark's feeble attempt to prevent this catastrophic inevitability. I see a flicker in El-Zurak's eye as he glances at Hussein. In a heartbeat, Hussein produces a gun, raises it, and pulls the trigger. The bullet hits Clark in the side of the head, pushing him down to the left and sending him skidding lifelessly across the floor. He stops in a pool of blood close to Matthews's feet.

I look away and curse to myself. That fucking idiot! What was he thinking? I look back over at Clark's dead body, lying contorted on the floor with blood still pumping out of the hole in the side of his head.

Matthews smiles and turns back, watching the screen like he's at the movies. Then he leans forward and presses a button on the console, and the screen starts flashing red. The white trajectory lines turn yellow, and small symbols of rockets begin moving slowly across the screen in all directions.

I feel my shoulders slump forward, and I drop to my knees.

I've failed.

I've just witnessed the end of the world.

39

"Don't feel bad, Adrian," says Matthews. "You've just witnessed a turning point in the history of mankind. Your grandchildren's grandchildren will thank us for this moment when they live in a world united by peace."

I can't find the words to either argue my point or say something derogatory. My heart feels heavy.

Next to me, I sense Raynor move. I look up to see him standing to his full height, looking over at the trio of Matthews, El-Zurak, and Hussein. "So, what happens now? Are you gonna shoot us?"

Matthews takes a deep breath and glances over to the ten-man unit he brought with him. I see him nod at one of them before stepping off to the right side, almost behind me.

I frown.

Something's not right...

The wheels kick in and start to turn again. I forget for a

moment the nuclear holocaust that's befallen half the planet outside.

What was it Matthews said? The public needs someone to blame... someone to hate. He went to all this trouble, paying the Armageddon Initiative to work for a full year toward this moment—to take control of the Cerberus satellite—only to make it look like everyone else is to blame.

Someone to blame...

Then it clicks.

I look up as time slows down. The men in the CIA unit level their weapons and fan out, opening fire as they do. With clinical precision and lightning speed, they shoot and kill every terrorist in the room, except El-Zurak and Hussein.

I look on as bullets fly and bodies drop. The familiar smell of gunpowder fills the air. I turn to look at Wallis, who's moving slowly down to the ground, covering his head with his arms. Next to me, Raynor's doing the same. I just stay still, kneeling amidst the chaos.

Time resumes its regular speed as the last body crumples to the floor. Matthews walks back into the center of the room, stepping over the dead bodies at his feet. He looks over at the two remaining members of the terrorist organization I mistakenly thought was behind this. They back away into the far corner, looks of anger etched on their faces. In his hand is a gun, which he aims at Hussein. "You gentlemen have served your purpose flawlessly. Your efforts in helping this world reach its potential will never be forgotten. They just won't be documented."

He fires four bullets, hitting Hussein in the chest and sending him sprawling backward to the floor. His blood sprays over El-Zurak, who remains still—defiant in what I'm certain now is his last day alive.

The general takes a step forward. I look over at his men, who seem uninterested in the four of us. Sorry... the three of us.

Damn it.

I let out a heavy sigh and momentarily curse myself.

No one seems to care about us now. I think if they wanted us dead, they would have shot us when they wiped out the terrorists. I decide to take a chance.

I slowly get to my feet. "General..." He turns, and I hold out my right hand, palm up. "Please. Let me."

His eyes narrow. He regards me as if trying to decide if I'm crazy, brilliant, or a serious threat. To be honest, I'm probably all three. But the only thing I'm thinking right now is that I'm too late to stop the Cerberus threat, and there's a good chance I'm going to be dead by morning. After everything I've been through, I think I deserve the chance to put a bullet in the head of the terrorist behind it all—so to speak.

Matthews looks past me at his men. They shuffle behind me and take aim at me. I shake my head, sensing his concerns. "No tricks. I just think after everything, you owe me this much, at least."

A few moments pass. He finally nods and hands me the gun by the barrel. I take it in my hand, regarding it, then aim at El-Zurak myself. "You wanna know what happened to Clara?"

He says nothing. His right eye glares at me as he visibly shakes with rage.

"At the end, she begged me to let her take her own life. I beat her, and she was dying, and she wanted a warrior's death. And I cared so little about my history with her, I granted her that last request. She blew her own brains out in Pripyat. How does that make you feel?"

His breathing is fast and his fists clench with rage.

"Whatever happens after this, I want you to know how she died... how she *failed* you..."

He stares at me with his one eye, snarling through the anger etched on his face.

"But you know what? Despite everything you've planned —the conspiracies, the attacks on me, even kidnapping my girlfriend—the real reason I asked for this is because you took from me the one thing that truly symbolized my new life. Because of you, my dog died, you piece of shit. And now so will you."

He screams with a guttural hatred and takes a step toward me. I pull the trigger once, putting a bullet in his right eye, leaving a large black hole in his face. Blood sprays the wall and glass behind him as he falls to the floor.

I take a deep breath and release the magazine from the gun, letting it drop to the floor. I eject the round from the chamber and hand it back to Matthews. "Thanks. You can do whatever you want to me now. I just needed to do something to make me feel like it's not all been in vain."

I turn to look at Wallis and Raynor, who are standing side by side, staring at me. The ten operatives all have their guns trained on the three of us. I walk over and join them, then look back at Matthews.

He looks at one of his men. "Take them away."

April 18, 2017 — 11:57 EDT

We were marched at gunpoint down sixteen flights of stairs and ushered outside, where a large crowd, mad with hysteria, met us. News crews, FBI agents, local PD—everyone was there. I surveyed the scene quickly but couldn't see Josh or

Tori. I hoped to God they did the smart thing and got the hell out of there.

Our guards led us to a black van and loaded us into the back. They restrained us by our wrists and ankles before the door slammed shut on us.

Matthews stayed with the media to give a statement.

They drove us to Fort Benning, about two hours away, where we were unloaded and taken to a holding cell at the base. They removed our restraints and locked us up. Six of the ten CIA operatives stayed behind with us, guarding us at gunpoint just outside.

We've been here almost twenty-four hours now. We all got a little sleep, but really, how tired can you feel when you just watched half the world get nuked?

I'm sitting on a bench, facing the bars of the cell. It's probably twelve-by-twelve, with benches along all three walls. We're on the basement level of the main building at Fort Benning, which has been in Georgia since 1918. It's predominantly a training base for infantry, but there's an MP presence on site, and it's local to Atlanta, so it makes sense they brought us here.

What happens now? I'm convinced they'll kill us. We know too much to risk being left alive, surely?

I just can't shake this feeling of guilt... like I should've done more. Maybe there would be more people alive if I hadn't stood there and watched everything happen.

"Can you believe this?" says Wallis to no one in particular.

"Nope," replies Raynor. "This shit is beyond me."

Wallis looks at me. "You okay?"

I look up absently and nod. "Just worried about Tori and Josh. They weren't outside the ComForce offices when we came out."

"I'm sure they're fine. Josh is a smart guy. He'll keep your girl safe."

"Yeah, I guess you're right."

Raynor moves and sits next to me. He leans forward, rests his arms on his knees, and clasps his hands together. "There's nothing you could've done to help Bob. You know that, right?"

I smile humorlessly. "I know it was his choice. It was a *stupid* choice, but it was his. He thought it was the right thing to do, and let's be honest, he did more than the rest of us did…"

"But look where it got him."

I shrug. "Maybe it's better to die trying than live with the knowledge you were helpless when you should've been anything but. You know who I am, John. You know the things I've done. How could I not stop this?"

"Adrian, you were in a closed environment, surrounded by trained soldiers with automatic weapons. You wouldn't have made it two feet. Even you—the mighty Adrian Hell. You might be extraordinary, but you're not Superman."

"And neither was Clark. What the fuck was he thinkin', John? Maybe if I hadn't given him such a hard time throughout all this, he wouldn't have felt like he had something to prove. I dunno…"

Raynor scoffs. "You're a dumb, arrogant son'bitch sometimes. You know that?"

I smile again, weakly. "Yeah…"

"Quit blamin' yourself for what happened. This was all so big, there's no way any one man could've stopped it. So, deal with that and focus on the here and now. We've got a whole new set of problems to worry about."

A soldier appears in front of us. He has an MP armband around his right bicep. "On your feet, all of you."

He unlocks the cell and holds the door open. We walk out in single file—first Wallis, then Raynor, then me. The MP walks alongside us as the CIA squad escorts us through the holding area and up into the main barracks—three in front, three behind. They show us to an office and open the door before stepping back. We look at each other and walk inside. The door closes behind us, and I see through the glass that they've left us alone.

Inside, the office is nicely furnished and has a warm feel to it, which is rare on an Army base. File cabinets line the wall to the right of us. To the left is a black leather sofa with a TV mounted above it. There's a news channel on, muted.

There's a desk in front of us with a nameplate on it. Behind it is a walnut leather chair, occupied by Special Agent-in-Charge David Freeman. He's resting forward on the surface, staring at us. Standing to his left is Ryan Schultz.

I roll my eyes. "Isn't this a good ol'-fashioned family reunion. Nice of you to join us, Ryan. Where the fuck have you been?"

"Reel that shit in, son," he says in his Texan drawl, pointing his finger at me. "I've been bustin' my hump tryin' to save your ass."

I turn and look at the TV. As expected, it's showing images of the fallout from yesterday. I point to it and look back at Schultz. "And how's that going?"

He sighs heavily, perhaps realizing it's not the best time to argue with me.

I turn to Freeman. "And have you finally decided which side you're on, asshole?"

He stands and slams his hands on the desk. "Hey! Watch your tone, you piece of shit. I was doing my goddamn job!"

I take a step forward, seeing an opportunity to let out

some frustration by beating this guy's head into the desk. Wallis steps across and cuts me off, placing a hand on my chest. "Knock it off, Adrian. Nothing these two have done was wrong, and you know it."

I hold my hands up and walk away, staring at the TV.

"What do you guys know about what's happened?" Wallis asks them.

"I only know what I've been told by my superiors and what I saw on the news," says Freeman. "But when I found out the CIA had captured you all in Atlanta and were bringing you here, I came over for Wallis. Ryan found me and told me... quite a story—which I'm still finding hard to believe."

"Hard as it is to believe, it's no less true," adds Schultz. "And I've got evidence to prove it."

I turn around and look at him. "You have proof? Of what, exactly?"

"Of the CIA's involvement. Financial records track the funding of a renegade cartel in Colombia, as well as the original intelligence reports on the Armageddon Initiative that GlobaTech provided months ago as a courtesy. When compared to the briefings fed down to other agencies, it's clear that the information has been doctored to suit their cover story and make us all scapegoats for what they were helping Hamaad El-Zurak do all along. It then became all about stopping GlobaTech and apprehending anyone helping them, so they could carry on funding the Armageddon Initiative behind the scenes with no one looking in their direction."

"This is good news. How did you get all this?"

"I spent a lot of time with the NSA over the last week. I've learned a few things off your friend, Josh, so when we found ourselves in their crosshairs, I did a bit of digging.

Another thing I found was a report from the upper echelons of the CIA to their equivalents in the FBI, detailing how Yalafi Hussein was an agency asset currently in play and was to be shown discretion during any operations to apprehend us."

"Shit. That explains why the D.E.A.D. unit was sent to take me out. They said I stole government property when I took Hussein's laptop back in New York. If Hussein was listed as an asset, then technically, I guess I did."

"Exactly. They covered their tracks pretty well."

"But even if Hussein was working for the CIA, why would he be discussing a top-secret government satellite with the director?" asks Wallis.

Schultz shrugs. "My guess? They'll say he was gathering intelligence on terrorist activity, and they were using the satellite to verify it. Forget what Cerberus could do. *That's* what it was initially designed for."

"That's pretty weak," I say.

"I know it is, but it's still plausible. And I just thought of that on the spot. The most powerful and secretive intelligence agency in the world has had months to think of a believable reason."

"Jesus Christ..." I turn away and pace slowly toward the door, but the images on the TV catch my eye. "Hey, turn this up."

On screen is a live press conference from outside the White House. President Cunningham is standing at a podium on the front lawn, with General Thomas Matthews at his side. The indicator appears on the screen as the volume rises.

"...our thoughts and prayers are with the families of the victims and the survivors in the nations that were subjected

357

to these truly horrific attacks by the terrorist organization known as the Armageddon Initiative."

Along the bottom of the screen is a ticker, scrolling right to left, showing the number of deaths in all the countries fired upon. Over nine hundred thousand dead in China... three quarters of a million dead in Turkey... two hundred thousand dead in Pakistan... another half a million in South Korea...

My God!

"These unforgiveable attacks took us all by surprise," the president continues. "I will concede that our technology was manipulated in a way we didn't know was possible, and I have taken action to have Project Cerberus decommissioned with immediate effect. It was designed to help protect the citizens of our great world, but instead, it was used to hurt them. From this day forth, the United States will set aside all foreign policies and treaties. We will wipe all existing debts. We will help those who need it most, no matter how long it takes or how much it costs. We... will... make... this... right!"

He pauses as a thunderous round of applause and cheering breaks out.

"This is bullshit," I say to the room.

On screen, President Cunningham holds up his hands so that the audience will calm down. "Now, even in these darkest of times, there is light. Thanks to the efforts of our intelligence community and the brave men and women serving our country, we have captured the men responsible for these attacks. Many of the terrorists involved were killed during the operation, but I can now confirm to you that we have the leader of the organization, Hamaad El-Zurak, in custody at a secure location, where he's undergoing interrogation..."

"Bullshit!" I yell. "I shot the bastard myself!"

"I would like to personally thank the Director of the Central Intelligence Agency, General Thomas Jack Matthews, for working to bring this evil individual to justice."

President Cunningham turns and shakes Matthews's hand, then waves to the crowd.

Unbelievable.

He's managed to turn the biggest terrorist attack in history into a goddamn publicity stunt... and the people are loving it! He just admitted it was American technology that caused all this, and they're fucking applauding him!

Jesus fucking Christ.

I turn to face everyone. "Schultz, have you heard from Josh and Tori?"

He nods. "They're safe. They slipped away in the chaos back in Atlanta."

"Good. So, what's your plan?"

"I need to make a call—try to get everyone released."

I shake my head. "There's no way the CIA are going to let us go when we know so much."

He reaches into his pockets, pulls out a USB flash drive, and waves it at me with a wicked smile on his face. "But they don't know we can actually *prove* anything. Let me do some negotiating. With Freeman's help, I'm sure we can make them see it's best if we keep quiet and all this disappears. The world's got enough to worry about, right?"

Schultz walks out of the room, followed by Freeman. Wallis and Raynor both sit down on the sofa in the corner, but I remain standing, staring at the TV screen. The scope of this is beyond comprehension. Millions of people have died. The last twenty-four hours ranks up there with the first two World Wars and smallpox.

I pace back and forth, unaware of the time. It doesn't

seem long before Schultz and Freeman re-enter the room. They look flustered.

"Okay, we're going," says Schultz urgently.

I frown at his tone. "With or without permission?"

"With... sort of. Come on. We don't have much time. There's a chopper waiting for us out front."

He turns and practically runs out of the office, with Freeman close behind him. The three of us exchange looks of confusion, then file out after him. We walk down the corridor, ignoring the accusatory glances of the people we pass, and step out into the open.

Sure enough, there's a chopper on the front lawn. Schultz is just climbing aboard. Freeman is on the ground, signaling us over. We all break into a jog and duck as we approach. The noise of the spinning rotor blades is deafening. We climb into the back, and we lift off before I even have chance to sit down.

"Where are we going?" I shout to Schultz.

"The safest place I know," he replies cryptically.

40

The safest place he knew turned out to be GlobaTech's main headquarters in Santa Clarita, California. The chopper took us to Atlanta International Airport. A private jet was waiting for us on the runway, fueled and ready to go. Vowing to myself that it was definitely the last time I ever traveled on one, we climbed aboard and were soon in the air.

The flight took a little over eight hours, during which I tried to get some sleep but failed miserably. We touched down at Whiteman Airport in Pacoima and made the half-hour drive from there to the GlobaTech building in a chauffeured limousine that was waiting for us.

The site is at the base of a small mountain range, and it's enormous. All the years I've had a relationship with them, I never knew just how big of a company they are. We drive in through the main gate and across what feels like a small town surrounded by a fence. Three- and four-story buildings are scattered around the site. Operatives parade around the grounds, kitted out and armed. There are helicopters and even fighter jets standing stationary, all bearing GlobaTech's red and black emblem.

We make our way over to one of the largest buildings around, which I take as their main office, and stop out front. We all pile out of the car. As I stand and stretch, I see Tori and Josh waiting for us. My girl runs over, jumps up, and wraps herself around me. I kiss her with as much passion as I can and guide her to the ground. Josh follows behind her, holding a laptop. We shake hands, and the group exchange pleasantries. Then we head inside to Schultz's office, where we sit around a large conference table and catch everyone up with what we know, right up to the point where we left Fort Benning.

"So, the CIA agreed to let you all go?" asks Josh. "Just like that?"

Schultz squirms awkwardly in his seat at the question and doesn't immediately answer.

I frown. "Yeah, Ryan, what was the story with us getting out of there?"

He hesitates another moment, his gaze rapidly flitting around the room. Everyone stares back at him. "I spoke to a guy at the CIA. I was given him as a contact when I was going back and forth with the goddamn NSA. I said that, under the circumstances, they can't justify holding Globa-Tech responsible for anything now that they've announced to the world El-Zurak has been captured. The guy didn't exactly admit what they've done, but he said they still need to be seen bringing the people responsible to justice."

"Sorry if I'm missing something," says Raynor, "but I thought they'd done that already?"

"They still have a whole lot of paperwork that we know they can't own up to, which says the people in this room played a large part in it all. They have to justify their intel, should there be an investigation."

My spider sense starts tingling. I look around the room at everyone. Schultz is sitting at the far end, looking flustered and out of breath. On his left, Tori looks tired, like she's spent a long time crying. She must be running on fumes right now, the poor thing. Next to her, Josh is sitting upright, tense and alert, listening to Schultz. By the look on his face, the cogs are turning inside his head. His laptop is on the table in front of him, closed.

Wallis is next to him, and Freeman is at the opposite end to Schultz, both looking positively disinterested, which I can understand. Wallis is back in the FBI's good books, so there's no pressure on him anymore. They'll just be anxious to get back to work and put it all behind them.

Opposite Tori, on my left, is Raynor, who still looks like he's trying to wrap his head around everything. He's a smart man, but he's old school. He likes to take his time, and I think this is taking a bit longer than normal to process. Again, that's understandable.

Then there's me. I have no official ties to the real world, apart from a bar in desperate need of renovation in a backwater town in Texas. I have no affiliation with any government agency. Out of everyone in this room, I'm the one with the least to lose.

Maybe I'm just being paranoid.

"I got them to agree that no one associated with Globa-Tech in any capacity will be held accountable for anything that's happened," continues Schultz. "They're dropping any charges against this company and releasing all of the assets they seized back to us. We're business as usual, effective immediately."

"What about me?" asks Tori, speaking for the first time since we all sat down. "I don't work for you."

"Sweetheart, you were the victim of a kidnapping by a known terrorist. You're fine."

"And me?" asks Raynor.

"You were a consultant, acting in an advisory capacity because of your knowledge and experience in dealing with the terrorists," says Schultz. "You're fine too."

The room goes silent, and Schultz shifts uneasily in his chair. Josh leans forward, pushes his laptop further out in front of him, and rests his elbows on the table. "And what about Adrian?"

Everyone looks at me, and I look up at Schultz. I already know the answer to this question.

I shrug. "Tell them, Ryan. It's okay. It's not your fault. I brought it on myself."

"Tell us what?" asks Tori, her voice quivering slightly. She turns to Schultz.

He sits up in his chair and fidgets with his hands in front of him, searching for the words.

"They... ah... they said—"

"They said that because I killed over twenty NSA agents and a couple of CIA guys to boot, I get to be guilty of pretty much whatever they want," I say, interrupting him. "Am I right?"

Schultz sighs heavily. I get up and walk around the table, taking a deep breath as I stand next to him.

"Adrian..." Tori stands and walks over to me. "Can't you just go to the authorities and explain what happened? You have proof that things weren't what they thought. They'll believe you."

I can hear the desperation in her voice. It makes my heart hurt, knowing she cares so much for me.

I look at Schultz. "Give me the flash drive with the evidence on it."

Reluctantly, he hands it over. It's small, maybe three inches long and an inch wide. It's like a fat pen—gray plastic with a cap that unclips to reveal the USB connector. I regard it for a moment in my hand, then turn to Tori.

"I can't turn myself in, baby. Not after what I've done." I show her the flash drive. "But this evidence proves the CIA masterminded a terrorist attack on American soil. It'd bring the whole country to its knees in minutes. Realistically, this information can't ever come out. But the threat of exposure is enough to give me some space, should the CIA get too close to me. They're going to make me public enemy number one, and the only thing I can do about that is run. I'm gonna have a lot of people looking for me for a long time. This evidence is my only protection."

I put my hand on her head and hold her close to me.

I look at Josh, hoping he has something insightful to say that will make everything all right. Just as he's about to say something, his laptop starts beeping, and everyone turns to him. He frowns and opens it up, examining the screen. "That can't be right…"

"What is it?" I ask.

"You saw Cunningham's press conference, right? After he said Cerberus had been decommissioned, I ran a program to try to hack the mainframe. I figured all the security would be down, and it'd be easy to walk right in. It was a shot in the dark, but I was seeing if there was any information from the attacks stored on there that we could use to help further prove what really happened."

"Sounds like a good idea. Did you find anything?"

"Well, no... that's the strange thing. The program didn't work because all the security is still in place." He looks up, but silence greets him. "That means Cerberus isn't deactivated..."

Freeman stands and walks behind him. "But the president himself said it was. That makes no sense."

"Exactly. Why would he lie? Just give me a minute here." He falls silent as he rapidly taps away on the keyboard. We all exchange confused glances. "The servers are fully functional, which means so is the satellite. Someone has to be in control. I'm trying to trace where the servers are being accessed from now."

"Surely, it'll be from ComForce?" asks Raynor. "That's where it's all based, right?"

Josh nods. "It is, but that building's on lockdown and still likely surrounded by the media. No way a team big enough and smart enough to operate a satellite could get in without anyone asking any questions."

"So, it's being accessed remotely?" I ask.

"Yup," he says as his laptop beeps again. "And it's being accessed from..."

He's silent for a moment, transfixed on the screen with his jaw slackened in clear surprise.

I raise an eyebrow, suddenly concerned. "Josh?"

He looks up with a bewildered expression on his face. "It's being accessed from the White House."

A palpable silence falls in the room. My mind is screaming at a million miles an hour in every direction. A thousand snippets of information flood to the forefront of my brain all at once. I pace up and down the room, trying to make some sense of the chaos inside my head.

Someone in the White House is using Cerberus right now.

The president lied about scrapping the satellite.

"This doesn't make any sense," says Wallis.

I hold up my hand. "Quiet, I'm thinking..."

I feel everyone's eyes on me. I'm standing near the door, and I turn to face the room. I meet Josh's gaze and see his cogs working like mine.

The president lied.

He also said they'd captured El-Zurak, which was bullshit. I assumed Matthews had told him that as part of his master plan, but what if he didn't? What if President Cunningham *knew* El-Zurak was already dead? He certainly put a good spin on it for the media. I know the guy's good, but was that speech a little too rehearsed? Or am I reading too much into it?

Matthews's plan was extravagant, to say the least. Could he have done it alone? It's possible, I guess. But it would've been a lot easier with approval...

My paranoia is giving way to reason. The more I think, the more it makes sense.

I turn to face the room. "This was a set-up from day one."

"We know," says Wallis. "Matthews admitted it to us, *and* you have the evidence."

"Correct, except Matthews lied about one thing."

Josh slams his fist on the desk, startling everyone. "Cunningham..."

"The president?" asks Raynor. "Are you saying he knows about what the CIA did?"

I sigh. "I think he's more than just aware of it. I think he's behind it. All of it. I think Matthews was a pawn."

Freeman stands and walks over to the window opposite, staring out at the expanse of GlobaTech's empire. He turns to face me. "Adrian, that's a pretty big claim, and you have no evidence. I know you're facing a lifetime on the run from the CIA, but don't you think you're clutching at straws here?"

I shake my head. "Look at the facts. Cerberus was commissioned by Cunningham to be built by NASA and GlobaTech, right? We already know features were added to it afterward, giving it the capability to steal other country's nuclear weapons. Who would have authorized that? Since he was elected, Cunningham's made these amazing changes and given the U.S. an unrivalled time of prosperity. But how did he do that? I remember reading up on it days ago. It was unprecedented, having such a massive reshuffle in the White House. He appointed his own directors in the CIA, FBI, NSA... he appointed new people in every position in the National Security Council—including the Secretary of Defense."

I cast a sympathetic look over to Schultz, who's listening intently.

"He then legalized cocaine and prostitution. No president in history has even dared to *think* about doing something like that, yet he suggested it, and it was almost unanimously approved. As soon as he did that, it took a couple of months to stop all crime. No more drug cartels because we're suddenly selling coke over the counter at Walmart. Then I came along and stumbled across a cartel running guns for the CIA. Matthews himself admitted it was perfect using them because they're not meant to exist anymore."

"Cunningham's behind everything, isn't he?" asks Josh rhetorically.

I shrug. "I think so, yeah. I think this is a clever and elaborate plan made and implemented by nothing more than a glorified dictator."

"But there's still no hard evidence," Freeman persists. "Without proof, we have nothing more than the CIA's admission of guilt."

"Stop thinking like a federal agent, Freeman. The fact there's no evidence *is* proof. The president's *too* clean. There's no way the director of the CIA could organize all this on his own without the president either finding out or approving it. Wallis, you heard Matthews's speech back in Atlanta. Either he'd been at the Cunningham Kool-Aid, or he was quoting someone else's vision. I think the president's behind all of this."

Silence falls again as everyone processes what I've said. Josh is staring unblinkingly at his laptop. "Adrian, if Cunningham has control of Cerberus..."

I nod regrettably. "I know, Josh. He's essentially used it once, so we know he's got no problem sacrificing anything to achieve his goal of creating a brave, new world for us all. He's crippled the planet, made himself the most powerful man alive, and currently has access to every remaining nuclear warhead on Earth."

"Oh my God..." says Tori, who's gone pale. "What do we do?"

"This has an *end of the world* feel to it, Boss," says Josh, looking more worried than I've seen him in a long time.

"We still need to find—" starts Freeman, but I cut him off.

"If you say *evidence of the conspiracy* one more time, I'm going to shoot you."

I pace back and forth once again as I play out every scenario in my head. Twice. After a few minutes, I stand and face the room, letting out a heavy sigh. I look at each one of them in turn.

"I can only think of one way out of this."

I put my hand in my pocket, feeling the USB drive. I walk to the window, replaying everything one last time in my head to make sure I haven't missed anything. I turn and face them all once more.

"I have to kill the president of the United States."

THE END

A MESSAGE

Dear Reader,

Thank you for purchasing my book. If you enjoyed reading it, it would mean a lot to me if you could spare thirty seconds to leave an honest review. For independent authors like me, one review makes a world of difference!

If you want to get in touch, please visit my website, where you can contact me directly, either via e-mail or social media.

Until next time...

James P. Sumner

CLAIM YOUR FREE GIFT!

By subscribing to James P. Sumner's mailing list, you can get your hands on a free and exclusive reading companion, not available anywhere else.

It contains an extended preview of Book 1 in each thriller series from the author, as well as character bios, and official reading orders that will enhance your overall experience.

If you wish to claim your free gift, just visit the website below:

linktr.ee/jamespsumner

You will receive infrequent, spam-free emails from the author, containing exclusive news about his books. You can unsubscribe at any time.

Made in the USA
Columbia, SC
08 August 2023

21420359R00228